APOLLYON

APOLLYON

To Glo,
my long-time
dear friend,
with warmest
personal regards
and love!
Bob
11-9-85
Duluth

A NOVEL BY
ROBERT STEIN

THE MÆCENAS PRESS 1985

Library of Congress Cataloging in Publication Data

Stein, Robert, 1933–
  Apollyon.

  I. Title.
PS3569.T374A86   1985   813'.54   85-13723
ISBN 0-87414-037-4

For about a hundred people —
but especially for Betty

And they had a king over them, *which* is the angel of the bottomless pit, whose name in the Hebrew tongue is Abaddon, but in the Greek tongue hath *his* name Apollyon.

—Revelation 9:11

PART
ONE

I

ABADDON! DAVID MIKHAEL ABADDON! Only son, only child of Saul Judah Abaddon, a Sabra, and of Sarah Vida Klein Abaddon, a New York City Klein.

David Mikhael Abaddon, all the world before him at twenty-two when he graduated from N.Y.U. with a double major. Degrees in nuclear physics and computer science. Only there was this: the same day he graduated from N.Y.U. he became a second lieutenant in the United States Army. David Mikhael Abaddon, Distinguished Military Graduate of the Army Reserve Officers Training Corps. Being a young scientist and Phi Beta Kappa wasn't enough for him. He had to prove as a young American that he could be a scholar and a soldier, like some of his family's Israeli friends.

This is what that kind of ambition led him to. They sent him to Viet Nam just in time for the Tet Offensive. From Saigon they sent him to Hue. And from Hue to a little outpost for Khe Sanh called Lang Vei. How some twenty-two-year-old with a flair for physics and computers got to Lang Vei, almost into Laos, only Westmoreland's personnel office in Saigon knew. They weren't looking at files too closely then. They needed officers on the line, up north. Lang Vei wasn't even Army—"I" Corps Marines! And four or five hundred grunts from the Army of the Republic of Viet Nam. Lovely scenery: mahogany, teak, and boojum trees—jungle, with an earthy smell. A Montegnard village. River. David loved the Montegnards on sight. Ugly little bastards. Tough. But tough, tough! Independent. He felt the Jew in him responding. But, what the hell and Jehoshaphat was he doing here? The camp was practically impregnable—thick concrete bunkers—lots of concrete—and supplies galore. They put David in charge of artillery.

He learned on the job, though he didn't have much time for

learning. One night the NVA attacked with Russian-built rockets and tanks, with napalm and tear gas. Who would use tanks in these ominous hills?

What happened at Lang Vei has been written about, but David had his own little holocaust to remember now for the rest of his life. He was walking out on the perimeter when the attack began and, running, got back to his bunker just in time to see the flames shooting from it and the others, and he somehow knew it was napalm. His artillery was helpless against tanks at such close range, in the dark. What the hell could you fire at? Someone got lights turned on to try to see who was who. David saw gooks coming right at him. Charlie everywhere. He blasted away with his .45 automatic, saw them go down. And then an American voice shouted, "Don't shoot!" David shot anyway, and started running. He tripped and fell. His legs and feet would not respond. Everything was in slow motion. And then he lost it. He lost all of it!

When he came to, he was walking in the jungle. An awful smell now, damp and cold and oppressive. There was someone ahead of him, and someone behind him. There was some light. Where was he? He thought maybe he was in training camp. He wanted to laugh out loud. Something told him this wasn't a time to laugh. He didn't have much of a sense of humor anyway, not the usual kind. Whatever he did have, now wasn't the time to start screaming his head off at something he thought was funny. Like, how did he get here? And who were these guys he was with? *And who the hell was he?*

And then it was daylight, and he was being hefted aboard a helicopter somewhere in the middle of the jungle along with the other guys.

How was this happening? Hey, where the hell are we anyway? Now in the helicopter he broke loose in a flood of talk. He couldn't stop. He thought about telling some Woody Allen jokes. And giggling. But the others were looking at him, not laughing, not saying anything. What was wrong? Didn't they like his borrowed jokes? He liked the way he did Woody Allen. He even looked like Woody, he'd been told. Hey, where were they going anyway?

Then he had a flash and remembered some things—the screams from the bunkers. God! Those horrible screams! *Ovens. Ovens again!*

He started shouting, now, in the helicopter. Then someone was putting a needle in his arm and he felt okay again.

Soon he and the others were being taken out of that chopper and herded into another. David flashed again. Choppers were taking them! He hadn't ever thought, he didn't think it was going to happen again, never again! But it was, and it was happening to him! They were sending him somewhere, those people he thought were his friends.

He started screaming again, uncontrollably. And someone was sticking a needle in him again.

He woke up in a hospital room, somewhere. . . .

He couldn't see anything but a white blur. The movie was out of focus. Couldn't someone help? His eyeballs hurt like hell. He tried to make out something, tried to bring something into focus. He was not on the chopper anymore, that he knew. The noise had stopped. There was no noise at all, not a sound. Maybe he was dead?

He tried to move, but could move only a little. He couldn't move hands, arms, not at all. Could only roll. Then he found it. He was in a goddam jacket. He was restrained. In a bed. He forced himself to really open his eyes. Blur. A vague blur. Steel bars on the bed. Cage.

He started shouting—at least he thought that's what he was doing. He heard a voice he didn't recognize as his, David Mikhael Abaddon's. He didn't think he had ever shouted in all his twenty-two years. He wasn't the screaming type. He, whoever he was, was shouting now though.

There was a squishing noise, and a woman's voice saying, "There, Dave, there now. You'll be okay. We'll take care of you, now." He tried to open his eyes wide and bring at least the voice into focus against the white blur.

He felt himself being rolled over, hands fumbling at his pajamas. Felt the jab in his buttock. Her voice was kind of crooning away. Like Diana Ross, singing the blues. Nurse rolled him onto his back. In an instant flash of focus, before he went out again, he saw this lovely pair of blue eyes telling him he was alive and she was going to pull him through, whoever he was. "There, Dave. You'll be okay," she crooned.

He went off somewhere, into oblivion.

When he awoke this time, he could see—like the scene at the end of *2001:* the room, white on white, clear, hard, a super-real photo. Three beds across from him—bodies. Hell, he was in a fucking mortuary, laid out. He was in a corner bed, bars still up, restraint jacket still on.

He lay there absorbing the scene. There was no panic this time, no wanting to scream his head off. What was the use? They'd only stick him again. This was the way it must have been when he was six months old in the crib, waiting for Poppa Saul to pick him up, hold him, murmur something in Hebrew.

He felt tears come. Crying at the thought of his father. Oh, shit! What was this?

He wanted to pee. He laughed through the tears. And a nurse was going by, squishing as she walked.

"Nurse," he called. She turned. She wasn't Blue Eyes. "I'd like to. . . ah, you know . . . ah, get this thing off!" His own voice surprised him, more like the one he grew up with.

"Oh, you're awake," she said.

"I'd like to, ah, you know what . . ." he repeated. Jesus, why couldn't he tell her he just wanted to take a piss.

"Just a moment," she said.

She went on down the ward. A few moments later she came back and talked to him like she was making sure he had come back for good and wasn't going to do violence to himself, or others, so she could take the restraint jacket off.

She let the bars of his bed down, took off the jacket. He stretched his stiff young arms over his head, the dark hair matted with sweat, flat on his broad forehead. He put on his glasses and did a quick aerobic and then another while she watched in admiration. He let her help him out of bed just to feel her hands on him. Good!

"I'll bring you a bottle if you like," she offered.

"No, thanks. I want to walk." He stepped into the Army Medical Supply regulation slippers and tried to walk. He faltered. She reached to help him, arm around his waist now.

He felt like he was coming back from having been a long way away, in strange places.

At the door to the men's room he turned to her and smiled. "I can . . . ah . . . go by myself," he said. She laughed. He felt like a child, going way way back to mother and his potty. She always hovered over him. He hated that.

"I'll wait. Just in case," the nurse said.

In the men's room he broke out in a sweat when he saw his face in the mirror. He looked so dumb. Why did he say that to himself? Something he had to remember. He was dumb. He trembled all over, and tried to get ahold of himself. He walked to the urinal— and dribbled over his hand. Hell! Peeing on himself! What was wrong with him?

He took it slow going out. Easy. She was there, waiting for the patient. He tried not to let her see he'd wet his pajamas. "You okay, now?"

"Sure."

She put an arm around his waist. He was glad to lean against her on the walk back to his bed, which she made up quickly while he sat on his chair. Five other beds in the ward. Not a stir from any of them. The place was so quiet. Not even a snore, if any of the other guys were asleep. He wanted to think so he could ask the nurse some questions. He was so tired. He just couldn't focus his mind. He didn't even know what he wanted to ask. But he did want to ask something. What?

"There now," she said, and helped him into bed. He felt weak again. The nurse gave him a pill and some water. He wanted to ask something, but his mind began to slip away.

When the nurse was gone, he just lay there. There was something he had to think about. Something? What? And then, there was nothing.

For the next couple of days David just floated in and out of reality, intermittently, like he was in a soupy fog, floating and flipping around. Sometimes he clearly saw blue sky, heard voices talking a vaguely familiar language, heard guys in the ward talking. He didn't understand. And there was a doctor who visited, tried to talk to him. David just couldn't make the effort to open his mouth. He knew he was supposed to. He couldn't. He didn't want to.

Then, one morning he awoke, and he was out of the soup, out of the haze and in a clear sky. Blue sky. And his first clear thought was: I have done something terrible. I've done something awful. I know I have. I've done something. . . . He pressed the call button. A nurse came right away—an old bag.

"What happened, nurse?" he asked. "Where am I?"

"Oh, now, you just don't worry. And go back to sleep."

David looked at her. Thoughts of his mother came vaguely into focus. Nurse had the same heavy face framed in greyish hair, an oval.

He pulled himself up on one elbow. "How come I'm here?" He asked, "Where am I?"

"We're not supposed to talk about that just yet," the nurse said.

David tried, again, to think. It hurt! It hurt to try to think. Jesus! What had happened? Where was he? How did he get here? Wherever here was. He couldn't remember.

"Pretty bad news, eh?" he said, slumping back down in bed.

She watched him for a moment, then went away.

He was still clear in his head when the doctor came. He sat up. "I'm trying to find out why I'm . . . ah . . . here," he said, surprised he was able to control his voice so well.

Doctor Campbell, a miniature Marcus Welby type in khaki, looked at David. Campbell ran his hand across the hair he'd combed from where it was to where it wasn't, and said, "Well, you're coming back to us." David waited. The doctor checked his tongue and then took a quick look into each eye. "We'll have a talk later," he said. "You were at Lang Vei. . . ."

The name hit David like a bullet in the head, and he felt numb. He'd heard that name before. He vaguely remembered now. Lang Vei. Lang Vei!

"I was?" he asked. "When?"

The doctor looked at him. "You're going to need a lot of rest. We'll keep you here for a short time. Then you're going Stateside. You'll get all the help you need there. They'll bring you out of this just fine. You'll be okay."

Panic crowded out the numbness in him. He sat up. The doctor, studying him, stepped back.

"Can I see a rabbi? I'm Jewish."

The doctor never took his eyes off David. "A rabbi?" He nodded, as if surprised. "A rabbi?" he repeated. "Not a psychiatrist?"

David looked right at him. Shook his head. "No." He felt good, human for the first time in a long time.

Doc hesitated. "I'm afraid we don't have a rabbi assigned here. Our Third Field Hospital chaplain is a Catholic. Sorry," apologizing quickly, with a half grin. "If you'd like to have Father Kelley stop by . . ." He shrugged, not knowing how offended David might be at his suggestion.

David frowned, puzzled. Why had he asked for a rabbi? The request had just popped out. He hadn't thought he had to think how. Why, why, why? And then, it just sort of popped into his head why. Something horrible had happened! He'd done something terrible.

He began to fall apart again. He tried to say something but just grew more rigid, his fists crumpling the bed sheets. His pallor changed to cold white. Doc rang for the nurse. In moments, David was getting a needle in his arm. Minutes after, he was relaxed enough from his panic attack that they could settle him back in the bed. Then he blacked out.

Something lay deep in David Mikhael Abaddon's memory, waiting to come to the surface, up to a level where he would recognize that he had blazed away with his automatic at human forms in the darkness, not knowing at all who those men were in the confusion and panic. He had shot, not knowing whether he shot at Viet Cong, or his own men. Did it really matter? For him, he'd shot his own men. He saw it and knew it that way.

It wasn't real now. It would get real, though. Later.

"Hey, kid. Wake up."

A heavyset man in khakis, with gold crosses, stood beside David's bed. He had wavy red hair and wore Pinocchio glasses that gave him an incongruous, almost comic-looking appearance, like some huge lineman on a football team, except for the head of curly hair, which turned him into a late sixties cherubic hippie.

"Hey, kid. Wake up. You'll never make it this way, kid." He bent over David, who turned and stared at the heavy face of Father Joe Kelley, ex-football lineman.

"Hey, smile, kid. It ain't so bad as all that, now is it? A smile a day keeps the devil away. My mother used to say that."

David hauled himself up slowly onto one elbow, watching Kelley like he was some apparition. "Ah, you're the . . ."

"Yeah. I'm the Pope's man here at Third Field." He paused. "You know, kid, you look like . . . sheol."

David had to smile.

"Mind if I sit down?" And Kelley sat on the edge of the bed, depressing it quite a bit. "One of these days . . ." he said to himself. He looked at David, and slapped himself on the belly. "The bod . . . the old bod . . . ain't like it used to be."

David watched this performance, fascinated. Any stereotyped notions he had had of Catholic priests vanished.

"Terrible what all this fine Vietnamese-French cuisine will do to a fella, if he doesn't watch out."

"You like food, Father," David said, finally able to say something. He often thought later how odd that these were the first words he said to Kelley. Calling him "Father" didn't seem right, not to a guy who wore a major's gold leaf on one side of his collar and a cross on the other.

"My curse, I'm afraid, David." He said the name like they'd been friends all life long. "I know a couple of fine restaurants here in Saigon. We'll honor them with our presence, God help us, as soon as you can get out of that bed. Are you kosher?"

"No. Mother is. When I'm home . . ."

The second he said the word home, a shot of pain ran through David's head, the pain of a memory returning. He had been so far away during the drugged sleep, he had lost all sense of his life in that other world.

"Where's home?" Kelley said. "Mine's Chicago!"

David talked then of Brooklyn, hesitantly at first, as if the memories coming back now with a rush would split his head wide open. He told Father Kelley about Mother—a power in everything, over everything—arbiter of manners, taste, class, culture, charity. "You name it. She's in it. A real Queen . . ." David was surprised at his own lack of reticence. He was talking family to a Catholic priest, someone who wasn't a rabbi. It felt good to be talking. He talked, too, about Poppa Saul. "He doesn't say much. He's a realist. For him everything is Israel. That's his religion, his life, along with that of his family. He'll do anything for its survival. Anything. God, he's tough!"

"Do they know I'm hospitalized?" David asked after a moment of quiet.

Kelley nodded. "Probably. Are you up to writing?"

David said, "Think so."

Kelley got notepaper and a pen and brought them to David. He sat up and wrote a very simple letter home saying he was hospitalized, but not wounded, and he'd be stateside in about a week, and not to worry.

Kelley took the letter from him and said he'd mail it, and promised to come for a visit every day until David left.

"I'd like that," David said.

Kelley went around to each of the other beds in the ward and chatted a while with the guys, and then left, nodding to David as he went out. "Looking good, kid, you're looking good," he said, laughing.

This was the beginning of a friendship that ripened fast. There was something appealing about Kelley that cut through David's drugged mind. After Kelley's first visit David lay there in his bed with an awesome headache, but, somehow, he felt good. His head was splitting, but he felt good. He had gone on and on talking family to Kelley. Why? Like he had found some long-lost brother. Growing up alone as he did, an only son, only child, he'd often fantasized an older brother. It was always an older brother, never a younger. That year he'd spent in the kibbutz, after his bar mitzvah, he'd made lots of friends among the boys there. Everyone was a friend. Suddenly, after growing up being on his own so much, he had lots of friends in the kibbutz, and it took him a while to get used to having so many, boys and girls, you were with all the time, even naked in the shower. David was shy at first. He'd always had everything at home for himself alone: his own room, with bathroom; his own records and record player; TV. Growing up, he even had a black Nanny to look after him. He didn't have to share anything. In the kibbutz, he had to share everything. He didn't even have his own bar of soap. And he didn't like it, at first. He'd grown up with a terrific sense of his own privacy. Gradually, the other boys and girls in the kibbutz broke him down. They got through his defenses by just being nice and kind and helpful, at all times. He couldn't believe it. He kept testing them by being nasty, and by going off on his own. They'd leave him alone. He'd come back. Play. Work. Soon, an incredible sense of security enveloped him. He felt part of a family for the first time in his life. He had real brothers and sisters in the kibbutz. Sisters who put their arms around him, hugged him. Brothers the same. The physicalness of the kibbutz was disarming to him. And there was no one around like Mother or Poppa Saul expecting things of him. He'd grown up under pressure. Performance was expected of him. Everything from the viola lessons to school to the Torah—something was always expected of him. And performance was discussed at length. Mother was a critic. In the kibbutz, all that was over for a year. He found brothers and sisters who just accepted him, no matter what he did. And he tested them, oh did he ever, those first few months. He thought they would ask him to leave, but they left him alone. When a boy or girl came to talk, mixing Hebrew and English, they'd usually invite him to explore something, or join in some work or a game.

He began to like the hard physical labor, and just feeling tired, with his brothers and sisters.

When he did go home to Brooklyn, he had a new confidence about himself. He didn't belong to Mother or Poppa Saul anymore. He had brothers and sisters in Israel, in the kibbutz. They loved him and would always love him. He had found a home and a family there.

His kibbutz conversion was total because he had grown up in a world in which he had been so solitary, in which he had, as a young Jew, felt defensive and alienated. You never knew when people would turn against you, no matter how friendly they seemed. You never knew. He had cultivated black friends going to public school and he felt safer, somehow, with them.

After the kibbutz, he did not feel so alone and alienated. He had found in the kibbutz that the whispers of *holocaust* and *genocide*, the words that caused the silence of terror, were now stilled. He was not haunted anymore. The fear went away. He was exposed to love, a whole community that accepted and loved him. They spoke Hebrew, which he learned quickly. It was for him a language of the love of others.

In his talks with Father Kelley, there were some of the long-buried feelings of his kibbutz days. He saw Kelley as a brother. He made him one, in his soul, when he looked up into that comic-looking face with the glasses, the mad smile. And that voice, like one he'd remembered Danny Kaye using in the movie *Hans Christian Andersen.* He'd seen it as a child. "Hey kid, wake up," he imagined hearing Kelley say.

When Kelley finally dropped by the Quiet Room late morning, next day, David was wide awake and waiting for him. He had to fight off the effects of whatever it was they were giving him, to stay awake to see Kelley. He wanted to see his brother.

Kelley gave him a quick sharp look from those big blue eyes, smiling. "Hey, kid, how's it going?" And he sat down on the edge of the bed.

"Okay, ah . . . Father." David gave the word a little action.

Kelley caught on. "Whyn't you try Joe next time? Not hard to say." He looked around. "Sure is quiet in here." He laughed at his little joke.

David said, "They give us these little, ah, bennies . . . " There were guys in six beds in the ward, all knocked out except David.

From outside, they heard the chug-chug-chug of a helicopter. Kelley glanced up at the window above David's head.

"Pretty bad out there?" David asked.

"Ain't gonna tell you, brother, " Kelley said. "And you ain't supposed to ask!"

David turned off. He collapsed. This was not the way it was supposed to be. He'd fought off the drug all morning just to stay awake to talk to Kelley and find out some things he wanted to know. Like, what the hell had happened to him?

"You gotta take it easy, Dave. Forget what the fuck is going on out there." He spoke in a hard whisper. "This is R and R time, buddy. Take it!"

The chugging of the helicopter faded.

"Something happened. I want you to help me remember," David said. He gave Kelley that long soulful look he'd been noted for in college, when he wanted things to get serious and the kidding to stop.

"I can't give you any images from the outside. This is supposed to be the Quiet Room, Dave. You're supposed to be *quiet,* here. I'm whispering, you notice. I don't want to get you flaking excited. Hell, I could do with some time in here myself."

David couldn't fight off the drug any longer. He collapsed.

Kelley was standing close, giving him little punches on the shoulder. "You can't get back in that fast. You gotta pace yourself, or you'll get slaughtered. Hey, Dave. I'll be back. You hear? I'll be back!"

They kept David on a light diet. After supper, Nurse gave him a sleeping pill and his regular yellow Thorazine. He was drowsing when Kelley slipped in and pulled up a chair. He sat and didn't even say hello. There didn't seem to be any need, now. And he started talking quietly.

"Listen to me, Dave. You're not crazy because you're here. I know what you're thinking, but believe me, you're not crazy. So, you want to find out what happened? Everyone else seems to want to forget!"

"I lost something," David said from a deep place.

"Hell, you lost nothing. You're alive."

"I did something terrible. Something horrible happened."

Kelley bowed his head. "I can't come here, if you keep blasting off. You're supposed to be sedated."

"I can't control it. I get this flash and feel like I'm going to be blown away."

Kelley reached out and gripped his hand. They were silent a while.

"I say Mass pretty early in the morning, in the hosptial here. You could come and just sit, and remember from Hebrew School—the synagogue—stuff you had to memorize. You can chant that to yourself. Gets you off your ass and out of bed anyway. Waddya say, bro?"

He had brought it back to David again. After the disappointment of this morning, David had lapsed into the zombie state, all the fight gone.

Now, it was back again. Kelley had included him in, wanted him in.

"I'd like that," David whispered.

"I'll tell Nurse. Won't she be tizzled. Pick you up early. So long, friend."

David cried quietly a while and then fell asleep.

Early the next morning Kelley appeared in the Quiet Room pushing a wheelchair. David was awake, waiting. He thought he could walk, wouldn't use the wheelchair. "I'm not wounded," he whispered. After taking two steps, he tottered. Nurse and Father Joe helped him into the chair, and Father pushed it out of the room and down the corridor.

At the end of the long corridor there was a small chapel to one side. Even at this early hour there were some people waiting— guys in bathrobes, a few civilians, some Saigonese. Sunlight poured in through clear windows. Father Joe left David at the back of the chapel. "I'll be about half an hour. Holler if you can't stand it, and we'll get a nurse to take you back." He winked. David smiled. Father fished in the pockets of his khakis. He pulled out rosary beads. "Thumb these. Worry beads. Take it easy." David took the beads, let them slide around in his hands. They felt good. Father Joe went up the aisle toward the altar, where two candles had been lit. The odor of lighted candles brought back the memory of the synagogue to David. He began unconsciously thumbing the beads.

Father Joe walked to the front of chapel, disappeared behind some curtains, and then emerged in a few minutes clad in gold vestments, trailed by a black-haired Vietnamese boy. Father faced the people and blessed them. He looked down at David, and then bowed over the altar and began the murmur of the Mass prayers, answered by the high lilting voice of the small altar boy in clear, beautiful English, and the congregation gave the responses.

David found some Hebrew phrases floating through his mind, effortlessly, even though he hadn't spoken Hebrew in a long time.

"Thou shalt love the Lord thy God with all thy Heart, with all thy soul, and with all thy might. And these words which I command thee this day shall be in thy heart."

"Praised art Thou, O Lord our God, King of the universe, who createst the fruit of the vine. Praised art Thou, O Lord our God, Ruler of the universe who hast sanctified us through Thy commandments and hast taken delight in us."

And as Father Joe began to serve Communion to those who wished to be a part of it, David's thoughts went to the prayer: "Blessed art Thou, O Lord our God, King of the universe who bringest forth bread from the earth."

The peace that passeth all understanding descended on David Mikhael Abaddon. He was not aware of time passing. One might have called it praying; he would not have called it that. He wasn't conscious of praying to anything he might call a god. Sometimes, the chants in his mind seemed to go on in unison with Kelley, as the priest murmured the Mass prayers at the altar and the small congregation responded.

When the Mass was over, Father Joe stood in front of him in khakis again. "That wasn't too bad, now, was it?" he said with a glint in his eyes. David smiled. "Not quite kosher, but not bad."

Father pushed David back to the Quiet Room. Kelley talked then about how nice it was to be back in Saigon. He'd done a tour of duty up north, too. In the highlands near the Laotian border. "Went out a few times on patrol. You lose non-combat status lightning fast up there. Never saw such jungle. Got that Agent Orange shit all over us. Christ! Pardon my French, and right after Mass, too."

Memories stirred in David, but he kept the panic down. Back in the Quiet Room, he got back in bed and asked Nurse when he could have some decent food. Kelley laughed. He touched David on the shoulder and promised to drop by in the afternoon. Before he left, Kelley walked quietly around to each of the other beds in the Quiet Room ward and spoke briefly to anyone who was awake.

David began to attend Mass every morning now, with Father Joe. Sometimes memories of something that had happened flashed in his mind, and David would break out in a cold sweat, grip the wheelchair till his knuckles turned white. The voices of the congregation responding helped him calm down. He thought once, being here in this chapel was like being in the kibbutz, not the synagogue. He'd kept the rosary beads and got to like the habit of thumbing them. Father Joe said he ought to make up little chants in his mind to go along with the thumbing. "Great therapy. My mother, God rest her, had the most peaceful mind. She thumbed the beads, reciting her Holy Marys and Hail Marys. I offer you Mother Kelley's cure. Make up your own chants."

Kelley came for a while in the afternoon, and brought a little pocket chess set, and they played some, but David could not concentrate very well. His head hurt with the effort. Having to pick up and then move the extra small pieces left his fingers shaking. Once, he had a severe anxiety attack at Kelley's aggressive style of play. He was an excellent but deliberate player himself. Kelley's style made him break out in a sweat, and then he began to go rigid. Kelley grabbed his hands. "Hold it down, hold it down," he muttered. And then, Kelley said something strange. "I'll take it, David. Give it to me. Give it over, over man." And David relaxed slowly, coming out of his panic, feeling he was really letting go of something.

"Thanks for that, Joe. You do that kind of miracle often?"

"Ah, just a little trick I learned from a fella once. Your move, Dave."

Doctor Campbell informed him one morning when David had been in the Quiet Room for a week that they were shipping him stateside to the Walter Reed Army Hospital in D.C. There he'd get the kind of treatment he needed on an extensive basis. "You realize, David, you will need lengthy treatment before we can evaluate you for return to duty or for discharge," Doctor said. David was quiet. He just nodded. And then a voice inside him said something very final: "David, you're never going back on duty with the Army. They won't let you." He tried to suppress the panic. Tears came to his eyes. Campbell said, "You'll get the finest kind of treatment at Walter Reed. You're not psychotic, you know. You're rather a sound young man, in my judgment, but you'll have to learn to deal with these anxiety attacks. This Army Field Hospital in Saigon isn't the place to deal with that problem, Lieutenant."

Kelley came to say good-bye. David tried to hand back the rosary beads. "Keep them. They're yours. Don't let your local rabbi see you with them. So, you're going stateside!"

David nodded. "I have to bring up some stuff for the shrinks at Walter Reed. Like what happened at Lang Vei."

Kelley glanced at him, then looked right in his eyes and said, "So, you're remembering? Look, old buddy. Lang Vei was bait, and so were you. The Army used all you guys. You were meat—so much meat in the trap. Anything that happened there, well, you'd better forget it."

Tears filled David's eyes. "I survived. I'm a survivor. You know what that means. I've got a responsibility."

Kelley took him by both hands. "I'm going to tell you something, fella. And you remember it, now, you hear? *I'll remember Lang Vei for you.* Someday you'll be strong enough to remember it for yourself. We've all got to stay as healthy as we can. We can't let this happen again. We've got to stop this apocalypse. You go back there and get healthy, and start doing something so Viet Nams won't happen again. You hear? Get strong! Be strong!" He shook David gently. "We've got a world out there that's great to live in and be alive in. God bless!"

Kelley was near tears himself. He bowed his head. David bowed his. They prayed together for a moment. Kelley embraced him tightly, then left quickly.

2

On a brisk sunny day in early March, Lieutenant D. M. Abaddon, U.S. Army, got off a C-141 four-engine Air Force jet transport at Andrews Air Force Base, southeast of Washington, D.C. The flight nurse had told him the nickname for the jet was "Starlifter." David didn't feel at all like a star. The flight had been pure hell. He had thought he'd never make it.

David had to share his seat on the flight across the pond, as the Air Force crew had called the Pacific, with two Marines who were going back home. They'd finished their one-year tour of duty. And all they could talk about was the drying out process they'd just gone through to get all traces of drugs out of their systems. David tried to sleep, but he just kept yawning. Then he got a pain in his chest and turned on the air vent. Couldn't seem to get enough air. He was hungry for air. Finally, he just couldn't stand it. He pushed the button on his seat that called for the nurse. When the uniformed flight attendant came, he asked to see a nurse, barely able to talk. The nurse came at once, and saw immediately what was wrong. She motioned to the Marines to get out of their seats, so that she could roll up David's sleeve and give him an injection. The two Marines, with typical butch haircuts, watched with sly grins and nudged each other. The nurse gave them an ironical look when she was through. They both shook their heads. David began to relax. "Hope you feel all right, sir," one of the Marines said. David shook his head. If they were being funny, he was in no mood for it. Soon he fell into a fitful sleep. He woke often, sweating. Half asleep and half awake, he somehow thought he was talking to Father Kelley, and Kelley was saying something comforting. What was it? "This holocaust must be stopped. David, you'll have to stop

15

this holocaust. You have to be strong. You have to get strong, David."

On the ramp at Andrews there were five olive-green Army passenger buses, each able to carry forty-two grunts, and a truck for luggage waiting. David thought, "That's typical. Five buses waiting for an airplane that was carrying only about 150 patients that are ambulatory." Even the nurses, who'd made comments to the passengers about the maximum load the transport could carry, snickered about that. "God," they'd said, "it's always such a waste of money." So the grunts got on any one of the first four buses. The air crew took the flight line shuttle. The fifth bus was empty.

The buses and truck were all driven to Walter Reed. David had gotten on the first bus and was sitting up front, trying to hold himself together. He was acutely aware that he was being watched. The men were watching him. He was an officer, after all, maybe a sick one but nevertheless an officer. He wore bars, didn't he? They hadn't taken the rank away from him. He had to, somehow, hold himself together.

At the admissions desk inside Walter Reed, the officers were led to a separate area, away from the wounded enlisted men. David moved, like a zombie, to his admissions area following a nurse who kept saying, for some reason, "This way, sir. Follow me, sir." He did, noticing in a detached kind of way that she had a cute butt.

He sat in the private reception room, with a few other officers, waiting to be admitted. The room was quiet, except for the Muzak. The Muzak played on and on. A nurse-receptionist huddled over a computer terminal, from time to time calling out a name. One of the group would answer, and gradually their numbers dwindled, as that officer would go off down the corridor.

David just waited, not even wanting to pick up one of the magazines on the coffee table right in front of him. Suddenly, the Muzak stopped. "Lieutenant David Abaddon, please report to the main desk immediately." The voice repeated the message. David was vaguely aware he was the person being paged. It was somehow strange hearing his name over the loudspeaker system, listening to it echo down the corridor. He was slow in making the connection between the message and some action he had to take.

He went up to the nurse at the desk. "I'm Lieutenant Ab . . . Abaddon."

"Oh," the nurse said. She picked up the phone, pushed a button, and said, "Lieutenant Abaddon is in the officer's reception room." Then she huddled over the papers in front of her.

David walked back to the stiff straight-back plastic chair and sat down. What was all that? Didn't she know it was an effort for him to move? He just wanted to rest.

The door of the reception room burst open, and there she was, this big woman who was his mother, running toward him with out-stretched arms, screaming, "My David, my David! What did they do to you, what did they do to you?" He half got out of his chair and then she was upon him, smothering him in a fierce embrace. "My boy, my son, my David! Oh, you're here!" David had fallen back in-to his chair under her onslaught; she knelt and continued to embrace him. Her expensive perfume floated in the air around him. He was caught in it. He just surrendered, as he always had to. He let himself be hugged, caressed, and cried over.

Over her shoulder, he looked up and saw Poppa Saul, bare-headed, carrying the hat. For an instant, David hardly recognized his father. He'd forgotten about the moustache, and, somehow, he hadn't remembered Poppa being so bald. He was smiling down at David, who was still engulfed in his mother's embrace. Poppa Saul reached across and put his hand on David's head, muttered something, and then withdrew it.

"Let me look at you, let me look at you," she said finally, still on one knee before him. She held him back from her. "You are not wounded? They said in the telegram you weren't wounded. Did they say the truth?"

David drew a deep breath and tried to speak. He had to keep drawing deep breaths for a few moments. Finally, he felt he was in better control of himself. "No, Mother. I'm not wounded."

She turned to his father. "See, Saul. He is not wounded." And then she remembered that that wasn't the point.

"They said it was acute environmental reaction response. What does this mean, David? What really happened, David?" She explored his face with her passionate dark eyes, and caressed his damp hair.

A nurse came by. "Lieutenant Abaddon, will you come with me, please."

Sarah Abaddon stood up as tall as she could and looked right at the nurse with an imperious stare, as if she were about to say, "This is my son, David. I'm going to take care of him. I will see he has the best care. Not you. You little nurse nobody from nowhere." Saul touched her arm, just before she exploded. David stood up shakily, and was led away by the nurse. Sarah started crying. Saul put his arms around her.

David disappeared down the corridor, and Sarah regained con-trol of herself.

"What will happen, Saul?"

"They will admit him, and put him through some tests to find out how he is. Then, they will see. I'll get in touch with Henry."

She sat down and the expensive leather purse she carried slipped off her shoulder. She picked it up and rummaged in it, took out a mirror. She glanced quickly at herself, then put it away.

"I want him to have private treatment, Saul." She looked around. "I don't trust . . . this, Saul," she said, giving a heavy shrug that spoke more than words. "We must bring him to New York." She spoke now as if she didn't care who overheard. "We'll bring him back with us."

Saul took her by the arm. "He's the Army's, Sarah." And he led her out of the reception room. "The Army has priority right now. We'll see Henry. I've made an appointment."

Doctor Henry Grevengoed, Chief, Psychiatric Division, Walter Reed Army Hospital, had had a call that morning from the senator from New York. The senator mentioned that the Abaddons would like to see their son as soon as possible. The senator said they would appreciate a few moments with Dr. Grevengoed, if he could take time just to keep them informed about what was going on with their son. The Abaddons were close personal friends of the senator. And the senator would appreciate it if Dr. Grevengoed would send him an account of what actually happened with the Lieutenant, over there.

And so it was that Saul and Sarah sat on the leather couch in Dr. Grevengoed's office, listening to him tell them that there was not much he could tell them, at the moment, about the condition of their son. On the wall behind his large polished wood desk hung pictures of President Lyndon Baines Johnson and Secretary of Defense Robert Strange McNamara. The doctor was a short chubby man in his early sixties, an administrator, soft-voiced, calm, smiling. He told Sarah and Saul he was putting one of this top-notch doctors in charge of this case. Sarah looked at Saul when Grevengoed said that. She did not speak. Grevengoed went on to say he would keep them informed of the diagnosis, treatment and prognosis, "within certain limits, of course, as the patient's privacy must be protected." He felt sure, though, there was nothing to worry about. David had the three qualities they looked for in such cases. He had youth and intelligence and at least some insight. And he seemed to be resilient. With proper treatment, he would be out of there in no time at all.

"What are you hiding from me, Doctor?" Sarah said, interrupting his patter. "I'm Jewish! I'm not afraid of the truth!"

"Hiding? Ah, yes. There is nothing to hide, Mrs. Abaddon, since we don't know much. Your son suffered acute environmental shock in action. Battle fatigue, we used to call it. He'll need a lot of rest and quiet in a controlled environment, at least for a while. That should get him back to normal."

"My son is not crazy," Sarah said quietly. "If he is, this damn war has done it to him. It's doing it to all of us. This genocide . . ."

Saul patted her hand after the outburst. Dr. Grevengoed waited.

"I'd like a report of his condition as soon as it is available, Doctor," she said. "Sooner, if possible."

Dr. Grevengoed coughed gently into a small, delicate hand, the only evidence he gave of trying to control himself.

"I will be staying in the Executive Suite at The Marriott, here in Washington. I'd like to see my son, now, please."

Grevengoed picked up the phone, pushed one of the control buttons on his call director and talked. David had been admitted. Dr. Samuelson was in charge of the case. David had refused a private room, to which an officer was entitled, and was now in a semi-private ward. Grevengoed hung up the phone and gave the Abaddons directions on how to get there. Saul shook hands with the doctor and thanked him. Sarah turned sharply and just walked out into the hallway.

After they had left his office, Dr. Grevengoed got right on the phone to Dr. Samuelson. "George," he said, "we got trouble on our tail. We'd better cover everything. You'll understand in a few minutes. She's on her way there now."

The charge nurse showed Saul and Sarah into the small ward where David had been admitted. There were four beds, all occupied. It was even more silent than the quiet room in Saigon.

Nurse had to shake David awake. "Your mom and dad are here to see you, David. Wake up!" She turned to Sarah as if to explain something, decided she had better not, and left. David turned over slowly and looked up at Sarah and Saul. He put a hand above his eyes and then sat up quickly, still staring at his parents as if wondering, "How'd they get here? And, how'd I get here?"

"David," Sarah said, embracing him again. This time Saul took each of David's hands in his own and squeezed. David still looked confused.

"We saw the doctor," Sarah said. "Don't worry about a thing." Looking around she asked, "Wouldn't they give you a private room?"

David hesitated, then said, "I like this."

Sarah glanced at the other three men sleeping and said, "For the company?" unable to resist showing off her wit.

She looked at David, seriously, passionately. "What did they do to you over there, my son? What terrible thing did they do to you?" Saul made a gesture with his hand, as if to stop her asking the question. David turned away. There was a long silence. Beads of sweat broke out on his forehead, and he could not look at either Saul or Sarah.

"Never mind," Sarah said. "You're home with us again. That's all that matters. We'll have you out of this place in no time."

She looked around. The sparseness of the hospital room offended her sense of life. She turned to Saul. "We must do something . . . this . . ." Sarah shrugged. Saul smiled. "I'll get you something to read." She touched the rough cloth of David's hospital gown and said, "I'll pack some things for you next time I come." She sighed and looked around again, her whole being offended by the sterility of the environment.

Dr. Samuelson walked in, a short dark curly-haired man with heavy bifocals. Sarah gave him a sharp, quick look. "*Samuelson* . . . Jewish?" He looked right at her. He had to answer this one. "Yes, Mrs. Abaddon." He turned quickly to look at David, felt his forehead and took a hand. Then, "I think we should let David sleep," he said. "If you'd like to come with me?" He gestured toward the door and bowed slightly.

He led them to an office just outside the ward. It was as military and sparsely furnished as the ward. A picture of the president hung on the wall. Dr. Samuelson offered the inevitable coffee. Both Sarah and Saul declined. He began his spiel, folding his heavy hands on the clean desk. He explained that he didn't have David's records from Saigon yet. "Things are a little confused over there . . . at present . . . to say the least." He paused, and then continued. "A preliminary diagnosis of David's condition is that he's suffering from acute anxiety and stress. Something we all have to cope with . . ." And he breathed out a little laugh. He went on to say he did not know how serious David's condition was. On the basis of a brief examination, he'd say, fairly serious. "He had a very bad flight from Saigon. The closer David came to us, the more stressful he became." Doctor Samuelson explained that he would proceed with a more detailed assessment of David's condition in a few days, when David had had time to rest and get adjusted to his new environment. They'd give him some tests, probably beginning with the Minnesota Multiphasic Personality Inventory, then do the Rorschach Test, and some Thematic Apperception Tests and sentence completions. In the meantime, David's medical record would arrive from Saigon. He planned, of course, to continue David on the medication he had been getting in Viet Nam.

Sarah and Saul listened politely to this narrative. Sarah's heavy face betrayed no emotion. But behind that cold stare, she was quickly assessing not only what Samuelson was saying, but Samuelson himself.

"Any questions?" he concluded.

Sarah stared at him, slowly focusing on the silver eagle of a colonel on his shirt collar. "I want private treatment for my son," she said. "I want him under my personal physician. I will have him transferred to New York."

Dr. Samuelson smiled at her, and then at Saul. "I must remind you, Mrs. Abaddon, your son is . . . well, the responsibility of the Army—that is, until he is discharged." This wasn't going to be easy. "I must also, Mrs. Abaddon, caution that at present, until David's condition is improved, we must limit all visitation hours."

Sarah stood up. And puffed up. Her immense physical presence seemed to fill the office. She was shaking. Saul took her arm.

"I think I can see about that," she threatened.

Dr. Samuelson opened his arms, turned the open palms of his hands toward her and shrugged. "He is our patient, Mrs. Abaddon. We got him into this mess. And we have a right to try to cure him as best we know how."

"I do not trust Army psychiatry," she said, and walked out of the office, her husband guiding her through the door.

Dr. Samuelson crossed his arms on the desk in front of him and put his head on them. The battle had been joined. The imperiousness of this woman broke through his professional calm and struck a little chord of panic and fear in his heart. He'd need more than just professional skill to prevent her from interfering with his treatment of David—who, he guessed, was a lot more traumatized than he had told her. He felt sorry for the lieutenant, for a number of reasons.

For the next few days, until he would receive David's file from Saigon, Dr. Samuelson kept a very low profile. He visited twice a day to chat and observe his general effect, and to attempt to establish a rapport with David before beginning treatment. He was in no hurry; he'd made a broad diagnosis after the first interview. David's condition wasn't unusual in Viet Nam vets—the incidence of anxiety neurosis was extremely high. "Post Viet Nam Syndrome," they'd been calling it. "Higher incidence than for any other war we've been involved in," he guessed. The reason? Softer generation, with little or no real preparation for fighting the kind of jungle guerrilla war being fought in Nam—another oriental war. MacArthur had warned about that, except that this time we were fighting on their territory and our guys were exposed to some pretty raw stuff, fast. And they broke faster than his, Samuelson's, generation, or so he had observed. David was just one more kid who had had a terrifying experience he couldn't cope with. Samuelson would have to try to help him put himself back into some sort of shape again, so that he could function in the world out there, and Samuelson guessed it would not be in the Army. David would never be the same twenty-two-year-old hotshot, at whatever he was hot at, that he had been before he went to Viet Nam. David didn't know that yet. And that would be one of the first steps in the long-range therapy the doctor saw ahead—to get David to see his condition now and what was causing it, then to get him to begin the slow process of building a new self, *for* himself.

A few days after that first meeting, Samuelson met Sarah Abaddon as he visited with David. She had been coming every day, he knew, and staying an hour or two, and then coming back in the evening. He had the report from the nurses on duty. He did not try to curtail her visiting hours. He didn't want a confrontation just yet. Once therapy had started, though, something would have to be done about her.

She was sitting in a chair, pulled up close to the head of David's bed. He was lying down, apparently asleep. She was reading *The New Yorker*. She glanced up at Samuelson, and their eyes locked in hostility.

"Doctor Samuelson," she said, letting him know she remembered.

He bowed slightly in acknowledgment and turned to David, who had opened his eyes. He asked a few quick questions to test his patient's reality orientation. "Who is President?"

"Johnson."

"What year?"

"Nineteen sixty-eight."

"What month?"

"March," David answered slowly.

Sarah interrupted. "'What are you treating my son for, Doctor?"

"At the moment, Mrs. Abaddon, we're just letting him have a good rest."

She shifted her enormous weight in the chair. Her dark tweed two-piece suit added to the impression of bulk and weight. "And drugging him day and night so he can hardly talk. Is that your idea of treatment, Doctor? I suppose you're planning electro-convulsive?"

Dr. Samuelson liked electro-convulsive therapy. It worked quickly, calmed patients down so that he could begin regular therapy. "I adapt my treatment to the needs of each patient, Mrs. Abaddon."

David listened to the exchange, then closed his eyes. He turned on his side, drew his legs up into the fetal position and pretended sleep.

Dr. Samuelson left. He reminded himself that he must be careful not to let his hostility of David's mother spill over into his relationship with David—that would be disastrous for effective treatment. So he timed his visits to David when Mrs. Abaddon was not there. He did not mention her, though he thought David might want him to do so.

Eventually he'd have to do something about the mother—he could not imagine what, short of severely limiting her visiting hours, which he should be doing already. It was apparent to him that David did not want to talk to her, and she was blaming the drugs.

When Dr. Grevengoed handed David's medical file to Dr. Samuelson in his office, they talked about the case. He'd heard again from the senator's office. Was there a possibility the case could be moved to a VA hospital in New York City? They would have to consider that possibility, being under some pressure from Mrs. Abaddon via the senator's office. Samuelson shrugged. In New York she'd have her own personal psychiatrist consulting on the case. He didn't care. It was actually none of his business since, at this time, David wasn't really his patient yet. "There isn't anything special about the case, is there?" Grevengoed asked. "Once he's reassured the threat of going back into a combat zone is minimal . . . with time . . . a few weeks of psychotherapy . . . medication . . . he should be able to control his anxiety," answering his own questions.

Samuelson took the file and glanced through it quickly. David had impressive credentials. Whizzed through N.Y.U. with a double major, computer science and nuclear physics, Phi Beta Kappa, Distinguished Military Graduate. How the hell did someone with his background ever end up in an outpost like Lang Vei? Someone must've screwed up in Saigon. Do you need experts in computers to fire artillery at guerrillas hiding in a jungle the size of New York? The report of the attack at Lang Vei during Tet and the events written in the file were abbreviated: "Night attack. Rockets. Tanks, with napalm and tear gas. Helicopters. All unexpected. Outpost overrun. Abaddon escaped into jungle. Picked up AM, confused, unfocused. Airlifted to Army Field Hospital, Saigon, under sedation. Transferred Walter Reed, March 7. Official." Not much there. Samuelson read between the lines, and it was there! The horror, the confusion of a night attack, napalm exploding orange fire into the night sky, men trapped, burning, in bunkers.

Samuelson shivered. *Ovens again.* He had his memories, too!

Yes, David had seen some stuff all right. And there was nothing psychiatry or psychoanalysis could do to blot from memory what had been seen. To *cope*—that's all Samuelson could help him with. And if they had to use electro-convulsive therapy to help him forget, they would.

Before leaving Grevengoed's office, Samuelson outlined the treatment strategy he would take with David. He wanted David off Thorazine, as soon as possible. He'd use Librium. Daily interviews. Might give him the MMPI. "Try to open him up as best I can, let him get some stuff off his mind. If they want him in New York, I suppose there's no reason they can't have him. But . . . that mother is something else. She's suffering some kind of shock herself, seeing her son—out of it."

Grevengoed nodded. "Do the best you can. Keep in touch."

David sat in the windowless office and looked at Samuelson across the clean desk, where the medical file lay open. Rushes of panic flooded through him, and yet, somehow, he sat in the chair, immobilized, fighting off the desire for flight. Where would he go?

Samuelson had tried to keep him calm. "I understand what you're going through. Please trust me. You've been through some awful shit. You and a lot more guys. I'm here to help, and I believe I can." He glanced at David sitting across the desk from him, in a silk bathrobe that surely must've come from Fifth Avenue, probably Saks. Clean shaven. Did his mother . . . ? "I want to reassure you first of all, David. You are not crazy." He smiled at the word. He touched his thick-rimmed glasses, and fingered the file. "What I'd like you to do is simply talk about what happened. Not right now, though. Today, we'll just do some personal history. Where you grew up. What your life was like. That sort of thing—the good stuff. Let's start off remembering some of the good stuff!"

In this way, Samuelson hoped to establish a sound rapport with

David and help relieve, for now, the anxiety he surely had, anxiety he'd have to allow to surface when they would bring back the memories of Lang Vei. "Another thing. I want to reassure you that your chances of going back to Viet Nam are . . . practically nil."

Then David did a strange thing. He began to talk about Lang Vei. Doctor tried to stop him. "Are you sure you want to . . . you're pushing yourself . . . In know some of what happened . . . it's here in your file . . ."

David stared at him, paused to take a few deep breaths. Samuelson watched him closely. The young, gaunt face screwed up with the effort of will to get this thing over with.

"I was on night duty," David said. "Out on the perimeter. We had some special rockets—new ones—very sophisticated. Guidance was pre-set. They were launched by computers. That's why I was there. Ground-to-ground rockets. Surface-to-air missiles." He continued to breathe hard.

Samuelson offered, "I can give you something to relax you."

"No, thanks, Doctor. Let me try. If I need, I'll ask . . ." And he went on to tell how he'd been the first to hear the rumble of tanks, and thought, "What the hell am I imagining? At midnight, on the side of a ridge? *Tanks?*" Then, unmistakably, he heard the chug-chug-chug of the rotors of helicopters. Suddenly, there was an orange flash behind him, in the direction of his bunkers. And then, the whistle of shells in trajectory. Mortars. Rockets. He recalled racing back toward the base, shouting to his men at the rocket stations, "Get back! Get back!" He carried an automatic, at ready, and then the night just simply exploded all around him, flames shooting high into the sky. He rushed back into base. Flames were roaring inside and shooting out through the openings of the bunkers. Guys were running in every direction. Shooting started. Bodies were being blown up from rocket explosions, right in front of David, and there were cries of horror from burning men trapped in the bunkers. Everyone was running.

David's chest filled with a rush of panic. There were men in front of him. He saw them in the flames. He didn't know who they were. They looked like Gooks. He started firing and running, firing and running. He just cleared a path for himself right through whoever they were, and headed for the jungle, after the other guys. Lieutenant David Abaddon bugged out, like any other grunt.

Samuelson listened closely to the account, ready to give David a shot if he needed it. He was amazed at the effort of recall and remembered detail. The guy was pushing himself, to get it all out. Well, the story was pretty grim, but not really unusual for Nam.

Samuelson had heard some like it before.

He gave David time to recover after the story was finished.

"You can't blame yourself for bugging out of there," Samuelson said.

David stared at Samuelson. Dully then, as if he were making one final effort to get it all out—the truth. "You don't understand. I would have killed anyone. I did kill . . . maybe, my own . . . I don't know . . . I ran . . . I killed . . . I escaped. . . I survived . . ."

He collapsed then, slumping into his chair. Samuelson called for the nurse. They helped David back to bed, and shot him in the butt with sodium amytal.

Samuelson went back to his office and sat alone looking at David's file. He dictated notes from the interview into his transcriber. Now he understood something he hadn't before. It wasn't the fear of being in Viet Nam, or of the war, that caused David's anxiety, or the fear of going back there. It was the thought that he, David, had betrayed himself. That was what was breaking him. He wasn't responding to any threat from the outside—that wasn't the problem—it was the danger from within that had shattered him. David Abaddon's problem was much more complex than Dr. Samuelson had originally thought.

3

DR. SAMUELSON had assumed that David's original trauma was in response to the horrors of the young man's experience. He saw his strategy of treatment as simple. Since David was already removed from a dangerous and threatening environment, part of the treatment would be to keep reassuring David that he would not go back there. He would do a complete physical to strengthen that reassurance, and then some psychological tests and a few weeks of interviews to relieve David's anxieties and to reassure him that he was not crazy.

All that treatment strategy now had to be revised. He just didn't know how deeply David had been traumatized. Now he was going to have to get into a lot of personal and family history. Samuelson didn't really like psychoanalysis. Patients in his office sat in chairs, not prostrate on a couch. There were too many men to be got back on duty to get into psychoanalysis with each one. His main aim was to get men functioning and back in the Army as soon as possible. If the case was too severe, he recommended medical discharge. He didn't like spending time with cases. There were just too many of them piling up. He felt tremendous pressure just from the sheer numbers of patients he had to see every day. It wasn't easy to give the individual attention they needed and deserved. He tried to do his best.

Samuelson got a call next day in his office from Dr. Grevengoed. It seemed that the senator's office had inquired why Lieutenant Abaddon could not be transferred to New York. Samuelson went to see Grevengoed. He didn't want to talk over the phone.

In Grevengoed's office, Samuelson sat and worried. He was now a physician caught in a political move, not able to make a decision

about his patient on purely medical grounds. He put the case to
Grevengoed. Lieutenant Abaddon might need extensive psychoanalysis and psychotherapy to get him to the point where he could
function again, not only as a Army officer. "Just as a person, I'm
afraid," Samuelson said. "He's fighting, now. I think I can help if we
keep him here. It's neutral ground. If he goes back to New York . . .
well, he won't stand a chance."

Grevengoed played with a pencil at his desk. The small chunky
man looked immobilized by Samuelson's news. He hated politicians interfering in his medical world, Russian style. "Any suggestions what to do?" he asked.

Samuelson told him about the interview with David. "An incredible performance. Without breaking down. He's going to punish
the hell out of himself if we don't help," Samuelson said. "Why not
lay it on the line to the senator's ffice. Tell them what really happened to the lieutenant. We respect Lieutenant Abaddon's right of
confidentiality. We might play around with it. Smash the ball back
at the senator's office. Let them decide." He paused, and then went
on, "The senator can get the lieutenant transferred. If he wants to
. . . if he's foolish enough to let the mother . . ." Samuelson threw
up his hands. "I'll continue keeping David on medication—no more
interviews until I hear from you. Of course, I'll continue to try to
enhance rapport."

Grevengoed realized Samuelson's suggestion was bordering on
the unethical. What did it matter, really, if Lieutenant Abaddon
was transferred to a Veteran's Administration hospital in New
York for treatment? It would be one less patient they had to deal
with.

He thought a while. Samuelson waited for his decision. "Could
you write me a report of the interview? Appreciate it if you by-
passed your secretary. Bring it to me as soon as possible. We'll see
what can be done." He smiled the nervous smile of a bureaucrat
about to make a play against the powers that be, to assert and hold
onto some vestige of the integrity of his medical profession, without much hope that he would succeed.

Samuelson smiled at him, too, glad he had decided to make the
play and not leave them seemingly helpless and powerless.

When Dr. Grevengoed phoned the senator's office to provide a
medical report on Lieutenant Abaddon's real condition, the senator was out. He left a message with the secretary to have the senator phone him, spelling his name for her. He felt that ought to be
enough, without going into any reasons for urgency.

The senator's office called back soon after. "The senator is on the phone and wishes to speak to you, Dr. Grevengoed." Grevengoed had had some experience in this sort of power struggle, but his palm was sweating and his heart beat faster as he held the receiver and waited for the voice that would say, "Hello, there, Henry! How's our little project going?" He hoped he could control his own voice.

And here it came, the thick, heavily accented voice, confidential yet not, in his ear, getting right to the point.

Dr. Grevengoed got right to the point. He avoided medical terminology and told the senator that Lieutenant Abaddon had had a deeply traumatizing experience in Viet Nam, one which threatened to break down his whole personality to the point where he would never again be able to function very effectively, either in military life, or as a civilian. An extended period of therapy was called for. It would be better not to have Lieutenant Abaddon moved to New York. The pressure on his personality structure at the moment would cause him unacceptable stress.

Grevengoed finished with that word. Everyone understood that word these days. Stress, stress, stress. Buzz word. What did it really mean? Most people thought it was a physical condition. Like hell!

There was a long silence at the other end of the phone during which Grevengoed could hear the senator breathing deeply—a bronchial or asthmatic breathing. He wanted to ask the senator if he smoked.

"Henry, are you saying the kid has gone crazy on us? Is he a basket case?"

"No, Senator, not at all. Nothing of the kind." Grevengoed let the senator have the whole story then, told him what had actually happened to David Abaddon at Lang Vei, gave him David's account of his own actions.

"And so, Senator, what we have is a young man who is suffering because he betrayed himself, as an officer. He betrayed his men. He possibly even thinks he's a killer. In cases like this, patients have even been known to identify with the enemy; they want to *push the button,* so to speak."

The breathing stopped at the other end of the line. Nothing like some good old fashioned deep trauma mental stuff to scare politicians.

"Hell, Henry, I can't tell his mother this. We're old friends. Family. We go way back. This is serious stuff you're telling me, Henry! How'm I gonna break it to her? You got files on all this stuff?"

"Yes, Senator. They're confidential, of course."

"Confidential, my ass. I want a complete report of this in my office by tomorrow morning."

Dr. Grevengoed held his breath and prayed silently for control.

"May I suggest, Senator, that we treat the matter very confidentially and not put anything in writing until you speak to the mother. We just don't like too much paper floating around, from our end, on such a sensitive matter involving one of our officers. If the press got hold of it. . . ."

That scared the senator, suggesting a leak to the press. Yes, he'd take the matter up with the mother. And get back to Grevengoed later.

The senator had an aide call the Senate Dining Room, on Capitol Hill and reserve a private room. It would not be easy to break the news to them about their son. The senator decided he couldn't just talk to them in his office about such a personal matter. He wanted Saul to be present at the lunch also, so Sarah had to call New York. Saul Abaddon took a day off from work at the United Nations to fly to Washington. Saul was deeply into details involving the U.N. Security Council's November twenty-second agreement on requirements for a Middle East peace settlement after the 1967 war. And, of course, as David's Poppa he had been acutely aware of the long siege at Lang Vei, Khe Sanh, and Hue. Saul Judah Abaddon had much on his mind as the three of them sat at the luncheon table.

In the private dining room there was a pervasive air of quiet, controlled elegance. The senator had chosen the place deliberately. If Sarah Abaddon was going to make a scene when she heard the news about her son, she'd have to make the scene in a place she knew didn't like scenes. Sarah was a passionate Anglophile. The senator knew this. He liked to prove how shrewd he was even in minor matters. Besides, they served a smoked salmon with delicate sour cream sauce and cold potato soup you could get nowhere else in Washington. All three declined the bean soup. A specialty of the Dining Room, it had ham in it.

The senator was always happy to see the Abaddons, not only because they contributed heavily to his political campaigns—they were key people. If they did not know what was going on at many different levels of New York society, they could find out. Sarah was on more committees than you could name, everything from activities of B'nai B'rith to her Brooklyn Heights Synagogue to several Jewish hospitals, the Museum Committee, the New York

Symphony. She and Saul regularly attended the Bernstein parties, though she didn't approve of the too liberal political views of the Bernsteins. Or religious views, either, for that matter. However, for the music, she forgave them, and helped Felicia in various efforts whenever she was asked.

Saul Abaddon gave the senator certain information and a point of view on international affairs which the senator found indispensible in developing his own broader perspective on world events. He had often been able to make political use of Saul's inside information, particularly on the Middle East, during the Kennedy presidency, and now with Johnson. And since the odds were that there was going to be a change, he'd be able to advise Nixon on foreign policy as well. The senator was a nominal Republican. He and his wife had been in politics so long now that distinctions between Democrat and Republican, at the level at which they played the political game, were purely *pro forma*.

At lunch, the senator apologized for his wife's absence. She was in the Middle East on business. To ease the tension, he told the latest Jewish joke about Arafat. Saul had one for him on Idi Amin from the U.N. They talked in subdued voices, making wry grimaces, not laughing at the jokes. Sarah indicated dry, matriarchal amusement at the male character of the jokes. She shared in the grossness in an aloof kind of way. She knew there would have to be talk like this before the senator got down to the real purpose of the visit. She was impatiently patient.

They all ordered the soup, salmon, and the canelloni. They drank Carmel President's Sparkling white wine, especially imported from Israel.

The senator talked about the coming Republican and Democratic National Conventions. He leaned close to them over the dining table, as if imparting secret information. "The war," he wheezed, "has just about finished the Democrats. *Coup de grâce.* We'll get in. And bring it to an end, this terrible . . . holocaust." He gave the word weight. All three were silent at the table for a moment, aware of the bitter irony that the nation which had won a war against holocausters and genociders was now itself involved in that very action. Of course, genocide against Vietnamese didn't count—they were *orientals.*

The senator cleared his throat and looked at Sarah, put a hand on her arm. "I have some good news . . . and some not so good," he said.

He told Sarah and Saul a modified version of what Dr. Grevengoed had told him. David would not be going back to Viet Nam.

What had happened to him there had been much too serious, too traumatic. It was going to take him a long time to recover. In the opinion of his physicians, he should be allowed to remain at Walter Reed, not be transferred to New York where there might be too much of a temptation to get back into things too quickly. He would be under too much pressure in New York. Things could not be hurried.

Sarah listened. She knew he was concealing something. "Senator, they will destroy him here. They will destroy his mind. All those drugs. No one knows the real effects. Electro-shock. They will leave *nothing* of his mind!"

The senator knew it wasn't going to be easy. He was sitting on top of something that could explode, like a hand grenade, and the fragments could go any which way.

There was a knock at the door. The *maître d'* entered to inquire if everything was to their satisfaction. The senator was glad for the interruption. It gave him a chance to make up his mind what to say next.

The *maître d'* left. The senator looked at Sarah and decided there was no point in trying to deceive her about the real nature of her son's illness.

"What I'm going to tell you, now, Sarah, is confidential." The senator looked at Saul. "Your son told his doctor . . . you understand," and he told Sarah and Saul then what had really happened at Lang Vei. "David is under the illusion—true or not, I don't know— that he killed some of his own men running. They napalmed the bunkers. Some of the men were roasted inside . . . terrible! . . . David ran into the jungle. He was picked up muttering something about a holocaust. . . ."

The senator watched Sarah as he spoke, ignoring Saul. Her strong face whitened, all the blood drained from it. She sat up straighter, as if to keep herself from falling over by an effort of will.

Saul had his hands folded, clutching his napkin on the table. He watched Sarah, too. He made as if to get up. "Are you all right?" he said to her.

She nodded. She touched her lips with her napkin. "Will he be court-martialed?" she managed to ask.

"No. There's nothing on his official military record, except, of course, in his medical file."

"The fool! The fool! Why did he have to tell. He didn't have to." She caught herself in the outburst and put a hand to her mouth. Saul bowed his head.

"I'm sorry, Sarah," the senator said. They'd been in many tough diplomatic and political spots before. He'd never seen her so shaken.

"Terrible," Saul said. "Terrible. For one so young. He wanted so much to show . . ."

The senator waited. He was used to being patient. He didn't feel nervous with silence. He wanted this thing settled. He didn't want Abaddon to go to New York. The case was too sensitive. He wouldn't try to persuade Sarah. He knew better than that. She'd have to come to her own decision, and then he'd take it from there.

"I don't want any publicity," she said. She bowed her head as if ashamed.

"Don't worry. When the case is closed, I'll have the files transferred to my office. There will be no record." He reached over and touched her hands. "There is nothing to be ashamed of. It happens."

She stifled a sob.

It was arranged as simply as that. For the rest of the meal they talked in a quiet way about what would happen if the press got hold of the story. They might try to use David for part of the anti-Viet Nam campaign against Johnson. Then, too, David's friends in New York would want to know details. They wouldn't be easily satisfied. And they spoke what, until then, had been unspoken between them: David was a Jew who hadn't measured up! There were certain elements that would take delight in retailing that juicy piece of ethnic gossip.

The senator knew Sarah was struggling with herself to normalize the situation so that she wouldn't betray her real feelings. Saul was more open than Sarah. He thanked the senator for all he had done. He hoped the senator didn't have to expose himself. Saul understood political power and the senator's position. You could never know when the senator's interference in David Abaddon's case would come out, be whispered about in a campaign, used by enemies. Saul Abaddon appreciated the senator's help. "I suppose we ought to see him before we leave," he said. The senator nodded. He read Saul Abaddon's feelings in that heavy face—there was sadness there. The senator knew why. He'd known the Abaddons long enough. For Saul, Israel came first, then, his son. And his son, though an American, was an ally for Israel. Saul would have liked David in the State Department or the Foreign Service, or at Harvard or Yale, an academic expert in some area of foreign policy related to Israel. He could influence the making of foreign policy even if he could not make it himself.

34

If he were given a psychiatric label, there would not be much chance for David to advance in the higher echelons of government. His career would be over before it began. Every man and woman of any importance in public life that Saul knew had private physicians who helped them through stress and depression with various drugs. That was not on their records, though. These depressions didn't happen before their careers were underway, and when they did, there were ways to conceal.

David had a psychiatric record now. Even if the senator held the record, the Army would know something—the senator wasn't that powerful. There was no clean slate for David, and Saul would have to adjust his ambitions for David to that fact.

Saul and Sarah were driven to Walter Reed in the senator's limousine. They were all silent on the drive. What could be said? The senator could sympathize with their personal tragedy. In the light of the whole of Viet Nam, it wasn't much. He had to give his time to these two people on a personal basis. He could not let an aide take care of it. He'd personally follow through on it for them.

He embraced Sarah and shook Saul's hand with both of his. They trusted him to take care of what would happen to David's records. Nothing would get out to the press, or beyond the Army.

Sarah led Saul to Dr. Samuelson. He talked to them in his office before taking them to see David. He could see that Sarah was measurably more subdued than before. He gave them a very general diagnosis of David's illness and tried to explain something about the nature of anxiety and stress. Sarah waved a hand. "I know," she said. "I have my own physician." Samuelson withheld the urge to tell her that her version of anxiety would be light years away from what her son was suffering. He turned to Saul as if to say something and looked hard into those grey eyes beneath the bushy eyebrows. He had the feeling that Saul understood. Samuelson had made some inquiries. Saul had been a Kibbutznik. He was an Israeli. Sarah was a New York Jew. There was a difference.

"What can we do to help?" Sarah said.

This was the time for Samuelson to bite the bullet. "I'm afraid at the moment there is little either of you can do, except, ah, to let him know you love him, and trust him. And, ah, believe in him."

Sarah squirmed. She wasn't used to this kind of spiel from a psychiatrist. She would have preferred something more concrete in the way of suggestions. "I thought of taking an apartment in Washington," she said.

Saul touched Sarah's arm.

Samuelson bit the bullet again. "Mrs. Abaddon, I'd advise you against staying in Washington—perhaps a visit on weekends, after a while. He'll have to come back to you on his own." He tried to make that sound tough and final. He hoped his nervousness before this woman wasn't obvious to her. She was used to total professional competence and the absolute manner that went along with it. He didn't want to falter. If he did, she would get her way with David, and whatever help he might be to David depended on his success in keeping the mother at a distance, at least, for a while, until David got some of his self-assurance back.

There was a long drawn-out silence now in which Sarah measured Samuelson's firmness and toughness in maintaining his position. She could bluff. Samuelson could not forbid her to stay in Washington.

"May I see my son?"

Samuelson led the way to David's ward. David was lying flat on his back with his eyes open. He turned his head at the footsteps. He frowned. Samuelson took his hand to reassure him. "Your mother has come to say good-bye," he said.

Saul came up to Sarah and put an arm around her. He could feel the tension in her body. She wanted to throw herself at David. Saul held her.

"Everything is going to be all right, David," she said. "We'll have you back in New York in no time. It will be over. We'll bring this . . . this . . ." She was at a loss for words.

"We'll have peace," Saul said leaning toward him. "Peace! You hear, David? We are working for it."

David's face brightened. "Okay, Poppa. Let's . . . let's, ah, go get it . . . that peace."

"You call, David, and I will come," Sarah said. "Anytime."

He frowned again, as if puzzled. "Yes, Mother, I'll call." She took his hand, caressed it, then dropped it.

"Take your time. Get well," Saul said. "We've got lots to do. Don't worry about anything. Get well."

Samuelson led them out of the ward. "Please give me a few weeks before you visit," he said, directing the comment to Sarah.

She looked right back at him. "I want reports. I want daily reports on his progress. *I* will decide when I visit."

Samuelson held the door for them as they left. "Of course, Mrs. Abaddon."

David lay back and closed his eyes. He did not sleep. He felt peaceful being alone, and, suddenly, greatly relieved.

He felt something around his neck and searched to see what it was. Dog tags. There were there—but, also, the beads he'd gotten from Father Joe. He began to thumb them, whispering prayers—and fell asleep.

Dr. Samuelson planned the strategy he would use for treating David with more than usual care. He wasn't sure he'd taken Mrs. Abaddon out of the picture completely. A woman like that, you just knew she wasn't going to surrender so easily. First of all, he was going to spend time establishing rapport with David—no pressure, no therapy or tests just yet. Privately, Samuelson didn't think there was that much he could do for David, anyway, to help him control his attacks of anxiety without being paralyzed by them. After meeting Sarah and Saul Abaddon, Samuelson was of the opinion that David would need longer treatment than he could get at Walter Reed. It wasn't just Viet Nam David had to be able to cope with and understand; he'd have to come to grips with his parents, also. That kind of psychotherapy would take a long time. It wasn't the Army's business. Samuelson liked David and felt great empathy for him, deepened because he was a Jew. But, he reminded himself, he was not a miracle worker. He was still amazed that David had opened up about what happened at Lang Vei. That had taken a lot of sheer will power and control. He could have knocked himself out for good with the effort.

The doctor started dropping by twice a day for brief chats with David. He didn't want to give any impression that he was probing. He talked basketball, the Knicks, David's favorite team. David roused with interest, asked after some of the players, their percentages, what the season had been like so far. Samuelson was pleased at his interest. He wasn't out of it altogether, like some of the guys who'd come to Walter Reed from Nam.

One day David said to him, "You, ah, handled my mother pretty well."

Samuelson smiled. "A piece of cake." He wanted David to forget about his parents, for a while. "Tell you about it sometime. If you want to know."

"Think I might," David said, smiling, too.

After about a week of small talk and laying the groundwork for mutual respect and rapport, Dr. Samuelson decided he might begin more formal therapy with David. David was ambulatory. A nurse told Dr. Samuelson he was beginning to wander the corridors a bit when he went to the bathroom. That was a sign of something. He wasn't afraid. Maybe getting the parents out of the picture was the first strategic move in putting David on the way to being able to handle his anxiety and stress. Any sign at all that David was beginning to have confidence in himself again was encouraging for Samuelson. He told the nurse not to stop David if he wanted to walk around in the hospital, just to keep an eye out, keep him away from newspapers, magazines, and TV for a while yet. Didn't want him hearing any Nam news, or seeing any demonstrations on TV.

David came to Dr. Samuelson's office in regulation Army pajamas, bathrobe and slippers. His mother had sent him a package with all his old civilian bedroom stuff, but he wore the robe only once, then asked the nurse to store everything for him.

Samuelson's office was spartan: no couch, vinyl armchairs, filing cabinets, a regulation office-type desk—no luxury. Picture of President Johnson. Diplomas. Medical books. David liked its drabness.

Samuelson stood up and shook hands with David when he came in. "Good to see you," he said. He meant walking around. David smiled. The guy had to say something. Samuelson opened his file on the clean desk. David sat in one of the vinyl armchairs and leaned slightly forward. He didn't want to slump.

He had begun to grow a beard and mustache, scraggly and free, uncombed. His hair was growing long. He just didn't want to think about Army regulations and grooming anymore.

Dr. Samuelson observed, sat down, and made a little note. The assessment of his patient had formally begun. Upright posture. Hands clasped. Head slightly lowered. Eye contact minimal.

He asked David a few questions about how he was feeling, just to get David talking so he could test the quality of his communication: Hesitant. Much clearing of throat. Fragments of sentences. Voice quality: flat, tight. Samuelson wished there was some way he could get David to relax.

He stopped making the notations in the file and leaned across the desk. "Look, David, I want to help in any way I can. I don't want to be just your Army physician. Let's talk." He came out from behind the desk and took a chair across from David. "Coffee?"

"No, thanks." He let the silence continue between them for a time.

Samuelson said, "We've got a long road ahead, David. I know you want to lick this thing. You impressed me, you know. You're facing it already. But you can't do it alone." He stood up and went over to David, put a hand on his arm. "I want you so you'll be able to stand up again, to anything, and feel confident that you won't break."

David looked up at him. "Is that possible, Doctor? You can't do that, can you?"

Samuelson sat down at his desk. "I can't do it alone. With your help, I can. I don't want to sound overly optimistic. You're in for the fight of your life. You'll *have* to fight for it, if you want it. I can help. Others will have to help, too."

David shifted in his chair, uncrossed his legs and stared at the floor. "Can I . . . would it be possible for me to leave the hospital . . . on a pass or something . . . maybe just for an hour . . . just to walk around?"

Samuelson sat back at his desk, amazed. His first thought was to say no. In the distant future, David would have to test himself in the world out there, but not now. If he went back too soon he could drive himself over the edge into total breakdown. He watched the young face, strained and intense. He wouldn't say no directly.

"How about waiting a week or two? We'll see how you're doing with the medication. We'll meet for an hour every day, to start with. There's a lot of stuff I have to get from you—personal history, how you really feel about things, in general, not just what happened in Nam. We have to put that in perspective. You think you can stand that kind of talk?"

David nodded.

Samuelson concluded the interview for that day and made an appointment for the next. He watched David carefully for any signs of stress in his posture or attitude. He could see none. He was amazed again at the effort to control. The medication undoubtedly helped. Still, the guy was fighting through on his own.

David shuffled out of the office and back to his room. He thought he would break down. And then he remembered something Kelley had said to him. "I'll take it for you, till you can take it for yourself." He found himself whispering as he walked along the corridor, "Take it, Kelley, I can't stand it for now. Take it. " And somehow Kelley took it, and the moment of anxiety passed, and he was in control of himself once more.

4

Samuelson kept rethinking it. He had at least two options in working with David. He could do the complete battery of personality tests, dig up a total family history, personal history from childhood on up, and do a lot of mental status interviews so that he'd have a myriad of observation notes. Somehow he didn't want to do that with David. He felt it would be a waste of time, and, anyway, Samuelson wasn't that sure he wanted to get into David all that much. He had a son four years younger than David, and felt he himself was already undergoing a touch of countertransference. He could easily see, if he did extended psychotherapy with David, how he might begin to use him for some of his own guilts about Viet Nam. Samuelson wasn't suffering. His son wasn't going to go.

He decided his best bet with David was to keep him on drugs and do intensive insight therapy so that he'd put what happened at Lang Vei in its right perspective, give him some insight into himself so that he could accept what happened in its own unique context. It wasn't his true self—any man would have acted as he did. Stories like David's were coming out of Nam every day. He'd have to understand that he wasn't an exception. In fact, Samuelson had a few more Nam vets he was treating, and he had a notion he might get David together with them later on for a little group therapy.

In his next session with David, he started out by asking him to tell once more what had gone on at Lang Vei, and how David felt about his own conduct.

David took a deep breath and began the story again, pausing to take a deep breath every once in a while.

"Now, tell me how you see yourself in all this," Samuelson said.

"I was an officer—that first. I betrayed my men. Look, I shot at them. Fuck it. Can't you understand? I *shot* at them!"

"You think you did. You don't know."

The sweat broke out on David's forehead. "Second thing," David said, "I wanted to escape. I wanted to bug out of there. I'd have killed anyone that got in my way. Do you understand that? That's not conduct becoming an officer and a gentleman."

And so it went in that session. Samuelson kept him talking it out. From time to time when David was exhausted, Samuelson would just point out to him how normal his reactions were under the circumstances. David whispered, "I ought to be court-martialed. I survived. And I'm getting away with what I did."

Samuelson wound the session down. He was exhausted himself. They hadn't even gotten into David himself yet, his own deeper feelings about himself. And then, there was his mother, and ultimately, Samuelson knew, they would get into the Jewish thing.

It was going to be heavy. At the end of that session, when he was making his notes, he thought to himself that he really didn't know how much help he could be to David, how much help anyone could be. All he could do was maybe lend an ear, keep him talking, and hope time and the drugs would help.

Over the years, his faith in psychiatry and psychotherapy had lessened. He could do some things. He was no miracle worker. Even if he got David to the point of understanding the ego, super-ego, and maturing to the point of understanding his own, David still might not be able to carry the understanding into his practical life. From the couch to the street was the long step some patients couldn't, or wouldn't take.

For two weeks, Samuelson met with David every day. He knew he was putting him under terrific pressure. David seemed to hold up. Where the kid got the strength, Samuelson didn't know. Samuelson noticed David held something in his hands, beads of some kind, that he kept thumbing. Worry beads. Samuelson didn't ask about them.

David was only a kid—he *looked* like a kid. That's what Samuelson couldn't get over. This was no battle-scarred veteran. This was a traumatized twenty-two-year-old kid trying to hold himself together so that he could get back into the game of life.

Samuelson decided the best current strategy in their talks was to avoid talking about Nam for a while, so he encouraged him to talk about his childhood. "Start from day one," Samuelson had said. "Start as far back as you can remember. Talk about anything, anything that comes into your head."

For a few days, David was practically silent on the subject. Samuelson had to make all the overtures, prodding with questions about childhood—how did he like school? Did he have many friends? What games did he play? How did he feel about his parents?

David said to him one day, "You saw them, Sarah and Saul. You met them. You know where I'm coming from. I was brought up in an upper-middle-class New York Jewish home. I was protected and sheltered. I was supposed to become someone. I always knew that. I was supposed to become someone." He was silent after that outburst, and Samuelson let him go early that day.

Samuelson encouraged him thereafter just to remember scenes from his growing up—not the painful ones, just scenes, especially ones he liked remembering.

The picture of David he saw emerging was of a shy, serious boy growing up in a household where something official always seemed about to happen. There was always some public event that had its repercussions in the huge home run by women who spoke Spanish, and David himself was taken care of by Martha Ann, a black woman who was part cook, part nurse.

The worlds of music and politics came into the home with the numerous parties his mother gave. It seemed to him his mother was always giving parties. His father was there, but his father's friends always seemed quieter than his mother's.

David remembered being introduced around at the parties as if he were something special. He hated it.

He decided to go to N.Y.U. over the objections of Sarah and Saul. They wanted him to go Ivy League. He wanted to stay in New York. He'd joined a club that flew radio-controlled model airplanes. He didn't want to leave the club. He didn't tell Sarah and Saul this, but that was his main reason for staying in New York. He loved his club.

Samuelson continued to meet with David in hour-long sessions. After a few weeks, David became more articulate. He seemed looser, relaxed. There wasn't anything really that painful in his past. He was very normal, except for the influence of growing up in a home where both parents were public figures and had very little intimacy to share with their child. David got that from Martha Ann, his black nanny. He didn't seem to want much. That wasn't bothering him. He accepted his life and accepted the unspoken feelings his parents had about him. He was destined for something.

One day, David said to Dr. Samuelson, "Look, ah, I'd like to get permission to go out." Samuelson stared at him and shook his head. "You've come a long way, but not that far." David glanced at him behind the desk. "I gotta try. I gotta test myself."

They talked it out. All David wanted at first was to be able to walk around the hospital grounds. If he didn't panic, then maybe he could get a pass to get off the hospital grounds.

Samuelson reminded him that they hadn't even begun to get into treatment yet. David was still on medication.

"Look, Doctor . . . ah, I respect your looking out . . . for my welfare." David took a deep breath. "I'll never make it back, where I want to be, talking to you. I gotta take it . . . outside."

Samuelson nodded. He understood. Still, he felt it was too soon, too great a risk of David's self-control, to let him outside this early. He compromised. He'd let David outside the hospital building for an hour. He must be able, the doctor insisted, to keep tabs on how David was holding up. David agreed.

He reminded David that it was still late winter out there, not yet spring. Spring was coming late that year.

David nodded and thanked him, and left. Whatever would happen to him, he had to take the chance and get out. He would heal himself out there, not in Samuelson's office.

David's hands shook as he dressed himself. His uniform hung loose on him. He had lost weight. He had to force himself to tie his shoelaces. Maybe going out on the grounds wasn't such a good idea after all. He forced himself. He sat on the side of the bed for a while to rest after dressing. And then he left the room, walking slowly, taking the first steps toward being a human being again and not a patient. He signed out at the nurse's station. She said how nice it was to see him in uniform. David had a bad moment. Yes, the uniform. He'd almost forgotten he was still in the Army.

The air was gentle outside, no wind. He smelled spring, though the grass was nowhere near green. The trees were still bare, but he thought he saw little buds.

He walked around for a while just getting the feel of being able to walk and feeling secure about it. He grew less and less anxious the more he walked. There were cars going by in the drive. No people anywhere.

And then a plane passed overhead. Immediately he tensed, then froze for a moment until the sound was gone. He tried to control his panic. There was a tree close by. He stumbled over and leaned against it for a while until the attack passed. A car was coming.

The driver stared at him. "For godsake, don't stop," David prayed. The car drove on. David went back inside the hospital for his meeting with Dr. Samuelson.

Samuelson had some news for him. His mother had requested permission to visit that weekend. Samuelson felt he couldn't refuse. He had kept her away from David longer than he thought he could. She'd called him for reports on David's progress. Samuelson tried to be honest with her. What was wrong with David might take years to get under control. David was making progress. "Of course he is," she said. "What did you expect, Dr. Samuelson?"

David heard the news with dismay. He just didn't want to see her. It wasn't that he didn't care for her. He did. He admired her, respected her—and was afraid of her. She intimated him.

He felt unable to cope with her now. He was trying to survive. Sometimes, he told himself, he was like a Jew who'd escaped the ovens. He had been spared. And now he had to survive. What he'd been through was enough to deal with for now.

He looked at Samuelson. "I might'a been better off if I, ah, you know, got wiped out." He sat hunched over in his chair, barely breathing. Samuelson got up. David raised his head and waved a hand.

"I'll be okay."

"I can ask her to postpone the trip another week. You've come a long way. I don't want you to fall back."

Samuelson was afraid he had transferred a great deal of paternal feeling to David. This could be his own son, Nathan, who was lucky and hadn't been sent to Viet Nam. "I can't put you under this much pressure," Samuelson said.

He told David he'd try to put her off. David wasn't able to stand at the end of the interview. He had simply become paralyzed. Samuelson called for a nurse. She gave David a shot. He relaxed after a while, and she wheeled him back to his room.

Mrs. Abaddon insisted on coming. Samuelson had to tell David. He had the look of a young man condemned to the chair. Samuelson explained that there was nothing he could do. He'd had a call from the senator's office.

David shared his room with a guy who seemed to be knocked out all the time. The nurses kept the curtain drawn between them. The guy was being fed intravenously and seemed to be hooked up to some life-support systems. No one came to visit him.

Sarah came on a Saturday afternoon, accompanied by Dr. Samuelson. She bent and kissed David, who just lay there, sedated. She sat down and took David's hand. The rich odor of her perfume filled the room. She had sent flowers. Dr. Samuelson left them together, telling her that if there was anything she needed she should press the call button. There was a nurse on duty.

Sarah Abaddon sat and held her son's hand and tried to talk to him. She asked him how he was and got no answer. Samuelson had warned her. After a while, she didn't talk anymore. She just sat holding his hand and crying silently. From time to time she let go of his hand and dabbed at her eyes with a handkerchief, taken from her huge leather bag.

At last she said "Are you asleep, David?" There was no answer. She felt his forehead and caressed his hair. She stood up and, out of curiosity, looked behind the curtain at the man in the other bed. She was so shocked she gasped. She turned back to David and bent over him and held him a while. Then she left, not looking back as she went out of the room.

She met with Dr. Samuelson before she left for New York. She had repaired her makeup and looked her imperious self as she confronted him across the desk. "I am not used to feeling helpless, Dr. Samuelson. I am the kind of person who gets tings done. I am helpless now, for the first time in my life. " She paused. Samuelson tried to say something. She shut him off with a wave of her hand. "My son is . . . mentally ill . . . he is a broken boy. He is finished." She muttered something in Hebrew. "He will have to be kept . . . away . . . the rest of his life?"

Samuelson was moved to see this so proud woman on the point of breaking. Would she measure up and be able to help her son with his needs, not her needs through him?

"Your son will get well, Mrs. Abaddon. All he needs is time. He has to fight to get control of his life and himself again. He has to do a lot of the struggle by himself. We can help. *You* can help, but only a little, I'm afraid. Most of it he has to do for himself. Give him a month or two before you try to see him again. Write, by all means. You know what to say. Keep reminding him of the good things. Think of those, Mrs. Abaddon. Things that were good for him and made him strong. And your husband . . . he should drop a line. When David is ready for a visit, I'll call."

She stood up, and they shook hands. She thanked him. There was respect in her manner. They were both surprised.

It took David nearly a week to recover from the attack. He felt life flowing back into his body. He was able to move with more ease. Samuelson came by every day to check his progress. He told him about the talk with his mother. There would be no more pressure from home until such time as David felt he could handle it. Samuelson would take the initiative the next time—no more surprise visits.

David was up and able to come to Samuelson's office for talks. He wanted to walk, though he was still shaky on his feet.

"Remember, David, you've got to stop trying to prove anything. You don't have to prove a thing to me."

David relaxed in the chair by the desk. Samuelson came out from behind it and sat nearby in an old armchair.

"I know, " David said. "I appreciate that. And how you handled Mother. I'll recommend you for . . . a Medal of Honor."

Samuelson laughed. He was surprised. This was the first bit of humor he'd heard from David.

They were silent for a moment.

Samuelson let him talk about whatever came into his mind, and if he didn't want to say anything, that was okay, too.

After a while, David began to talk. It was as if he decided to trust Samuelson more now. He told him some things, let him in. "You see, ah, I see Nam as a kind of American holocaust. We were the Nazis this time. I was an officer . . ." He began to breathe hard.

"Don't, if you don't want to," Samuelson said.

"I have to," David said, getting himself under control again. "I have to say the way I saw it. I was an American officer. I am a Jew. I didn't ever think much about it. I was a Jew involved in genocide. You understand, Doctor?

"Yes. I understand." David was the first Jew who had come at Samuelson this way. The atmopshere between them was charged.

"I am also a survivor," David went on, gaining strength as he talked. "I am also a survivor. I am a Viet Nam Nazi—Jew survivor. I have a responsibility."

"Please don't hate yourself," Samuelson said, very intense now. "You did not know. You were used. No one really knew the Viet Nam thing. It just seemed to happen and to go on and on. No one, nothing was able to control it."

David knew he was in deep now, and saying stuff that he really meant. He could say it to Samuelson, and he'd get it all out and never say it to anyone again. That was what was driving him.

"I am a survivor, Doctor. And the only thing left in life for me . . . is to make sure this kind of holocaust doesn't happen again." He took a deep breath. "That's what I want to get well for. I want you to help me to get well. I want to join whoever it is out there fighting to stop the next one." David was opening and closing his fists. Samuelson noticed the worry beads. David saw his look.

"Catholic rosary beads. Friend gave them to me. Sometimes odd things help." He shrugged and was silent.

Samuelson let the silence go on. Then he said, "We'll talk some more later. You got a lot out for one day." They shook hands, and David left, a fragile figure making an effort to walk steadily when Samuelson thought that he ought to fall.

David trusted Dr. Samuelson; he put no pressure on David in the way of formal psychoanalysis. Their meetings were more conversations between an older and a younger man. Samuelson saw the danger of the transference and knew that somewhere down the road it would have to be broken for both of them. He'd face that problem when they came to it. Anyway, what they were into was a lot bigger than both of them, and they both knew it.

The one real positive core Samuelson had to work with was David's fanatical desire to get well and get back into life so that he could begin working for peace in the world. The negative pole he had to confront in David, and the one that David had to confront in himself, was his own self-hatred and self-doubt after his actions at Lang Vei. David said over and over again, "How could anyone who did what I did . . . how could I work for peace in the world when I might be the one pushing the button? No one knows what they can do. . . .

Samuelson didn't ask David to come to grips with that problem head on. He just let him say it out, and then asked him more questions about his life.

One day David talked about the year in the kibbutz. Saul had sent David there after his bar mitzvah. David hated the bar mitzvah. His mother's family made a big thing of it. David felt he was being treated like some kind of prince. He didn't like that. It made him anxious and self-conscious, like he got when he felt something was expected of him, that he had to be different.

He liked the kibbutz. It was strange at first. He was very shy. Living in the dorms, taking showers with everyone, boys and girls together, the dining halls where everyone ate were new and strange experiences. And someone was always reading letters or sharing thoughts, or discussing work, or telling stories about working.

A girl became friends with him. Ruth Tobias. Dark eyes, hair and skin—Mediterranean. Her parents had sent her. David began spending all his time with her. They worked in the orange groves together, and they talked and talked. They showered together. Trying to make love together for the first time came about naturally. David was talking with her, sitting on her bed in the dorm, down the hall from his room. She was in her pajamas. The lights went out. She took his hands and helped him undress.

He slept with her that night. They didn't make love. They just touched. He got up early in the morning so that the others in the dorm wouldn't see him, and went back to his own room. He tiptoed all the way. He thought he was going to burst out of his skin.

The memories of that year flooded out of him now. Samuelson saw the energy coming back into the eyes and the body. David became flexible. He talked of Ruth. When he left the kibbutz and went back to New York, he promised to keep in touch with her, with all of his people. He thought of them as his people, his loved ones. He thought of them that way.

He wrote diligently for a while, for a year. Then the pressures of school took over, and he was getting more and more involved in the model airplane club. The letters became harder to write, and he delayed longer in answering her. Finally, he didn't answer at all.

"That was the best thing in my life. Ruth. The kibbutz."

Samuelson had found a power source. For the next few weeks he encouraged David to talk more about Ruth and the kibbutz, every little thing he could remember. Samuelson prompted him. David associated freely, and his memories were strong enough to drive out the horror of Nam.

The other thing David talked about was the model airplane club. It was a secret kind of thing. He wanted to keep it from Sarah and Saul, his being in the club. There were four of them in it. He was the only Jew. Actually, David was just helping out this guy. He was building a scale model Cessna. It would be radio-controlled, flown remotely, from the ground. The guy didn't want to fly figure-eights or anything, he just wanted to build for speed. After school, David would go to his friend's basement, and they'd put in a couple of hours' work. He began reading up on planes and aerodynamics, types of models, the works. He became so absorbed he forgot himself. And he forgot himself talking about it to Samuelson. Again, Samuelson found a source of positive energy he could exploit. He thought of a way to see how far David had really come.

Samuelson knew of a model airplane club in Washington. There was a park where some of the members met and flew. "You think you could handle it?"

David paused a long time. He'd been walking around the hospital grounds so much it was getting boring, and this was a chance at something different.

"Sure like to give it a try," he said.

"You don't think all that noise will bother you?"

"Well . . . all we can do is wait and see."

The following Sunday Samuelson took him to the park to watch some model planes in action. People were flying kites. It was a bit windy for the planes. Samuelson introduced David to a friend, and David watched him put a little P-51 Mustang up in a cloud of smoke and backfires. The noise was deafening.

Samuelson felt that if David could stand this, he had come a long way. David was absorbed. He showed no reaction to the rifle-like detonations going off all around him. He watched, smiling, at ease. He began talking engine size and ground effect with Samuelson's friend. You could see he wanted to take over and fly the P-51.

Samuelson thought they'd had enough for one day, and they drove back to the hospital. David talked freely, really opening up on aerodynamics and plane design. He fantasized about designing a plane that would take off, escape gravity, and move about in space as easily as a plane goes from city to city on earth, and he told Dr. Samuelson about his fantasy.

"You should'a been in the Air Force," Samuelson said.

David tensed. "I'm a Planet Earth guy," he said, tensely. "If we can't make it here, we ain't gonna make it anywhere else."

Samuelson didn't push the point, but he had an idea. He said nothing to David. He wanted to talk the idea over with Grevengoed first. It was very simple. He'd encourage David to learn to fly a plane. The idea was radical enough that it just might push David completely back into control of himself. He was almost there. If David took it slowly, he might finally find in flying the healing he needed. Of course, the idea might backfire, too, and set David back. It would depend on how he, Samuelson, handled it. He had a friend, a pilot, who'd flown in Nam, and scrubbed out in a rice field. Made it back, somehow. Now he was sympathetic to all-Nammers.

Grevengoed thought the idea was risky, but said Samuelson knew the patient well enough. If David wanted to try, take it slowly. It would get him out of himself, anyway, and active again.

When Samuelson suggested flying to David, David thought for a few moments and then, with a shrug, said, "Why not? If you think I can make it . . ."

"Don't see it as a challenge. You'll only get uptight if you do. This is for fun, for pleasure. Think of it that way."

David's eyes brightened. "Yeah, that's nice. I gotta stop seeing things threatening me."

The following week Samuelson drove David out to Hyde Field in Clinton, Maryland. And there they met "Mac" McCallum, who took David for his first flight in a Cherokee "Archer" N38394. The plane was the property of Capitol Flying Service, the company that ran the fixed-base airfield operations there. Samuelson went along for the flight. He thought it would normalize things that way, and he'd make sure David was seeing the flying as pleasure, not as a challenge.

The day was one of those soft, bright late spring days, with about five knots of southwest wind and plenty of visibility. They leveled off at five thousand feet and flew over Washington. David relaxed, looked down, and began to pick out places on the ground—Washington Monument, Lincoln Memorial. He showed no trace of anxiety whatsoever. Samuelson was amazed. The reaction was nothing short of sensational. But, in cases like this, you never knew what would bring on a sudden attack again. David was secure now in his hospital routine, and with Samuelson. He was not threatened by anything, and the flying was fun. He did not seem to associate it in any way with his Nam experiences.

So David took up flying with McCallum during the summer. McCallum wanted to get in flight instructor time. That was the way he put it to David, and David was welcome to pilot, too. David learned flying casually and easily. He'd piloted enough by the end of the summer that he could have flown the plane himself, if he had wanted to. He'd logged almost fifteen pilot hours. He could easily have soloed.

Samuelson had been corresponding with Sarah and Saul weekly, giving them accounts of David's progress. Now and then, Sarah would get impatient and wonder when they could come and visit. Samuelson had cut off all direct communciations with David—not even a phone call. Any communiation had to come through him. Sarah accepted the conditions when she perceived David's remarkable improvement after talking to him once, and briefly, on the telephone.

Now, however, Samuelson decided he was really going to test
David. If he got through it, he'd invite Sarah and Saul down to
Washington and begin discussions of getting David a medical discharge. In spite of the improvement, he did not think David should
be submitted further to the pressures and demands of being an
officer on active duty.

Dr. Samuelson had in mind a few sessions of group therapy.
He'd had three patients meeting in a group for some time, and they
were beginning to handle themselves quite well, expressing deep
personal attitudes and needs and feelings. They were able to take
discussions by others within the dynamics of the group.

When Samuelson suggested group therapy to David, he was
quiet for a while. David understood what Samuelson was up to. He
couldn't stay in this neutral, sheltered environment forever. "If
you think I need them," he said at last. Samuelson explained what
he hoped to accomplish. "If you can take them, we'll think about a
medical discharge. And getting you back to New York. If that's
where you want to go."

The thought of getting out of the military and getting back to
civilian life gave David a big lift, a happy one. He thought, "Christ,
I'd do anything . . . I'd go through anything to get back out." Samuelson read his face. "Okay. We'll set you up with the group. Nothing is demanded, just participate as you want to, say what you
want to. Get into the habit of communicating as you go, not like in
a structured situation. If they ask you questions, answer as you
like. It's a group, you know—a kind of kibbutz."

At the first few sessions with the group, David was shocked at
their raw approach to each other. All three were about David's age,
and each had been through some bad stuff in Nam. One guy had
been through a hazing episode. He'd placed a grenade in the pup
tent of an unpopular officer and almost killed him. The guy had
been high on dope at the time. There was a cover-up, and nothing
happened, but later, *he* got booby-trapped, and lost a leg. What
haunted him was the memory of the lieutenant he'd almost killed.

The group waited for David to talk through all of the first few
sessions. Samuelson was present all the time, moderating, and
simply calling things off when the stuff became too raw, or someone in the group was threatening to lose control.

As the sessions went on, David felt a desperate urge to say something, he didn't know what. This wasn't "Dear Abby" stuff he was
hearing. He thought of Kelley back in the hospital in Saigon, what
he had said. He'd take the Nam thing on for David until David

could bear it on his own. David wanted to say something like that to these guys in his group, now. But he knew he couldn't take on anyone's troubles, his own were enough. He still saw himself as an officer who'd betrayed his men, maybe even shot some of them, and, even worse, as an officer in an Army that was involved in genocide. He couldn't talk about that, not in a group.

But, one day, he did. One of the guys just turned to him and asked, "Well, how did you fuck up?" And David found himself talking. He wasn't even tense. Maybe he'd been conditioned by the previous sessions. Maybe it was because Samuelson was there and had heard it all before. So, David told them about what happened at Lang Vei, and what he did, and how he felt about the war, as genocide and holocaust.

He was sweating profusely when he finished. The three guys were watching him. Samuelson had gone out in the middle of the recital, leaving David to go it alone.

"Shit, man, that's hardly nothing," one of the guys said. "You got scared shitless and started shooting from the hip."

David let go then. He started screaming and cursing, and jumped up and began pounding at the walls. "You guys ought to kill me, you hear? You ought to kill me with your bare hands! Why don't you? Come on! Let's get it over with!" He challenged the three guys. They just looked at him. "Do you know what?" he yelled "I'd a shot you guys! I'm just a little gutless wonder, a shit, a pure shit! You hear?" He beat on the walls again. Samuelson came in and took him by the shoulders. "Okay, guys, enough for today," he said calmly.

The others left, and Samuelson sat with David waiting for him to calm down. He wanted to put his arms around him, but he did not dare.

When, at last, David was calm, he asked, "How do you feel?"

David looked at him. "I'm . . . ah . . . I feel a lot better than I thought."

After that incident, Samuelson kept David in the group for three more weeks. He was preparing a report to the Army Medical Advisory Group recommending a medical discharge for David with twenty percent disability. Meanwhile, he got in touch with Sarah and Saul and told them they could come and see their son, anytime. Samuelson informed David of this. David said he was ready. He wanted to continue with the group, though, until he was ready for his final discharge.

Mac McCallum had volunteered for overseas duty again, to Viet

Nam, to fly for Air America on CIA missions, so the flying was over for David. He missed it, and promised himself someday he'd go up again. He would have liked to take the flying exams and get his private pilot's license, but that was not to be. His medical history precluded that. Even if he wasn't crazy, he was now and always, according to the record, someone who might need help from a psychiatrist.

Sarah and Saul came on Saturday. Sarah cried as she enfolded David in her arms. Samuelson turned away. Saul looked at his son and pointed at the beard. "You will pass for a rabbi, son," he said. David shook his father's hand firmly, then they embraced.

The three of them went downtown to the Hilton for diner. Sarah linked her arm in David's. She would not let him go. He was quiet. He could bear her nearness. It occurred to him, looking at her across the table at dinner, that he was losing his fear of her. The realization came as a pleasant shock. He smiled at his mother, and then at his father.

"You've come through, son. I knew you would," Sarah said, her eyes filling with tears.

David faked a cough. He was hesitant to speak, but he had to tell her.

"Mother, I will never be really cured. You must know that. My record will have an account of the treatment. I will still be counseled on an outpatient basis in New York, at a VA hospital. I cannot put myself in any situation that might bring on an attack. I've . . . well, I've got to watch myself." He felt tense while he was talking, and really relieved when he had finished, as if he'd passed his biggest test so far.

Saul said, "Don't worry, son. There will be no pressure. Whatever you want to do, you do it. There is no pressure."

David looked at his father and knew he spoke the truth. But he also knew Sarah. She would accept with part of her mind that her son was now a mental casualty of war and would never be whole again. There was another side to her, however, David knew well. Sarah had faith in medical science. David knew that she clung to the belief that the doctors would eventually make him seamless again. He knew that would never happen. That was his salvation. He would watch himself and know now when he was in over his head and being threatened. He had just acquired strategies for coping.

His first piece of news for Sarah and Saul was that he would not be living with them. He had decided that after talking it over with

Samuelson. When he told them across the dinner table, Sarah bowed her head.

"They have given you back to me. And now you are taking yourself away again. You will not live with us?"

David steeled himself, looked toward Saul for help. He got it.

"Momma, why don't you try looking for a nice apartment for David when we get back. He will need our help."

David threw his father a look of gratitude. It was settled like that. Sarah would look for an apartment for him. She'd call and let him know what she found. She wouldn't take anything until she could show it to him when he came home. She began to make plans. David didn't mind, now that the main point was settled. He'd have his own place. Even if it was close, still it would be his place where he could withdraw, if need be. He needed a sanctuary. That's what he would make of his place.

When they left him at Walter Reed, Sarah insisted that she would come down to Washington to pick him up when he was released in a week or so. "I wish you wouldn't, Mother. I'll call you so you can pick me up at Kennedy." She hesitated, then kissed him.

That was the way it was going to be between them from now on—little compromises, concessions, little bargains made. David would have to give in, some of the time, for he didn't want any total confrontations. Sarah also knew she mustn't pressure him. If she wanted to have any kind of a whole son at all, she'd have to be very careful how she handled him.

They were making peace.

Before he was discharged, David went out and bought himself some clothes. He did appear at the medical hearing in his uniform, smooth shaven, and heard Dr. Samuelson present an official diagnosis of his illness, and the prognosis. And then, the recommendation. The Army medical doctors asked him a few questions, which he answered easily, except for a slight hesitancy in his speech.

They asked him to leave the room. Dr. Samuelson came out in a few minutes and shook hands. "Sign the papers on my desk on your way out, and you're a free man." He put an arm around David. "And don't let me ever catch you in a uniform again, young man."

David shook Samuelson's hand. "Thanks . . . for all of it. You're, ah, pretty great, you know."

"Don't tell them," Samuelson said. "I like my privacy."

They said good-bye. "By the way. Your medical records go to the senator's office. Some very general stuff goes to the VA in New York. Enough to let them know you can come in on an outpatient basis, and to get medication. Okay?"

"Okay!"

On his way to Dulles Airport, David thought of Sarah's power. The real record of his service in the U.S. Military would be buried forever in the senator's private files, never to appear until perhaps they were all dead. He wouldn't forget his own record though. He couldn't wipe that out.

When David walked into the terminal at J.F.K. Airport, he was met by Sarah and Saul. They were chauffeured in the family's rust-colored Cadillac to the Klein mansion, in Brooklyn Heights. There was a quiet celebration that night. Zada Klein was proud of grandson David having served his country in Viet Nam. Zada didn't know what had really happened there.

David stayed only the week in his old home. Sarah had found an apartment for him, partly furnished, in Brooklyn, in a brownstone building. David took it on sight. He did not want to stay too long at home with Sarah. He kept out of her way during the day, contacting old friends and people he knew through his family. One of them recommended he try International Computer Machines for a job. He applied, and was hired without fuss. His vita and computer experience with the Army were impressive. No one questioned him about his discharge. The ICM family was not that sympathetic to the Viet Nam War. Everyone he'd talked to treated him with a kind of sensitivity when they found out he was a Nam Vet. He was assigned to the Systems Research Institute in downtown Manhattan, where he'd be working on computer design, training under a Jeff Piedmont, who seemed nice enough.

Sarah insisted on decorating his new apartment, and he let her—another compromise. Then he moved in. His parents had all his electronics stuff moved from home for him. Most of his other things came along, too, though not all. Sarah would not hear of having *everything* moved—essentials only. David felt he could wait, and make a clean break later, slowly.

He called the Brooklyn Veteran's Administration Hospital for an appointment, and talked to a lady on the phone who had a voice that sent shivers through him. She was the nurse receptionist to a Dr. Silber, whom David was to see.

David started working at International Computer Machines. For the next four years, he consolidated his position there. His relationship with his parents, even with Sarah, mellowed. David was able to maintain an independence he'd never before enjoyed. And he met a nurse named Janet.

PART
TWO

5

DAVID, ANXIOUSLY·PACING, rode the subway train toward the Brooklyn VA Hospital Psychiatric Clinic. He wasn't going to panic, so he paced and thought of his first visit to the clinic in September, 1968.

David moved quickly through the main lobby and stopped at the information desk to ask for directions to the psychiatric clinic.

"It's on the ninth floor," replied the volunteer from her seat behind the circular counter. Smiling, she pointed to the bank of elevators at the far end of the lobby.

The elevator was crowded with people as it left the first floor, but when it got to the seventh floor, the last two remaining passengers got off, and David rode to the ninth floor alone. As he stepped out of the elevator, his eyes darted back and forth until he found the clinic door standing open. He was glad as hell to be there at last because the terrible ache in his stomach had returned the instant he had seen that damned bumper sticker. It had just happened, outside, in the street in front of the VA hospital: US/USSR NUCLEAR FREEZE NOW! "It never fails," he thought. "Every time it just reminds me of the holocaust thing again."

Calming himself, David marched into the clinic and up to the reception desk and asked, "Would you please tell me where the men's room is?"

The nurse smiled and said softly, "It's right over there," pointing to a door on the opposite side of the room.

David thanked her, turned and walked straight across the room, went inside, locked the door and vomited into the urinal. He wiped his mouth with a paper towel, washed his hands and face, went back out, and sat in one of the orange plastic chairs lined up against the walls.

Doctor Louis Silber glanced quickly through the medical history in the file in front of him. Then he called on the intercom to the nurse in the waiting room.

The nurse looked at David and asked, "Are you David Abaddon?"

"Yes." He felt uneasy at her glance.

"You may go in now. The doctor is waiting for you."

As he went past the reception desk, he glanced at the nurse. She deliberately looked away. He read the nametag pinned to her uniform. J.L. Schreiber, R.N.

As David came into the room, the doctor rose and stuck out his hand.

"Hello. I'm Lou Silber," he said.

David shook hands with him and sank heavily into the big vinyl-covered easy chair. They talked for almost an hour. "Let's just get acquainted," Silber had said.

When David got up to leave, Silber handed him a prescription and smiled. David thanked him and left. The nurse was talking on the phone as he walked past the reception desk. He nodded at her. She smiled. Later, while he was waiting on the second floor, at the pharmacy dispensing window, he thought about her. She was attractive. Looked like Elke Sommer. He hadn't thought about women in some time. He got his Librium and left.

Walking to the subway David thought about the session with the doctor. It wasn't anything like talking wifh Samuelson. It didn't need to be, of course.

Riding on the train back to ICM, David thought it would be nice to have Silber there. Silber reminded him of Kelley. But, that nurse! He knew that sooner or later he would have to ask her out. He'd have to take it easy, though.

That was in '68. It took time before he could trust himself to ask— a long time—some years, in fact.

Today, he'd slept in. He was taking the day off. His plan was to do his jogging, and then to go to the clinic to visit with Doc. What he really intended to do was ask Janet to go to lunch with him. He'd asked her before. She was always polite, but said no. Seemed like she was always busy, or had other plans.

On the calendar on his desk he wrote, *"Ask her again today."* He noted the date: May 29, 1972.

He took a quick shower, put on his brown and white jogging

stuff, and took the subway to Central Park. It was a twenty-minute ride. As he got up to street level, he saw the tiny silver-haired lady sitting motionless at the Park's entrance, waiting to sell her flowers. Admiring them as he walked up to her, David looked at the petunias, peonies, pansies, iris, and the last of the tulips, but his eyes fell on the tiny red silk roses. He asked, "Did you make those yourself?"

"Yup."

"How much are they?"

"Two seventy-five each."

"I'll take one," David told her, reaching into his pocket for the money and handing it to her.

She gave him the tiny rose, and his change, and returned to stoic.

David walked away remembering that for a long time he had been sure she was blind. He had watched her often whenever he was near that area in Central Park. She always wore the opaque sunglasses,even when there was no sun, and it seemed to him that she almost never moved. She just sat, motionless. But once, while jogging close by, in the summer of '69, or maybe it was '70, he saw a little dog walk over and lift his leg to pee on her ankle. David smiled to himself remembering how the little lady moved her foot, almost imperceptibly, bumping the dog away. Funny lady.

David tucked the little silk rose carefully into the pocket of his jogging top, and put the change in his pants. He ran three miles in and around Central Park. As he was about to trot over to the subway station and go to the VA, he noticed a large group gathered around a woman. From a distance it appeared that she was standing on some kind of platform, shouting into a bullhorn. David moved in that direction until he could hear what she was saying.

"If we must, we will. We'll have a thousand peace rallies, just like this, and put a stop to the nuclear madness all around us. Those politicians in Washington won't listen unless we do it. If we fail, they will blow up this planet."

David flashed. He saw Viet Nam, and the perfectly shined symbolic combat boots, placed in front of the officers and men of the corps standing at rigid attention, boots that were meant to honor those killed in action, whose bodies had already been shipped to the States—in bags.

He started quickly toward the subway station stairs. He had to get to the VA at once. He needed Doc.

The Flower Lady watched with curiosity as she saw the dark-haired young man race past and away from her. As he disappeared down the stairs to the subway across the street, she thought, "Strange. He always before just jogged or walked quietly alone in the park."

David burst into the waiting room in his jogging suit. Janet was startled, and knew instantly something was wrong. She spoke into the intercom.

"David, Doctor Silber will see you now," she said.

Silber always greeted David in the same manner. They were more friends than patient and therapist. They had talked about many things—agent orange, opium poppies from the Golden Triangle in Southeast Asia smuggled into China, then to Anywhere, USA, nukes in artillery shell boxes David thought he saw once in a truck in Nam. Just one big fucking mess, the war.

David sat down and tried to regain control of himself. Then, he talked.

"Protesters were gathered around this shouting female in Central Park, Doc. She had a bullhorn. You could hear the noise all over. She was hollering about blowing up this whole god-damn planet. Raw. Awful. Raw shit." He paused for a deep breath. "I almost got sick again, like in '68, the first time I came here to rap with you. Anyway, I had to see you!"

Silber listened, thought, "It'll take about forty minutes, and then he'll run down." He was surprised. David had been doing much better, going longer and longer between panic episodes. The last one was months ago. That group in Central Park must've been something else. He let David talk himself out, and then tried to calm him with talk of peace and all those working for it.

"David, why don't you make another appointment with Jan, and come back next week to see me again? Okay?" he said.

David felt better, thanked Doc and left. He went out to the circular counter in the waiting room, leaned across it and said, "Hi."

Janet Schreiber had been nurse-receptionist in the Brooklyn Vet's Hospital Psychiatric Clinic since 1968. In four years she'd seen a little of almost everything. She looked up from the stack of paperwork in front of her as David spoke. She smiled. "Hello. Again."

He was working at seeming to be casual. "Will you go to lunch with me?"

It didn't work. She knew he was anxious. It showed. She hesitated. He looked very upset. She had never dated a patient. It would be okay, if she wanted. He really looked upset.

"Where will we go?" she said. Just like that.

He half sang the jingle, " . . . to McDonald's!"

Janet smiled. "Meet you in the main lobby in fifteen minutes," she said, looking at her watch.

David waited for her in the main lobby, his jogging suit attracting some attention. And at last there she was. All he could think of to say was, "Hi." She grinned as they left for McDonald's.

Traffic was heavy. David thought there must be a thousand cars lined up. They waited at the corner for the light to turn green.

"Tell me about yourself," she said quietly.

David looked at her, and just then the light changed. They started across the street. "Graduated from N.Y.U. in '68. Double B.S. in nuclear physics and computers. Been at ICM since the fall of '68. September. About six months after I got back from Nam." He hesitated. "That place was hell. Someday when the Lord's ready, He'll give the earth an enema starting at Lang Vei."

She laughed. He thought, "She's fantastic!"

McDonald's was crowded, and when they finally worked their way to the front, he ordered a hamburger, fries and coke, "Times two."

David paid. Janet picked up the tray, and walked outside. He followed. They sat at a picnic table with a canopy. "God, they're good," she said. He nodded, eating and watching her eat.

When they'd finished, they just sat sipping cokes. Suddenly David said, "Governor Wallace was shot two weeks ago. They got the creep who did it right away. A guy named Bremer. Bastard! Shot four people. Wallace is completely paralyzed now." He paused, gulped some air, then, "Why would anyone do that? He must be bananas!"

Janet smiled at him. "I don't know either. People do funny things. Life doesn't always make sense, David."

He studied her face, wishing he could see her eyes better. The sunglasses hid them.

"We'd better start back. I should be at my desk by one."

Their shoulders brushed as they stood to leave. She didn't move away from him as they walked out, forgetting to empty their trays and stack them.

"You're New Yorkers?" she said.

"Mother is. My father was born in Palestine. He's a Sabra."

"A what?"

"A Jewish person born in Palestine—now Israel."

"Where does your father work?"

"At the UN. He's on the Staff of the Israeli Delegation."

Janet turned to look at him as they walked. "He must be important."

They waited on the last corner for the light to change. A car stopped in front of them. The radio was on. Roberta Flack was singing, " . . . the first time ever I saw your face . . . "

David looked at Janet. She glanced at him, then turned quickly and stepped off the curb. When they got to the main entrance, he said, "Will you go to see *The French Connection* with me tonight?"

She hesitated, thinking. "Call me later this afternoon. Thank you for lunch, David."

She went inside, rode the elevator to the ninth floor, walked straight into Doctor Silber's office. "May I speak to you, please?"

"Yes. What is it, Jan?"

"David Abaddon." She closed the office door.

"What about him?"

"We just had lunch. He's asked me to go to a movie tonight. I'm a little worried."

"Why?"

"Well . . . his . . . condition. I don't want to . . . you know!"

Silber smiled. "You've seen his file. He's okay. He needs friends."

"I don't want him to, well, you know . . . get serious."

"You know what's in his medical record, Jan." Silber got up from his desk and walked over to pat her arm. "My personal feeling is that he is a very fine young man."

"He really is very nice. Gosh, I've known him so long."

"Sounds like you've decided something."

"Guess I have. Thank you, Doctor."

David took the subway home, showered, shaved and dressed. Later, he dialed the clinic and made a date with Janet for that evening.

He was waiting at the theatre before six forty-five. She was a little late, but she came. It was the first time he'd seen her out of uniform. She was stunning! "You're beautiful," he said. He got their tickets and bought a bag of popcorn as they walked inside.

They both liked the movie and thought Gene Hackman deserved the Oscar.

Later, they walked to Hamburg Inn and sat in a booth and had coffee.

"What are you thinking?" she asked.

"Vietnam. When we used to patrol in the jungle at Lang Vei, we'd see caravan after caravan of South Vietnamese carrying backpacks, moving north. Once we followed one for a while. We had to turn back. They went on into Laos. We later heard they go on up to the Chinese border to barter. Those guys were carrying opium poppies that end up in Hawaii and L.A. Want to know what we called that?" That was *The Chinese Connection.*" He added, "The drug problems in Nam were covered up pretty well, Jan. But we knew how bad it really was."

"It's bad all over, now," she said.

He brought her to her subway, and said goodnight, not even trying to kiss her. It had been so long he didn't think he could remember how.

Next morning, he woke angry at himself! And frustrated. He should've asked her for another date right after the movie. Now the days until his next appointment at the VA would just simply drag by.

He called her at work. No, she didn't feel up to another movie so soon. Perhaps some other time.

Thank God for Jeff Piedmont's support at work. Doing advanced computer projects for ICM was easy compared to figuring women. Jeff was not only a great boss, he seemed to know females. David went to Jeff's office and told him, "Last night we got along fine. Today, it's like she doesn't even care. I can't compute it."

"Welcome to my world," Jeff said. "I've been married over ten years. Got three sons. Audra is the greatest, but the only thing predictable about her is that she's unpredictable."

They laughed together.

Jeff's secretary heard. She glared at them through the open office door.

David left and walked back down the hall to his computer console, wishing it was next Monday and VA time again.

Father Donovan was waiting for Janet in his study, in the Brooklyn St. Thomas More Church. Her call from work that afternoon was almost mysterious. Said she was anxious, that she'd explain everything at seven o'clock. Her faithful attendance at Mass and gentle manner made her easy to like. Father Donovan often thought, "She could easily be Irish, except for her name. Schreiber's so German. Thank the Lord she didn't end up a Lutheran."

Janet was over fifteen minutes late. She apologized, explaining that she'd missed the six-thirty subway train. Standing before Donovan in his study, she said, "Father, I'm seeing a Jewish boy. What do you think?"

"Why don't you have a chair, dear, and we'll talk about this," he said gently. She sat in the easy chair, right next to his.

"There. That's much more comfortable for both of us," he smiled. "Now. What's this about a young Jewish man?"

"Well, Father, for the last several years this young Viet Nam veteran has been coming to the psych clinic for counseling. We've been looking at each other for years. You know what I mean. Anyway, he gets counseling from my supervisor. Doctor Silber likes him, too, and told me it would be okay to date David. So. I went to lunch with him last Monday. Then we went to *The French Connection* that night. Now, he's been calling me at work. He wants to go out again."

"Something more?"

"Yes, Father. I've read his medical record. Just as a part of my duties. It's not really very bad. Not in the sense that he'd do anything to me. Or to anyone else. David is nice. But . . . well, he got overly tired and worried in that awful battle at Lang Vei. You know, the Tet Offensive, in February of 1968. Our poor soldiers fought with the Communists for seventy-seven straight days. So far, that's still the longest battle of this war. I like him, Father but . . . he's . . . not a Catholic."

"Is that what's really bothering you, my dear?"

"Yes! And I just know if I keep seeing him, I'm going to start caring for him a lot! He makes me laugh. He's such a riot when he tells Woody Allen stories."

"Your judgment is always fine, Janet. I'm a little concerned too. Do you think he'd come here and visit with me?"

"I think he would, if I asked him to."

"Well, now. Why don't you talk to him, and then call me."

He stood up. "Is there anything else I can do for you?"

Janet got up. "No, I don't think so, Father. Oh—thank you for staying late tonight to talk with me."

"You're quite welcome, dear. Good night."

"I feel much better now. Thanks again. Good-bye, Father."

From the study, Janet walked into her favorite church. She genuflected and knelt down. On the kneeler, she said prayers, for David and for herself. Then she rose slowly and walked out of the church and across the street. Down in the subway, she got on the train and all the way home promised herself that she'd go out with David Abaddon again only if he would agree to talk to her priest. Janet had been going to Mass at St. Thomas More since she first got to New York. And Father Donovan had been like a second father. He always knew best!

On Monday, David was early for his appointment at the clinic. He had thought the day would never come. He hurried to the ninth floor and into the waiting room. He looked around. Janet wasn't there. No one was. Disappointed, he sat down in a stiff plastic chair, and waited for someone to come into the room. At last, Doc Silber came out of his office and invited David in. He followed the doctor through his office door and closed it. He tried to be casual. "Hi, Doc. Isn't Miss Schreiber here today?" he said.

"Yes. Janet's here, Dave. She must've stepped down the hall for a minute," Silber smiled. "I understand you're seeing her."

"Yes, sir," David said.

"I'm sure she'll be back in a few moments." He paused. "How've things been this past week?" He sat down and motioned to David.

"I really need to talk to Janet," David said. He sat down. "Things are okay. The news makes me tense. All the nuclear stuff with the Russians. The talks won't come to anything." He looked around. "We'll have another holocaust. I've told you about my own grandfather. My Zada. He died in an oven at Auschwitz. They caught him in Warsaw. He was just visiting from Palestine. He got caught in Hitler's blitzkrieg. The Nazis herded all the Jews into trains and took them away. Like cattle. That was it! My Zada, burned up." He felt very agitated.

Dr. Silber listened with interest. No matter what conversation started their sessions, invariably they'd end up on some phase of holocaust: of WW II, of Viet Nam, or of the new holocaust—nuclear war.

David slowly relaxed. Talking it out did him good, but he kept looking at the door, and Silber released him early.

Janet was at her desk filing some medical records. David walked to the counter and said, "Hi."

She walked with him to the elevator. "David, I talked to my priest, Father Donovan. He wants to meet you, and talk to you. Will you come with me to see him?"

"Sure. One of my favorite people, anywhere, is a priest from Nam. His name is Joe Kelley. That man supported me in the hospital. I didn't want to do anything. I'd lost it all. I owe him a lot! Anyway, when can we visit Father Donovan?"

"I'll make an appointment for tomorrow right after work, if that's okay," Janet said.

"You bet."

David handed her the red silk rose. He'd been so excited the last time they were together, he'd forgotten to give it to her.

"I love it," Janet said. She asked him to call.

He nodded and left, very happy. He couldn't compute her, but at least they were together again.

In the office, Janet phoned Father Donovan and made an appointment for the following evening. She wanted to tell Doctor Silber the good news. When his last patient left, she went right into his office. "Doctor, David has agreed to visit with my priest. And I've just made arrangements for both of us to see him tomorrow after work. May I leave a little early to be sure I'm there to meet David?"

"Of course, Jan."

"I like David. He's nice! But . . . if I'm going to have a relationship with him, well . . . I promised myself I'd go out with him again if he'd just talk to Father."

"Jan, I think it's an excellent idea to have Dave see your priest." He didn't want to say too much at this point.

"I do care about him, Doctor. And I feel fine about us now."

She knew it was going to be serious with David. It was all happening so fast. But, no—it had really been happening for a long time!

The phone rang moments after seven, and of course it was David. "Father agreed to see us tomorrow at five-fifteen. Is it still okay?" Janet asked.

"Sure thing."

"David, I forgot to thank you for the rose. Where did you get it?"

"Oh. In Central Park. I sometimes go there to jog. There's a little old lady who's always selling flowers on a corner there. She watches me from behind her dark glasses. And I watch her. We never speak—at least not till last week. She's funny. Kinda weird. She made that red silk rose herself."

"It's great. Thanks, David."

She was silent. Then, "I've got to hang up now. My mother is going to call me from Ithaca. I'll be going home in a few weeks, and she wants to talk about that. So, I'll see you at the church. Bye-bye."

"Okay—so long. See you." He could hear the smile in her voice.

David's phone rang almost the second he put it back on the receiver. It was his mother. "So—how are you?" she asked.

"Fine. How are you and Poppa?"

"Just okay. You know. It's that time of life for me. Your father is fine. What have you been doing?"

Janet. He thought of her instantly. Better not say it though. "I've been reading a lot." He paused. Then, "Right now I'm starting a new book by Irving Stone. *The Passions of the Mind.* It's kind of a biographical novel about Doctor Sigmund Freud. Have you heard of it?"

"Of course. I've read it. When are you coming home? Your Zada wants to see you!" David did not visit very often recently, so she called to talk.

"I'm not sure. Please give him my love. And tell him I'll try to be there the weekend after this next one."

"Why can't you come home this weekend?"

"I'm going out with a friend. We're going to see *The Godfather.*"

"Is this a girl, David?"

"Yes, Mother. She's a nurse, at the VA hospital. We're seeing each other . . . ah . . . as friends. You'll like her," David said, forcing calm into his voice.

Sarah paused. Then she said, "A shiksa, I suppose!"

"Mother . . . *please.* And then he said, "Her name is Janet!"

God! Sarah could make him mad in a flash!

"David, I've told you before. You should not spend time with gentile girls. It will only lead to trouble in the end." Breathing heavily, "You should come home this weekend and see your family. Be with Jewish people. It's better for you."

"Mother, I'll try to be home soon. I'd better go now and get my dinner off the stove before it burns. Tell everyone hello. And love. I'll be seeing you. 'Bye."

"Good-bye, David. And you should listen to your mother."

He hung up and went out for something to eat, downtown, away from the telephone.

Tuesday dragged by. Janet couldn't wait for four o'clock to come. For David, at ICM in midtown Manhattan, it was even worse. Jeff Piedmont, his boss, finally told him, "Leave, and go see her!"

Janet was standing on the front steps looking for him. They hugged. Then she led him to the study.

Father Donovan was reading a book when they came in. "Hello, you two."

"Hello, Father, this is David Abaddon."

"How are you, David?" he said, standing to shake his hand.

"It's nice to meet you, Father," David said as he glanced at the thick snow-white hair, and the priest's pale blue eyes, so penetrating in their intensity. Donovan's rosy cheeks gave him a healthy looking countenance, and when he spoke he seemed, somehow, to glow. David thought, "God, those Irishmen!"

"Please sit down, young people." They did, as Donovan sat in a chair in front of his desk. "Well. Tell me about David," the priest said.

David talked about himself for a while.

"Do you, ah, go to synagogue?" Father Donovan asked.

David explained his growing up, his bar mitzvah, and spending a year in the kibbutz. "I am a Jew, Father. But my religion is the brotherhood of man." Father Donovan nodded. Janet smiled.

"I'd like to know more about Catholicism," David said.

"I'm sure I can help you," the priest said.

"I met this Father Kelley in Nam. He was really important to me."

Father got up and went around behind his desk. He reached into his top center drawer, removed a pamphlet, and handed it to David. *On Becoming a Catholic,* by Father Peter Schmidt.

"This should answer some of your basic questions, David. If you'd like to, let's talk after you've read it," Donovan said.

"I'd like that."

David leafed through it quickly. No pictures, except the one on the cover—an arty crucifix, Christ clearly depicted.

"He was one of our boys, you know, Father," David said smugly. The three of them smiled at each other—easily, genuinely.

As they all stood, Donovan extended his hand. David shook it.

Janet watched them, feeling quite pleased.

"God bless you both," Father Donovan said.

David and Janet left, holding hands. She took David into the church. Janet genuflected and crossed herself. Then she sat down in the pew and motioned for him to sit next to her. He did, and took her hand. Looking around, she whispered, "Isn't it beautiful?"

David nodded, as he glanced around. The large cross up front, with the crucified Christ hanging there, caught his attention. It seemed a harsh and cruel image to represent a religion.

Janet whispered prayers, and they left.

Outside, David asked why she was whispering in the church. Janet explained, "It's a mark of respect. It's traditional." He smiled and nodded. David Abaddon understood about tradition.

They walked across the street, into a small cafe, and ordered iced tea with lemon.

As they sat in the booth she said, "Thank you for coming, David. It means a lot to me."

He was silent.

She asked, "Why are you so quiet all of a sudden?"

He paused. "I think about you so much, Janet Schreiber. As soon as I get up. When I jog. And at work. All the time. I just always want to know you're all right."

She was silent now. They drank and left. She put her arm through his, and they walked the rest of the way to Shakey's Pizza without speaking. Inside, they ordered a cheese pizza, with extra cheese, to go. She carried it on the subway and to the front of her apartment building. Janet opened the front door, and they walked up two flights of stairs. She unlocked the door to her apartment, and they went in.

David glanced around the room. Soft blue velvet sofa, matching easy chair, small writing table and chair, wall-to-wall shag carpeting, navy blue, sheer curtains on three windows on the front. African violets on each of the sills—color-matched decor. And immaculate.

She led him to the kitchen, where he sat down at the table. Janet said, "We'd better eat the pizza before it gets cold."

She sat across from him at the small table, and they ate half the pizza.

Then they took their tea and went to sit in the living room on the sofa. *All In The Family* was on TV. They laughed at Archie, Edith, Meathead, and Gloria. "They're insane," David said.

After it was over, she turned the set off. He said, "I can't believe what they get away with."

Janet said, "It's getting late. We both have to work tomorrow."

"I know. But I hate to leave."

They walked to the door then. He took her face in his hands and kissed her gently. She asked, "Will you call me tomorrow?"

"You know I will. I'm calling every day from now on."

Janet smiled at him, and closed the door as he disappeared down the stairs.

When he was down in the street, in front, David turned and looked up at her windows. Janet was standing in the center one. She waved to him.

"Goddamn, she's beautiful!" he said. Later, on the subway and in bed, he kept thinking of how sweet her mouth tasted—even after pizza.

As soon as David got to work at ICM next morning, he called Janet, and told her how much he had enjoyed the evening.

"Thanks, David," she said.

They made a date to see *The Godfather*.

"I told my mother I was seeing it with you." He took a deep breath. "She got mad at me! So, what else is new!"

Janet sighed. She knew this was trouble.

David called Janet every day, faithfully, sometimes twice. She'd answer, and wait for his voice to be there. He told her he felt comfortable, happy.

Both of them were anxious for Friday to come, and it finally did. David met her at the Manhattan Hyo Tan Nippon restaurant on East 59th. A Japanese hostess with tiny shuffling steps led them to a small, low table. They took off their shoes and put them to one side. They sat down cross-legged, on floor mats right next to the table, to be served. The sake wine they sipped was not exactly what they had in mind, but they drank some anyway. While they waited for the food to be brought to their table, David described the new ICM computer. Janet talked about plans for her trip to Ithaca, and told him about her parents. He watched her mouth form words. Once when she paused he said, "You're beautiful." She smiled shyly, and thanked him in a whisper.

They shared a salad with some awful-tasting dressing on it. Then the waitress brought out a shrimp dish with rice. Delicious. But what they liked most was the seclusion. Before six it was very private there, almost exclusive.

He paid the waitress with his Diner's Club card, saving unnecessary conversation with the waitress, who spoke with a heavy accent.

As David signed the credit slip, Janet put on her shoes. After the waitress shuffled away, Janet handed David his jodhpur boots, remarking on their shine. He just said, "Let's go."

Outside, he said, "I'm really into the Systems Research Institute work now. We've finished the design on the new ICM 370. God, would the Russians like to have our computer stuff! We can run circles around anything they have. Our whole missile system is based on advanced computer technology."

David watched, then whistled for a cab. It didn't stop. He waved to the next taxi driver coming toward them. The car stopped in front of Janet. They climbed in and David said, "RKO Theatre."

After the movie they crossed the street and went into a liquor store. She chose "The Blue Nun." Outside, he got the first taxi to stop. On the way to her apartment David asked, "How did you like Marlon Branflakes in the movie?"

She ignored that, and said that Al Pacino and Robert Duvall and Brando were great actors. "Academy Award performances. Weren't they?"

David nodded.

The cab stopped at her brownstone. David paid the driver, and they went up the stairs and into her kitchen. She said they could put ice in the wine to cool it. He nodded. It was hot.

Janet motioned for him to get the ice cubes and put them in the drinks. She walked into the living room and turned on her window air-conditioner. David brought the wine in and sat down on the blue velvet couch. She sat next to him.

The wine mellowed them. David reached for her face and turned it toward him. She kissed his cheek. He kissed her mouth. He pressed closer.

Janet relaxed, letting herself gently away. He lifted his wine glass, took another drink. Then he put it on the coffee table in front of the couch and motioned with his hand for her to move to the far edge. She did. He lay down, putting his head in her lap. His eyes closed almost instantly.

He awoke, suddenly, and sat up rubbing his eyes. "I really fell asleep," he said.

She stood, smiled, and got his glasses. While he was sleeping, she'd taken them off and put them next to his wine glass.

He put his glasses on and stood up. They hugged, kissed good-night, and he left. David took the stairs two at a time and was outside in seconds. He turned, looked up, waved. He knew where she'd be standing. He thought, "God, I love her."

6

In the morning, first thing, David called Janet and invited her to his apartment. He gave her directions, and she was there in less than an hour. She rang his apartment bell from downstairs, outside, by pressing the "Visitor Alert" button next to his name, under the mailbox.

"Hi. Is that you, babe?" He put his face next to the speakerbox on the wall just inside the front door of his apartment, but he had already depressed the access control button, and the buzzer was sounding downstairs. She pushed the first floor security door open and climbed the stairs to his second floor apartment.

His door was open for her. She stepped just inside and they hugged and kissed. A neighbor walked by, smiling. Janet shut the door.

"It only took about fifteen minutes to get over here on the subway. And then it was a three-minute walk to your front steps."

"I'm so glad to see you! Let me show you my apartment."

They walked through together. Older furniture, she thought, but how clean everything was—polished linoleum in the hallway, vacuumed throw rugs in the living room. The brown two-cushion couch was worn some, but spotless. "An incredible guy," she thought. The air smelled of Pine-Sol in the sparkling kitchen, and in the bathroom. "He'd be so easy to live with," Janet imagined.

"Lieutenant Abaddon, you pass muster. Inspector's grade is nine point five."

"Ma'am, a question. Why didn't I get a perfect ten?"

"Well—the inspector got only one kiss!"

David took her face in his hands and turned it gently to kiss the left cheek, then the right, and finally, the mouth.

"Funny, you don't look French to me," she giggled, "but you get a ten from the inspector now."

Janet glanced down the hall and asked, "David, what are those two rooms back there on either side of the hallway?"

"On the right, toward the street, is my bedroom. Want to visit?" he asked, smiling.

She nodded, and they went back to the doorway. Light blue spread on a big double bed with a single headboard. On his nightstand, next to the phone, there was a copy of *The Passions of the Mind*. Easy chair with his black jodhpur boots neatly placed on the floor, right under the front fringe. Both closet doors were closed. Not a stitch of clothing in sight! Everything perfectly placed.

She turned around, pointed to the closed door across the hall, and asked, "What's in that room?"

He opened the door and went in. She followed.

"My God, David, where did you get these computers?"

"Surplus from the institute. They give it away for almost nothing, at least to me. I bought the rest."

"But, isn't it terribly expensive?" She hesitated. "How can you afford it?"

"My mother. She gives me as much as I want."

He sat down at the mid-point of the console, equipment on either side of him stretching wall to wall, about eight feet. Janet told him she'd never seen anything like it.

"Show me how it works," she urged.

He turned the system's master switch to "ON" and entered his password.

"David, why did you type my name on the console?"

"I use 'JANET' as my password. Know what I'm saying?"

"Tell me."

"For security reasons, a computer is always programmed to give no information at all unless the correct password is entered, and it has to be right at the beginning—the first transaction, or the computer just won't function at all." He paused. "Okay?"

"Okay. We have that at the VA. But I didn't know you would have it here."

"Sure," with emphasis. "It's good practice."

Then David typed on the keyboard, pushed "ENTER" and information appeared on the viewer. It was "Daily Quotations" from the New York Stock Exchange, selected data he'd already programmed. "Works just like ICM, IBM, Hewlett-Packard, Burroughs, Control Data, and AT&T," he said.

He entered new commands and the screen cleared. At once, a chess game was on the viewer. David typed in his move. Instantly, the computer responded with its play. Suddenly, the two were involved in rapid-fire action. Janet was spellbound.

"David, are you a genius?"

"I once scored one-sixty on the Stanford-Binet, an IQ test they gave our class in high school." He turned to look at her.

"Isn't genius anything above one-forty?"

"I think so." He turned back to the keyboard.

She asked him to put the stock quotes back on the screen. They spread across it. "My Dad would be fascinated with that. He's always trying to make a killing, as he says, on the Exchange. Would it be okay to tell him that it's your hobby?"

"Sure." He paused. "I'd like to meet your family." David turned his face toward hers. He stood and put his arms around her and pulled her to him. "I'd like to go to Ithaca with you, some time."

"I'd like that."

They kissed. Again. Then she told him she was hungry. He offered to fix omelets, turned, and pushed the system's master switch off.

In the kitchen Janet laughed as he put on an apron. Her laughter stopped him, and he turned to look at her. She apologized. "David, I'm sorry. But you do everything so perfectly. I didn't mean to hurt you. The act of putting the apron on—that's what seemed so funny to me. I wasn't laughing at *you*."

He shrugged his shoulders and turned back to the kitchen counter. She came up behind and hugged him hard. Her hands and arms and body against his felt good—David Abaddon was in love.

He got the eggs and cheddar cheese and milk from the refrigerator. Pointing for her, he asked that she get the large frying pan from the bottom cupboard. She did, and put it on the stove. Then she found the plates, silverware, cups and napkins and set the table.

He made two omelets. Perfect. Coffee, and two bagels from the breadbox on the counter. They were delicious with the cream cheese and grape jelly. Janet said she'd not had such a good brunch in a long time. And they were content to just sit there and sip more coffee.

David broke the silence. "Why don't we go to Central Park and walk around some? It's almost eleven o'clock. I'll show you the little old lady who makes the tiny red silk roses."

She nodded. They stacked the dishes in the sink, and cleaned the table.

They walked out of his apartment, down the stairs and to the subway station. Inside, they arrived just in time to see the train they wanted to take pulling out. So they waited and watched the others who were waiting—a normal pastime in the New York subway.

Suddenly, a lady screamed, and they turned at once in the direction of the noise. The lady was about a hundred feet away and stood pointing at them. A blur, and then they saw a young boy who couldn't be over fifteen race toward them. A woman's black leather handbag dangled from his right hand. David moved in front of Janet to shield her from whatever was about to happen. The boy must've seen David move. Suddenly the thief veered sharply left and ran up the station stairs and out of sight.

"That's awful," Janet said.

"Happens all the time, Jan," he said.

"He must be desperate."

"Probably Puerto Rican. Maybe he needs bread for a fix. Who knows?"

She put her arm through his, and hugged herself close to him.

Their train came at last and they rode to the park stop without saying much, but Janet held his arm the entire time. It felt good to them both.

They walked up the station stairs, across the street, into the park. David pointed to the flower lady. She was sitting there, staring straight ahead. Flowers were placed, as always, in a horseshoe around her. She never moved her head—as usual. They walked over to the stand, and walked past her. She didn't move. Her sunglasses were opaque, and you couldn't see her eyes—as usual.

They turned, came back, and stood right in front of her. He asked, "How much are the red silk roses?"

Silence. Then, "You know!"

Janet and David looked at each other, then back at the lady. They both smiled at her. She didn't move.

They walked away, and didn't look back at her.

"God—she is weird, David. She never moved her head or her eyes, but she must've remembered you." Janet stopped to look back, and asked, "Is she always that way?"

"Yes, and I'm sure she watches me jog, too. I like to study her."

Janet thought it was the flower lady who liked to study David and told him so.

"You jealous?"

Janet laughed.

They walked then into Central Park, and stopped to buy pop-corn to feed the ducks near the shore of the lake. Her arm through his, they went past Hans Christian Andersen's statue, and Alice in Wonderland's. They walked into the Children's Zoo and didn't want to leave. The excitement of the children over all the animals and birds and real scenery and everything, they agreed, aroused memories of when, as children, their families had come here, probably at one time or other on the same day. And just maybe, they had passed close by each other.

Later, as they walked to the subway entrance, David pointed to Temple Emanu-El and said they would visit there sometime. She nodded as they went into the subway station.

Her train had just pulled in, and they hurriedly agreed to meet later and go out to eat. She got into the train and called to him over her shoulder that she'd phone him later. The doors closed with a "clack" and her train rolled away.

David boarded the train that had just pulled into the station and sat across the aisle from two young couples. Without realiz-ing it, he was entertaining them by the look on his face as he whistled and hummed, "The First Time Ever I Saw Your Face." One of them whispered to the others that he looked just like Woody Allen. And they asked him to tell them something funny. He did. He was used to that. It'd happened to him before.

He was waiting impatiently at his apartment, when the phone rang. Janet wanted to meet as soon as he could. David, too.

They met at the subway turnstiles under the World Trade Center. It took eleven minutes to get to the Journal Square stop. They walked upstairs, out of the station, and took the bus south into Jersey City. David wanted to take her to Braggadocio's. He promised it would be the best Italian sausage sandwich—and wine—she'd ever had.

They got off the bus and walked the two blocks to Braggadocio's Italian Restaurant. The hostess seated them in a hardwood booth near the front door. The smells of tomato sauce and cheeses and garlic filled the air. They agreed that you got the real thing only in a place like that.

Both of them ordered the sausage sandwich and the red house wine, with big tossed salads and creamy garlic dressing. They talked about the scenes in Central Park and those of the bus ride. Their orders came in ten minutes, and they ate as if famished. Jan told David he'd been right, it was the best.

As they walked to the bus stop, David mentioned how fast she'd eaten. She told him she'd wanted to get back to her apartment, where they could be alone.

The ride back to Brooklyn and the walk to her building took an hour. They opened the downstairs security door and went up to her apartment. The couch was wide enough, and they lay together to watch TV. They fell asleep.

When David woke he was on the couch alone. It was daylight. He was still in his clothes, his shoes off—his glasses too, but they were on the coffee table. Janet wasn't anywhere in sight. He put his glasses on and found his shoes near the easy chair. His watch read seven.

Softly, he called, "Janet?"

"I'm in the kitchen, having coffee. Want some?"

He got off the couch, put his shoes on and walked to the doorway. She was sitting at the table in her sheer light blue nightgown and matching peignoir. Drinking coffee, and reading the Sunday paper. "Beautiful!" he thought.

She smiled up at him. "You were sleeping so soundly when I woke up at two, I just couldn't wake you. So, I snuck your glasses and shoes off and then went to bed. How do you feel?"

He walked over, knelt on one knee, and they hugged. David told her he'd had a perfect sleep, one of the best, but now he had to use the bathroom. She pointed down the hallway. He felt perfectly at home. He'd come a long way from Lang Vei.

When he got back to the kitchen, she'd already poured a cup of black coffee, and put a piece of buttered toast on a plate.

He sat down and sipped coffee from the steaming cup. Taking a bite of toast he said, "You know my mother is going to just kick up a shit-fit when she finds out how much we're together, don't you?"

"Why, David?" Janet asked. "Why doesn't she understand about us?" Her face started to flush. "Just because I'm German? Or is it because I'm Catholic?"

"It's that you're not Jewish. She'll call you a shiksa and tell me I'd better keep away from you—or else!"

"Or else wha . . . *what*?" she stammered.

"First, she'll make mild threats. Like she won't call me or speak to me. And then it'll get worse and she'll tell me, 'You'll not get one penny of my money.' Things like that."

David tried to explain about the family "of the House and Lineage of David, the King," and about being "the Chosen" for over five-thousand years, and that, until 1948, for twenty centuries they did not even have a country, and still they remained a nation on God's earth.

Janet listened and, when he was finished, went into the living room and stared out her front window. David followed, came up behind and gently turned her around. The tears were streaming down Janet's face. "Doesn't she know how much I care about you?" She choked down a sob. "No other man, except my own father, has ever slept here! *Never!*"

He just held her then, and she laid her head on his shoulder until she stopped sobbing.

David was sorry he had mentioned Mother and all the rest of it. "But," he thought, "she has to know what lies ahead, for both of us." It would be damn tough. He just knew he'd be into it, goddamned heavy, the next time he saw Mother Sarah.

They walked back into the kitchen together, sat down at the table and finished the toast, and drank their coffee, but didn't say anything.

Then he told her he had to leave and get back to his apartment, and that on the way he would be stopping at the drugstore. Said he had to do some laundry.

They kissed briefly. Then he walked quickly down the stairs and to the subway and got on his train.

He was glad she'd seemed to believe him about having to leave. It wasn't true. But, he needed time alone, to think, about how fast the relationship was developing, where it was leading, and about the almost overwhelming problems they'd encounter now that they were in love. Oh sure, she'd never said the words. But, he knew how much it all meant when she'd said "no other man." He was proud. Goddamned proud. Why shouldn't he be!

On the train, and for the rest of the day, he thought about their relationship. He couldn't think about anything else. And when he'd tried to play chess with the computer, always a good pastime, it just didn't work. Simply put, Janet wasn't Jewish, and his mother would never accept her. That was that! A confrontation with Sarah was inevitable.

He called Janet just before going to sleep. They spoke only briefly and then said good night. He could tell she had been crying again.

Almost as soon as he got to ICM next morning, he called Father Donovan and made an appointment to visit at the chapel study right after work. He'd been thinking about Donovan, after reading the pamphlet on Catholicism.

Then David phoned Janet and said he'd see her at noon when he would be coming for an appointment with Dr. Silber. She was very excited when he mentioned that he was going to see Father Donovan.

The meeting with Dr. Silber went beyond the usual boundaries of doctor and patient. David confessed his love for Janet, and the potential trouble with his mother because of the Jewish issue.

Dr. Silber spoke warmly of Janet, and thought the relationship had done wonders for David. "Stick with it, David. That's what I say. You're able to cope now. I'm sure you can influence your mother. You must get them together."

David felt better after their talk.

On the way out, he made a date with Janet for that evening, after he had been to see Father Donovan.

After work, David took the subway to the chapel and walked quickly back to the study. He told Father of his interest in Catholicism. It had happened even before Janet. It went back to Saigon and Father Joe Kelley. He wanted to learn more, satisfy a curiosity. The priest said he would help in any way he could. They talked then about the details of the pamphlet David had studied. He told the priest how affected he was when he'd read the part about the crucifixion and death and burial of Jesus. And then, how he had gotten "a funny feeling in the back of my neck, when I read about the resurrection of the Son of God."

Father patiently explained some of the details of the significance of Christ rising from the dead, and he briefly touched on Communion as Catholics practiced it.

David seemed to grasp and understand the meanings of the many abstractions almost too easily. Father said, "David, have you studied about this before?"

"No, Father, not really. It just seems to come to me. It's like I am reviewing for a test in college. The material isn't new to me. Somehow, it's almost like I've been exposed to all of it, somewhere, before. Know what I mean?"

Smiling, Father said, "Not exactly, but that's okay for now. Let's keep studying it, together. When can you come back?"

"Tomorrow. Right after work, again. If that's all right?"

Donovan grinned and agreed to meet then and every day, at the same time, for the rest of the week. David shook his hand and left. He was doing this to be closer to Janet. It had been easy so far.

Janet was sitting on the steps of his apartment waiting for him.

He took her hand as they went quickly up the stairs. He got out his keys, opened the security door, and they walked up to his apartment. Only when they were inside, with the door shut, did he take her in his arms and kiss her. He didn't want to let go and neither did she.

The he led her into the kitchen. "That's the last time you'll ever wait there for me. I'm giving you my extra set of keys for both doors." He opened his junk drawer and got them. When he handed the keys to her, she smiled. "I didn't think you had a 'junk anything' in this place, mister." He kissed her again. Her taunts didn't matter. Not as long as she cared and was there with him.

They helped each other make salad and sandwiches—roast beef, with mustard. She made iced tea, and both had Italian dressing and breathed of garlic. Neither noticed, not when they cleaned up the dishes after finishing eating, or when they took second glasses of iced tea into the living room and sat on the couch to watch TV, not even when he hugged her close and said she should stay with him.

Janet said she probably shouldn't. She didn't have anything to sleep in. She did think, though, that one of his short-sleeved summer shirts would do fine. And she did have the small toothbrush in her purse, and the makeup she'd need in the morning.

"What will it mean, if I say yes, David?"

"It will mean that you will sleep with me. We'll be together. And I'll do whatever you want."

She buried her head in his chest then and hugged him around the waist. When she looked up there were tears in her eyes.

He kissed her, got up and led her down the hall. He turned on the bedroom light and sat down on the edge of the bed. And he glanced at the chair, his eyes urging her to sit in it and try to relax. She sat down and crossed her legs, and folded her arms. She looked right into his eyes, and he knew she'd be staying with him but that they'd be just sleeping together. He had to remind himself how proud he'd been, just the day before, when she told him what he already knew. *"No other man! Never!"*

He went into the bathroom first, closed the door. He washed quickly and brushed his teeth. When he came out, Janet had gotten her purse, put it on the table and had taken off her shoes and white pantyhose. She was waiting to go into the bathroom. He smiled at her, but she walked past him into the bathroom and closed the door.

She rinsed her pantyhose in the sink and hung them over the

towel hanging on the bathroom door rack. Then she undressed and took a quick shower. When she had dried off and put her panties back on, she opened the door to the bathroom just a crack. She was going to call for David. But he was standing right in front of the door, and he handed her a blue short-sleeved summer cotton shirt. Janet closed the door and put the shirt on. She carefully put her uniform on a hanger on the back of the bathroom door. She crumpled her bra and was squeezing it in her hand when she walked out of the bathroom. She went over to the table, put the bra in her purse, and then moved quickly around to the other side of the bed, got in and pulled the sheet up around her neck.

David was fascinated, watching this performance from the opposite edge of the bed. He spun then and sat cross-legged on top of the sheet, grinning. She just looked up at him. He leaned forward to kiss her, but when she turned her head slightly away, he had to kiss her on the cheek.

"Is something wrong, babe?" he asked, embarrassed.

She just said, "Get under the sheet and turn out that light."

He did. She was waiting to put her arms around him. He held her. And they fell asleep, in each other's arms.

When she woke at six, he was not there. There was the smell of coffee. She got out of bed and walked into the kitchen. David had set the table with orange juice and coffee. He'd slept in just his pajama bottoms and now had an apron over them. Janet giggled and he knew why, so he chased her into the bedroom. They jumped on the bed at the same time. He reached for her. She let him catch her, and they hugged close. It felt so good—to both of them!

She reminded him about work, and said they'd better go back to the kitchen.

After juice and coffee, they got dressed and took the subway to Brooklyn center.

When David got to his desk at work, he found a note to call his mother. He dialed, and she picked up the phone after one ring.

"Hello, Mother. It's me. How's everything?"

"When are you coming home? Your grandfather wants to see you."

"I'll be home this weekend. Okay?"

"Of course. Who do you think has been calling and asking you to come home?"

He disregarded that, and explained that he would be there on Friday night, as soon as he'd run an errand. He talked, gently, about Janet, mentioned casually his spending time with her, told his mother that Janet wanted to visit them. Then he said that he had to get back to work on the new ICM computer.

Sarah ignored his words. Said she hadn't been feeling well, and that they'd see him Friday evening, after his grandfather, she, and Poppa returned from Sabbath services.

David did as Janet wanted. He would see Father Donovan evenings after work. Then she and David would eat and spend time together. They would sleep in their own apartments. David, reluctantly, agreed.

On Friday Janet went by bus to Ithaca as soon as she got off work. David talked with Father Donovan about Communion. David said he understood, saw the reasons for it. He promised to come back next week.

David took the subway to Brooklyn Heights, walked to his parents' home, and let himself in. He was waiting when the two of them and his maternal grandfather returned from the Brooklyn Heights Synagogue. He hugged them, and they each in turn embraced him. That they really loved him was one thing David had never doubted. He just couldn't be Jewish in their way.

Zada, as David called his grandfather, went into his own room at the far end of the huge mansion. The Kleins owned property in many places, and this home had been theirs for over forty years. Immaculate grounds, maintained by two gardeners, surrounded the house built more than a hundred years ago. The street in front was tree-lined and attractively preserved by the city. The three-story home was cleaned daily by three maids. There was wall-to-wall carpeting everywhere and more rooms than David could remember. Brooklyn Heights was for the elite!

Mother, Poppa, and David sat down alone together in the front room study. David had shut the sliding doors at the room's entrance, and he faced his parents. "I'm seeing Janet Schreiber, the one I've told you about. She is special to me," he said.

Sarah's eyes narrowed, and she looked at her son and said, "What are your intentions regarding this Catholic?"

"Mother, I asked before that you call her by name. It's *Janet*! And my plans are to spend lots of time with her, and *only* with her."

"Do you intend to marry her?" Sarah Abaddon's voice was cool.

"Maybe. I don't know if she would marry me even if I did ask her. Does it really matter so much, Mother?"

She stared at her son for what to him seemed like an eternity, and then she got up, walked out of the room, went to the elevator and pushed the call button. When the elevator came down to the first floor, the cage safety door opened automatically. Sarah got in, the door shut, and she was lifted to the third floor. She walked directly into her private bedroom and slammed the door.

Poppa Saul got up slowly and walked over to the couch. He reached out with one hand and placed it on the shoulder of his son. David had his head bowed. Slowly, he lifted it and looked into his father's eyes and saw the tears.

Saul Abaddon sat down beside his only son. He put his arm around David's shoulders. For a long while neither of them spoke.

After what seemed to David to be much too long, his father said, "You have to be more gentle with her. You have to work harder to try to understand her. You are her son. You are the light of her life. This family is all she has. Please consider her feelings, and mine, too, and leave this young girl. Let a nice gentile boy find her. You can find a nice Jewish young lady and spend lots of time with her. Okay?"

Poppa Saul—always the diplomat, ever ready to smooth things over for the family, and for Israel—so predictable. Jewishness came before all else, before everything.

And David said, finally, "Not this time, Poppa. This time I'm going to do it my way. This is my life. And Janet is going to stay in it. All of it that I can get her to agree to stay in. Do you understand?"

Saul looked at his son for a long while. Then he rose slowly, and left the room, and David was alone.

David had known before he got to the house that this might happen, and maybe that was best—to get it over with right away. Then they could spend the rest of the weekend being angry and hurt and pout and not speak to each other unless it was absolutely necessary.

So when he left, only his grandfather was at the door on Sunday night to hug David and say good-bye.

He walked to the subway and took the train to Janet's stop. He found a pay phone and called her. She answered after one ring, told him to hurry. David ran up the station stairs and all the way to her brownstone and pushed the button.

She answered his ring without asking who it was. David rushed through the downstairs door and ran up the two flights of stairs to her door. She was standing in it, waiting for him. He went into her arms with such force that they fell off balance and had to release each other momentarily to regain it.

"I've missed you so much!" she said.

David couldn't speak. He just took her in his arms and kissed her again and again and again—tenderly at first, and then with more intensity. As he pressed close to her, she responded, as does the lady who has had time to think about what she really wants to do with the one when he is there at last.

They didn't want to eat. They weren't hungry. They wanted to be together, alone, for the night; but not at her place, she told him. Janet folded a uniform, packed some things, and got her small makeup kit. They took the subway and then walked to David's apartment.

They went down the hallway into the bedroom and took off their clothes. He led her to the shower and turned on the water. They got into it, together, and hugged and kissed, and David washed Janet, and she washed him. When each had explored the other, they let the warm water run over their bodies and rinse them. Then they took one large soft blue bath towel and each dried the other.

David picked up his lady and cradled her in his arms. He carried her to the bed and put her down in it, and he lay down beside her and softly kissed her mouth again. She reached for him then, and pushed his head down so his mouth was kissing her breasts. Gently, he touched her with his fingers. She began to shiver, just a little. Then a trembling started, so he took his hand away. But she said to touch more. He felt her hands and fingers grip his back and head, almost too tightly. And her throat had little sounds in it.

Her hands found his face, and she pulled now so she could kiss his forehead, and then his cheeks and his mouth. She urged him toward her, with strong hands, and they were together.

Afterward, he whispered, "I thought you said you didn't have any experience at this?"

She said slowly, "I read a lot."

And they slept.

The following week David continued his chats with Father Donovan after work each day. Then Janet and David would meet, and they'd eat together. Either at his place or hers. They wanted each other again, but she told him it was not a good time right now.

Everything seemed perfect for the two of them. They were in love, and knew it. They couldn't have been happier.

Janet told him her parents wanted both of them to come for a visit the following weekend. David was happy. It made up for what had happened at his home, but he didn't mention that.

On Thursday evening they were sitting on the couch in David's apartment watching TV, eating pizza when the visitor's ring sounded. Janet started, nervously.

David walked over and pressed the intercom button and asked, "Yes, what is it?"

"This is your mother. Please let me in." David pressed the access button.

"You are about to meet her," he said to Janet.

She put her pizza down. Suddenly, she wasn't hungry anymore. She turned off the TV. It had to come sooner or later. She might as well face it.

David stood in the open door of his apartment waiting for his mother. She came up the stairs, puffing like a steam engine, he thought to himself. From the look on her face, he guessed she was ready for battle.

She marched right past David, without speaking, and went to the easy chair and sat down, staring at Janet.

At last she said, "So. You are Jan—" She never finished the word. Instead, she turned to David and said, "Are you going to marry her?"

He paused. Then he said, "Yes, I am, Mother. If she'll have me!"

Sarah rose and strode to the door. She stopped, turned and said, "You are no longer my son. To me, you are dead." She left, slamming the door behind her and clomped down the stairs.

Janet began to cry. David went to her and put his arms around her. They sat like that for a long time.

Later, they went to bed. Janet said she wasn't sure about marriage. They would have to talk to Father Donovan. "Father Donovan will know what's best," she said.

David said, "I understand." And he told her, "I love you. And I want to marry you."

"I love you, David," Janet said.

7

As soon as they woke, they talked about leaving that night, right after work, for Ithaca. Neither mentioned Sarah. Some things were better left unsaid for now.

The day at work dragged for each of them. When they finally did meet at the bus depot and got on the way at five-fifteen, they sat right behind the driver and talked about work. He told her more about ICM and the 370. He hadn't been able to do much all day. He wanted to be with her.

"Me, too," she said.

She fell asleep, and her head slipped onto his shoulder. He cushioned it, moved only when he had to, so as not to wake her.

They arrived at the Ithaca bus depot a little behind schedule. Jack Schreiber, Janet's father, was waiting for them. Janet hurried over to hug him and kiss his cheek. She turned then and said, "David, this is my father."

"Hello, sir. Nice to meet you."

John William Schreiber mumbled something as he looked down at them and shook hands with David, who stared up into a pair of blue eyes that matched Janet's, and at the silver hair, thick and wavy, that made the tanned face soft and gentle. He looked every bit the part of a Cornell professor of English. Jack seemed to lean back on his six-foot-two frame to measure David, almost as if he were thinking about whether or not to buy something at some kind of show or auction. That made him seem . . . well, distant . . . at least to David.

Janet talked quietly while the three walked to the baggage claim and waited. When the luggage came, David grabbed her small bag and his own, and they went out to where Jack had parked the station wagon. David put the bags in the back, closed the tailgate, and got into the rear seat. Janet sat down in front, moved to the center next to her father and motioned for David to sit with them. She held his hand, so her father could see.

David had never been in Ithaca before. Jack Schreiber talked about Ithaca. "It's the county seat, and our population now is over 20,000. We're right in the center of the Finger Lakes, David. We'll be going sailing on Cayuga Lake tomorrow. Of course, we think it's the best one, with Seneca probably a close second."

Many of the trees along the highway were apple-bearing, but there were maples, too. The thought of maple syrup made David's mouth water. They hadn't eaten earlier when the bus driver announced the rest stop at Binghamton, and now he was hungry. He felt absolutely no pressure, no tension, and he was surprised at his composure.

Jack slowed the car just then and turned onto a gravel driveway along a white wooden fence, and in just a little over a hundred yards they came to a stop in front of a two-story home, obviously built a long time ago.

"This is our antique," Janet said, laughing. "The Schreiber place."

Lisl Schreiber kissed her daughter and hugged her. Then, she casually hugged David. Janet had warned him that her mother was always very affectionate. "My mom is a small, plump, almost always happy person. Just like you'd expect a Pennsylvania Dutch girl to be." And David agreed, now that he saw her.

"Would you two like something to eat? Or drink?" Lisl asked.

Janet looked at David. "I'm dying for a ham sandwich and milk," David said.

All three of them laughed, breaking what little tension there was. Jack came in quickly, asking what was so funny. Lisl told him. He looked at David, smiling.

After they'd eaten, all four of them sat at the table and talked. David told about his work at ICM, quietly, making light of its importance.

"Computers, eh?" Jack Schreiber said. "Must get you to talk some more about that."

David felt at home, welcomed, happy. They accepted him.

When he got up the next morning, David looked out the window across Cayuga Lake, to the far shore and the steepled and stone buildings of Cornell University. Such a beautiful place, he thought.

David smelled coffee and bacon. He dressed and hurried downstairs and into the kitchen. Lisl gave him a cheery good morning,
poured two cups of coffee, and they sat down together at the kitchen table. "You and Janet seem happy," she said.

David talked about when he first met her. "Fall of 1968, when I
first got back from Nam. She'd just come to work at the VA, and I
was getting some treatment there."

"At the psychiatric clinic?" she asked.

"Yup. I had some of that post Viet Nam syndrome they're all
talking about. Her boss, Doctor Silber, was my physician."

"I've read about that syndrome, David. I'm really sorry," Lisl
said.

David had more coffee. Lisl changed the subject to the university.

Janet came down the stairs, two at a time, in her bare feet. She
had on a white terrycloth halter and matching shorts. "You look
like a movie star," David told her. That made her blush. She
walked up, hugged him from behind and then sat next to him at
the table.

"Ready to eat, you two?" Lisl asked.

They both nodded. Scrambled eggs, bacon and toast were ready
in no time. The three of them ate, and then Janet and David went
outside. Her father was near the small white wood barn, hooking
the trailer hitch to the back bumper of the station wagon. A
twenty-five foot sailboat was carefully tied down to the trailer.
Jack Schreiber loved to sail!

"Hello, you two. Wanna sail this morning?" he asked.

"Of course, Daddy. But first we're gonna pet the horses," Janet
said.

David asked softly, "What should I call your mom and dad?"

She hesitated. "I don't know. Play it by ear."

They went to the paddock to see the colt and two mares. Janet
called to them and held out a sugar cube she'd brought. All three
trotted over to her. She told David, "The red mare, with the white
star on her forehead, is Bittersweet. She's four. The colt is Sugar.
He's about six or seven months old. He's Bittersweet's. And the all-
black mare is Lady. Aren't they beauties?"

David and Janet patted them. Finally he asked, "Can we ride
them sometime? I'd love that. I rode in summer camp when I was
a boy, in Israel in the kibbutz."

"Sure we can."

They went to help Jack with the sailboat.

Lisl had packed a picnic lunch for four, and Jack was finished hitching the trailer to the station wagon by the time Janet and David got there. So they all got into the car, and Jack drove to Cayuga Lake.

Jack backed the trailer onto the slip. The other three climbed into the boat, carrying the food and a thermos. Then Jack released the boat so it floated at the shoreline. He reparked the car and climbed aboard his sailboat to take command at the stern.

The one-horse outboard pushed them slowly out of the inlet and into open water. Minutes later they'd hoisted the jib and mainsail and were sailing under clear sky, across blue water. David had never sailed before. The beauty of the lake, and Janet, her parents' warmth filled him with a sense of well-being he hadn't known since his kibbutz days.

Janet insisted on taking command. As she and her father changed places at the stern, Jack nodded to David and said, "Hang on now!" Suddenly Janet pulled the mainsail rope tight against the side, and the boat sharply picked up speed. It became obvious to David: Janet Schreiber was a daredevil when she sailed. She had a faraway look in her eyes, and seemed oblivious to anything but the thrill of sailing.

They dropped anchor in a small cove, and waded to the beach for their shore lunch. Janet and Lisl spread the blanket and put food on it, and four famished sailors devoured almost all of it.

They repacked what food remained, put the baskets in the boat and sailed back to the inlet. David took the sails down, as Jack deftly eased "JANET ALIVE" to the slip with the outboard. All helped put the sailboat back on the trailer, and Jack drove toward the farm. David remarked on their name for the boat, and said he'd used Janet's name, too—as the password to activate the programs in his computers.

When they pulled up next to the barn, Jack said he'd put "her" away. Janet said she and David would be going riding. She ran into the house and got on jeans and sneakers. When she got back to the barn, David had saddled the horses. Janet rode Lady. "This is my Lady," she said. "She's almost thirteen. I got her for my twelfth birthday." David said he liked Bittersweet.

They started slowly, then began a canter. Suddenly, Janet said she wanted to race. David looked at her face as she urged Lady to a faster gallop. The oblivious-to-all-else look came over Janet's face again. As she raced past, David thought, "Chutzpah personified! My God, she is audacious!"

They turned onto a narrow trail on the next farm, out at its edge. They slowed the horses, and walked them to the top of a small hill. David and Janet climbed down. David tied both bridles to the branches of an apple tree and then lay on the grass, beside Janet. She kissed him, and they held each other close, hands caressing. That beautiful, overpowering feeling surged in both of them, and they struggled for a moment with her jeans. Then, she courted him with her fingers. He responded. That carried them. Perfect — for both.

After "mellow-time," as David would call it, he told her she was great. She punched him in the ribs and then jumped up, vaulted into the saddle and made Lady gallop back down the trail. David followed on Bittersweet, as fast as he could, but Janet had ridden out of sight.

When he rode Bittersweet down the gravel driveway of the Schreiber farm, David could see Janet sitting on the top board of the paddock fence. He jumped down and ran to her. Looking up into her face he said, "Your eyes are shining, your cheeks and lips are rosy. I'd say you have the fresh-loved look!"

Janet jumped off the fence, put her arms around his neck, hugged him close, and said, "I love you, David Abaddon."

In the house, Lisl told her husband sitting at the kitchen table, "I like that young man. He's got honest eyes. You know how I am about that. And he passes my eyes test." She poured more coffee for both of them and then sat down again across the table from Jack.

"I'm still not sure about it," he worried. "Janet is all we have left. I couldn't stand not having everything fine in her life. Looks as if she's already made up her mind." He was silent. Janet was the only child. He would not lose her.

Janet came in and the happy, healthy look of his daugher was clear to him. "After all," he thought, "it's her decision, not mine."

When David came into the room, Jack said, "Tell us about this computer business you're in, David. Sounds fascinating."

David talked about the Systems Research Institute at ICM, where he was helping with the programming for the new 370.

Jack listened to every word, and then asked, "Do you see any practical uses, for scholars?"

"Of course," David said reassuringly. "I'd say such things as format and word counts and spelling and lots of other applications could be available to you through the computer."

Jack hesitated, then said, "I think some of my colleagues are afraid of the things. I call it computer fear. It surfaces very subtly, but it's there. And I'm not sure why."

David nodded. "I think that's probably true—and natural. There are a lot of people who don't understand computers, and so they fear 'em. But knowledge is power! The computer can be fed information about all of us. If someone, especially a person who is destructive, is privy to such information, it could be damaging to any one of us. I think that's what causes a lot of the fear of computers."

Janet told her father about David's hobby of playing with the stock exchange data. Jack, very interested, leaned toward David. David told how he would keep several years of stock trends of certain Fortune 500 companies in his home computers, and of how he'd predict, at various times, when those stocks would go up sharply, or down. Jack asked how David had done. David blurted out, "I'm a millionaire, several times over!" He laughed.

Janet had told her parents about David's family on her last weekend visit, and that Sarah was the daughter of the department store Kleins, so Jack wasn't sure whether David was kidding or not. Jack thought better of pursuing the subject, at least for now.

He said, "I understand you're a chess player, David. Would you like to play?"

"Sure," David replied.

They went into the living room and set up the chess pieces on the board built into the card table, and the two of them played chess and drank beer.

In the kitchen, sitting together at the table, Lisl told her daughter, "I like him. I think he's honest. And he cares very much for you. When he looks at you, there's love in his face."

"I love him, too, Mom. I think I'm going to marry him."

Lisl Wichterman Schreiber thought back to when she'd first met a handsome young man on the Cornell campus, and of how concerned she had been when she'd gone to tell her parents about John William Schreiber. Her parents had asked every question they could think of, and then they told her that she was taking a chance marrying someone like him. "How wrong they were," she thought. And she told Janet, "You must decide for yourself. Just don't be in a hurry. And I'm on your side. You know that, dear."

Janet looked at her mother, at the blond hair now turning gray, and at the cinnamon-brown eyes and ready smile. "How lucky I am," she thought, "to have her for my mother and not someone else!" And she got up and hugged Lisl warmly.

Janet looked into the living room. The two men were both sitting there, staring at the chess pieces before them. Obviously, they did not want to be disturbed. Janet walked back and sat down at the kitchen table opposite her mother, and they smiled at each other. Both of them knew it would take time for Jack to accept it all, but it wouldn't be that hard for him. He'd accept it, in the end.

David won the chess game. He suddenly attacked with his Queen, and that put Jack's King in checkmate, and the game was over. The suddenness of David's attack surprised Jack. He complimented David.

As they were putting the chess pieces away, Jack said, "Do you think it would be good timing for me to invest in some ICM stock right now?"

David hesitated. He knew that 1972 would be the year of the 370. The exact date of its release was yet to be decided. Such information could mean the difference between making a lot of money, or just some. He had to be loyal to ICM. On the other hand, he did not know the exact release date. Slowly he said, "I'd do it—soon. Don't wait much longer." And the stock-split gossip flashed through his mind. He thought, "It couldn't happen to a nicer gent than Janet's father."

Jack Schreiber thought maybe he'd take David's advice and buy some ICM stock.

Janet told her mother all about David's seeing Father Donovan every day after work, and his interest in Catholicism. Lisl was very pleased. She had converted to Catholicism. It had so upset her parents when she'd talked to them about young Jack Schreiber, a Catholic, and then about marrying him. But she had done it! And, as far as she was concerned, that had been the best decision she had ever made. And she reminded Janet of both of those things and then told her to go join the men in the living room. "I'll finish getting everything ready for us in here, dear," she said.

Jack and David were still sitting at the card table talking about computers when Janet came into the room.

Casually, Janet said to her father that David had been chatting with Father Donovan.

Jack Schreiber knew what she meant. It was serious with these two.

Lisl announced dinner and they sat down at the kitchen table, ate pork chops and homemade applesauce, mashed potatoes and gravy, strawberry jello with bananas for salad, and asparagus spears and mayonnaise, Lisl's freshly-baked bread and her raspberry jam. She had made peach ice cream. David said, "That was a meal fit for a king and his family."

That evening they sat in the living room, made small talk, and watched a rerun of "The Mary Tyler Moore Show," and then some of "The Partridge Family." They all went to bed early.

Next morning they had quick cups of coffee, and drove to Ithaca for Mass in Saint Bernard's Church at Scipio Center. Father Karl Schultz led the service. He looked out into the congregation when he blessed those attending Mass, and it seemed to David that his eyes made it personal for the four of them!

When the prayers were being murmured, and the responses were being said, and the altar boy's voice could be heard, David remembered the Third Field Army Hospital in Saigon, and Father Kelley and all he meant to him. David had tears in his eyes, and Janet took his hand in hers and squeezed it.

When the Mass was over, they stood in line to shake hands and talk briefly with Father Schultz. Janet hugged Father and introduced David to her parish priest.

In the car riding back to the farm, she told David he was the priest who taught her catechism when she was a girl. "He gave me First Communion and led everything at my Confirmation class."

Janet softly hummed, "The first time ever I saw your face . . ." and she thought, "He will officiate at my wedding, also."

When they got home, Janet and David packed, and Jack drove the four of them to the bus depot in Ithaca. Janet hugged and kissed her parents. Lisl held David close for just a moment, and then Jack shook his hand. Each squeezed the hand of the other, to subtly signal that they both knew there would be more.

In the bus on the way back to New York, Janet told David that she was sure the visit had gone very well for them. Her parents would accept him, no problem. Then, they slept, his head on her shoulder.

The bus pulled into the Brooklyn bus station on time. They got their bags right away, then took the subway to the stop near David's place. She suggested something to snack on, so they walked to the pizza parlor, and he ordered a cheese, with mushrooms and Italian sausage to go. They hurried, since it looked as if it might rain. They went up to his apartment and turned on the air-conditioner. They shared beer and pizza.

He wanted her to stay all night, but she told him she'd have to go to her apartment and get a uniform and everything else for work in the morning. David said he'd go along.

When they got back to his apartment, he locked them in. They showered together and got into bed. It was perfect love. And again.

When David got back to his apartment the next day, after he'd visited with Father Donovan again, he found a letter in his mailbox. It was from his mother. She said that he should call her as soon as he received it. He did, and she told him she wanted to come the following evening to talk to him, and that his father would be coming along to listen. David agreed, knowing that it probably would be best to just give way and let it all come out into the open. It was going to anyway, so now was as good a time as any.

On Tuesday evening, when he got to his building, Sarah and Saul were standing in front. "Waiting," she let him know. David ignored that. He opened the security door, and they walked up the stairs in silence.

Inside his apartment, after David had closed the door, Sarah said, "Have you made up your mind about . . . her?"

"Yes. I have, Mother. I'm going to ask her to marry me."

Sarah paused, then said, "What about your being Jewish? And your family? And our traditions?"

"I'm thinking of becoming a Catholic, Mother. I'm taking instruction. I know this isn't easy for you to understand, but it's best for me. I want you to know, I'm more at peace with myself right now than at any time since I got back from the kibbutz when I was fourteen!"

Sarah stood as tall as she could and so did Saul. She glared at David, and she reached across her bosom with her right hand and gripped the sleeve of her dress just below the shoulder. She yanked, as hard as she could, ripping the cloth at the seam. Then Saul tore his shirt, too, and mumbled some Hebrew. David's mother said, "You have made your decision, and so have we. You are no longer our son. We will bury a casket, and put a headstone on the grave. To us, you will be dead!"

Sarah turned sharply, stomped to the door, and walked out. Saul followed closely behind her. He glanced back at David once, and then closed the door behind them. David heard their footsteps, as they slowly descended the stairs. David wept.

Later, he called Janet and told her what had happened. She reassured him again and again. Then she said they should talk to Father. David said he would be glad to. They would meet at his apartment the next evening, about seven.

Late that night, David woke up in a cold sweat. It had been weeks—he couldn't even remember the last time—since he'd had the nightmare. Holocausts. Lang Vei's bunkers. Auschwitz's ovens. What was the difference? It always added up—man butchering man—bigger and better ways to kill each other! The Great Hate! And David wondered, "Why am I thinking these things all of a sudden? Why now?"

Then his thoughts raced to Janet and the uncertainty of the relationship with her parents, and to the demands of becoming a Catholic, and the pressures of marriage to a gentile. There, he'd finally focused on it. Even if it was just to himself, he had his doubts, too. And it wouldn't be easy, a mixed marriage. Oh sure, there were always optimistic philosophers ready to say, "Times have changed." Don't count on that. He'd still be the Christian-Jew that everyone talked about—and Janet—and their children, too.

His mother had said to him, "You are no longer our son. To us you will be dead."

Poppa Saul? The man had never even had a chance to get a word in or express an opinion. "How does he feel about me?" David asked himself.

The pressure in his head became almost unbearable, and he began to think about . . . Nuclear war! The new Holocaust! He started to tremble.

He stumbled and almost fell in the dark as he raced for the bathroom and to the medicine cabinet. He got the bottle of Valium open, took two tablets and gulped them down with water. After he'd taken about ten deep breaths, he felt along the walls in the blackness until he'd reached his bed. He fell into it, exhausted, sweating.

He tossed and turned, but sleep finally came—it was fitful, but he slept and was able to turn off for a little while.

The next day at work at the Research Institute, he could only go through the motions. By eleven o'clock he had called Janet, and she managed to squeeze him in, so he could see Doctor Silber right after lunch. She asked David what was wrong, but he told her he would explain later.

His level of stress was apparent to her when David walked into the psych clinic waiting room. Janet asked him right away to please tell her what it was all about. He tried to impress her with how calm he was, but her instincts read him. She told him so. David said he'd tell her later, after he had talked to Silber.

He visited with Doc for over thirty minutes and told him about the weekend at Ithaca and how perfect all of it had been, and then Sarah had gotten back into the picture, and everything had changed. He explained the Lang Vei-Auschwitz nightmare again. Doctor had heard it all before and had thought, just maybe, it'd gone away. He now saw otherwise.

Doctor Silber and David agreed that he should resume visits in the psych clinic again, if that made him feel more comfortable. David said it would. They also discussed the stabilizing influences in his life, and agreed that David should pursue them—Janet—and Father Donovan, his boss and friend, Jeff. And, in David's opinion, Lisl. In the near future, he was sure of a closer relationship with Jack, too.

David thanked Doc, took the Valium prescription from his desk and walked out to the reception desk. He told Janet he felt much better, said she should come to his apartment that night and stay with him, so they could talk about all of it. She said she'd be there at seven, as planned. He got the prescription filled at the VA pharmacy and left.

All the way back to the ICM offices, and for the rest of the day, he thought over and over, "How lucky I am to have her right now, and the others in my life who care about me."

8

JANET LET HERSELF into David's apartment before seven and was sitting in the easy chair, waiting for him, when he got there. He bent to kiss her and then knelt beside her. They hugged. "How are you and Father Donovan doing?" she said.

"Just fine. I've decided. I'm going to take formal instruction soon. Then, I'll take First Communion and be confirmed. I've asked Father if we could do it privately, in his study, and he said we could."

Janet cried. Happy, content, she hugged David.

He sat on the floor and they talked then about who would be there with them for the ceremony. David said he hoped just Lisl and Jack would come. Janet promised she would phone home and ask them to come, the minute he knew when.

Then she said he ought to go lie down and rest. She told him, "You look worn out." He hesitated. Janet said she'd get their dinner ready. So he lay on the couch and fell asleep right away. And he began to dream. The one about the new holocaust, about his morbid fear of mankind's surge toward total destruction—Armageddon, the final battle. He'd had nightmares before about ". . . and fire shall rain from the heavens . . . the flesh shall fall from their bones."

He sat up, wide awake, in a cold sweat, remembering what he had just dreamt. The balance of power, between the haves and the have-nots in the nuclear world, was for David Mikhael Abaddon the balance of terror. And the "nuclear parity thing" was just so much bullshit to him. It was starting to bubble up in his brain again—too often—and he was not sure what to do about it, except to keep it from everyone.

Janet came in from the kitchen and told him dinner was ready. He said he'd be right back and walked down the hall to the bathroom. The sound of his urine splashing in the water at the bottom of the stool seemed too loud, so he directed the stream to the side, where it was quieter. And he thought to himself, "I'm a bunch of nerves all rolled up in one guy. I've got to stop this worrying shit. It's all the time these last couple of days. I've got to cut it out—somehow—and Janet is not going to know. Ever!"

He promised himself that he would really try to reprogram himself to worry less. And he washed his hands and walked into the kitchen and sat down at the table across from Janet.

They shared hamburger patties with onions, macaroni and cheese, toasted garlic bread, and lettuce salad, with an herbs and spices dressing she'd mixed. She teased him when he asked for the ketchup for his meat. She said he always used it to cover up the taste of some dish he really didn't like. He smiled, just a little, but her taunt went unchallenged. There wasn't much fight in him right now.

When they finished eating, they cleared the table and helped each other clean it all up and put everything away. Then they sat on the couch in the living room and watched TV. He didn't mention anything about what was really bothering him, when he tried to explain his feelings and behavior of the last several days. David told her everything he could think of, but he never said the words "new holocaust," or "gentile wife," or "mixed marriage."

Janet reassured him, again and again, of her love and respect for him, and of her determination, but she said nothing about her inner feelings, either—the one she had, sometimes, inside, like a tiny inner voice that only she could understand, telling her to "look again, Janet. There's more to this than you're able to see."

She thought then of how she would get such a feeling, when she was about ten, when her parents were talking about some subject and she was not supposed to get the real point or meaning of what was being said. She had a kind of sixth sense, she'd always told herself, and she was getting it now, while David was telling her his innermost thoughts. She said to herself, "There's more to this. Find out what is really going on here. He can't hide it from me forever." And she thought, "I'll pick up on it. And soon!"

David said they should get ready for bed, and she agreed, with the promise from him that she could shower first.

She went to the bedroom, undressed, and then went into the bathroom and showered.

David went into his computer room and shut the door. He locked it from the inside and turned the master switch on. He typed the password 'JANET' on the keyboard. Then he asked the computer to put up the last two years of data on the stock trends of ICM. It did. He entered several figures and percentages and asked the computer to predict ICM's stock value for the next twelve months. The viewer went blank. Then it printed in computer-type words what he wanted to know. David's advice to Jack Schreiber was correct. Now was the time to buy ICM stock. Jack should have his broker purchase common stock, right away. "And," David thought, "that prediction does not include a gossiped-about stock split when the 370 comes on the market."

Janet knocked on the door and said softly, "David?"
Instantly he erased everything on the screen and keyed in a chess game. He entered his play. Then he got up, opened the door and let her in. She glanced up at the screen momentarily, then at his eyes. She smiled and asked, "Did you beat him?"
"No. Not this time," he said. "And it's *her*," as he tried to smile back at Janet.
Almost in a whisper, she said they should go to bed soon and maybe he'd feel better after a shower. He agreed, turned off the master switch and then the lights.
Janet walked back to the bedroom.
He went into the bathroom, took a quick shower, dried off, and got into bed next to her. She had the sheet pulled up to her neck, and had turned off all the lights except one. She reached up and turned that one off, too.
David leaned over gently to kiss her good night. Janet moved toward him. She was naked. He forgot all that stuff he'd been thinking about.

Next morning they had quick cups of coffee and took the train to work. All day, David tried to concentrate on programming the 370. He just couldn't. His thoughts kept flowing back to Janet. "She and I are *love*," he thought. He felt certain that for the two of them there was no love except what they had. And he told himself, "If anything ever happened to her, I would want to die."
David finally decided that he had struggled long enough about his parents. And, after he'd eaten lunch, he called his parents' house, hoping his grandfather would answer. He did. David asked if he could come to talk. They agreed on after seven that night.
When David had finished his instruction with Father Donovan,

he took the subway train to Brooklyn Heights and then walked to the house. He let himself in. As arranged, he walked to the back of the house on the first floor and knocked softly on the door to his Zada's room.

"Come in," the old man said.

David quietly opened the door and walked into the room. His grandfather was sitting in a rocking chair, reading the Torah. David walked over, kissed him on the forehead. And the old man smiled up at his grandson.

"Sit down, please," he said to David, as he laid his readings on the small table next to the rocker.

Slowly, David sat down on the edge of the single bed, right in front of his mother's father. David looked directly into his Zada's eyes. Then he said, "Zada, is there any chance for me to make it up to Mother and Poppa?"

Samuel Abram Klein had been born ninety years before, in the city of Wroclaw, Poland, not far from the border of Germany. Even in the 1880s there was the feeling in the Jewish community there to "get to America," and he and his parents had settled in New York City when Samuel was still their only child. And they worked—hard. Samuel's father, Aaron, was a tailor. The family started a clothing shop. Then it became a store, and they borrowed money from friends, Jewish friends, to expand it. By the time Samuel, and then his brother Jacob, finished at Columbia University, the Klein Department Store empire was legendary in New York. The tiny family had come to America poor. They had labored mightily to become one of the most respected and wealthiest families in the city.

Zada Samuel Klein was the last of the original "American" Kleins, and his only child Sarah had assumed control of the business. And now David Mikhael had become the apple of his Zada's eye.

David had adamantly refused to work in the Klein Stores, but in Samuel's mind now was the overwhelming problem of this Catholic girl, and Samuel Klein said to his grandson, "What is it that you want to do with your life?"

David looked at the old man's wrinkled face. He saw the bald head under the yarmulke, the sad look in the eyes. And David had no answer to give. He just could not bring himself to make the man feel even sadder than he already was. So he said, "I want you to accept me as I am. Will you help me with Mother and Poppa?"

The old man stared at David for a long while, and then he asked, "Will you marry the young girl your mother has been telling me about?"

David hesitated. Then he lowered his head so his grandfather couldn't see his eyes, and they both knew the answers to all the questions that Samuel and Sarah and Saul had in their minds.

David rose slowly, and he kissed his grandfather good-bye and walked out and stood in the foyer. There he paused, looked into the study, saw his mother and father talking. He could hear the low tones, but not the words being said. Saul glanced through the doorway at his son, and as Sarah did the same, she stopped talking. She simply walked to the study door and quietly closed it, but to David it sounded like a rifle shot, and the echo rang in his ears.

David let himself out the front door of the mansion, and as he walked down the street to the subway station, the tears came. He could remember being that sad only a few other times in his life.

Ruth Tobias got off the El Al jet at the John F. Kennedy International Airport and walked to the first pay phone she saw. She put down her shoulder bag and dug in her purse until she found the little book and dialed the number she read in it. The soft-spoken lady on the other end of the phone told her that David Abaddon no longer lived at that number, but he could be reached at a new one, and she gave it to Ruth.

When his phone rang, David almost didn't get up from the couch to answer it. He had slept very little the previous night, and the day at work had been painful for him. Now he was resting, alone in his apartment. He hadn't even wanted Janet to come to be with him. As far as he was concerned, that was about as depressed as he could get—he didn't even care to have his lady there. But he picked up the phone anyway—from force of habit more than anything else.

"Hello," he said.

"David, this is Ruth Tobias. Ruth, from the kibbutz at Kinneret."

He felt dull, as he forced his mind to race back to 1960 and Israel and some of the best days of his life. Then he almost shouted into the phone, "*Ruthie!* Is it really you? Where are you? When did you get here?"

"Please, David. One question at a time. I just got to the Kennedy Airport here. I came on the night flight from Lod Airport. You remember, the one we saw you off at when you came back home in 1960? Anyway, I'm traveling to Chicago to see my relatives. But I'd like to see you before I go there. Is that possible?"

"Of course it is. Let me see," as he thought of how to meet her. He decided it would be best for her to take a cab to his apartment. He told her that, and gave her directions.

David dialed Janet's number, and she picked up the phone after one ring. When he had explained the situation, she agreed that it would be better if Ruth stayed with her, and said she'd wait up until the two of them got there.

David watched through his front window for the cab to stop in front of his building. When at last it arrived, he rushed down the stairs and out the security door to meet Ruth. She had just paid the driver and was turning around when he reached her. She grinned up at him, and they both giggled a little, and then they hugged each other, again and again. He kissed her on each cheek, as he would any of his sisters from the kibbutz.

Ruth was a Sabra. She had been born in Jerusalem in 1946 and had never left Israel before. Now, she was telling him, she had completed studies for her master's degree at the Hebrew University in her home town, and her parents had given her a trip to America, to visit relatives, as a graduation present. She'd decided, "I will stop in New York City and see my kibbutz brother, David."

David told her how excited he was to see her, as they went upstairs. He carried her two pieces of luggage and led the way to his apartment. He let them in, closed the door and pointed to the easy chair and motioned for her to sit down.

As she sat in the chair, David studied how much she'd changed since she and the other sisters and brothers had said good-bye to him in Tel-Aviv. Ruth had always been petite, he recalled, but now, with only a bit of makeup to highlight them, her black-as-ebony eyes sparkled, and her hair matched them in color, glistening in the table lamplight. "Her tanned skin is beautiful olive, as smooth as silk," he thought. And although her outfit was a bit wrinkled from the long trip, she was perfectly dressed in white blouse and cotton poplin two-piece suit the same blue as the Star of David in Israel's flag. David said, "You've become a lovely woman, Ruth!"

"Oh, thank you. And you are just as charming as ever, Mister Abaddon," nodding to him.

"Please tell me about our kibbutz," he urged.

"I want to," she said. "It's still the best one of them, I think. I haven't been back there for about two years, but the last time I was there it had changed very little. The center building, where we all lived together, was freshly painted that same shade of pink.

And it still had the red-tile roof. The other buildings all around it were exactly the same, too. I think their oranges are the best grown in Israel. And the rows and rows of sugar beets were being cultivated by the young people, just like we all did. The last night I was there, the full moon was shining on the Sea of Galilee. We sat near that set of rocks on the hill and watched its reflection slowly move across the water. It's still the prettiest sight you've ever seen. You know! Kinneret is so lovely at that time of summer."

David sat, listened, transfixed. Then he asked, "Did you go into the building where our group lived?"

"I walked inside the first day I was back, and I went upstairs to the second floor and walked down the long hallway past my room—and yours, too, now that I think about it. Some young people were in the rooms, visiting, just like we used to. They seemed to be really close to each other, like our group was."

"So, all the children and young people are still raised together, separately?"

"Yes. And they seemed to be enjoying it as much as we did. I just loved that when we were there, and I think they all do now, too!"

David marveled at her command of English. When he had first met her in 1959, she could speak only a little, but now, she was saying the words that should be said easily, though with some trace of accent. He asked, "Where did you learn to speak English so well?"

"I started taking it in school during the fall term, right after you helped me, David. Your patience with me, when I could barely understand any of it, made all the difference. That inspired me to study harder. And to learn it the best I could. I knew, even then, that someday I would come to see you here in America. And also, I felt I'd use it in lots of ways in my work and everything."

Then he remembered the time he'd asked her to tell him what a Sabra was. She had to struggle with her broken English to tell him. She had to use some Hebrew, too, and then he understood her. "Sabras are Jews born in Israel. The nickname comes from the Hebrew word for cactus fruit. It is very prickly and hard on the outside. But it is really sweet and tender on the inside," she had said. Later David learned that Sabras are fiercely independent, full of energy, and very tough. They are proud to be Jewish, but they are even more proud to be called Israeli. And they take great pride in their new, young country. They would defend to death the land that was now theirs!

"What did you study at Hebrew University?" he asked.

"Political science, with a minor in English. And, I took a masters in it, too. I'm planning to go to law school, but when I get back to Jerusalem I'll work and study in my father's law firm—at least for a while."

Later, David looked at his watch and told her they should go catch the subway. He suggested that it would be better if she stayed with his friend, Janet, in her apartment. Ruth asked him why, since they had practically lived in the same room when they were thirteen. He told her he'd explain it on the way to Janet's. Ruth asked who that was.

He carried the luggage. They walked to the subway station and took the train. On the way, he explained who Janet was, and why it was better for Ruth to stay with her. Ruth smiled, but he was not making her understand. Ruth had been raised in the kibbutz, in Israel, and here in America, well . . . it was different. To explain that, in one conversation, was more than even David Abaddon's silver tongue could manage.

So he decided to change the subject, and he asked what it had been like to be in the Six-Day War.

Ruth told him that it had all been okay, until May 1967. Then, Egypt's President Nasser had demanded that the United Nations withdraw its emergency military forces. When they were gone, the Egyptian military went back into the Gaza Strip, and Nasser closed the Gulf of Aqaba to all Israeli shipping. On June fifth, the Israelis seized the Gaza Strip, and in a total of six days they occupied the Sinai Peninsula to the Suez Canal and captured Old Jerusalem, the Golan Heights from Syria, and Jordan's West Bank. Finally, by June tenth, the UN arranged a cease fire agreement, and the fighting stopped.

"Where were you at the time, Ruth?"

"My father forbade me to go out of the house, for any reason. We were lucky. The fighting was across the city from our house, and we only heard the sounds of the guns, for about three days, and then it was all over. No one in my family was hurt, even shot at. Thank God!"

"What about the kibbutz? Did they get involved in the war?" he asked.

"Yes. When the fighting was going on with the Syrians, the adults were all carrying weapons. And the Israeli tanks were all around Kinneret. The military officials made the children and young people hide in the underground dugouts. Remember when we had to do the practice drills and hide in them? It was fun then, but in the Six-Day War, I thought about the children, and I didn't think it would be so much fun. Not when there was real gunfire in the distance."

They arrived at the exit for Janet's area, and he motioned for them to get off. While they walked to the apartment building, Ruth told him that the Israelis had won a smashing victory in '67, and that he would have been proud to be there. He smiled at Ruth and told her that he *had* been proud, even though he had been here, in New York.

He led her up the stairs to Janet's mailbox, and he rang the visitor alert. Janet asked over the intercom who it was, and he said into the speaker, "C'est moi." Janet buzzed so the security door could be opened, and Ruth and David walked up to her apartment door.

Janet greeted them at the door. David introduced the two women, and then all three went into the living room. He stayed long enough for them to get acquainted, and then said good-night and left to catch the train back to his place. Riding to his apartment, David thought, "Ruth is a smash. I wonder how Janet will like her."

David rose earlier than usual the next day and, noticeably excited, called Jeff Piedmont to tell him all about the surprise visitor from Israel. Jeff gave him the rest of the week off, on vacation, and he invited the three of them to come over to the house on Saturday evening, "for a small party!" David was delighted, because of his affection for both Jeff and Audra. He thought, "That will be a great chance for Ruth to see a nice New York City family, in their own home." And she'd be able to see how Americans really live. Janet would enjoy seeing them, too, he knew.

The rest of the week, David spent all day, each day, with Ruth. He started her tour at N.Y.U., showed her the physics and computer science facilities. She was impressed. He took her to Central Park and the two of them went every place he'd been with Janet, just a few short weeks ago. Ruth saw the Flower Lady and said she couldn't figure her out, either.

They went to Tiffany's and Radio City Music Hall. He took her to Rockefeller Center, then showed her the United Nations Plaza and U.N. Headquarters. She saw the Waldorf-Astoria and Macy's and Gimbel's.

On Thursday afternoon, they visited the Jewish and Guggenheim museums. And that night she was visibly awed when he showed her Manhattan at night, from the Empire State Building.

She said that her favorite was the Statue of Liberty, and that Emma Lazarus had said it all, in her ". . . give me your tired, your poor . . . ."

David took Ruth to Janet's apartment each evening, and the three of them ate together, either there or at a nearby cafe. The two women slept at Janet's, and he at his apartment. He was content, and felt that it was all working out very well, although he did miss seeing Janet, and he had a few guilty feelings because he'd not spent one minute with Father Donovan all week.

On Friday, Ruth asked if she could meet David's parents, and maybe they could go together to worship. David made an excuse about that, but suggested they join the congregation at Temple Emanu-El.

Jewish people at worship filled the synagogue. David and Ruth felt serene. They had been greeted, led to their place for the services. It was a prayerful, coalescent congregation.

The cantor's melodic baritone was passionate, moving, as he led the Shma. When the congregation joined in, David was stirred by the beautiful echoes of "Hear, oh Israel, the Lord our God, the Lord is One."

David felt like weeping. That prayer had been drummed into him before his bar mitzvah, and now he had anxious thoughts of leaving all that behind, to convert, to marry Janet. He prayed. He needed calm.

The Rabbi's sermon was an open plea to end the Viet Nam war. The verve with which he delivered ". . . our moral responsibility to end war's madness . . ." struck a harmonious chord in David and Ruth. The Rabbi had challenged them.

Later, at coffee, several members of the congregation spoke to them, and the Rabbi shook the hands of each as they said goodbye. They had been welcome!

David suggested they go to the theater. Ruth thought that would be fine, and told him to call Janet and tell her to meet them. When Janet answered the phone, he said, "I love you. Will you come and go to the theater with us?" She seemed distant and cool to him, somehow, but said she would meet them in front of the theater. Waiting to hail a taxi, he could recall other times when Janet had suddenly been aloof for no apparent reason.

Ruth and David arrived at the theater to find Janet waiting for them. The marquee read, "The Prisoner of Second Avenue." David bought the tickets, and when the usher had seated them, he told Ruth that the play had been written by Neil Simon. It starred Peter Falk and Lee Grant. He explained that it would be a comedy about a typical middle-aged couple who "suffer" like almost all urban apartment dwellers. He suggested that they should all watch for the big catastrophes and tiny annoyances a couple would experience in such a setting. David felt he should give Ruth some background, because this would be her first such adventure in an American theater.

Ruth and Janet and David had laughed so hard that their jaws ached when they came out of the theater. Ruth said it was the funniest play she had ever seen, and Janet and David told her that was true for them, too. He took them out for pizza and beer. Then they split up at the subway station. The women went to Janet's, and he went home alone.

On Saturday, David slept in. He thought that the two of them might just go shopping, and that he could relax some. It worked. By the time he'd shaved and showered, they had been to several of New York City's largest department stores. They called to tell him they were back on Broadway, where the Avenue of the Americas crosses, and would he come and meet them. He said he'd be there in half an hour.

They met about one, had lunch, and then they walked into Central Park. All three of them said they were tired and would be content to just sit by the lake and watch the ducks and birds. It is always in vogue to watch the other people sitting, or passing by. "That's allowed, in Central Park, in the world's greatest big city," David said.

Late in the afternoon, they went to Janet's, and as soon as they got to her apartment, David lay down on the blue velvet couch and fell asleep.

The two women sat in the kitchen, at the table, talking. Janet had been very impressed with Ruth's ability to speak and understand English. Janet told Ruth about being a cheerleader for her high school football team. Ruth said she could not understand American football, that soccer was her team sport.

Their conversation wandered from law to nursing to military service for women in Israel. Ruth vividly described the humorous side of life in the kibbutz. Janet responded with equally funny tales of living in the nursing students' dorm at Arnot-Ogden Memorial Hospital in Elmira.

David woke at six and called Jeff on the phone, and Jeff invited the three of them over. He told David not to bring anything, but David insisted they would bring some beer, so on the way to the subway they stopped at a deli and got two six-packs of Heineken's.

Jeff Piedmont was brilliant with computers, but what his hard driving bosses at ICM really liked best about him was his ability to supervise. In their opinion, he was the best technically trained supervisor they had. For that reason, Jeff Piedmont ran the Research Division of the Systems Research Institute for ICM. Sure, it was a long ride every workday, commuting to the 200 block of Manhattan's East 52nd Street, but he, and especially Audra, wanted a family atmosphere for their three sons, and Jeff felt that the sacrifice of getting up early each day to commute was worth it for his sons and his lady.

David had been to the Piedmont's before, and it was with some pride that he led the two ladies, one on each arm, to his boss's beautiful home in Forest Hills Gardens. It took a while by bus to get to the center of Queens from Brooklyn. "This looks like a good family living place for the wealthy. Is that so?" Ruth asked.

Both Janet and David assured her that she had that correct, and as they walked along, Janet pointed to the attractive shopping center. She guessed that Audra probably did her shopping there.

David rang the doorbell of the two-story frame house. It was large, and looked as if it had been painted an off-white just that summer, the shutters a deep brown. Jeff loved the browns and greens of earth and summer, and his suits and sports clothes followed those patterns of color.

Audra opened the front door. Her face was lighted by shining green eyes, David thought, and was always cherub-like. She seemed to be constantly smiling, and the moment you met her, you felt as if you'd known Audra Piedmont for a long time. She greeted Janet with a hug, and David also. She turned to Ruth and said, "I'm Audra. Welcome. Please come in, everybody."

Ruth followed Janet through the door, and David went in last. Audra closed the door, just as Jeff came around the corner into the foyer and introduced himself. Then, he looked at David and said, "Now I know why I haven't heard one word from you all week. You found the two prettiest women in Brooklyn and forgot all about the rest of the world."

David grinned. He had been having a fantastic week with the two of them, and it must be showing in his face.

Jeff continued, "You look as if you'd just died and gone to heaven, Dave, and surrounded yourself with a couple of angels!"

Audra looked at Jeff, as if to caution him to not move too quickly with Ruth. After all, Audra seemed to be saying in her look, you've just met the lady from Israel, and she might not understand your hearty American ways.

Ruth instantly sensed it, and she put them all much at ease by saying, "Jeff, you remind me of some of the other young American guys David and I were with in the kibbutz. They always said such nice things to us, too, and made us feel that we were special."

David asked where the boys were, and Audra said that she'd decided to let them stay at her mother's for the night. "That way," she said, "the five of us can spend all our time visiting and getting to know each other better. We'll show them off to you when you visit next time."

"So thoughtful, always so thoughful of others," David thought to himself, as he handed the six-packs of beer to Audra. "She's the perfect wife and mother and friend."

Audra put the beer in the refrigerator and invited all of them out to the fenced-in patio, and they sat facing each other on lawn chairs. The picnic table nearby was loaded with various dishes, each carefully covered with foil. Jeff said he'd just finished putting up the natural wood fence, and they all now had the chance to celebrate the Piedmonts' new-found privacy.

Jeff offered drinks all around, and got Ruth the gin and tonic she asked for. The others said they wanted one of his margaritas. "Oh, you'll like them!" Audra assured them. "That's one of the three things he does best."

When they'd tasted their drinks, each nodded and smiled and said they were fantastic, and David asked, "What are the other two things he does best, Audra?"

She grinned broadly and said slowly, "Well, the guy can really boil an egg. And, ah, well, ah, God, can he mow the lawn!"

The five of them laughed, and Audra was pleased to see Ruth was very much with it. And so was Janet. Audra was like that. When you were in her home, you were special. She genuinely wanted you to be a part of her life, and the lives of her husband and sons, too. Ever so subtly, she checked in on that, because she wanted things to be just right, for everyone. Audra cared, and everyone loved her for it.

After a second round of drinks, the cooking was begun. Audra's freshly baked buns were perfect with the hamburgers and cheese, covered with barbeque sauce. There was potato salad, and hot baked beans steaming in an electric pot. While they ate and drank, David thought, "She has probably been working most of the day on all the good stuff we have to eat now." When she brought out two kinds of homemade pie, he knew it was so, and he ate two pieces of the cherry. Ruth and Janet had the apple, and so did Jeff and Audra.

When they were all sitting quietly, after everyone had helped clean up and clear away the dishes, Ruth told them that was the best cook-out she'd ever had. "And," she laughed, "it was also my first."

"Right on, right on, right on!" they all said, laughing.

All too soon it was after eleven, and David reminded, "We should probably start back for our pads." Jeff told them to not be a bit concerned, because after they each had said the "thank yous" and "just wonderfuls" and "good-nights" and been given hugs all around by Audra, he drove them to their apartments.

9

ON SUNDAY MORNING David called Janet, and when she answered he made small talk for a moment or two and then asked to speak to Ruth. There was a dead silence on the other end. Finally Ruth took the phone and said, "Hello, David. Did you sleep well?"

"I really did. I'm so glad you came through New York. I was really depressed, for many reasons, before you came. Now, I feel like trying again. Thanks for that!"

"Oh, David. I'm the one who is thanking you. And, as always, your patience never seems to run out. You are special to me, you always will be."

Janet sat in her living room easy chair and listened. She heard Ruth tell David that it was the noon flight on American Airlines that she would be taking to Chicago. Janet Schreiber had had a long week. Work had been slow, and then Ruth had suddenly descended from the sky and had been in New York all week. Janet liked Ruth. She was a nice person, well educated, very articulate with languages. Ruth was sophisticated, easy to talk to, not to mention the fact, of course, that Ruth Tobias was absolutely beautiful—stunningly beautiful—but she had enjoyed Ruth just about as long as she could stand it.

Ruth called softly to Janet, who took the phone to talk to David. She agreed to bring Ruth, and her luggage, to JFK. They would meet David there, for quick cups of coffee.

The American Airlines counter at JFK was packed. Even more than an hour and a half before take off, it took almost thirty minutes for Ruth to make her way forward to the ticket counter. Because she'd purchased her ticket in Israel, at Lod Airport, it took extra time to verify her reservations, but it was all worked out, "with the wonders of modern science and a computer or two" David said. Only Ruth reacted with a smile, he noticed.

Ruth said she would feel better if she went to the boarding area and waited there for the flight to Chicago to be announced. Janet and David walked with her to the area, and the three sat in stiff interconnected multicolored plastic chairs. Not much was said, except by Ruth, who commented on the large number of huge jet airplanes rolling back and forth on what looked like super highways.

At eleven-forty, the American Airlines attendant behind the counter announced Ruth's flight number and said it would be leaving in about twenty minutes. His voice seemed louder than normal to David as he listened to the speakers just above their heads. "But maybe," he thought, "it just seems that way because both Ruth and Janet are so quiet."

They made certain that Ruth had all her belongings, and she and Janet hugged. Janet turned away quickly, walked over to the small counter where the attendant was and stood waiting for David and Ruth to say their good-byes. After all, she was thinking, they have been close friends since they were thirteen. They'd each said so four or five times, and they probably had a few more friendly words to say to each other that no one else should hear.

"Good-bye, David," Ruth said. "God bless you for being so sweet to me. You are the nicest guy I know."

David could not speak. He was like that. When things got really heavy, he just couldn't say anything, and this was one of those times. "God knows," he was telling himself as the two of them stood face to face, "when we will meet again." And suddenly there were tears in his eyes.

Ruth saw them and was touched. She was a tough-as-hell Sabra, but when there was open love expressed for her she was always moved. She reached up and kissed David's mouth, and she lingered there. He kissed her back, and hugged her warmly.

Ruth Tobias turned and went down the ramp, walking to the jetliner that would take her to Chicago

When David turned and looked at Janet, she just stared at him. He tried to smile at her, but it didn't seem to him that she was being very responsive, so he said they should probably go back to the apartment and relax. They walked in silence down the long corridors of the terminal building to the bus stop. The Carey bus arrived and they got on. After paying their fares to the driver, they sat side by side in the first seat. Not a word was spoken during the entire long ride. When the bus reached the Grand Central Station stop, they got off and walked to the subway.

They climbed the stairs to David's apartment, went in, and closed the door.

"Why have you been so quiet?" David asked, so softly it was almost inaudible.

Janet only stared at him. Still standing, she walked a step or two in one direction, and then turned and walked a couple in another. She was almost walking around in a circle, and he said she should sit by him on the couch and they could talk.

She sat in the easy chair across from him and glared, for what seemed to David an uncomfortably long time, and then said, "You and Ruth certainly made a nice looking couple, kissing and hugging at the airport! Did you kiss and hold her every night in the kibbutz like that?" she asked, clenching and unclenching her fists.

He took a deep breath, realizing fully now what had happened. He almost whispered, "No. That was the first time I've ever kissed her. I look at Ruth like she's a sis—"

"Sure you do!" Janet shouted, interrupting him.

She stood up, stiffened, turned sharply and walked to the window. She looked out at nothing for a few seconds and then spun around. She picked up a small pot of tiny green ferns and smashed it to the floor. Then she started to sob.

David got up, slowly, and walked over to her and said, "Ruth's an old friend. She is like a sister to me—just a kibbutz sister. She came to visit, at just the right time, and helped me out of a bad depression. Okay?"

Janet pounded her fists on his chest, not hard, but hard enough that he knew there was really nothing he could say to make her feel any better, at least not right then. Ever so gently he put his arms around her, and pulled her close.

David led her to the couch and asked her to lie down, and he lay next to her. After a while, he whispered to her, "You are my love." And they both slept.

When he woke, she was up on one elbow staring at his face, and he looked into her eyes, and she said, "I'm so sorry. I don't know what happened to me. Everything was fine, all week, until this morning when I heard Ruth talking to you on the phone. And when she said you were so special to her, and those other things, I got all upset and now I feel terrible!"

David kissed her and when he did it again, she pressed close to his body. She had a way of doing that, he was discovering, to let him know what her inside feelings were. It was her own way of telling him that she wanted him very much, and right away!

He got off the couch, took her hand, urged her to come with him. They walked to the bathroom and took off their clothes, as fast as they could, and Janet set the faucets for a warm bath. She motioned for him to get in the tub, and to sit down. David grinned at his nurse as he did. She lathered and rinsed him. He reached out for her then, and pulled on her arms until she got into the tub with him. She sat down facing him, and he got up on his knees and bathed her gently to the waist. When he'd rinsed off the soap, he put his hands under her arms and tried to lift her. She smiled, and stood before him. He bathed her, touching softly, caressing. After the rinse, he hugged her and she stood motionless, until she felt the kisses of his tongue. Then she held his head and he heard those sounds she made, coming from deep in her throat. Suddenly she gripped his head so hard it hurt, but he ignored it because she was trembling so.

When she relaxed her hold on his head, David stood and kissed her mouth, and she returned his passion.

They dried each other and went back to the bedroom. Janet pulled the spread loose from around the pillows and folded it on the end of the bed, and they got under the fluffy blue blanket and began to touch, all over. Both of them filled with the warm flow, that most overpowering of all feelings, those of a woman and a man, wanting each other, desperately, hungrily. They went with it, and experienced it, and it possessed both of them.

"Now it's mellow time, " he whispered, breathing heavily. They rested together. He always held her close afterward, because he loved her so, and he felt that little touch of affection would be noticed and appreciated, even though what he really wanted was to turn over and drowse.

Janet said she had to tinkle, and he watched her as she walked away from the bed, down the hallway. "God, she is so beautiful naked," he thought. "I would do anything for that woman. Anything."

When Janet came back to the bedside, he reached out to her and she scrambled into the bed next to him. He said to her, "You are my love. The only love. And I will do whatever makes you happy. No matter what it is!"

She snuggled up to him, kissed his cheek. Then she said, "I'm really sorry I got so jealous of Ruth, and threw such a fit. But, I just couldn't help it. She is so bright and beautiful. Ruth's perfect. It's there for anybody to see. And, well, I was jealous."

David said thoughtfully, "Ruth isn't perfect. I'd say she's, oh, maybe *just a bubble away!*"

Janet punched him in the ribs, just hard enough to let him know that it was time to change the subject, and he did. "Has your dad bought the ICM stock yet?"

"Oh, I forgot to tell you. Or, rather, I never had a good chance to talk to you about that," she said. "He bought several thousand shares a few weeks ago—and he told me to tell you that if it didn't hit, he'd throw you overboard when we go sailing next time."

David was silent for a few moments and then explained the tight spot he'd been in regarding the new computer, and that when he and Jack had first talked about the possibility of buying some ICM stock, the loyalty thing bothered him. But now he could tell her, and Jack, too, that there was probably going to be a two-for-one stock split and that, happening almost simultaneously with the introduction of the new 370 computer, would probably send even the split stock sky high. It was just possible that Jack would, indeed, make a killing.

Janet hugged and kissed him, and said, "I really respect you for that, and you should know that my father likes you! I know, because he never would joke about throwing you overboard unless he did."

They got up then, smiling, and took a quick shower together, and dressed and went out to eat.

While they were eating, Janet brought up the matter of Ruth again. She asked, "Are you going to keep in touch with her?"

"Yes. I plan to write to her from time to time. Is that okay with you?"

"Only if I can censor your letters, and read all of hers," Janet warned.

David smiled his little smile at her, thought to himself, "I like it. I like it a lot! I like it that my love is jealous!"

Father Donovan took a folder from his private files in the bottom drawer of his desk. In the privacy of his study, he examined the "Record of Instruction" of David Mikhael Abaddon. He read over the notes and the accomplishments recorded there. He double-checked each entry to be certain that he had not overlooked a single requirement. Perhaps some, even some of his colleagues, would say he was one Catholic priest who was "hidebound by tradition." It didn't matter. The ministration of the Gospel of Jesus Christ to all of God's children was his job, and by God he'd do it his way!

Robert Lee Donovan had been a priest for almost thirty years, had wanted to be one even when he was a boy. Serving on the altar had been a delight for him. Even when his friends skipped, he went to the cathedral. He never missed, not even one Mass, not even when he felt sick. He went anyway! He could remember studying about the seven Sacraments before he was confirmed, at the age of ten. Robert Donovan had had tingles in his neck when the priest told them about the Holy Orders.

The checklist on his desktop showed the thirteen Areas of Instruction for David, and there were check marks by eleven of them, indicating completion. Those were Salvation History and Church History, the Life of Jesus Christ and the Catholic Church of Jesus. David had carefully studied the seven Sacraments, and wanted to be confirmed. He'd memorized the Ten Commandments, and the Laws of the Catholic Church. Baptism and Holy Communion and Mass, in particular, interested him.

So, Father noted, there were two to go. The Confessional, and the symbols, rosary, prayer booklet, and their significance had yet to be studied. Then David and Janet, too, must be instructed on Matrimony. Then, he felt, all would be ready for the two young people he so much enjoyed. "Yes," he thought, "it won't be much longer now. It'll be just a matter of another week, maybe two."

David picked up the phone in his apartment, took a deep breath, and dialed. Janet sat across from him, in the easy chair, and waited to hear what would be said. On the way home, after eating, they'd talked about his making one more attempt to reconcile with his mother and father.

"Hello. Who is this?" Sarah Abaddon said.

"It's me, Mother. David. How are y—"

"You should not be calling here," Sarah said, cutting him off. "Your father and I have told you already. You have made a choice to be a gentile. You are living with a gentile girl. You have become a Cath . . . ." She could not finish the word.

"Mother, please let me come to the house and try to explain to you why . . . ."

She cut him off again, this time by grunting into the phone something about Judas and crazy and shiksa. And she said, "Your father and I have told the Rabbi to bury a casket, with certain of your things in it, in a Jewish cemetery. The grave is to be marked with your name and dates of birth, and death. To us, you are dead. To Saul and Sarah, it is as if you died in September of 1972. Don't call here anymore. We don't want to talk to you. Understand?" And Sarah Abaddon hung up the telephone.

David was very quiet, but Janet coaxed him to talk. He told her, slowly, what his mother had said—about the casket, and certain of his things, and about being considered dead. He could not keep back the tears. Janet held him, and said she would never leave him. No matter what happened, she promised David she would never, not ever, go away from him.

As soon as work was over the next day, David went to Father Donovan's study and told him everything. Father calmly said, "I've had several other Jewish converts while serving in this church, David. In most cases, the parents do eventually relent and accept both parties, and the conversion to Catholicism, too."

"You don't know Sarah Abaddon, Father. She's the queen. What she says goes. It's always been that way, and, I think, it always will be."

Father suggested they go ahead with the instructions for that evening. David fingered the rosary beads and told Father Donovan that he'd memorized the Lord's Prayer, and he recited a "Hail Mary" perfectly. When the session was over, David mentioned the beautiful statue of Stephen the Martyr which stood just inside the front door of the church, and Father Donovan made a mental note of that, for David would need a confirmation name.

That night, even with Janet sleeping at his side, David had the nightmare again. It started, it seemed to him, the minute he closed his eyes. He saw a new car going down the street, and there was a sticker on the back bumper. It read: NUKES—*NO*, SCHOOLS—*YES*. That set him off. He ran after the car. It was fast and almost got away, but David did get close enough to see that it was a station wagon filled with children. Their faces seemed to be horribly scarred by burns, and *they were all blind*.

He awoke with a start, heard the sound of his own voice as he cried out. Janet was shaking his arm, he realized. He felt sweaty, and was shaking.

Janet soothed him, and they embraced and fell asleep again, but not before she'd thought that he seemed to be having bad dreams more and more often. "If only his mother could be a little easier on her only son," Janet worried to herself. "What a woman that Sarah is!"

Father Donovan called Janet at the VA Hospital and invited her to come with David to his study the next two evenings. She agreed to be there, said she would be happy to share in the instructions about Matrimony.

"Matrimony," Father explained to Janet and David, "is one of the Seven Sacraments. We believe that, once you've been joined in marriage, you will remain so until one of you dies."

David questioned Father then about the possibility of having a marriage annulled. Donovan told him that such a procedure was very difficult to accomplish, and that a number of criteria had to be met, in order for the Vatican to grant one. Janet looked at David with a strange, almost unbelieving stare as he asked about that.

So David said, "I'm just curious about all of the aspects, dear. Please tell her, Father, that there have been many such incisive questions during the instructions."

Father said, "There have been many such incisive questions during the instructions, dear."

Their laughter released the tension that Father had felt since they'd begun the session. He continued, "You must abstain from sexual intercourse until after the marriage ceremony. This is a requirement of the Church. Now, once you are married, you may engage in sexual relations as often as you wish. However, the only method of birth control recognized in the Catholic Church is the rhythm method. Simply put, it means that you not have intercourse during those times of the month when Janet might become pregnant. Again, it is the only acceptable way to prevent her from conceiving. The use of contraceptives, in any form, is strictly forbidden."

Father studied their faces for a few moments, and then said, "Do either of you have any questions about the parts of matrimony that we've discussed?" They shook their heads, smiling.

"Good," he concluded. "Tomorrow, as soon as you get off work, why don't you both come here to the study. Then, we'll talk about the marriage vows and the ceremony itself, and that will finish up all the sessions of instruction that I had in mind. Sound all right?"

David and Janet stood up. They both nodded, and thanked Father Donovan. They said goodnight and left.

As the two of them walked out into the main lobby of the church, David pointed to the statue of Stephen the Martyr. He told Janet it was his favorite. She smiled, and nodded when he whispered that the sculpture was one of excellence and great beauty.

That night, at David's apartment, Janet said she'd thought she should go right to sleep. Father had reminded them both, she said, about total abstinence until after marriage. David thought, "It's going to be a long, cold, dreary Brooklyn winter!"

The following evening after work, they went again to the study and discussed matrimony with Father Donovan. Both Janet and David said emphatically that they were ready to make a total commitment, together, to the Catholic Church. Father Donovan smiled broadly.

He finished by talking of David's completing the fifteen sessions. "You have been one of the brightest, most attentive young people I've ever worked with. I think congratulations are in order, Mister Abbadon."

"I want to thank you, Father. You've been really patient with me. I sincerely appreciate that. It's been my good fortune to have had you as a tutor," David said.

Father promised then to conduct David's baptism, when it was mutually convenient; then David could take first communion and be confirmed.

"Father, as I mentioned, Janet and I want to have her mother and father there, too, so we'll call them, and then be in touch with you. Okay?" David asked.

Donovan smiled in approval, said he looked forward to seeing Lisl and Jack Schreiber.

As they left the church, Janet said, "I think I'll stay at my apartment tonight, and I'll call my parents from there."

They were silent as they walked toward the subway station. Janet knew David was more than a little disappointed that she wasn't staying with him that night, so she took his arm and walked as close to him as possible. She asked, "Should I ask them to come for everything?"

"Yes. Please do," David said softly. "Ask them to come next Saturday. I'd really like to do all of it on a Saturday morning."

Janet called David about two hours later. She said, "Hi. What are you up to?"

"I was just reading a good paragraph in *Passions of the Mind*. It's the part when Freud had the tumor removed from his mouth and almost bled to death. It's really an interesting biographical novel."

She thought to herself, again, that he certainly could suddenly become detached from immediate things. After all, wasn't her call about them, the instructions, and her parents coming really most important? But she kept her frustration to herself and said, "My parents can come a week from this coming Saturday. They can't come this weekend because my dad has to attend a convention of some sort in Albany. Does that sound all right to you?"

"It sure does," he said. "That's a turn-on."

He was sure she was grinning into the phone when Janet said, "My dad said to tell you that he'd need the extra time anyway, to count all the money he's made on ICM stock. He said he was sure you'd want to know how much he's made."

"God, am I glad that worked out! I don't know what I'd have done if it hadn't."

David told her he'd call Father Donovan and set up everything for a week from Saturday, at nine o'clock.

The morning news on the NBC show "Today" was a shock to David. He was getting ready for work, and there it was. Israeli airplanes had flown into Syria and Lebanon and had "attacked military targets." They'd done so to retaliate for the slaying of the Israeli athletes who had been murdered in the Olympic Village in Munich three days before. He'd had one of those awful Armageddon nightmares that night, and he wished that Janet would relent and sleep at his apartment once in a while and maybe he'd not have those awful dreams.

He thought, "Maybe I should postpone the conversion, and everything." He called Janet and she agreed to come and spend the night with him.

That night they talked about the significance of what he was about to do. Janet told him again and again that, just because he was becoming a Catholic, it didn't mean he was forsaking all that he and his family had ever been. She reassured him that to be a Christian-Jew was, well, somehow, really special.

David's eyes filled with tears. He remembered that when he was about twelve his mother had made some horrible comments about the son of a friend. He remembered that she said they really believed the guy was crazy, and that his parents had told the rabbi to bury a casket and mark the grave to show him as dead. Maybe Janet Louise Schreiber thought it was "somehow, really special to be a Christian-Jew," but David knew the Jewish community would think otherwise.

They went to bed, and she held him until he fell asleep in her arms. When they got up in the morning, she reminded him that he had slept the whole night through, without as much as a whimper.

During the days that followed, they spent almost every moment together. Except for the time spent on the job, they were inseparable. "My mom and dad will be here late tonight," Janet said to him as they were having wake-up coffee at his place Friday morning. "So, I'll be going right to my apartment after work to wait for them to come."

David frowned, and asked, "Why can't I be there with you? I can stay until they arrive, and we can visit some, and then I'll come back here to sleep. Okay?" Janet nodded.

They met after work at her apartment and made ham and cheese sandwiches for themselves. She fixed a tossed salad and iced tea. They went into the living room and sat on the couch to eat. The TV held little interest for them, until another story came on about Bobby Fischer besting the Soviet Union's Boris Spassky for the World Chess Championship. David turned on, and talked chess to Janet until they were both sleepy.

About ten-thirty, her visitor alert rang. She went to the intercom, asked who it was. Her father's voice came on, and she pressed the access button.

When they heard her mother and father coming, she and David walked out to the landing. They greeted each other warmly and then went back into the apartment. David asked about their suitcases.

"They're downstairs inside the security door, next to the wall," Jack said, adding that the car was parked a block away. David went down to get the bags.

While he was gone Janet told her parents, "David has some doubts right now. I'm sure he loves me. He wants to go through with everything in the morning, but he is anxious. Can you help me?"

Lisl and Jack assured their daughter that doubts, at that time, were normal. They told her they'd do what they could.

When David came through the door with the luggage, Jack said, "Thanks, son. You're always doing things for others, not the least of which was the suggestion that I buy some ICM. There's been a stock split. I made the killing I've always dreamed of." Lisl winked at David.

As David left Janet's apartment, he had a broad smile on his face. On his way home, he thought again and again that Jack had said the magic word—only once—but Jack had said it: son.

David went to his apartment, got undressed, and flopped into bed. As he was going to sleep he thought, "The rest of all this'll be all right. Somehow, it will all be okay, for the four of us."

David Mikhael Abaddon got to the priest's study of Saint Thomas More Church in Brooklyn at nine o'clock. Father Donovan and the three Schreibers greeted him.

Father closed the study door, and asked David to kneel on the velvet-covered pillow. David did, and Lisl stood behind him, Janet on her left, and Jack to her right. The priest baptized David "in the name of the Father and of the Son and of the Holy Spirit."

Donovan took communion himself. Then he served First Communion to David and, in turn, to the others.

He asked if David believed in the Father, the Son, and the Holy Spirit, to which David said, "I do!" The priest then confirmed the young Jew from New York.

"Congratulations, 'Stephen,'" Donovan said, bestowing the confirmation name on David.

David stood up and the priest shook David's hand. Jack, and then Lisl, did the same. Janet kissed and hugged him.

They had coffee, and David said, "It was easy." The whole "everything" as David had been calling it, took just over thirty minutes.

They all thanked Father Donovan, then went to the subway station and on to Janet's apartment.

They talked about having lunch at Braggadocio's. Jack said they should all go in the station wagon, and then he and Lisl would drive back to Ithaca from the Jersey side.

They walked to the car and drove to Jersey City.

At Braggadocio's they sat in one of the large wooden booths. Each ordered the Italian Sausage sandwich and salad with house dressing and red wine.

Everyone raved, so David didn't bother with his Woody Allen bit about it being the best.

After lunch, they walked to the car and said good-bye. Janet said she and David would probably be coming home for a weekend soon. Lisl hugged David and told the two of them that they should come to Ithaca and stay for a week, not just a weekend.

Janet kissed her parents, and David shook hands with them and hugged Lisl again. Janet stood waving as they drove away. She turned to David, in the middle of the parking lot, and said, "I love you. Very much. And, I'll marry you David Abaddon." David's eyes filled with tears of wonder and joy.

They went to David's apartment, and closed and locked the door, and they forgot about everything, except that they were engaged to be married, and very much in love.

10

Rabbi Jacob Goldman stopped his car in front of the Klein home in Brooklyn Heights. He got out slowly, walked up to the door, and rang the chimes. The door opened at once, and the maid let him in. She led the way to the study, motioning for him to follow. Sarah rose to greet him, and sent the maid away.

"So, how are you, Rabbi? she asked.

"I'm just fine, thank you, ma'am," he said. He paused, and she sat in the center of the couch, pointing to a nearby chair. He sat in it, and said, "I've completed all the details you gave to me on the phone. It's all done."

"Good," she said with finality. "Send the bill to me and I'll mail you a check."

He tried to smile. "Would you like to know where the grave site is?"

"No, I would not, and neither would my husband. It's over. That's it, and that's all."

The rabbi started to say something more—twice—but he was so uncomfortable that he said he had other important work back at the synagogue and asked to be excused, almost as if leaving the presence of a princess.

Sarah rose, walked ahead of him to the door, and bade him a curt "Thank you, and good-bye."

As Goldman drove away, he thought to himself how glad he was to have all of that behind him.

When Saul got home that night from the U.N., Sarah was waiting at the front door. As he entered, she said, "It's done. Rabbi Goldman was here and told me all about it. It's over."

"Did he tell you which cemetery it's in?" Saul asked.

"No, he did not, and I told him we didn't care to know any of the details. It's done! And, that is it!"

Saul didn't care to eat, saying that he'd had an off day at the U.N.

Sarah ate a hearty meal and two desserts. "What the hell," she thought, "I'm eating all alone anyway."

Saul Abaddon was called to a phone in a private office in the United Nations building. He listened as the Israeli ambassador to the U.N., Yosef Tekoah, came on the line. Saul's eyes narrowed a bit as he listened to the ambassador and looked out the window at the Goldwater Memorial Hospital on the tip of Welfare Island. He let his eyes slowly drop then, until he saw some choppy waves on the East River. It looked cold outside, and he shivered involuntarily.

He hung up the phone, then changed his mind and dialed the Israeli U.N. Delegation offices. He told his secretary, "I may be a little late in the morning."

Saul took the elevator down to the first floor, and walked out of U.N. headquarters to his waiting car.

Riding in the chauffeured limousine, Saul's mind flashed back to the early days. He remembered his father talking about emigrating from Poland to Palestine, and of how all of them in the late 1800s and early 1900s had drained swamps and sunk wells and irrigated the deserts. They had planted farms with foods that grew in the now fertile soil, as far as the eye could see—and forests. They had made the desert bloom. Saul thought about the war, and about his many activities in supporting the Zionist movement, and about the great leaders he'd served. He thought of Ben-Gurion and Eshkol and now Meir, and of Dayan, *the* Sabra. He remembered being with Moshe, and with Menachem, in the Haganah. Begin and Dayan were Saul Abaddon's idols.

Saul had been sent quietly to the United States by the Zionists in 1945. It had been his responsibility to live in the United States, to marry, and become a part of the Jewish community there. Life with Sarah had not been easy, not at all, but he had a mission to perform for Israel, and nothing was going to stop Saul Judah Abaddon from getting it done. As it later turned out, the United Nations became his field of battle.

The chauffeur drove to the Klein home. He jumped out from behind the wheel and went around to open the door for his employer. Saul thanked him, said to put the Cadillac away for the night, and walked to the front door.

Inside, he called for the maid to get Sarah. She came down at once on the elevator. The two of them went into the study, and he shut the door.

Saul said, "Mrs. Meir wants me to return to Israel at once. I can't imagine why. The ambassador called me and said he'd tell me all about it in the morning."

Sarah bristled. Why, after all these years of fine service, did Israel's Prime Minister want her husband back in Israel? It just didn't make any sense—at least, not to her. She demanded, "Find out why, Saul!"

Saul knew she'd want him to take the direct approach. Sarah always took the straight-ahead route to solve any problem. "You know I will," he said.

Sarah was troubled. She had wondered many times what it would be like to live in Israel, but she had never imagined it might be required of her, of the two of them. She stared, as only Sarah could, at Saul.

They had stood during the entire conversation. Now they both felt exhausted. She motioned for them to sit down. Saul welcomed the comfortable feeling of the easy chair. Sarah continued to stare at him, but he was accustomed to that.

The next morning Saul waited at the office of Israel's U.N. ambassador. When Mr. Tekoah arrived and walked into his private office, Saul followed. They exchanged brief cordialities, then the ambassador said, "The Prime Minister wants you back in Israel, in the Ministry of Defense. The chief of the Intelligence Division had a heart attach yesterday morning. You are to take over the responsibilities of that position next Monday. It is a temporary appointment. You are to fly out tomorrow night. Your wife and son may follow you later, if you wish."

Saul could only stare in disbelief. The short reply he made was simply, "Mrs. Abaddon will be going with me, if that has your approval. My son will remain in the United States."

The ambassador consented and said to be certain to let him know if there was ever anything he could do for the Abaddon family, either in Israel or in the United States.

Saul thanked the ambassador and left. He began to feel an excitement he hadn't felt for years. It was like the old days, he told himself. Suddenly, there was action. Things were happening. He was going home!

Flying now, the El Al jetliner was filled to capacity. The departure and climb out from JFK International had been uneventful. Even Sarah, who had grumbled through all the preparations for the journey, seemed peaceful now. The seats in first class, and the service provided by the multilingual Jewish stewardesses, were outstanding, Sarah had said. She told Saul, quietly for a change, "I'm excited to be going there. We'll undoubtedly be meeting many influential people, high in government."

Resting in the large comfortable seat, Saul had mixed emotions. On the one hand, he'd been in San Francisco in April of 1945, to quietly be a part of the U.N. Conference on International Organization. True, Israel was not yet a nation, but Zionists knew it was only a matter of time, and to have one of the "low key" members of the Haganah already stationed in the United States was routine. His role was to watch, listen, learn, and to get involved, swallowed up, in the Jewish community. His permanent visa had been arranged for—he was a visiting Zionist, lobbying quietly for what would be a new State of Israel.

So, flying home now, he felt mixed emotions. Yes, on the one hand he'd looked forward to being at the convening of the twenty-seventh session of the U.N. General Assembly. It would be on the nineteenth of September. He had met U.N. President-Elect Stanislaw Trepczynski soon after his election. Saul wanted to get better acquainted with the man from Poland. Poland! Suddenly Auschwitz came to mind. That is burned deeply into the minds of all of us, he thought, and the face of Saul's murdered father flashed almost life-like in his mind.

On the other hand, he was going home. It was only a guess, but it seemed to him that if the Grand Old Lady-in-Charge wanted Saul Abaddon back in Israel, it had to be for an important reason.

Saul looked at Sarah. She was sleeping, with her head turned away from him. "Eating, sleeping, and talking—those are things she can do well," he thought. He fully recognized Sarah could be beyond belief to deal with, but, he rationalized to himself, he'd done it for Israel. Israel came first. Face it, being married to Sarah Klein had given him a perfect cover. He was assigned to the diplomatic service and, eventually, to the United Nations. He was, furthermore, married to an American. Saul had the best of everything—free access to all levels of government, society liaison with America's finest, and, thus, to all sources of information both in and outside of the United Nations. And all of it for Israel!

Saul rested comfortably then. He'd accomplished his tasks well, they had told him. As he began to doze off, he told himself, "It was a challenge. Being the perfect spy for over twenty-seven years, for Israel, was a special calling, and all had gone well!"

As soon as the Boeing 707 came to a stop at Lod Airport, a stewardess in blue and white came to assist them. She helped the Abaddons gather their carry-on bags, and then escorted them through the exit to a steep flight of auxiliary stairs. They had been pre-positioned by the Lod Airport Service. Only a special diplomat would be allowed to disembark that way, to a waiting car at ground level.

An army colonel was standing next to the rear door. He opened it for them, saluted and said in Hebrew, "Welcome home, sir. Ma'am; it's good to know that you'll be here with us now." Sarah got into the back seat, and Saul followed. The officer quickly slipped into the front seat next to the driver. They drove from the airport and headed down the highway.

Saul nodded and smiled at Sarah, but his tired eyes were glowing. Sarah looked away from him and at the back of the colonel's head. She was fluent in Hebrew, and she thought, "Judging by what that officer said, it sounds as if we may be here for more than just a little while."

It was snowing and David was bundled up in winter clothing, but he shivered a bit as he walked into the Church of Saint Thomas More. He took off the warm clothes and laid them on a chair outside the confessional. He took a deep breath, and went in.

He sat down, as he closed the door, and said, "Bless me, Father, for I have sinned. This is my first confession."

The priest on the other side of the screen responded, then questioned David.

David knew it was Donovan. He answered, "I have had sexual relations with my fiancée."

"How often?" asked the priest.

David swallowed hard and said, "Two or three times a week during the months of October, November, and till now in December."

"For goodness sake, Dav . . ." Donovan stopped, reminding himself that he was not to be personal. It didn't matter that he had carefully explained all of it to Janet, that abstinence had been covered during the lengthy instructions with David. "Hadn't he learned anything?" Donovan silently demanded.

Holding back his Irish anger, Donovan said, "You should come to confession about once a week, and you must stop the practice of sexual relations with your fiancée. You have to stop now!" He cleared his throat, and then asked, "Understand that?"

David lowered his head, and said that he did, and said that he had no other sins to confess.

The priest assigned penance, and David heard again Donovan's explanation of " . . . a sacramental rite involving contrition, the acceptance of penalties, and absolution." David knew that. He also was thinking he'd be quite a while completing the penance assigned.

He promised the priest he would begin at once, and he rose and left the confessional. David walked to the front of the church, lit candles, and genuflected at the edge of the pew. Then, he got down on the kneeler and began to say the Hail Marys and the Lord's Prayer—over and over, and again and again.

When David realized he would never finish in any sort of reasonable time, he stopped reciting. He had to meet Janet. And, he told himself, "I'll just have to come back tomorrow night after work, to finish. Or I'll do them at the apartment—or maybe I'll just skip the rest for now."

He stood up and moved into the aisle, and genuflected again. Then he turned and walked back to the chair near the confessional. He picked up his scarf and put it on. As he was putting on his winter coat, he glanced toward the study. Father Donovan was standing just inside the doorway, looking out, and he was staring right at David.

Turning quickly, David walked out of the church and to the subway station. He rode the train, thankful for the warmth inside, to his stop, then hurried to the apartment. Janet opened the door, explaining that she had been watching for him through the window.

"Kiss me, dear," she said.

He did, but only as he passed by to hang his coat in the closet. After he'd done that, he turned around and said, "Father Donovan was in the confessional, and even though I knew he would be, I was very uneasy."

David went on to say that the long penance assigned about equaled the length of time since September, when he'd been confirmed. "It'll take me an aeon to say them all," he said.

"Don't worry about all that now," she said. "Let's go cuddle together."

David told her they shouldn't right then, and that maybe they ought to just go to the kitchen and fix something to eat. They did, but Janet looked at him unbelievingly. He heated some soup, and she made Swiss cheese sandwiches, and they ate. But, she said over and over to herself, "He's never said *no* to me before." Later, when they were in bed together, she knew he was really upset about something. He had made excuses all evening, and now said, "I just want to go to sleep!" And she wondered what in the world it was that had him so shaken up.

They fell asleep almost at once, in each other's arms, and David began to dream. It was the new holocaust dream again. He dreamt that he was walking at the foot of the Golan Heights in Israel. Suddenly, out of nowhere, a child came walking toward him. He stopped, waiting to see what she was going to say or do when she reached him. When they were face to face, he looked down at her, and she stared up at him. Then it happened. *She started to melt.* Right there, before him, she was slowly disintegrating! Her beautiful face became at once ugly and twisted in pain. He reached out to try to hold her, to soothe her, but she just simply disappeared—vaporized!

David woke, moaning. Janet was sitting beside him saying, "Easy now. It'll be all right, David. Just take it easy for now." His thoughts flashed back to Father Joe, and Nam. Kelley's face, focused now in his mind, was smiling, and David felt better, as he remembered Kelley's promise. Kelley would keep it. He'd keep it all, until David was better able to handle everything.

"Please, David, you must tell me what it is that's bothering you so much right now," Janet begged.

He paused, a long pause, and knew he would have to tell his lady something, but decided in an instant that he'd only tell Janet some of it.

"There are really two things on my mind right now, babe," he began. "First, Father Donovan came down on me really hard about you and me getting it on. You know. The bit about before the marriage vows have been said. He just overwhelmed, yes, intimidated me about that. Then, I've been concerned a lot lately about the nuclear problem. I know I've really not said much to you before, but I'm worried as hell as I keep hoping for some sort of breakthrough on a permanent nuclear freeze agreement. Or maybe something can be done if ever the Strategic Arms Limitation Talks got off dead center. Janet, I am worried that there is going to be a nuclear war, and I'm convinced that it will begin because of some ridiculous folly on the part of a careless or irresponsible third-world nation."

"I never knew that was troubling you, David. Why haven't you told me about this before?" she asked.

He became noticeably pensive then, but after a while he said, "I never told you anything before now because I was hoping it would all resolve itself, somehow. But obviously it hasn't." David took a deep breath, sighed, and went on. "I'm certain, in my mind, that the Russians and the United States are too smart to start an exchange of nukes. They've got enough moxie to avoid that. Look back at Korea, Cuba, and now, Viet Nam. They're not going to begin a holocaust of nuclear proportions—no way! No, it'll be some stupid asshole in a third-world country that'll begin something awful. And my worst fear is that Israel will be drawn into it."

She hesitated, and then asked, "Why in the world do you feel that Israel is so threatened by nuclear war?"

He took her hands between his and said, "You must never repeat what I'm going to tell you. Promise me!" She did.

He continued, "My father came to this country first in 1945. He got a temporary visa, through the British. Later he got a permanent visa. Anyway, he was really sent to America as an agent of the Zionists. Poppa Saul was a long-time member of the Jewish underground, the Haganah, and I'm pretty sure that he helps the Mossad. But, he was put here to get things done for the Jews."

Janet interrupted to ask, "What's the Mossad?"

David explained their being the elite. "They are Israel's secret intelligence and counterespionage agency."

And he said, "My father never has suspected that I've guessed, but sometimes I'd look in his briefcase, at home. I'd do it at night, after he was asleep. He wouldn't usually lock his papers up. He'd put them in the center drawer of his desk, in the study. Anyway, I'd see papers from the Israeli Embassy. They were in envelopes, already opened, labeled *Most Secret*. And I read those."

Janet stared at him, in disbelief. "Oh, my God," she whispered.

David took a deep breath, then said, "You know what the Biblical writings predict. And now, the Israelis have nuclear power. They have a plutonium-producing facility. It's in the Negev Desert, at Dimona, near Beersheba. They make plutonium there that's pure enough to be used in atomic bombs."

She shuddered and couldn't believe the look on David's face. It appeared to her that he might be sick at any moment.

Rather than breathing evenly, David started gulping air. Unsteadily, he continued, "Now the Arabs have money from the oil they sell all over the world. You can bet, and you'd win, that they'll try to buy enough plutonium to construct their own facilities, to produce the pure stuff, for atom bombs."

Janet could only shake her head in disbelief. And she asked him where the major threat might originate.

"If I said, I'd only be guessing, but remembering some of the messages in my father's desk from a few years ago, and from my gut feelings, I'd say Syria or Iraq or Iran—maybe all three. They've got to be trying to get plutonium. And I'm really wary of the French. I'm just not sure about them. India, too. It's really hard to say."

By then they were both so wide awake that she said, "I'll make some hot cocoa. Okay?" He nodded. They got up, put on robes, went into the kitchen together and sat down. Both were thinking that something had to be done about such madness.

They began nightly discussions of things important to them. Either Janet or David would bring up something to talk about. It was winter then in New York, and it was more convenient for them to meet after work at David's. One of them would fix their meal, or they'd do it together, and they would talk. Sometimes it would be about marriage plans. Janet said she wanted to marry him in Ithaca, at her church, with Father Schultz performing the ceremony. David grinned and said, "Of course." He wanted a little boy. She told him that two children had always been what she'd hoped for.

So it went—work during the day, and nights and weekends just being together. Once in a while David went to talk to Doc Silber, but it was mainly social. Janet was there. David told Silber he really had never felt better about his personal life, and that he and Janet were to be married in June. Doc seemed pleased at that. He told David so, and later he mentioned it to Janet. "You'll be happy," he said to her. It was clear to Silber that David had adjusted well, with some considerable help from his head nurse. The doctor wrote in his medical record, ". . . there clearly has been a significant behavior modification, in this instance." Silber was sincere, and honest with himself, in stating what he felt about David Mikhael Abaddon. David had come back. He'd come a very long mile along the difficult road to recovery.

Settling down in the land of his birth was a joy for Sabra Saul. Everything had been arranged. Fall had been so pleasant, and Sarah and Saul saw people he had known long before World War Two.

Living in Jerusalem was something Saul Abaddon had looked

forward to when he knew he'd be returning to his native country. The Israeli government provided a safe house for the new Chief of Intelligence and his wife; and, just as she always did, Sarah got her wish. There was a welcoming party, and the Abaddons met most of the leaders of Israel. Saul told himself that Sarah had been so charming and pleasant that he almost didn't know her. It had gone well, for both of them, during the first few months. "Back home," Saul kept saying to himself.

Saul sat in his office in the Ministry of Defense and thought of his first meeting with Mrs. Meir. She had asked that he come to see her in her office. He was overwhelmed, as they sat there together, when she said, "Welcome home, Saul. We need you to serve with us here now. Your record is impeccable. You have done our country a great service. I look forward to seeing you often."

He thanked her, and told her that he would, of course, serve wherever she wished. As he left, she smiled that famous smile at him. "God, I love her!" Saul thought.

Saul remembered then that first September night when he and Sarah had walked near the Knesset building. On a low hill in Jerusalem, near Hebrew University, the home of the Israeli Parliament was always brilliantly lighted at night.

Sarah had said softly, "It is simply beautiful, with the floodlights all around making it glow."

The Ministry of Defense was guarded, everywhere, by Jewish Marines. They were the elite, Saul had been told, every one of them an expert with firearms, and highly disciplined. Their business was to make absolutely certain that only those people who were supposed to got into the building.

Saul was impressed. He had been escorted to his office on the morning of September twenty-fifth by an Israeli Marine major. The next day, he was driven to the Ministry in a staff car, and as they went through the gate he heard the guard call him by name, and greet him in Hebrew. "My God, they are efficient," he thought.

Saul Abaddon's duties were complex and varied. Intelligence is gathered by almost any means. Jewish people all over the world were loyal to the State of Israel, and, at the risk of their very lives, managed to get information to the government of Israel. Saul never dreamed of the amount of data he would be seeing every day, information accurate to an astonishing degree, on any of a thousand useful subjects. Saul was indeed proud that he had been asked to return to Israel, to serve the nation he loved so much.

Sarah had grown to accept their new way of life. She had the servants she'd been used to, now from West Jerusalem. Saul saw to it that she got what she wanted — it had become a habit. He took her to the important Israeli government social events. He thought, "She seems to be mellowing. Just a bit, she seems to be a little gentle."

The Christmas season was near, and Janet and David had arranged for two weeks of vacation. They both got off early on Friday, and met at the Brooklyn bus depot. The bus left promptly at one, and arrived in Ithaca on schedule. Jack and Lisl met them. After warm welcomes, they got the luggage and drove to the farm for a late supper.

Later, they all sat in front of the fireplace and talked, mostly about being family. It was December twenty-second, and they had two weeks, the four of them, together in Ithaca, at Christmas time.

Next morning it was snowing, gently. Janet got her figure skates out, and then called next door. She got the promise of the loan of some hockey skates for David to use. They put on winter parkas and walked to the Henderson farm, a little less than two miles away. David picked up the skates on the back porch, and they walked to the pond that bordered the Schreiber and Henderson farms.

Sitting on the bank putting on their skates, Janet told him why the Hendersons weren't home — they were ice-boating on Cayuga Lake. She said Jack would take them, too, if David liked. "Maybe later," he said.

Skating onto the ice, David fell. When he tried to stand, he fell again. Janet said, "You are about as steady as Bambi was, the first time he and Thumper tried the ice." They laughed together.

After falling so many times he lost count, David slid over to the bank. He crawled off the ice and sat down to watch Janet skate. She was gliding over the ice, silent and graceful, like an eagle soaring in flight.

She skated over to him, saying that was enough. They took off skates, put on their boots, and walked to the Schreiber farm. Later, when just the two of them were drinking hot buttered-rum, sitting in front of the fireplace, he told her, "You are poetry in motion when you skate like that. I love you dearly — for a thousand reasons." Janet smiled, kissed his cheek, and snuggled up to her man.

Christmas morning was picture perfect, as if taken from Irving Berlin's song, *White Christmas*. The blanket of white snow covered everything.

Janet went into David's bedroom at the front of the house. They walked to the window together, and looked out across the frozen lake at the way winter had repainted Cornell University. Beautiful! Simple beauty, they both knew, leaving it unspoken.

Lisl called to them. "It's Christmas, you two. Come down and see your gifts!" Janet whispered to David that her mother became a little girl again on Christmas morning. "My dad thinks so, too," she giggled. It'd been a real contest between the two of them, when Janet was small, she told David, as to who had the most fun, and, as he would soon see, Lisl had changed not at all.

The exchange of gifts early on Christmas had always been tradition at the Schreiber's. Gifts were shared all around—nightgowns and shirts, ties and socks, linens for the home, sports jackets for work, one for Jack and another for David. Everyone got handkerchiefs, and Janet got a popcorn popper for her apartment. She said she might let David use it sometime. His face turned crimson. Lisl changed the subject, ignoring what all of them knew.

Janet and Lisl got coffee and just-baked cinnamon rolls and they all sat down for a quick breakfast.

Later, Lisl said they should finish coffee with a song or two. She sat at the piano and played. Everyone sang what words they knew to Mel Torme's *Christmas Song* and then *Sleigh Bells*, and *Winter Wonderland*.

Jack and David sat in the living room, facing each other on the couch. They talked about their gifts. "I love the soft blue color of the suede sports jackets. They should be really warm for us," Jack said. David just nodded, thinking how wonderful it was that Jack accepted him.

Lisl and Janet finished preparing brunch and came to get the men. The four went into the dining room, sat down to eat slices of fresh-baked ham and candied yams. There were oven-warmed homemade bread and piping-hot mixed peas and carrots, grown on their farm. They shared a huge bowl of potato salad, David's favorite. Lisl said she had made it just for him.

"We're stuffed," everyone said.

They cleaned up everything, then all sat around the fireplace, talking about their collective hopes for the best for all the people, everywhere. And David thought to himself, "How lucky I am to have become a part of such a beautiful family!"

Next morning they all put on winter clothing, and pulled the ice boat to the lake with the station wagon. They didn't need chains on the wheels. The snow-plow had come through, and the roads were clear of all but the hard-packed snow.

They put the ice boat out, and climbed aboard. Jack was at the controls and was as skillful at handling it as he was at being skipper of his sailboat. They tacked back and forth with the wind.

Back at the shore, Janet changed places with Jack and took the controls. At once her daring showed, as she pulled the ropes tight, and the sail became rigid in the wind, pushing the craft precariously fast.

When Janet took them out too far, the ice looked thin to Jack. He insisted that she turn back toward shore, quickly. They decided to call it a day and go for home, to the fireplace and some toddy.

The days seemed to hurry by, and almost too soon it was time for their annual New Year's Eve party. Lisl told them she'd invited a few friends over, and things would liven up about nine o'clock.

A dozen friends partied, talked, and ushered in the new year. Janet kissed David and said, "It's 1973, and we'll be married this year." He smiled. That said it all.

Just before the group began to break up, Janet introduced David to Danny Henderson. David thanked him for the loan of the hockey skates and Danny mumbled something about that being no problem, and promptly switched subjects to say that he was a pre-med at Cornell and that he was in his sophomore year. Janet and David both noticed that Danny never really focused his eyes on theirs when they stood face to face talking. He seemed to stare blankly at them, in a kind of unfocused, spacy way. After Danny said good night and left, Janet told David, "That guy is weird. He's something else." David leaned over and said softly in her ear, "He really is. He's got the personality of a dial tone." Their quiet chortling went unnoticed.

Too soon it was time to bus back to Brooklyn. Neither wanted to, but bosses would be looking for vacation-filled faces on Wednesday morning.

Jack warmed the station wagon's engine to insure them lots of heat on the drive into Ithaca. At the depot, the four said goodbyes, and Janet and David got on the bus. They sat alone in the long seat in the rear, waving to Lisl and Jack until the bus took them out of sight. Then Janet turned to David and they kissed.

There was no one seated near them, so each let the warm flow, stored inside for two weeks happen, and when they reached David's apartment at last, they let themselves go completely.

Saul sat at his desk, poring over some reports on the relative strengths of Israeli armed forces versus those of bitter-enemy Arab nations. As the intercom buzzed, he picked up the phone. It was the Minister of Defense, Lieutenant-General Moshe Dayan. The two old' friends from the Haganah exchanged warm greetings. Then Moshe explained that the Prime Minister was planning a secret trip to Rome. She would be visiting with the Pope. It was unprecedented. It was critical that all go well. Saul was to have the latest information available to insure her absolute safety, and they had only until January fourteenth. She would be meeting in the Vatican with Pope Paul VI on the fifteenth!

Before dawn, on January fourteenth, Chief of Intelligence Abaddon was in the office of Minister of Defense Dayan. No one else was present. Saul came right to the point. Based on everything known, and upon the recommendation of the intelligence staff, he felt that the Prime Minister would be safe in Rome. However, he urged that she be subtly surrounded by her bodyguards whenever she was exposed to even a small number of non-Israelis.

Later, Saul was proud that her trip had been uneventful in matters of threats or violence, and Mrs. Meir and Pope Paul VI had a most cordial meeting. She told the Pope that the people of Israel intended to stay in Jerusalem, and keep it all. Also, she discussed the prospects for peace in the Middle East with the Holy Father.

Now it was all public knowledge. Saul couldn't help being pleased with the success of his first critical assignment. He had done his work well and recommended that she go to Rome. Congratulations would be on their way to him, from his many colleagues, soon.

The days at work passed too slowly for Janet and David. They would meet as soon as they could late each afternoon and eat out together or at one of the apartments. She insisted that they sleep at his place, always. It was not a matter open to discussion, David had learned. Once the lady made up her mind, that was it. He thought, but never said, "Hard-headed Germans."

The evenings and weekends passed much too quickly for them. During those times they talked about their June marriage, and of the house they would find that would be perfect, like that of the Piedmonts.

One night David began, "I've been reading again about this nuclear thing, babe. It's awful. The muscle-flexing with nukes that the Russians and Uncle Sam keep initiating is being misinterpreted by some third-world nations. They see their lack of knowledge about nuclear energy and having no source for plutonium as a weakness, and they are willing to pay any price to get some. That's what I was telling you was my worst fear, you know, just before we went to Ithaca."

"I know, David, but there isn't anything we can do. It's all being talked about and worried over at lofty levels. We'll just get silver hair too early if we try to keep it all in perspective. I say we have to let the powers that be keep the peace."

David said, "You don't understand. When I was in the hospital in Saigon, Father Kelley and I agreed that there couldn't be any more Viet Nams. I was the one who explained how it is in the kibbutzes. It's special there. I mean, the feelings that people have for each other, and the genuine love and affection that flows all around—people caring for people made by God. Nukes unbalance all of that. They tip the scales to the edge of madness. That is what I'm worried about. Not just another Viet Nam. I'm talking about the destruction of the world."

She saw that he was going into orbit again, as he had on many occasions, so she said they ought to go to bed and bundle. That worked. They took their shower together, got under the sheets and blankets, and afterward, during mellow time, she whispered that it had been warm and gentle and intensely satisfying for some reason. "Maybe we ought to talk about the nuclear thing every night before we make love," she joked quietly.

David turned away from her and stared at the wall, with his eyes not even blinking for so long that they were uncomfortable. When he didn't move or speak, Janet snuggled up to him and bent her body to conform to his, and she reached over and hugged him with the one arm. She was gentle, because she thought he might be asleep, but she knew she shouldn't have said what she had said—no jokes about nukes!

David sat at the console of the 370 in his office at ICM. Jeff walked in and sat down. "Dave, we've sold two new computers to the Israeli government. A small ICM staff is to go to Jerusalem, to the Ministry of Defense, and see to the installation and programming. Frankly, I want to recommend you as a programmer. First, you helped design the machine and you know what's inside it about as well as anyone, and you speak Hebrew like a native. That's important. The Ministry has a Hewlett-Packard 1000 now, and the compatability issue is critical. We must see that the two new machines are interfaced so that the defense staff doesn't lose a single byte of data."

David's thoughts went spinning. Israel. Jerusalem. The Ministry of Defense. Saul Judah Abaddon. Sarah. David had too many thoughts wildly flashing through his mind. "I'll have to think about it and get back to you, Jeff."

"Can you let me know in the morning? They want to know upstairs. You know. The boss is always looking around for somebody's ass to chew on, and we can avoid that by responding quickly."

Janet and David met for lunch at the McDonald's where they'd had their first date. They got Big Macs, french fries, hot coffee, and sat alone.

He told her everything Jeff had said. She was very quiet for a long time, then asked, "When? For how long? What about me? What about us?"

"Those are my questions, too, but the ICM front office has to submit the names of their team members. Then, the matter of security clearances being obtained from the Israelis must be handled. At that time the Israelis will answer questions."

When she looked at him completely puzzled, David added, "I have to say that I can't blame them. The Israelis have got to have an enormous amount of data stored in their computer, and they have to make every effort to be certain that it isn't compromised by people given access—not even a little!"

She seemed to relax. It did make a lot of sense, when she looked at it that way, but she said as they left the restaurant, "I feel very uneasy."

That night, after they'd eaten in Janet's apartment, he called his parents' home and asked the maid to get his grandfather. When he picked up the phone, David asked about his health. Then David explained that it was really important for him to talk to his father.

"You'll have to telephone him in Jerusalem," the old man said. "Saul and Sarah have been there since September, and they will probably be there for some time, according to what it says in your mother's letters."

David was stunned. He couldn't believe that. There were a few more words with his grandfather, a polite good-bye, and he hung up. He walked over to the couch, sat down next to Janet, and told her what he'd learned.

He said, "There will be no help from Saul on forming an opinion." There would be no one else to talk to. They were on their own, he heard himself tell her.

They discussed the situation long into the night. It came down to an agreement on two critical issues. He would go, only if they could go together, and they would go as man and wife. So, she said she'd go to Ithaca the next weekend to arrange for their marriage in March, and they would both go to Israel, and David would tell that to Jeff in the morning.

David slept with Janet, in her bed, for the first time.

Next day, early, David went to Jeff's office and told him the decision. Jeff frowned, and David questioned him.

"It's just not done that way, Dave. ICM's not going to like that, not at all. I really don't know how I'm going to explain it to them upstairs."

David said that his decision was final, and that he would appreciate it if his determination was expressed upstairs. Jeff nodded, as David left.

Janet took the one o'clock bus to Ithaca on Friday. David suddenly experienced a feeling of solitude he hadn't known since Lang Vei.

Early the following morning, David called Ithaca and got Janet out of bed.

"I just had to talk to you, love. I'm so lonely, I can't stand it."

She smiled into the phone as she answered, "I love you, David. I'll talk to Father Schultz and explain everything this morning. Daddy and I are going ice boating this afternoon, and I'll call you tonight and tell you all the good news. Now, please just go program your computers, or read *Passions*, or go to a movie. I'll call you tonight. Okay?"

David reassured her, said he'd be waiting for her call.

David sat in his apartment watching TV. He picked the phone up on the first ring and said hello.

"Mister Abaddon, this is Father Schultz, in Ithaca. There's been a terrible accident." He went on to explain that Jack had reluctantly let Janet take the ice boat out alone. Jack had stood near the shoreline. On a high-speed run, apparently too close to open water, Janet had crashed through the ice as Jack watched in horror. He had raced to the spot where the ice boat was floating, but Janet was gone—under the ice. They had just recovered her body.

David was numb, speechless. Father Schultz's words echoed in his mind. Then there was a deafening silence. At last, David managed to mumble that he would be in Ithaca on the next bus. He asked that someone meet him. Father assured him they would be there.

David called Jeff, explained about the tragedy, asked for the next two weeks off—emergency vacation. Jeff insisted the staff would cover everything in the ICM offices, urged David to try not to worry too much. "We'll pray for you, Dave," Jeff told him.

The Mass of Christian Burial was conducted by Father Karl Schultz, in Ithaca's Saint Bernard's Catholic Church. Everyone said he could conduct such a Mass as well as anyone. The church was filled during the service, and most went to the site of Janet Louise Schreiber's grave.

To David, it was all a blur, a white-out. He stood by Lisl and Jack and later vaguely remembered riding back to the farm, but his head hurt, and he had trouble focusing his mind. Like before, in Nam.

He stayed at the farm with Lisl and Jack. He kept thinking that Janet would walk through the door at any moment. So he talked and talked and talked, mostly to Lisl. She was a great listener, and he needed that.

After almost no sleep at all for two nights, David's head throbbed with pain. He had to go back to Brooklyn. "To see some other friends," he lied to the Schreibers, but he promised to keep in touch with them. He meant it. All the way back on the bus, he told himself that Lisl and Jack Schreiber were like a mother and father to him.

When the bus arrived, he went to a pay phone and called the VA Hospital Psychiatric Clinic. When Doctor Silber came on the line, David spoke briefly, then left the phone dangling on its cord, and walked over to the curb to hail a cab.

Doctor Silber had been at the funeral in Ithaca. He had seen the remarkable on-the-surface poise of David Abaddon, during what had to be another living nightmare for the sensitive young Viet Nam veteran, so when David called and asked if he could come over right away, it was not a surprise. Doc told David to come directly to the office.

David got off the elevator and rushed past the reception desk and into the inner office. He slammed the door and marched up to Silber.

"I don't know if I can make it, Doc. She was everything to me. I never loved anyone else. She was the only person I've ever felt that way about."

David couldn't think her name. He tried, but couldn't make out the word. If he did, he kept imagining, he'd lose it all. Lose all of it. Again.

P A R T
THREE

II

DOCTOR SILBER convinced David to admit himself to the Brooklyn VA hospital as an in-patient. David knew it was for the best. It would allow him time to try to focus, think, get his life together again—after Janet.

For the first several days Silber kept him on Valium shots every six hours and visited him each day for a talk. On the morning of the fourth day, in his private room, David seemed a little better. Doctor Silber had come in early to see him every morning since he'd been admitted. The day before David had mentioned his twenty-seventh birthday party. He was still unable to say Janet's name, but Silber remembered that Janet had talked to him about spending that anniversary with David. Silber tried to get him to talk about it now. David clammed up, and Silber didn't push it.

When he came back to David's room after lunch, David said, "Did President Johnson die? Were the Peace Accords signed in Paris, bringing the Viet Nam War to an end? Or am I imagining things again?"

Silber was pleased. Here might be the hoped-for breakthrough. "Yes, Dave. On January twenty-seventh, just after the death of Lyndon Johnson, North Viet Nam and South Viet Nam, the Vietcong, and the U.S. representative signed the treaty. The Viet Nam War is over."

David lay back on his bed. Silber could see that he was breathing easier, had relaxed some, but he was still worried that David would suffer a psychotic episode.

"How's the Watergate thing going, Doc?" David asked.

Silber said, "It looks as if some of Nixon's personal staff may have been involved."

David felt suddenly tense, and asked for more Valium so that he could sleep. Silber had a nurse give him a shot. David felt dreamy, as the nice high from the medicine took hold.

A strange feeling came over David. It seemed to be physically present in the back of his neck, but there were unexplained mental sensations, too, in his thinking—unknowns—unfocused thoughts.

He felt a rush of panic, and reached for the call button, to summon a nurse for more Valium. He hesitated, then stopped himself. He became angry, fiercely so. There was his imperious mother, the horror that was Nam, then his parents disowning him, and now the loss of his love. The adrenalin flowed and he felt energy surge through him, but the more he thought about it all, the more frustrated he became, and the rage was suppressed, and morbid depression swept over him.

David got another shot, but it had minimal effect. He whispered to himself that he'd be better off dead.

His mind, hazy as it was, suddenly produced a thought, then another, and he was able to effect a kind of focus: it became clear to him that he must build an atom bomb.

David awoke, sat upright in bed. Rubbing his eyes, he glanced around the hospital room. It wasn't just imagination. He had had those thoughts. There would be a bomb. He could do it. What a challenge! Triggering things, doing things, had always been his way. He'd do it—new preemption, by David Mikhael Abaddon.

Now the ideas in him were exploding with stunning force. He kept thinking it was crazy. *He* was crazy! So what? The thought of building a bomb filled him with awe, exhilaration.

He lay down, began to wonder whether it would take him a long time to design the bomb. He admitted to himself that he couldn't remember all the details of the two ways you could induce plutonium to explode, but he was sure the temperature at the center of the sun is around fifteen million degrees Kelvin, and he speculated that the temperature at the center of an atom bomb would be about that when it popped. "It's elementary physics," he whispered to himself, and he drifted off.

Silber came into the room just before five o'clock, just as David was waking. They talked briefly, and then the doctor said he was going to call it a day. David asked if he could go sit in the TV room with the other patients. Silber agreed, said they could walk down together. David got up, put on the blue robe with VAH printed on the back. He and the Doctor went to the TV room. There were three other patients sitting there, watching and listening to the national news. Silber waited until David settled comfortably into one of the folding chairs, then left, motioning a good-bye.

The four patients, all Nam Vets David was sure, were absorbed in learning of the release of the first one-hundred-sixteen U.S. military men who had been prisoners in Hanoi. It's high time, they agreed, and thank God that thing is over and our guys are coming home.

When a commercial interrupted the news, David got up and walked back to his room. It was time to eat, and he was hungry. The tray of food was on his movable table. He sat down, pulled the table to him, and cranked the handle until the table was at a comfortable level. He had a pork chop and applesauce, green beans, and a tossed salad. He drank coffee and ate two chocolate chip cookies. He left the mashed potatoes and gravy—they looked artificial.

A volunteer brought a pushcart to his door. David took copies of *Popular Science* and *Mechanics Illustrated*. "They're light reading," he thought. "I don't care to do a lot of thinking." At ten o'clock, he closed the door, got into bed, and turned out the light. He fell asleep. The next he knew the nurse was shaking him, asking if he wanted a pill so he could sleep.

"My God," he thought, "why doesn't she get in the bed, and I'll go be the nurse?" He fell asleep again, after taking the pill she insisted he needed.

The next morning Doc Silber came in at seven o'clock. David was up, had already showered, and eaten. "I've been waiting for you, Doc. I'm starting to remember some things I've been trying to think of. I feel better today."

"What kind of things are you trying to remember, Dave?"

"Things about Ja . . ." He tried to say her name. He'd been thinking of it yesterday, when he had to ask for more Valium. Now, it stabbed his mind to have the thought, but he knew he had to face it. There would be no way to get out of the hospital unless he took a chance. So he took a deep breath, and said, " . . . ah . . . about her. About Jan . . . et."

Silber took David's hands into his own, and squeezed them tightly, nodding for David to keep going.

"I know she's not coming back, Doc. I know I have to learn to accept that. It'll be hard for me, but I'll have to do it."

They talked then about what had happened at Cayuga Lake. They talked for more than an hour. When he left the room saying he'd come back after lunch, Silber wasn't sure who had been in the most pain through all of it — David or himself.

The next three days were filled with even more positive signs. Silber wrote in the medical file: " . . . patient is responsive, alert, controlled. Frequency of medication reduced." By Friday afternoon, Silber was thinking, "Probable release to out-patient status on Sunday."

David felt reassured because Doc had said he could be reached at any time. During the day David was instructed to dial the VA switchboard operator if necessary and have them activate Silber's beeper. Silber also gave him his unlisted home phone number and said, "Dial any time. If you feel the need, call." David could live with that. He told himself, "I'm lucky to have Doc in my corner — damn lucky to be in the care of this guy."

Silber was amazed. David was going to be fine. The recovery was remarkable. His patient was ready. The process of medication and counseling, providing a bridge of support for the patient, had been successful.

On Sunday afternoon, Silber stopped in the doorway. He asked, "How are you today, Dave?" David replied that he felt good, was ready to go home.

"You can pack. Go out-process any time you wish. Keep my numbers handy. Call the minute you feel the need to have someone there. Okay?"

David nodded, smiled, thought, "What a guy he is! I admire him." He got up to gather his few personal items.

Out-processing was easy for David Abaddon. He'd done it before, in Washington.

In just over an hour, he walked out into the mid-February cold of Brooklyn. "It's colder than a nun in a convent," he told himself. But at last he was on the way to his apartment and to the solitude he sought.

He took a quick shower, put on blue jeans and a sweatshirt, then called Jeff. He lied, said he had just come back to town from Ithaca, said he would be back at his desk at ICM in a week. David asked, "Will you and Audra pray for me? I need your prayers." Jeff promised they would.

Jeff said there had been no word yet from the Israelis on approving anyone to go to Jerusalem to install the two 370s. He asked if David would still be interested in going. David said he definitely wanted to go there now.

David walked into his bathroom, ran cold water. He took some in a glass, put a Valium pill in his mouth and swallowed. Thoughts of Sarah and Saul in Israel had swept into his mind. As always, the unknown or the unpredictable made him uneasy.

The effects of the pill came quickly, and he felt the calm settle over him. Then he called Father Donovan, and told Father of his lie to Jeff. "ICM has some very strict policies on security. If they find out that you've had any kind of psychiatric history, well, they restrict you—professionally, just as the federal government does. I'd never be allowed access to any interesting ICM projects, *never again!*"

Father Donovan asked David to come to see him, and they hung up.

Next, David dialed Ithaca's area code and Schreiber's phone number. They talked for half an hour, rambling on about Janet, and all the talking triggered David's mind and suddenly the idea broke through. He diplomatically concluded their conversation, and as they said good-bye, Lisl said to keep in touch—he'd promised he would, she said.

Next morning, David rode the early commuter train to Washington, D.C., wearing his Army officer's uniform. He took a taxi to the Library of Congress, and spent the day in research, taking notes from the Los Alamos Project documents. Now he was certain!

In the evening, he took a city bus to Walter Reed Hospital. He walked briskly to the radiology department. The rooms were deserted. He found a pair of lead-lined gloves, a special protective face and head mask, and a heavy lead apron. He emptied a laundry bag of its soiled linens and shoved in the stolen items, then he picked it up and walked out. No one paid any attention to the jaunty young officer—he obviously knew who he was, where to go, what he was doing.

Back in his apartment, David could think of nothing else. He knew it was crazy—that he was, too, but only about the bomb. It

154

didn't matter. He would build the bomb, just to do it—a David Mikhael Production!

David stayed in his apartment the rest of the week. All he did was write programs for his computer.

He went out once on Tuesday, to see Father Donovan. They talked briefly in the study, then David wanted to go to confession. There David said he really had no sins to confess, but he did want to tell someone, and he'd chosen Father, about his plan. He was designing an atom bomb—in his computers, in simulation, just to be sure he could.

"For what possible reason do you want to do a thing like that?" Donovan asked.

David said he wasn't exactly sure—just to do it, to keep his mind occupied.

"You must go back to the VA hospital, David. Talk to Doctor Silber about it. Will you promise me you'll do that?" Donovan urged.

"I can't, Father. If I do, the shrinks will lock me up. They don't deal with reality when it comes to something like this." Then David said he had to go back to his apartment, that he had some things he wanted to get done. He said a polite good-bye, and was gone.

Father Donovan didn't have any idea what to do! He didn't think David could or would go through with this plan, so he decided simply to wait and see.

On Sunday night, David went into the computer room in his apartment. He reached for the system's master switch and turned it on. David sat down in front of the console and typed the password JANET on the keyboard, then pressed Enter. Then he put another password into the computer: SHEOL. Suddenly a diagram appeared on the viewer. It was an engineering sketch, in the form of a perfect sphere. There were numbers and formulas printed in the margins.

The graphic in the middle of the screen showed a solid-core center, about the size of a softball. Around it was a drawing of a shield labeled *beryllium*, and that, in turn, had the outlines of small packets of explosives placed symetrically around it. Under it all was a label, spelling out in computer-type the words IMPLOSION DEVICE.

David typed a series of mathematical formulas on the keyboard. Instantly the graphic vanished, and the numbers and symbols he'd typed appeared on the screen. He asked the computer, by making one last entry, to use them and analyze the mathematical soundness of his entire simulation. The computer screen went blank. Then appeared the answer he'd been waiting for. It told David Abaddon that his physics and math in the main graphic were perfect, and that he had, indeed, correctly designed an atomic bomb.

He smiled, leaned back in his chair. He entered the date, then he turned the system's master switch off. After David had gotten into his pajamas and turned out all the lights, and was lying in bed, the date he'd put in the computer kept flashing in front of his eyes, like a neon sign—coming on, then off. It was *February 25, 1973.*

Next morning, David went back to work at ICM. When Jeff walked in, David followed him into the front office and shut the door. He thanked him for his support during the past few weeks. Jeff told him no thanks were necessary, that the workload had been assumed by several of their colleagues. "You may be going to Israel, you know," Jeff said.

"I'm ready to go, Jeff, whenever you want. I feel that some travel and a change of scenery would be good for me." He thought how strange it would be to go to Israel now.

Jeff was relieved to know that David was not totally depressed.

David went to his desk, and dialed Doc Silber. They chatted a while, and Doc Silber was glad to know that David was back at work.

"My boss just told me I may be going to Israel for as much as six months, and I need some way of getting my medication while I'm there. Do you have any suggestions?" David asked.

Silber hesitated. Then he said, "I can give you a six-month prescription, Dave. You can take the pills with you, but ... ah ... how will you get them through the Israeli customs?"

David said, "I'll take care of those customs people."

Silber said to let him know ahead of time by a phone call and the prescription would be waiting for him.

After he'd hung up, David turned back to the console beside his desk. He stared at it and thought, "Things are going to work out. Somehow, for me, things are gonna be all right!"

Evenings in his apartment, David planned and made a list of all the things he would need to build the bomb. He calculated how much beryllium he would need, and sized the thick reflector shield. He noted fuses, wiring, detonation devices, power sources, connecting pieces for the framework, to support the device during construction, and the high explosives necessary to crush the sub-critical mass of plutonium into a massive explosion.

David woke up late one night, his thoughts centered on his two major problems. When he placed the high explosives around the plutonium, they had to be arranged to virtual perfection. It was essential that the imploding shock wave compress the plutonium equally from all sides; otherwise, the mass would not become critical and one would get only the yield from the high explosives. His other major concern was radiation. Plutonium is pure poison. It is the silent, thorough killer. If he ever did get any plutonium, he would need to manipulate the stuff cautiously. Radiation protection equipment would become essential. He'd wear it with a kind of diabolical pride.

Well, there was always tomorrow, he thought as he drifted off to sleep again.

David now knew what was required to build the bomb. He was acutely aware of the myriad difficulties. It had never before been accomplished by one man. The challenge of it filled him with self-awe, inspiration. He felt driven to the task.

He thought long and hard about the problem of the explosives. The Los Alamos documents did not reveal what was used in the Japan A-bombs. The high explosives in "Little Boy" and "Fat Man" remained a mystery.

He considered simply guessing, but decided that was not good enough. He must build a bomb that *would* work. He became angry with himself. There must be a way, but imaging them, he was thwarted. Was it TNT, RDX, PETN? Nitroglycerin? Pentolite?

Where to buy it was another problem. He finally decided to telephone the Du Pont Company, say he was a graduate student in theoretical physics. He'd convince them it was all just a matter of curiosity about explosives. He knew he could use his best Woody Allen as a screen, if he had to.

David called the Du Pont experimental plant near Wilmington, Delaware. He guessed, "They probably get requests like mine often. I'll explain it's just theory I'm after. That won't arouse anyone's suspicions."

When the company switchboard operator asked who he wanted to speak to, David said he wasn't sure. He told her what he needed, and she said to wait a moment. At last, a man's voice came on the line. "Chemical Research Center. May I help you, young man?"

David moved in quickly with his story, was aggressive, got the answers he had to have.

He was smug about using a subway pay phone—no way to ever trace *that* call.

David followed the world news more closely than he ever had. He felt it was critical now to be informed on current events. "I must be knowledgeable about the things around me in order to appear as normal as possible," he kept telling himself. So, in early March, he noted the resumption of the U.S.-Russian Strategic Arms Limitation Talks. They'd been in recess since December of 1972, and now "new SALT possibilities" had to be anticipated. He heard on an NBC "Today" news broadcast that Syria had adopted their first permanent constitution, and he read that Egypt's new leader was Anwar al-Sadat. "Things are happening, and I'm keeping up," he assured himself.

During those weeks in March, David went to see Silber three times. He called each time and went during his lunch hour so he didn't have to ask for any more time off. And he just didn't want anyone at ICM to know he was seeing a psychiatrist.

He also went to confession and to visit with Father Donovan. Oddly, the two of them never spoke of the bomb when they were in the study. It came up as a major topic only in "the box," as David had come to call it, and, curious as he was, Father waited for David to initiate the subject. He thought, "If I mention it, that may scare David away. Then no one would be able to keep track of what's going on. At least this way, someone knows where he is, and what he's thinking." So he let David ramble about his life. There was something about a possible trip to Israel, seeing the VA doctor, being able to keep up with fast-changing world events. Father noted also that David never mentioned Janet's name, not in the confessional or in the study. Donovan thought on more than one occasion, "He seems so normal all the time, except for that awful thing he says he wants to do!"

Jeff buzzed David on the intercom, asked him to come to the office. When he walked in, Jeff said to shut the door and sit down.

"The Director just had me come to his office. The Israelis have approved the request of ICM that four of you be allowed to travel to Israel, and to stay in Jerusalem until you've installed the two 370s in the Ministry of Defense. Your visas will be good for only six months, but they can be renewed. I think the fact that you spent a year in the kibbutz—and speak Hebrew—influenced them very favorably, Dave. Central Administration was happy about that."

"When do we leave?" David asked.

Jeff explained that the four of them were to travel by El Al to Lod Airport, leaving the night of April ninth. He said ICM and the Israeli government were paying the expenses, for everything, for the six months. If that was the time it took.

David said he was ready to go, that time would drag for the next couple of weeks. He asked, "What about my passport and visa?"

Jeff handed him the application and told him to fill it out for a renewal. He told David to return it, with his expired passport, in the morning. "ICM will get all team members' passports and visas," Jeff said. And he told David he didn't know who the others were, but that they would have a meeting before they all left.

David grinned at Jeff, and left with the application. He filled it out at his desk and laid it aside. Then he called the VA, asked that Doc Silber be told David Abaddon needed to see him.

David walked quickly to the subway and rode to the VA. He went to the Psych Clinic, waited, finally got to talk briefly to Doc Silber. Doc wrote a lengthy prescription for Valium and handed it to David. After thanking Doc, David went to the pharmacy. They filled his order and handed it to him through the opening in the glass.

As he walked to the subway, and then on the train riding to his apartment, David thought "I've got my crutch. If I need to, I can use the Valium to get me through the days—and the nights, too—in Israel."

David slept as soundly that night as he had in a long time. Early the next morning he went directly to work. He'd remembered to bring his expired passport, and he put it and the completed application for renewal on Jeff's desk. Then he went to his desk, took a sheet of ICM stationery out of the center drawer, sat down at the typewriter and began typing a letter: "Dear Ruth—"

The following week David went to see Father Donovan. They talked for forty-five minutes or so about the trip to Israel. When Donovan asked, David said there was really no need to go into the confessional. "I have nothing to confess, Father. I feel fine. I'm down to two, and not more than three Valiums a day now. Things are looking good," David said, thinking of Father Kelley at just that moment.

Donovan thought, "So! He takes tranquilizers. Maybe he will soon forget this atom bomb idea!" But all he said was, "Have a pleasant trip, David. And be sure to drop me a line now and then. I'll look forward to that." David promised he would keep in touch.

Later that week he went to see Doc Silber, and they spoke only briefly. David said he would write. When the doctor put out his hand as they were saying good-bye, David hugged him. They both laughed, a bit nervously. David said, "You're the only shrink I've ever done that to." Silber smiled as David walked out.

That night David went to Manhattan to see his landlady, Leah Cohen. Leah's family had been close to the Kleins for over thirty years. In 1968, when Sarah had called to ask about something special in the way of an apartment for Son David, just out of the Army, Leah had said not to worry.

Now David explained about going to Israel for ICM for perhaps six months. He gave Leah a check covering the rent for that period.

Leah said, "Not to worry." She would make certain his apartment was secure, and as he was leaving she said, "I hope you can get back together with your mother and father." David said nothing, but nodded and said good night.

On Friday, Jeff brought David's passport, with a six month visa inside, and put it on his desk. David looked up and smiled. "About all I have left to do is pack, and call Lisl and Jack to say good-bye," he said. Jeff grinned at him, nodded and left.

David started packing on Saturday and finished on Sunday. He'd been told to take extra, and he filled two suitcases. He took plenty of soap, a dozen tubes of toothpaste, two combs, an extra hair brush and several bottles of shampoo. He emptied six small plastic bottles of multiple vitamins and refilled all six with Valium. Then he put them neatly back in the box the vitamins had come in. He resealed it, and packed the box under plenty of clothing.

He closed the two huge pieces of luggage and put them to one side in his bedroom. Then he dialed Ithaca and talked to Lisl and Jack for over an hour. They went on and on about Janet, work, the stock market. David told them about his trip, said he'd be leaving the next day. And he said, "I want you both to know how much I care about you. We have a great relationship, and I want to keep it that way." He promised to write. They did, too. Lisl told him they'd pray for him. He said he'd do the same. When the three were saying their good-byes, tears stung David's eyes.

The following day was the ninth. David went to work early, lugging the two large suitcases with him on the subway. He took a cab from the station exit to the Research Institute, and dragged the bags to his office, then went to see Jeff. They talked for a few minutes and then both went to the first meeting on the project. There were six people in the room. At the head of the table, always in charge, was the Director of the Systems Research Institute. He was Jeff's boss and, as everyone knew, as tough as they come. His management style commanded the utmost respect. He was William Corbett—W.C. for short. He was a professional Irishman—and a leader, one had to admit. He made the introductions while Jeff sat quietly with the others. There was James Bannion, who would be the project manager. He was from central administration, where he normally was an executive assistant to W.C. "Jim has the final say on everything," W.C. said. The chief engineer was Scott Curtis. His assistant, also an engineer, was Paul "Ace" Barker. Then W.C. asked David to stand. "Here's the best programmer we have. When you three get the machines installed, turn David loose. He'll program the goddam things perfectly for you," W.C. announced.

Over coffee W.C. told them the reason they'd not met until departure day. First, he said, there wasn't any real need to get together and talk about the 370. They had all been in on designing it. Then, he explained, he felt that if he treated the whole thing in a low-key manner, so would they. And, he concluded, the Israelis wanted just that. *Secrecy* was paramount. He pounded the table for emphasis.

The rest of the morning, and until mid-afternoon, everyone talked details—of the flight and arrival at Lod Airport, accommodations and food, security, and the Israelis' insistence that the four of them stay in plain sight at all times, unless, individually, they requested and had approval for any kind of travel. The four were each thinking the same thing then—"I'm gonna sight-see," but no one said so, not while W.C. was in the room.

The director gave the group one of his famous sermons about "The Project" coming first. ICM was his whole life, and he reminded everyone of that every chance he got. There were even private jokes about W.C. making it with the machines. *"Whatever'll get him off,"* they said.

A little after two o'clock, W.C. left, and the four agreed to meet at JFK, at the El Al counter, at six. That would give them almost two hours before take-off time.

Jeff took David out for a late lunch, and they spent the rest of the afternoon together, talking about everything in general, and nothing in particular. David wanted to hear about Jeff's boys, so he talked at length about Tad and Chip and little Charlie.

They went back to ICM and walked slowly up to David's office. That killed some time and got them some exercise, Jeff said. With the door to the office closed, Jeff urged, "Let me know if you need anything." David said he would. Then, he put on his jacket, got the suitcases and took them to the door. They hugged each other warmly, and David opened the door and left with tears in his eyes, and Jeff's, too.

The El Al flight took off on schedule. They flew to London, refueled, and then on to Athens. When, at last, the El Al jetliner landed at Lod Airport near Tel Aviv-Yafo, Abram Weisman, an Israeli Army colonel, met and helped them. Their customs inspections were accomplished in a private room, with the doors closed and bolted.

As two uniformed customs agents began the search of David's bags, he got a little tense. Every item was removed from both pieces of luggage. David stared nervously at the gray-haired agent when he picked up the box of vitamins. The agent shook it twice, looked at David, and put it on the pile of already examined articles.

When the officials had finished, they told Colonel Weisman, in Hebrew, that everyone could repack. Before Weisman could respond, David thanked them in Hebrew and told the other ICM-ers they'd been cleared. They all breathed easier, as the two customs agents walked out. They were cleared directly to passport and visa processing—that was routine.

Later, Colonel Weisman's driver pulled the army staff van up to the pile of luggage at the entrance of the terminal and they loaded the bags and got into the van. The three Americans sat in the back. Weisman and Abaddon sat side-by-side behind the driver, chattering away in Hebrew, as they drove to Jerusalem. *It was April eleventh.*

Colonel Weisman led the four ICM "gents," as he called them, to the Visiting Officers' Quarters, inside a maximum security compound, surrounding the Ministry of Defense. Each of the visitors had a private suite of rooms, a welcome sight as they walked in and looked around—spacious, and everything in its place, "spit and polish" clean, everywhere. They thanked Weisman, and he left. Later, when they compared notes, each found he had exactly what the others had: a sitting room, bedroom and bathroom, with military-type furniture throughout. Not bad, they'd said. "Now," Ace offered, "if we can just find hot and cold running maids, that'll do it!"

Excellent meals, all kosher, were available to the visitors. Ace called it "chow time." He was a West Pointer and had served a tour of active duty as an Army officer, but he'd become disenchanted after two tours in Nam, and he had resigned to work for ICM. Ace knew the military way and he pointed it out to the three others, accurately and humorously, and it was appreciated.

Gradually, as they got into their work patterns, it became apparent that it would be better if all of them wore military coveralls. They had no insignia, but were always required to have their Israeli identification cards clipped onto their collars.

David was their interpreter. His Hebrew served them well and often, although they found that many of the people they came in contact with spoke English, at least to some degree, and that was a help.

The computers were already in the warehouse when the ICM crew arrived; and the work of the ICM engineers, directing the Israeli computer engineers and their helpers, went smoothly, efficiently.

David's work pattern differed, but he helped the other three get things started.

After a week he decided to find Poppa Saul. There was no doubt as to where the offices were located. The restricted area was guarded around the clock by the elite Jewish Marines. It was not possible to simply walk up the stairs to the second floor and surprise his father, so David went to the young commander of the Marines, and told him the truth. He said, "I haven't seen my father since he and my mother came here last September. Can't you arrange an escort for me sometime when we're sure he's in?" The young captain said he'd see what he could do. He took David's ICM business card, with his local address and telephone number written on the back.

It took three days for the captain to get back to David. "Come to my office, the one just outside the restricted area, on the first floor. We can talk there," he said on the phone.

When David got to the captain's office, he wasn't in, but when he returned he apologized to David, explaining that there had been a suspected infiltration attempt.

The captain clipped a second identification card on David's collar. The new one was bright red and had "Official Visitor" stamped on it. With the young officer leading, the two of them walked up the stairs. As they went through the heavy double doors the captain had swung open, the Marines on either side snapped to attention. In moments they were in the inner sanctum.

David saw the closed-circuit television cameras and wondered where the monitors were, as they walked all the way down the corridor to the last door. The captain opened it, motioned for David to go in, and the escort followed. David went to the male secretary and introduced himself. The sergeant stood, bowed slightly, and shook hands with David. He said, "Your father is expecting you. Please go right in." David thanked him, turned and smiled at the captain, who sat down to wait.

When David went into the office, Poppa Saul stood and walked around his huge desk. He came toward David, as he closed the door, and they came face to face. Neither spoke. David's face was flushed, and he was uncertain as to what to say, how to act.

Poppa Saul said, "How are you, David?"

"Fine, Poppa. You?" David felt a cold sudden sweat beneath his outward calm.

Saul Abaddon didn't answer, his eyes measuring his son. It had been last September when the casket had been buried in Brooklyn, and now David stood in his Jerusalem office, apparently wanting to find a way back. Saul, too, was a bit uncertain as to how to behave toward this "dead" son.

Glancing at the conference table, Saul nodded. They each took a chair from its place at the table, turned it toward the other. They were only three feet apart, almost bumping heads as they sat down.

David couldn't stand the silence. Nervousness clearly in his voice, he summarized ICM's purpose for sending the four employees to Israel. Saul smiled, looked quickly away, stirred in his chair, and David knew suddenly that Saul Abaddon had been the key highly placed Israeli official who had, all along, been monitoring the development of the entire project.

David suddenly went to his knees in front of his father, hugged him around both legs and said, "Help me, Poppa. I love you."

Then David did something he would later wonder about again and again. He said, "I'd like to see Momma!" And he lied, "Tell her that I'm still a practicing Jew." David asked if he could go to services with both of them on Friday night.

Tears welled up in Saul Abaddon's eyes. He said, "My son has come back to me." He took the handkerchief out of his back pocket, unfolded it, put it on his head. Then he bowed his head murmuring the Hebrew prayer of thanks.

Saul and David stood. Saul took David's hands in his and shook them. Smiling then, he said, "Why don't you come to the house tonight. I'll call your mother and tell her everything. We can have dinner together, like we used to."

David was tearful also, and said he would be waiting in front of his building at six o'clock. Saul nodded, smiling.

When Saul and David came out of the office arm in arm, the secretary and marine captain stood up and came to attention. Father and son didn't notice, as they walked down the corridor and out of the restricted area together. David stopped only long enough to hand the Official Visitor badge back to the guard at the main entrance, then he and his Poppa walked down the stairs and outside, talking quietly.

The staff car pulled up in front of David's building promptly at six o'clock. As the driver spoke to him in Hebrew, David got in, and they drove off.

David got out of the car in the small circle near the door to his parents' house. Both Sarah and Saul came out to greet David. "For once," he thought to himself, "Poppa is getting equal time." They hugged him, and as they walked into the house, David thought, "She seems to have mellowed some—maybe."

The evening started slowly. David had to lie. He told his parents that he'd never completed the Catholic conversion. He said the relationship had been broken off, and that he'd heard Janet had drowned in an accident while she was ice-boating with her dad. David excused himself then, and asked for the way to the bathroom. He went in and locked the door. He couldn't look at himself in the mirror, but he managed a glass of water and a Valium.

Later, they had a marvelous kosher meal. The family's two maids served dinner. They started with borscht. David indulged himself, ate two bowls of it, explained it'd been too long since he'd had any. Then they had roast chicken, kreplach, vegetables, and

Carmel Sauvignon Blanc wine. David drank two glasses of it and started a third. He felt more relaxed then, as the pain from his earlier lies faded.

As they sipped black coffee, Sarah asked David if he would like to live with them while he was in Israel, and as she glanced at Saul, to see if that was all right, David couldn't believe what he'd witnessed. Saul was leading, and all three of them knew it.

Saul smiled, and gently asked, "Would you like to stay here, son?"

David hesitated, glancing first at one, then the other, and nodded.

Saul explained that all the arrangements would be handled from his office, after David was certain it would be permitted by the ICM team chief. "Jim Bannion won't care," David said. "I'll tell him, and the other two, that maybe we can all go sightseeing sometime. Okay, Poppa?" Saul nodded, said he'd see what he could do.

With that settled, the three spent the rest of the evening talking about where they would visit the following weekend, as soon as the Sabbath was over, on Saturday evening.

Bannion was delighted, and so were Curtis and Barker. They'd had a hunch that their "Jewish Connection," David, would set them free, and they had been right.

On Friday afternoon, David had his bags packed. Saul's personal car stopped in front of David's building. He carried the two heavy suitcases out to the car and put them in the open trunk. The driver closed it and got behind the wheel. David sat next to him in the front seat. They left the security compound's military atmosphere and drove to "the Chief's House," where David would be living during the remainder of his time in Israel. *It was April twenty-seventh.*

When the Jewish Sabbath began on Friday night, much of West Jerusalem closed down. The Abbadons observed this Sabbath with enthusiasm. David felt a special embrace from his father and a controlled hug from his mother. "Sarah, like this," thought David, "is at last tolerable." But he'd wait to see more, just to be more sure.

On Saturday evening, after the Sabbath, the three of them went to the Wailing Wall. Located on Mount Moriah, it was all that remained of the Jews' Holy Temple of Biblical times. The hundred-sixty-foot-long Wailing Wall had been the west wall of the court-yard of the Holy Temple. It was now *the* symbol of Jewish faith and unity. Poppa Saul and David borrowed prayer books and shawls at the wall and prayed together, but Sarah had to pray with the other women, separately—it was the ancient custom.

Later they drove through East Jerusalem, filled as it was with Arabs. They'd had their Moslem Sabbath on Friday, and on Saturday evening the cafes and other places of entertainment were mobbed. Signs in the streets and store windows, and languages being spoken, were mixed. You could take your choice, or use all three—Hebrew or Arabic or English.

Sarah asked to go home then. She'd had enough, she said. Poppa grinned at David and turned the car around at the next corner, and they drove back to West Jerusalem, and home.

There was a message waiting for David. He was to call Ruth Tobias at her father's law offices in West Jerusalem. He called her back the next evening, and after hanging up the phone, walked to the living room to rejoin his parents. He said to them, "I've invited Ruth over for a visit. She'll be here in about an hour." Quickly searching their faces, he asked, "Is that all right?"

Saul and Sarah looked at each other. Each could read the other's mind. "All right? He's asking if it's all right? It's wonderful, is what it is!" But all Poppa Saul quietly said was, "Of course. It's fine, fine, son." Sarah smiled, nodded approval, but was silent.

When Ruth rang the doorbell, the maid let her in and brought her into the living room. David met Ruth as she came through the door and they hugged, and he kissed her on the cheek, as she turned her face up for it. Then he introduced her to Sarah and Saul. They all mumbled a shalom and then sat down. As Ruth and his parents talked, David marveled again at her poise and perfect grooming, listening to his articulate friend explain how far back their relationship went.

"Tell us about your trip to the United States, Ruth," David gently urged. They all sipped black coffee Sarah had poured, as Ruth talked about her visit to America. She spoke about New York and Chicago as having been the best, and she told them all how much she appreciated David's taking care of her in New York. Ruth never mentioned Janet. David had told her of the accident, and his grief, in the letter he'd written some weeks earlier. Ruth would respect his wishes, David knew.

Ruth suddenly asked to be excused, explaining that she had to work the next day. She said good night to Sarah and Saul. Then she and David walked out to her car. He thanked her for not saying anything about Janet, and for coming. Ruth hugged him and said they should get together soon. She got into her car, waved, and was gone. "Abrupt," David mumbled as he went back to the house.

David got up early each day and rode with his father, in the ministry staff car, to the compound. The driver always stopped at the Ministry of Defense, and the intelligence chief went upstairs, into the highly restricted area. The computer programmer stayed on the first floor, and walked back into the secure area where the ICM team was assembling the 370s. At day's end, David invariably was ready to leave first, so he'd walk upstairs and talk to the marines on guard at the heavy double doors, outside the restricted area. Gradually, as the weeks went by and they visited in Hebrew on any of a hundred subjects, the marines became friendly with the American. His Woody Allen bits did nothing for the Israelis, but his easy manner and fluent Hebrew did. They even began to anticipate his visits, and to enjoy his stories about America, and they were soon on a first-name basis. All of them knew his last name as well, of course, but when his father's approaching footsteps echoed down the long corridor at the end of the day, the marines stiffened to attention to be ready as the "Chief" walked through. He always said good night to them, and then went down the stairs with David to the waiting car.

Sometimes hours during a day would pass, and David would not have to think about the bomb. Then suddenly his obsession with it would force all other thoughts out of his consciousness. He had convinced himself that preparing mentally for construction of the bomb was critical to maintaining his sanity, but he also rationalized, "Everyone has to be a little crazy about something. That's how we all stay sane."

David needed plutonium. He must get some. He'd find a way, in the inner sanctum.

David remembered his promises to write, and mailed postcards to the Piedmonts, Doc Silber, and Father Donovan, and, over a period of several days, he wrote a long letter to the Schreibers. He included his ICM address for any return correspondence. It was imperative that he hide even the slightest

168

reference to Janet from his parents—that relationship must remain covert, for now.

Every day in the Ministry David was with the ICM team. He had watched the unpacking and the systematic arrangement of the bits and pieces of the 370s. The ICM people in the United States had labeled everything, and that, along with the efficiency of the Israelis, was unbelievably effective. The Jews knew nothing about ICM computers, but with Curtis and Barker giving guidance, and Bannion providing leadership, everything went smoothly. And always there was David's ability to speak Hebrew flawlessly. He explained specifics, lent support to Bannion on public relations.

So it went—calculated, smooth, professional. Progress was ahead of schedule. Bannion thought that if all went well, the project could be completed ahead of schedule. The group was assembling each machine separately, but side by side, in the first floor secure computer room. Bannion observed every important move anyone made around the 370s. He'd been savaged almost to death by W.C., back in Manhattan, learning the business of ICM and how to operate; and he knew he'd have to get either a superior rating from the Israelis when it was all over, or all the scar tissue on his ass would be ripped open by W.C. So he felt compelled to make certain that everything was perfect.

Intelligence Chief Abaddon got passes for the Americans, so on weekends they went sightseeing with David as their guide. The four of them saw the Arab shops that line the narrow streets of the Old City of Jerusalem. They came to recognize a Jerusalem that is holy to three religions: the Moslems, the Christians and the Jews. That understanding was strengthened by seeing the Dome of the Rock Moslem shrine, the Church of the Holy Sepulchre deifying Jesus, and the Wailing Wall where ancient Jewish customs abound.

One Sunday morning, David led the group on a walk east on the Jericho Road. They passed the Damascus Gate, then went past Herod's Gate, then the four turned south and made their way past Saint Stephen's Gate. When they arrived at the Golden Gate, the three others told David he'd finally gotten them to something they knew about. Chuckling, Ace said it was time to go back and check on his maid.

David practiced his deception so well that no one guessed his real thoughts. What others saw was a confident, poised, articulate

Jewish-American, one who spoke Hebrew fluently, knew how to charm others, was the son of a ranking Israeli official. What David Mikhael Abaddon felt inside was an almost constant anxiety.

He'd lost the love of his life, the only woman he had ever loved, could love, and here in Israel he felt a new tension—another holocaust in the making, the New Holocaust, and that was the cause of all his constant inner pain. He'd decided that something the cause of all his constant inner pain. He'd decided something had to be done. The world had to be alerted to the threat. Now that he had been living in Israel for a while, he was really in touch with what the prophets in the Bible had written about. "The reality of Armageddon is here," David told himself.

He waited, and watched. He thought about building the bomb, but that was separate from the situation in Israel—it was just something he wanted to do. *It was June third.*

At the dinner table that night, Saul told Sarah and David that West German Chancellor Willy Brandt would be arriving in Israel on Thursday. It was the first such visit to their country by a German of that rank. Poppa Saul said there was still considerable anti-German feeling in Israel because of the Nazis. David stared at his father, and thought of his paternal grandfather, a man he'd never seen, except in photographs, who had died in the ovens at Auschwitz. And as David thought of the enormous evils man smashes down on his own kind, he could understand why there was still a considerable anti-German feeling in Israel. He said nothing. "I'll wait," he told himself.

The next day, David had nothing to do, once he'd given some Israelis instructions on where each of the programming modules would be placed when the 370s were fully assembled. The workers seemed satisfied and went back to their areas. David told Ace he was going to visit his father.

When David got to the second floor, two marines he'd talked to many times were standing guard, relaxed. They smiled at him and greeted him in Hebrew. He talked to them for almost an hour. No one went in, or came out of, the inner sanctum. One of the marines said he was going to piss. He walked downstairs. David asked the other if he could go in and visit his father. "Just a short visit," David said. The young marine hesitated. David moved toward the double doors. The marine shuffled, nervously, so David waited until the first marine came back, and the three of them talked about whether David should go inside. After David said he

170

wouldn't stay for more than a few minutes, the marines agreed.

As David pushed open the door and walked into the long corridor leading to his father's office, he smiled to himself.

Step 1, ever so important to the success of his plan, had been accomplished.

When David got to his father's outer office, the sergeant-secretary looked up. He stood and greeted David, who smiled and asked to see his father. The sergeant picked up the phone, pushed the call button and spoke into the mouthpiece. He hung up and told David to go right in.

David walked into his father's office. Saul was staring at some aerial reconnaissance photos. He turned them face down as David came in.

"How are you, Poppa?"

"Who let you come back here, David?"

David tensed. If Saul raised even a hint of displeasure, it would all be over. "I wanted to see you, Poppa. I'll only be here a few more months, then we're going back to Manhattan." David did a Woody Allen bit, which always amused Saul.

Saul said, "I think you do Woody Allen better than he does himself." He was laughing when David turned around and left the office. David grinned at the secretary, went out and down the corridor, through the double doors, and both marines seemed relieved to see him. David said his father had been very happy about the visit, and that was that. David said, "See you tomorrow," and walked down the stairs to the computer area.

Step 2 had also gone well.

David skipped going to see Poppa Saul the next day, and the two after that, because of the visit of Willy Brandt, but on Friday morning, David grabbed some papers with ICM letterheads from his desk and carried them to the second floor. He lied to the marine guards at the double doors, saying he must take the documents to his father. The marines waved David on through. He folded the papers after he was inside, walking down the corridor to his father's office, and kept them under his arm. "That looks official," he was thinking.

David visited with the secretary, about nothing in particular, and then with his father. He stayed only a short time, then walked out and through the corridor. Once outside the double doors, he thanked the marine guards and went down to the first floor, taking the stairs two at a time.

Step 3, the last one, had gone perfectly, he assured himself.

The pattern had been clearly established by the end of June. Several times a week David would subtly make his way in to visit with his father, or the secretary, if Poppa Saul was busy, or away at a meeting. The marines became more and more used to it when they realized the Intelligence Chief didn't care. Mr. Abaddon was being visited by his son—simply that. No one minded.

It finally happened! David was having lunch with Poppa Saul. Intelligence Chief Abaddon took a phone call on his special Hot Line. He was summoned at once to an emergency meeting being convened by the prime minister. David told his father to just go ahead, that he would clean up everything after finishing lunch.

Saul got up, walked over and opened a drawer in a safe that was labeled MOST SECRET. He removed several file folders, put them in his black briefcase and, instinctively, pushed the drawer to close it. It remained ajar, but in his haste, he didn't notice. He turned quickly and marched to the door telling David, over his shoulder, that he'd see him at home.

David watched his father leave, and heard him click the lock that secured the door to the corridor. David looked then in all the areas of his father's office suite. He was especially alert for closed-circuit television cameras in the offices. There were none. He was certain. He was alone. He walked to the safe and pulled the drawer open. There were Hebrew titles on each folder. David searched until he saw the one he was looking for: NUCLEAR.

Since early childhood, David had been aware of his "gift" of eidetic recall—photographic memory; he could "take pictures" with his mind. David opened the Nuclear file and willed the process to begin. There was a document that showed the most secret sale to Israel of thirty short-range attack missiles—SRAMs—delivered by the United States government. The nuclear warheads had been removed and replaced with a new, extremely powerful explosive, but all had nuclear capability.

He put the file back in place, and chose another: EMERGENCY DISPERSAL OF SRAM.

David opened it and carefully noted that the short range attack missile is launched from an aircraft already in flight. He laid out three pages from the file and began "imaging" again:

Page One: A map of Israeli air bases siting the dispersal point of each pre-positioned SRAM.

Page Two: The approximate airborne launch location, and primary target area (plus one alternative) for each missile, when the survival of the State of Israel was at stake.

Page Three: The computer Action Code Words and Computer Authentication Procedures needed to put the plan into action.

He returned the papers to the file, replaced it in the drawer, and locked it. He made certain that everything else was exactly as he'd found it. He cleared the table of the remainder of the lunch, putting what was uneaten back into the bags, which he took with him. As he left, he closed and locked the outer door. He walked down the corridor, noting again that the CCTV cameras were located only in that area. He went out through the double doors, smiling at the marines as he went by.

Bannion was talking to Ace when David came toward them in the secure computer area on the first floor. He asked Bannion if he could leave for the day to visit his mother. Grinning, Bannion nodded. David waved, walked away and out through the gate of the compound. He took a taxi home and told his mother he felt a little ill. He asked that he not be disturbed for a few hours, said he would be taking a nap.

He went to his room and closed and locked the door. He took a tablet of paper and pen from the desk drawer, sat down, and began to write, from memory. When he finished, he had three pages. *It was July fourth.*

12

THERE WAS A PHONE in the secure computer area near the desk that David used. He called Ruth as soon as he got to work the next morning. "Maybe the Israelis tap the telephones in the Ministry," he thought, "and if I am caught with a Sabra father and a Sabra lady friend, that'll look good."

When she answered the phone at her father's law office David said, "Hi. C'est moi. How are you?"

"Hello, David," she said. "I thought you might not call me for a while. You told me you were so busy with your work for ICM."

He explained that while the new computers were being assembled, he really had little to do, and the big job of programming the 370s for the Israelis would come once the machines were up. Then he asked, "When can we go out together?"

Ruth said, "Any time. I'd like to show you around some. Would you enjoy that?"

David said he wanted to go to Tel Aviv-Yafo to see the sights there, and visit Lod Airport, where the ICM team had landed in April. David reminded her that he hadn't had much of a chance to look around because they'd come in at night.

Ruth said she'd go to Tel Aviv with him the next Sunday morning, and David said he'd call early Sunday to reconfirm. They chatted for a while, then said good-bye.

At that moment, Bannion rushed in. "You must go see your father right away. He's just called for you. He said to tell you that the marine guards have instructions to let you through at once." Bannion paused, then said, "Let me know if there's anything I can do, Dave."

David noticed the painful expression on Bannion's face and wondered, "What the hell is it this time?"

He ran up to the second floor. The lone marine waved him on, stepping to the double doors, opening the one on the right for David. The marine, who had always had a smile for David before, didn't this time, so by the time David got to his father's office, he felt uneasy. He rushed into his father's office, closing the door behind him.

David's heart was pounding. Had he forgotten to put everything back in the safe perfectly? Had someone seen him? Had he tripped a silent alarm? Had he been observed on a hidden television camera? Or in some other way?

Saul Abaddon's face was ashen. "Sit down, son," his poppa said. "Your mother has had a stroke. She's in the intensive care unit at Hebrew University Medical Center. I want you to go over there with me now."

Walking down the corridor just two minutes earlier, David thought he might be spending the rest of his life in an Israeli maximum security prison for stealing information on what had to be some of the most secret capabilities the Jews had. Many people probably didn't even know they had nuclear material, let alone warheads ready for instant deployment, if the survival of the nation was threatened.

David stood. "Let's go, Poppa," he said, relieved even in the face of this crisis.

As Saul came around the corner of his desk, David met him and took his arm. They went out of the offices and down the corridor arm in arm. Both of them got into the staff car that was always waiting to take the Chief of Israeli Intelligence wherever he wanted to go.

The driver took the road past the Hebrew University and the Church of Saint John, and stopped before the entrance to Hadasseh-Hebrew University Medical Center. David took his father's arm, and they walked in together.

A woman at the information desk, smiling, gave them directions to the Intensive Care Unit. She said there would be someone there to show them to Sarah Abaddon's bedside.

David led his father to the ICU. "He can be so resolute," David thought, "but under certain circumstances, his very sensitive inner self cannot be disguised. That's Poppa!"

The head nurse directed them to Sarah's room. They tiptoed in. She was lying motionless on her back in the bed. Wires, secured to her head and arms and chest with medical tape, trailed across the bed and into two monitors. One was labeled EEG and the other EKG. The oscilloscopes showed a picture of her brain waves and heart beats. The fluorescent screens glowed with activity—the bright green tracings were a welcome sight to Saul and to a much relieved David.

Doctor Abe Solomon walked in. He introduced himself, and gave a guarded opinion. "We'll just have to wait, gentlemen. In cases such as this, time is the key. Nature will take its course. We must be patient now."

Later, David called Ruth to postpone their Sunday plans.

And they *were* patient. There was no other course, because for the next two months, Sarah remained, first in the hospital, and then resting at home. She cooperated with everyone. Sarah was gentle, kind, considerate. The personality change had been abrupt—an almost complete reversal. As her recovery progressed, in early September, her speech was a little slower than usual, and she walked deliberately, although there was a slight limp in the right leg. But Sarah had come through it, and Saul and David were attentive to her, during all of it. She loved them for that, and showed it whenever and however she could.

Doctor Solomon talked to Saul, asking if there had been an earlier stroke. When Saul said no, Doctor Solomon explained that sometimes a person could have a *slight* stroke, and it could go undetected. Saul said he didn't think that had happened to Sarah, or he would've noticed. Both he and Doctor thought nothing more of it.

Later, when Saul told David, he thought back to the scene at the front door of their home in Jerusalem when he'd first arrived, and Sarah and Saul had come out to hug and kiss him. David remembered that the thought had occurred to him that Poppa was getting equal time, and Sarah had seemed to be more mellow, almost gentle. Sarah, the Matriarch, had changed. David said nothing to his Poppa. But he thought, "Solomon probably got it right. Something had happened. Whatever, she's going to be all right, and God knows she's easier to get along with now."

While Sarah had been so ill, David lost some contact with the ICM team. He did manage to spend some time with them each day in the computer room, but it wasn't as it had been before his mother got sick, so when he returned to work full time in early September, he'd fallen behind.

David spent extra time and was "up to speed," Bannion told him, in almost no time. Further motivating David was the fact that

Bannion and the engineers were nearly finished with their work. Word was, Bannion hinted, that David would soon be able to start programming the computers.

"You'll be staying in Israel, alone, to finish the job for ICM," Bannion said.

David was ecstatic. "That has to be a nice vote of confidence," he told himself. "Maybe I'll even stretch it out a little. That way I might be able to stay with my mother, and Poppa, for the high holidays."

But David worked extra hours nevertheless, sometimes late into the evening. He wanted everything to be perfect. Performance was important. The Israelis, his people, had enemies on their borders, and within them. Constant vigilance was the price they paid to preserve their freedom, their way of life. David would do his best work, he had promised himself that. The computer he had helped design was a truly remarkable machine, and when it was working perfectly, it would be of immeasurable help in aiding the people of Israel—to remain free, and a nation on God's earth.

Working late, alone except for one Israeli in the computer room, David leaned back in his chair. He had studied and studied publications recommended in the latest ICM bibliography. "I've practically memorized the *ICM System/370 and Processors Bibliography*," he said silently, and as he'd known all along the difficult part would be the interface with the Hewlett-Packard 1000. It was a different machine, and the hookup with the 370s would be the focal point of the problems, if any.

"I need a break," David thought. He called Ruth at her parents' home in West Jerusalem. They talked for over thirty minutes. She agreed that to go to Tel Aviv the following Sunday would be a nice change of pace for both of them.

Sunday morning David drove his father's car to Ruth's home, and they were on the road to Tel Aviv by eight o'clock. It was only about sixty kilometers, but the traffic was always heavy the day after the Sabbath, so they got an early start and spent the day sightseeing.

Ruth told David all she could remember. "It's the largest city in Israel, and our major industrial center. More than half of our factories are here." She went on to tell him that almost all of the food-processing industry, the most significant branch of Israeli manufacturing, was in Tel Aviv.

She showed him clothing and textile factories, and they ended the day by touring a fruit-processing plant. Oranges were being waxed with a special coating of protection developed by Jewish scientists—it lengthens the time oranges can be stored without spoiling, they learned, and David was reminded that oranges are Israel's major crop.

As they drove from place to place, David watched for Israeli air bases. He passed as close to them as he could, and later, near Lod Airport, when they were driving southeast of the city of Tel Aviv, David took mental pictures of everything he saw. The airfields were some of the ones on the map, on page one, that he'd memorized. They would be critical in the emergency dispersal of SRAM. He stored the information in his head. "Just like programming a 370," he thought. *It was September second.*

Back in July, while Sarah had been so sick, David heard on the news that the French had defied an interim injunction by the International Court of Justice. France had ignored the Hague court and conducted in the South Pacific the first nuclear test of their current series. David had been fairly passive about it then, because of his mother's illness. Suddenly, the audacity of the French came into sharp focus in his mind, and he was livid. But this time he had no Donovan, Silber, or Janet to talk to. He decided he would just keep it inside, wait, try to work hard, not to think about it so much. Ruth being such a good friend helped, too.

David got to the ministry early next day. He concentrated on the last stages of the installation of the 370s, looked forward to the system generation and programming—SYSGEN and programming were his forte.

He knew better than anyone that computers can be frustrating. At times, they seem to have personalities of their own, they seem temperamental. But, as David always explained to others, computers do exactly—and only—what they're instructed to do, so it all comes down to one thing: patience! That virtue is essential, if you want to be a computer programmer.

Bannion walked over to David's desk, and David talked on and on about being in Tel Aviv the day before, sightseeing. Bannion smiled, then said they were about finished with the 370s, and that during the rest of the week they would be interfacing them with the H-P 1000. Then Bannion told David he could begin to program the three computers. "You can make them do something, for the Israelis."

David was ready on Friday afternoon when Ace came to his desk. The two went to the computer room, joining Curtis and Bannion. All was ready.

David went to work. He checked everything, and then sat down at the main console and began. He first created the test data base, then entered the test programs to access it. He had known from the beginning that the test programs he'd be entering in the 370s would be more sophisticated and intricate than the ones already in the 1000. Furthermore, he wanted the new ones to work more smoothly. He tested. They did. Both 370s worked perfectly.

Next, he checked the modem. If it was working properly he'd be able to send computer data over telephone lines. Everything was fine, but a modem requires a terminal monitor program. David verified that it, too, was ready. Finally, he ran the last test program, one that would take data from the 370 discs and send it over a telephone line. Perfect!

When he got up to leave, David suddenly realized he was alone except for one Israeli. David looked at his watch. It was almost midnight. "Now that really is sublimation," he said. He picked up a phone, called his father's driver and had him bring the staff car to the front of the ministry. As David went out and got into the car to go home, he knew he would have to invent a problem—either that, or he'd be done in a few weeks, and that was much too soon.

Monday morning David was back at the computers when Bannion and the two ICM systems engineers got there. David explained that everything had worked to perfection, and that they could probably begin thinking of making arrangements to go back to Manhattan, but, he said, he would like to stay in Jerusalem to train the Israelis, to answer their questions, and to assist the Jewish computer programmers until they were completely familiar with ICM's best.

On Tuesday, Bannion received word that W.C. had okayed the return of the trio to the United States. And he left "good luck wishes" for David, wonder of wonders!

Bannion had David call El Al Airlines in West Jerusalem to confirm the departure time for the three. It was to be the following evening, September twelfth, at six.

The next afternoon, David took his father's car and drove to the entrance of the Visiting Officers' Quarters. They loaded the trunk with luggage. Bannion sat in front with David, Barker and Curtis in the back, and David drove them to the El Al Airlines entrance, at Lod. They said their good-byes to David, and the three of them disappeared into the terminal.

David drove around the airport. It was dusk, but he could still make out the access roads, the entrances and exits with little difficulty. He hurried to Tel Aviv, restudied the roadways near the air base. All was as he remembered, except that he now had a perception of how it all looked at night.

On the drive back to Jerusalem David thought, "Somehow, I've got to find a way to enter the page three action code words in the computers, to see what happens, and to find out what their computers know!"

As David walked into the computer area next morning, he was deep in thought. He sat down in the chair at his desk, stared into space. It was one thing for the engineers to assemble the 370s, and to bring them together electrically with the H-P 1000, *but* the programming interface was something else. David wasn't in the least concerned, however—he saw that as an opportunity. He could "have problems" that would delay his departure, and, more important, that might mean that the Israeli computer programmers would have to give him some of their access codes to the 1000. Then, he'd wait, and when he got the chance, he'd enter the codes and find out what the Israelis knew—on a myriad of subjects.

Daniel Abrashkov interrupted David's train of thought. "David, when can we complete the final interface of all three computers?"

Born and raised in the Russian Ukraine, Abrashkov had fled to Palestine during World War II by himself. He had the admiration of all. Everyone knew the indomintable Abrashkov had walked out of Russia to escape the pogroms.

David turned, and smiled up at the six-foot-five-inch, salt-and-pepper-haired Daniel. "I'm planning on sometime before the twelfth of October. My visa runs out then," David said. He stood and they walked to the console and sat down. David was thinking how often he'd seen Daniel, and heard so much about him from the Israeli programmers.

David wondered why they'd met only a week ago. He made a mental note to try to find out. After all, the guy was the Israelis' head computer programmer.

Abaddon and Abrashkov checked every basic programming operation of the 370s. It took them the rest of the day, and evening, and all day until near sundown on Friday.

Monday morning, Daniel was already at the console programming when David walked in. They greeted each other, then completed incidental tests on the 370s.

"We need to be certain all the satellite terminals installed in the ministry are working properly," Abrashkov said.

David asked, "How do you want to do it?"

"You stay here and I'll go to each one and type in my password and some test data. Then, I'll call you on the telephone to see that you're getting the proper feedback on your CRT and from the printer," Daniel said.

The double-checks went like clockwork. Every ICM satellite terminal worked perfectly until late in the afternoon. Then, the one in the basement supply room wouldn't activate. Abrashkov phoned David and asked him to come to the terminal to assist.

David got one of the technicians to show him where the room was, and with David standing behind him, Daniel tried the terminal again. It would not operate.

Daniel let David sit at the terminal. It'd been a frustrating day for the Israeli, for some reason. When David asked for a password, Daniel unthinkingly gave him his own. David entered the password, got the computer to accept it. "Nothing to it," he said.

David and Daniel walked back upstairs together and had coffee. They agreed to finish the few remaining checks on the terminals the next day.

Abrashkov left for home. David had one last cup of coffee, and thought of the password: BRINA. It was probably his mother's name, or some other important lady in his life. David's thoughts raced then to Ithaca, winter ice, a skater named Janet. His eyes filled with tears, as he remembered that important lady. He got up quickly and walked out.

When Poppa Saul came down the stairs to go home, David was waiting at the landing. They walked together to the car. As the driver turned at the main gate, David said, "You look pensive, Poppa. What's on your mind, anyway?"

"I've just had a busy day, son. I'm trying to get everything done before Yom Kippur, so we can have family time. We're doing some assessments for the Prime Minister. She wants to *know* that it's going to be—how do you say it—'business as usual' during the holidays. How can any intelligence chief ever guarantee that?"

They rode the rest of the way in silence. With enemies on all their borders, the Israelis always had to be ready to fight, without warning.

Later that evening, Poppa and David were alone in the sitting room. David suddenly thought about always being ready. He asked, "Poppa, do we have any sort of weapon here in the house? You know, just in case?"

Saul looked at David without a change of expression. That always meant his Poppa had an option. Saul got up slowly, walked to the desk and opened the top right-hand drawer. He took out a metal case the size of a shoe box, turned around and walked back to the couch. He handed David the case, opening the lid just then. David's eyes widened as he looked inside at the most beautiful ebony-colored Luger he'd ever seen, a 9mm with four neatly placed boxes of ammunition in indentations along the inside edge of the case. David took the weapon in his hand and put the case aside. "Quite a contrast," he said silently. "A Nazi Special in a Sabra's house in Israel."

He examined the gun, then put it back in place, closed the lid and went to the desk. As he returned the case to the drawer, he asked, "Where did you get it, Poppa?"

His father glanced toward the doorway, as if to assure himself that no one else was listening, and told his son, "I took it off the body of one of those sons-of-bitches, in North Africa, during World War II. It was a pleasure. The bastard was a dead major."

David wanted to ask who had killed the Nazi, but he didn't. Saul Abaddon never talked about such matters.

As David got to the computer room next morning, Abrashkov was waiting alone to talk to David.

They went into the hallway and Daniel led David to a spot against the far wall, away from everyone. He said anxiously, "I gave you my own password yesterday. That is a breach of the Most Secret security clearance directives. Do you recall my password?" David remembered, and they both knew it.

Abrashkov hesitated. Then, "You are probably wondering why all the Israeli programmers stayed away from the System 370 Project until you were almost finished assembling the computers. Simple. The other three Americans are not one of us. You are, but the decision was made to keep a distance from all four of you, for strict security reasons, and yesterday tells you why. It takes only one slip, and there is compromise." Daniel stared at David for so long that it made him nervous. At last he said to David, "We have two alternatives. I can turn us both in to my superiors. That will mean punishment for me, at least a reprimand, maybe worse. They will have to change my password, and they'll direct me to do much reprogramming because my password, as head programmer, allows access to all data in the computers. The other option is to say nothing. *But,* if we choose that, you must promise me you will *forget* my password and that you will *never* use it."

They agreed on the latter. It would be much easier on everyone.

The checks on the satellite terminals were resumed. They finished the last of them bfore four o'clock and left.

David told Abrashkov the following day that he would have to call the ICM Research Institute in Manhattan. He explained that there was no way to complete the final programming connections between the H-P 1000 and the 370s by October fifth. It would take until at least the tenth, David lied. Daniel said to call from a more private telephone, pointing to one on a desk across the room from the computers.

David picked up the phone and dialed the international operator, who assisted. After two rings, the secretary in Jeff Piedmont's outer office answered. She spoke briefly to David after he identified himself, then buzzed Jeff.

"Hello, Dave. How in the world are you?" Jeff asked.

"I'm fine. How is everyone there?"

They talked for about fifteen minutes. Jeff mentioned a new project ICM had won from the Air Force. He said he'd tell David more later, said it was Top Secret, but he did say, "It's the space program—orbiting satellites." And he explained that David would be right in the middle of it, and added, "W.C. is still mauling the staff with his tongue, like the beast he is." Laughing with Jeff, David knew that all was normal at ICM.

Jeff ended the conversation abruptly, saying, "The hot line from upstairs is ringing." Before hanging up, he agreed with David's projected arrival in Manhattan on the tenth or eleventh.

David went back to Daniel's desk, and explained he would be staying until the second week in October, and added that he'd be in Israel for Yom Kippur. Abrashkov was obviously pleased for his young friend.

The rest of the week David and the programmers worked to complete assignments. By Friday afternoon all was on schedule, so Abrashkov told his Israeli programmers that was enough. They all left, except for David and Daniel. They sat side by side at the console, and entered one test program after another in the 370s and got perfect feedback. Then, Abrashkov decided to ask all three computers to respond, in consonance. He entered the commands. Everything worked flawlessly.

Daniel turned to David. "Let's go. There's nothing wrong, so let us not fix it." They said good night and walked out. *It was September twenty-first.*

On Sunday morning, David called Ruth at her home. He said, "Hi, Ruthie, it's your Yankee." She wasn't sure what that was, so he explained. "Let's go somewhere today. Okay?" he urged.

Ruth paused, then said, "Why don't you come over here for the day? My parents are visiting a family in Bethlehem and I'm alone. We can have something to eat and listen to music. I didn't really want to study law anyway."

Ruth was waiting when David arrived. As he got out of the car, she put her arm through his and they walked around back to the patio, where they spent the morning talking about her law studies and his work for the Israelis—and sipping Carmel Chenin Blanc wine.

At mid-day, she suggested they have lunch in the kitchen. They went inside and warmed leftover chicken soup and matzos, and Ruth made hot tea. They shared a huge orange.

Later, in the sitting room, Ruth played the piano with David sitting on the bench next to her. Ruth was perfection on the Steinway. She'd taken lessons, read music. Her "Tie a Yellow Ribbon 'Round the Old Oak Tree" made David smile. Then she did a slow rendition of "Touch Me in the Morning." When she finished that there was a silence in the room that made David uneasy. Suddenly Ruth kissed him, and he was so surprised that he didn't respond immediately. Then he did, and put his arms around her. They turned toward each other. Ruth suggested that the piano bench made things difficult, and nodded in the direction of the couch. Ruth sat on the edge, and David knelt in front of her. She spread her legs slightly, and he leaned in between them. She reached around his head and pulled him toward her, until his face was buried in her breasts. She sighed, softly, and David kept his face there. It felt *so* good, and to Ruth, too. She leaned all the way back, pulling him with her. He looked at her face; her eyes were closed. David released her, stood, took both her hands in his and said, "Your room?"

She got up and led the way. David shut the door and looked for a lock. She said it wasn't needed. Ruth took her clothes off and lay on the bed. David sat in the chair behind the door and took off shoes and socks, then stood, dropped his pants, and pulled the t-shirt over his head. He stepped to the side of the bed away from

Ruth, and sat down on the edge. Only then did he take off his shorts, and turn quickly to her. She grinned at him, pulling the two of them together. He was strangely conscious of her strength.

The touch of Ruth's naked body made David shiver as she began to caress him with her fingers. He tried to respond, reached for her hips with both hands. The soft flesh of the woman melted into his fingers. He put one hand on her stomach and moved it in gentle circles as he let it go lower and lower. Ruth made little sounds like a coo from a songbird. When David touched her, at last, Ruth began to undulate, and the sounds in her throat never stopped, and she reached for him.

David pulled away. Suddenly, he realized he didn't want to do that. He couldn't. His body was not responding. It seemed impossible, and he felt limp inside, too. He thought he might be sick.

Ruth turned her body and face to the far wall so David couldn't see, and her tears came quietly. She wondered what she'd done wrong.

"It's not you, Ruthie," he whispered. "It's me. I just can't. I don't know why. Forgive me."

David put on his shorts while still sitting on the edge of the bed. Then he got up, walked to the chair and finished dressing. He glanced toward the bed and saw that Ruth hadn't moved. His "good-bye" was said so softly, that in the car on the way home he was afraid Ruth hadn't even heard him. All he knew was that he just couldn't do that—she wasn't Janet.

When he got back to the house, he spoke only briefly to his parents, and said he'd had a fine time with Ruth, when Sarah asked. He told them that he really needed to spend time alone, and would appreciate it if he wasn't disturbed. He went to his room and lay face down on the bed with the door shut, and no one heard him crying softly, or saw him take two Valiums, so he could sleep.

On Monday morning, Abrashkov was already working at the console when David arrived.

Daniel and David explained to the Israeli programmers that they were going to run another series of tests to be certain the three computers were operating in perfect consonance. Abrashkov typed his password on the keyboard, and pressed the enter key. The computers were ready. He continued. The machines responded to perfection. This process continued for the remainder of the day, and throughout the next.

It appeared to the group that their American-Jewish friend would soon be going back to the United States, but David urged them to "be cool." He reminded them all that Yom Kippur was the following week, and that New York could survive just fine, even if David Abaddon didn't get home until the second week in October. The Israelis pledged support. Abrashkov told David they would concur with his choice of the *final acceptance date for contractual purposes* by both ICM and the government of Israel.

The remainder of the week was routine. Actually, there was nothing left to do except make absolutely certain that all security procedures had been followed, and to assure the Ministry of Defense bosses that all data was and would be secure. Abrashkov accepted that responsibility, said he'd do it next week.

David and Daniel wished each other good Sabbath, and Abrashkov left. David sat at his desk and thought about his next move. It was all like a chess game, he thought, and he decided he had to make his move that night. It might be too late to get any data if he waited until the following week.

When Saul came down the stairs to go home, David was waiting. They walked out to the staff car together. David said that he would have to return to the ministry that evening, to finish up some last-minute details on a program. It wouldn't take more than an hour or two, he lied, and asked if the driver and car could be made available. Poppa Saul nodded, and David leaned forward to explain to the driver he was to return to the house at seven o'clock.

Later, after eating, David excused himself and said he needed to study some final software. When Sarah asked, he explained that meant programs, procedures, rules and associated documentation. Hardware, he told her, was the actual physical equipment, such as the 370s.

His parents smiled at David as he left the room, and Sarah nodded approval. Their son had been a part of something important to Israel; and all along, his mother was saying, she had known it would turn out that way.

In his room, with the door shut, David took page three from the bottom of his suitcase and studied it. He was sure he would be able to refer to it later, if the need arose, but he'd learned the necessity of options. He folded the page and put it in his pocket.

Promptly at seven, the driver arrived. It took only a few minutes to drive to the ministry and through the gate. On the Sabbath, everyone was occupied otherwise and not concerned with the driver and staff car of the intelligence chief.

David closed the door to the secure computer area. He turned on only the lights near the computers and waved to the one attendant sitting alone in his office. After quickly checking the computers' responsiveness, David took a deep breath.

He put BRINA and then the first action code word on the CRT and pressed "Enter." He waited. The system demanded authentication. David followed the exact procedure cited on page three. While he waited for the computers to respond, he took the page out of his pocket to verify. He was correct.

Suddenly, the printer began its work. The sound startled David. It seemed to be making too much noise, responding at the rate of six-hundred lines per minute, but he told himself it probably just seemed noisy because he was in the room alone.

David stood, walked over to the printers. The one that had been running stopped just then. David advanced the printouts so that he could see all the lines. He only glanced at them, worrying about spending too much time, and that someone might come in. He removed all copies and laid them on his desk. Then he returned to the console and directed the computers to erase all inquiries. David walked back to the desk, dropped his military coveralls, folded the printouts and carefully put them in his jockey shorts. One could never be too cautious, he was thinking. Then he pulled his coveralls up, smoothing the front, looking down to see that there was no revealing bulge.

David waved to the attendant and went out to the waiting car. On the way home, and later when he locked the printout in the suitcase, he kept thinking how easy it had all been on that Friday evening, in Israel.

There had been widespread celebrations on May fourteenth. That day, Israelis had joyously observed their twenty-fifth anniversary as an independent nation; and so, as Yom Kippur approached, everyone was preparing for a special time. It would be the Jews' holiest festival, an extension of the unique feelings of all Israelis during their anniversary year.

Work had moved slowly for David, and for the other programmers, too. There was nothing more to do, so by Friday all of them were ready for the holiest of times—the Day of Atonement.

As the programmers bade each other good-bye, David could almost see the shared special feelings. He felt proud to have been a part of helping to make Israel a safer place for his people. He

wished the programmers a good holiday, said he'd see them next
week. All but the one programmer required for security reasons
were gone in a few minutes.

Then David and Daniel were alone again at the console. The two
of them looked into each other's eyes. They embraced. Nothing
was said—nothing had to be said. Daniel and David secured the
area for the weekend then, and walked outside together. Both
were prepared for the important day that tomorrow would be for
everyone of the Jewish faith.

When Poppa Saul and David got home, Sarah met them. She
was so happy, she said, that they would be together for the highest holiday. David smiled and walked to his room, closing the
door behind him. Quietly, he got his suitcase from the closet and
opened it. He dug to the bottom for the computer printout. He
spread it under the light on the small table next to his bed, and
read each word carefully. It gave him the highly classified information he wanted. If the nuclear warheads owned by the Israelis
were ever decentralized from their most secret Negev underground security facility, David had the routes.

"Knowledge is power!" he thought.

The scream of the jets overhead brought everyone to attention.
There was no doubt that danger was in the air, as wave after wave
of thundering aircraft shot across the Yom Kippur sky. "Thank
God," Saul said, "all of them have the blue six-pointed Star of
David on their sides and wings."

Then the silence was deafening. Something was very wrong.

The Arabs had attacked on two fronts. Simultaneously. Syrian
military forces attacked the Golan Heights, and Egyptians struck
across the Suez Canal into the Sinai. Arab allies quickly joined
the battle. Iraqi air units and ground troops came to aid the Syrians. Kuwait and Tunisia sent soldiers to the Sinai to join their
Egyptian brothers. Sudanese and Saudi troops helped, too; and
Lebanon aided the Palestinian guerrillas as much as they could.
Jordanian and Morrocan troops were fighting on the Syrian front,
and the Day of Atonement was being observed in full measure, de-
laying Israeli mobilization.

Saul Abaddon took the phone from the hand of his son, listened
for only a moment, then hung up. He explained that he would be
at the ministry, in response to the worried looks on the faces of
his wife and son.

David drove Saul to the ministry. After his father disappeared inside, David parked the car, then walked to the front door, and into the computer area. The room was a flurry of activity. "I'll just watch—and wait," David thought.

He did, all day, and far into the evening. Everyone sipped coffee, but ate little. The frenzy never stopped. Worry was thick in the fall night air. Israeli military forces were reeling, or holding their own at best. It was not a good time, not at all.

David went to the phone, called upstairs to see if Poppa Saul wanted to go home with him. His father wasn't able to come to the phone. The secretary said that his father had left instructions for David to go on without him.

On the way out of the building, and riding in the car to the house, David wondered if the Israelis would disperse their nuclear warheads if the tide of battle continued to go against them. He worried, "If they do decentralize the nukes, how will I know *when?*"

On Sunday morning, early, David drove to the ministry. When he got to the computer area, he saw only two people, and they were programmers he knew. "Maybe the war is going better for us," he thought. But when he asked, the programmers quickly told him, "It's worse, if anything."

Later, when the two Israelis were occupied at a desk at the far end of the room, David decided. With heart pounding, he sat down at the console and entered BRINA, then the action code words. Authentication was demanded, and he instantly complied. The printers chattered. No one looked toward him or the hardware. He imagined, "In all the commotion, it is almost certain nobody will make security checks of the computer runs—probably not for some time."

Casually, David walked to the first printer and tore off the printouts. Slowly, he went to his desk. He folded the papers and put them in the back pocket of his military coveralls. Moments later, he called "shalom" to the two programmers. They waved at him without looking up. Israel was at war. They were busy.

David walked quickly out to the car and drove home.

Alone in his room, David studied the printouts. Movement of the warheads would be that night. The exact time was not specified, but "after dark" was directed by highest authority. As he had anticipated, the air base near Tel Aviv-Yafo would be receiving plutonium bombs. The route of travel listed was simple, to avoid arousing suspicion or curiosity. The single truck, led by one jeep, would " . . . take the most expeditious roadways . . . " until nearing the air base. There, the drivers were to take a specified side road that would lead them to a remote area. Military police would be waiting once they arrived at the special entry gate, to allow the two vehicles to pass through security and onto the air base.

The lone identification on either vehicle was to be the Israeli Coat of Arms. It would be on the doors of the truck only. David thought, smiling to himself, that'd be easy, and he pictured in his mind the purple and white Menorah and olive branches, with ISRAEL spelled out in Hebrew at the bottom.

David refolded the printouts and put them into the front pocket of his coveralls, then he lay on his bed and fell sleep.

Before leaving, David went to his mother's room and explained that he might be out all night. He just wasn't sure, he softly lied to her, how long it would take him to assist the others with the computers.

Sarah promised David she would try to relax, remain calm.

Then David went into the sitting room, went to his father's desk and opened the top right-hand drawer. He removed the metal case and put it on the desktop. Opening it, he took out all the ammunition and put it in his pockets, and stuffed the Luger in his belt. Quickly he closed the case and returned it to the drawer.

On the drive northwest to Tel Aviv, David heard the distant sounds of war to the north. He flashed back to Viet Nam, Lang Vei, and panic rose in his throat. He fought it back with thoughts of Kelley and no more Nams, and of peace for all—like in the kibbutzes in Israel, he remembered telling Kelley.

David finally found the gravel road, near the air base, after a back and forth search. He drove slowly to a secluded place and parked his father's car, about a kilometer from the area where he planned to intercept the truck. He pulled the car well off the roadway, hiding it behind some bushes.

David grabbed his backpack and went around to the rear of the car. He got a hammer, screwdriver and pliers from the trunk and closed it. He put the tools in the backpack and hung it over a shoulder.

He started walking. He stopped at the only place where the specially marked single truck would have to be slowed for a sharp turn in the road. It was about four kilometers from the

special entry gate. There were trees in the area and he was reassured. At least there was that for cover as well as the darkness,
and, there was a war going on! It would all help.

He lay in the ditch, at the point where that last turn began.
"Now I know how criminals must feel before committing their
crimes," he thought. "Nervous and anxious. Almost not able to
stand the wait."

He loaded the Luger. If there was to be a small firefight, David
felt he was ready.

He waited. Watching one huge four-engine jet after another
come from the west with lights flashing and land. Others, also
with what appeared to be United States markings on them, took
off and flew west.

As he lay hidden in the ditch, David flashed again to Nam, Lang
Vei. Panic again! Killing the enemy in Nam had been a living horror. Killing his own had led him into a near black madness. He
had indeed looked into the abyss, and now he was again preparing
to be one of the Four Horsemen. Could he?

David calmed himself. He was a driven man, *had* to do this
thing. The only component he now lacked to build the bomb was
plutonium, and *if* he needed to kill again, even his own, he'd have
to do it. Someone had to bring to the attention of the world the
fast-developing nightmare that nuclear war would be.

David felt an inner peace. Ready.

There was no traffic on the road. If the jeep and truck did come
the way they were supposed to, David's problems would be sim-
plified. He would have to overcome at least four men. If that number had been increased, he'd probably have to abandon the plan
completely.

Then, they were coming. Their parking lights only were on, and
they were moving much more slowly than he had anticipated,
probably because the road was so bumpy, and they were undoubtedly being cautious.

The jeep came first, a little ahead of the truck, and went on
around the turn and the trees. Then, the truck with the coat of
arms on the door was almost opposite the place where David was
hiding. As it was about to pass his position he jumped up, raced
for the door. He leaped onto the running board, pointed the Luger
inside, ordered the Israeli to drive off the road *at once*, then, *stop!*
The truck lurched to a halt. David motioned for the two men to

put their hands on the dashboard. He watched their every move, his eyes telling them so.

Slowly, he opened the door and got in as the driver slid over to the middle of the seat, and as the roar of the engines of another U.S. jet taking off filled the air, David forced the Luger's barrel into the driver's gut, and pulled the trigger. The muffled shot was barely audible, but totally effective at point-blank range.

David killed the guard the same way.

He pushed the body of the driver down onto the floor next to the gearshift. He took the cap from the driver's head, and put it on. Then he forced the dead guard's body to a sitting position, propped it against the far door. By the time the jeep driver and guard came walking back to see what had happened, everything appeared normal.

As the two Israelis approached a point near the front fender, David lowered his head a bit. His face couldn't be easily seen. He slowly let himself over the side, slipping to the ground, and calmly pointed the Luger in their faces and ordered them to raise their hands high above their heads. Then he directed the two to go to the back of the truck. He followed. When they were at the rear, he had them lie face down on the ground.

David smashed the gun butt to the base of the skull of the one he assumed was the guard, then the other. He struck so hard that there was very little blood. "Those four will never tell anybody *anything*," David whispered, and he stuffed the Luger in his pocket and swung up into the back of the truck. He blinked away the darkness there. And then, he found them—three nuclear warheads, crated individually. That kept the sub-critical mass of plutonium in each container from coming too close to any other. God knows if the centers of any two of them came into proximity, a critical mass would be produced, and that was mushroom cloud stuff.

He jumped off the back of the truck and ran to the jeep that was parked on the road, around the corner. The motor was still running, the lights on park. He got behind the wheel, turned the jeep around and drove back to the point next to where he'd been hiding in the ditch, got out and found the backpack he'd left there. He rushed back to the warheads, took the tools from the backpack, and forced open one of the crates. There it was—a warhead! It wasn't as big as he had thought it would be, and he smiled at the thought that it'd fit into his backpack.

He picked it and the tools up and slipped them into his backpack and put his arms through the carrying straps. Walking to the jeep, he glanced in the direction of the base. "There's no activity, and it's a couple of miles to the security fence," he mused. And he smiled to himself again that he'd thought of the distance in miles and English, after he'd been speaking in kilos and Hebrew for so long.

He parked the jeep next to his father's car, shut off the engine and parking lights, and threw the cap onto the seat. He thought, "Anything else?" It was dry, so no problem with tire tracks. He hesitated. Then, satisfied, he grabbed the straps of the backpack and carried it to his father's car. He put it on the floor in front of the passenger's seat, and pulled the Luger out of his pocket and placed it on the seat next to him.

Driving the car slowly, David turned toward Jerusalem. There was little other traffic except for the military vehicles that went by on the opposite side or passed David, who was in no real hurry. He silently complimented himself. It had gone as smoothly as he could've hoped for. There were at least two reasons for that, and he smiled broadly. He had the Most Secret computer data, and no one knew. Furthermore, there was the element of surprise. "Oh, yes," he thought, "the fact that there is a major war in progress is a factor, too—a significant third factor."

When he got to Jerusalem, the dark streets were deserted. It was just after three o'clock as he pulled the car up quietly beside the house. He shut off the lights and engine, picked up his baby. "Funny to think of the warhead that way," he thought. "But in several ways, she is my baby."

Soundlessly he let himself into the house and tiptoed to his room. After carefully placing his baby on the closet floor behind the large suitcases, he closed the folding doors. He undressed, went to bed, and fell asleep at once. *It was October eighth.*

13

IN THE 1967 WAR, Israel had quickly won a one-sided victory. Things had gone so well for them, it had been rumored that the American Air Force had called it "the perfect tactical air war—the way to fight and win an air-ground war!"

Not so in 1973! The contrast was as day and night. The Arabs were exacting heavy tolls in Israeli fighting men and their equipment. Egyptian forces overran Israel's fortifications in the Sinai. The Syrians captured Mount Hermon in the north. Because of Yom Kippur, it took Israeli forces too long to regain the initiative. It was clear that Israel's torch of freedom flickered low.

The Arabs had been equipped and trained by the Russians. In particular, during the October War, Egypt and Syria were supplied by massive Russian military airlifts. The United States responded with an all-out airlift for Israel. Huge C-5 Galaxy aircraft, the largest cargo air-carriers in service anywhere in the world, flew into Tel Aviv with payloads of over 140,000 pounds. Around-the-clock resupply was not new to the U.S. Air Force— that had been done in the late '40s at Berlin, and in the early '50s in Korea, and again in the '60s and '70s in Viet Nam. In Israel, enthusiastic U.S. aircrews directed the off-loading as soon as each C-5 came to a stop. Cooperation between the U.S. and highly motivated Israelis was close to perfection. Resupply was critical, and all of them knew it.

David tossed and turned in his bed. He really couldn't sleep very well. While he was in the ditch, near the base at Tel Aviv, he had seen the huge cargo-lifters of the U.S. Air Force coming and going. He saw the red, white and blue stars on the fuselage and wings of each, and he remembered how the army grunts in Nam had called them "aluminum overcasts." But, if he was correct, each of them was carrying an enormous load of supplies and equipment for the Israelis. So. That was on his mind. Then, thoughts of the plutonium crept into his head. It was there, in the closet, he kept thinking. He wanted to take it out and look at it.

Suddenly, he felt a rush of panic. He'd forgotten the Luger. By morning, he knew the four dead Israelis and the jeep and truck would be found, not to mention a missing cannister of plutonium. David sat up in bed, then got up, pulled on his pants, raced down the hall and out to the car. The gun was in the front seat where he'd left it. "Thank God!" he thought. "Poppa Saul would've been able to trace the whole thing, if he'd had the Luger for his first clue." David went back to his room, closed and locked the door. He took a t-shirt from the dresser drawer and tore it up. He used a little sun-tan oil to help in the process of cleaning the weapon. When it was sparkling, he took it, and the ammunition, and put them back in the metal case in his father's desk. Then he returned the oil to the cabinet in his bathroom. As he went outside to throw the pieces of t-shirt into the trash, he said under his breath, "At least that is taken care of."

He looked at his hands. They were trembling. David walked quickly to his room, took a Valium and forced himself to suppress the thoughts darting around in his mind. "If I don't get my act together, I'll blow this whole thing," he worried. The glow of the pill came over him. He sat down in the easy chair and fell asleep.

About seven o'clock he got up and walked into the kitchen. "The domestic," as his mother called Naomi, the maid, poured coffee for David. He sipped some, nodded and went back to his room. After closing and locking his door, he got the warhead out of the closet. He sat in the middle of the floor with the cannister before him. Radiation, and the awful things that can come from an overdose of it, were foremost in his mind. One had to exercise extreme caution with plutonium, and no one was more aware of it that the honor graduate in nuclear physics from N.Y.U. He studied it, and, after deciding just what tools he'd need, he put the nuclear assembly back in the closet and closed the folding doors.

David drank the coffee, got up and went into the bathroom. He showered, shaved and dressed. Then he went to see his mother. Sarah and Naomi were in the kitchen having hard toast and drinking hot water from their coffee cups. David smiled at them, and walked out to the car. He was thinking, as he looked through the tool chest in the trunk, that many older Jewish people had that kind of breakfast. His grandfather had told him when David was a little boy, "It helps to get the morning constitutional moving." David grinned. "Sometimes we're funny people," closing his smiling eyes.

After gathering the tools he'd need, David closed the trunk of the car. He went to his room and again closed and locked the door.

Ever so carefully, David spent the morning removing the core from the device. It had been packed in protective material to insure that handlers wouldn't receive radiation burns. When David discovered that, he was much more at ease. Careful to keep the protective shield around the plutonium, David separated it from the rest of what he had stolen. He lifted the sphere in his hands, like a crystal ball, and stared at it. Everyone knew it was impossible to get what David Mikhael Abaddon held. He had thirteen pounds of plutonium!

He put everything in the closet and closed the folding doors. He needed time to think. He lay on the bed, and mapped plans in his mind.

Saul Judah Abaddon had been living at the Ministry of Defense. The war had been going poorly for Israel, and the intelligence chief had come under considerable fire because of the complete surprise of the Arab attack. Days and nights ran together for all on the ministry staff. In the south, the first wave of Egyptians virtually waltzed over Israel's Bar-Lev defense line along the east bank of the Suez. What the Israelis were certain would never happen *did* happen. In the north, the reinforced Syrians were joined by men with equipment from many of their allies. Reports in Saul's office cited assistance to Syria from Iraq and Morocco, as well as from Jordan, and Lebanon was aiding the Arabs to the best of their ability. Saul was under constant stress—something he didn't at all enjoy.

He had called home several times each of the past couple days to be certain that all was well, and each time either Sarah or Naomi had been able to reassure him. When he called on Monday, right after lunch, David answered. "Hello, Poppa. Are you all right?" Saul told his son that he was "tired and a bit irritable" and went on to explain that there were some very rough times ahead. David casually mentioned that he had been busy in the computer room, and at home, that he and everyone were just fine. Poppa expressed satisfaction with that. Then he cut the conversation short, saying the hot-line was ringing. They both hung up. David was more relaxed after talking to his father. Poppa was okay, and it was obvious that David's surreptitious actions had gone undetected. He thought, "I am a bit of a sneaky bastard," but it failed to amuse him.

After the phone conversation with Poppa, David walked to his room, closed and locked the door. He opened the folding doors of the closet and removed all the elements of the warhead. He laid aside the plutonium in its protective shield, and stuffed everything else from the warhead into his backpack. Then he got his suitcase from the closet and opened it. He put the precious softball-sized object into the bag, and locked it. He then placed it carefully under his other big pieces of luggage, in the closet.

David picked up "the rest," as he'd been silently calling what he didn't need, and saw that all was well concealed in the backpack. He put his arms through the carrying straps, and walked out into the kitchen. His mother and Naomi were ready to go to downtown Jerusalem, and he offered them a ride.

David helped the ladies get into the back seat. Then he put his backpack in the trunk. During the drive to the market, David cautioned them. Rumors were everywhere about Arab terrorists. "Be very careful to stay in the Jewish sector," David urged. Each nodded to him as he looked at them in the rear-view mirror. When they asked to be let out at the next corner, David pulled over and let them out by a Barclay's Bank sign, and said he would pick them up at that same place at five o'clock. Sarah and Naomi smiled at him, waved and walked the other way toward Havoy's.

David headed the car south, out of Jerusalem, on the road to Bethlehem. He went through it and on toward Hebron. When he was well away from everything except highway traffic, he turned east on a narrow unpaved road. When he was sure he'd left everyone well behind, he stopped the car, got out, and opened the trunk. He picked up the backpack, closed the lid and walked east on a trail. "The Dead Sea is out there," he told himself. Once in the wilderness, David dug a hole in the sandy soil with a small piece of metal he'd brought, and he buried "the rest."

His step was much lighter, his walk quicker, going back to the car, and on the drive back to Jerusalem he caught himself humming "The First Time Ever I Saw Your Face."

David drove to the Ministry of Defense. When he got to the main gate of the compound, the marines on duty stopped him. They demanded identification. David replied brusquely in Hebrew, as he handed one of them his compound identification card. The more senior of the two stared at him, said he knew who David was, but he said *everyone* was being asked for identification now. The pre-emptive war was the cause. With hordes of Arabs warring at their borders, Israelis were taking precautions. They were sure that David understood.

When he got inside David walked straight to the computer area. Abrashkov and a full complement of programmers were busy. The hardware and software available to the Israelis in those rooms were critically important now, and the staff worked feverishly to take full advantage of the data they had. They pored over long reams of computer runs—statistics of weapons systems and materials available on October fifth, and what was at the ready now, after losses: numbers wounded, dead.

David was not surprised when Daniel and the others spoke only briefly to him, and Daniel said, "Not really," when David asked if he could help.

Saul Abaddon sat at his desk busy with some papers he had just been handed. The ring of the phone startled him. "Nerves a bit on edge," he thought. He picked up the phone, listened. When he hung it back on the hook, Saul's face was ashen. He reached for the intercom, buzzed for his secretary. As the sergeant came through the door, he sensed the worst.

"Find David for me. Now," Saul directed.

The secretary returned to his desk and called down to the computer area. David answered, listened while the sergeant told him that his father needed him at once.

David hurried to the second floor security entrance and explained the phone call he'd just had from his father's office. The two marines looked at each other, decided silently that one of them would escort David to his father's office. When the two of them got there, the secretary nodded to the marine and he left. David walked into the inner office and closed the door behind him.

Poppa Saul sat at the desk, his face buried in his hands. David walked around the corner of the desk, touched his father's shoulder and asked, "What is it, Poppa?"

Saul Abaddon looked up and said, "Your mother has been killed. In a bomb blast. It was apparently set off by a terrorist who was blown up when it exploded. Naomi was critically injured, too. She is in the hospital, in a coma. Head injuries."

198

David was stunned. Here was torment again, that awful feeling inside when the worst has happened. The blackest sort of pain filled his stomach, and there was no stopping it. The agony of Nam, the anguish of Janet, the pain to now bear because of a murdered mother. Who was tormenting him? Why had he been chosen to suffer so?

He asked to be excused, went into his father's bathroom and vomited into the stool.

Jewish tradition dictates a very clear course of action: when one of the congregation dies, burial has to take place within twenty-four hours. It was not a matter for discussion. Embalming Jewish people just wasn't done. Putting the body to rest, immediately, *that* was done.

Saul explained that he could not possibly leave Israel, not in time of war, when the tide was so much against their people, so David would have to take his mother's body back to New York for burial.

"I was going to have to leave anyway, Poppa. Please let me take this one for both of us," David said feeling a slight surge of strength—from Kelley, or somewhere. "I'll make all the arrangements for Mother with the rabbi. Can you get us some transportation by air?" David asked.

"Let me see if I can get the U.S. Air Force liaison commander at Lod to agree to fly you and her home." Saul's voice broke, momentarily. He told David where the body was being prepared, and they walked out together, to the waiting staff car, and the driver took them to Sarah.

Air Force Colonel Jack Logan agreed that it would be acceptable to fly the body of the wife of a ranking Israeli official to the U.S. Sarah was an American citizen, and so was her son, who would be escorting. "The C-5s are going back empty anyway. There's plenty of room on any one of them," the airlift boss had said.

So it was arranged. Both Saul and David would go to Tel Aviv with Sarah's body, and see to it that all was ready for the flight home, and David would fly with her. Saul had to stay in Israel, and with his critical duties.

Saul told David that all American citizens had just been ordered out of Israel by the first available means of transportation. David said nothing.

Saul and David stayed at the funeral home for a short while, then walked out to the waiting staff car.

"I've got to get back to the ministry, son. Why don't you stay here for a while longer?" Saul was clearly despondent.

"Please let me drop you at the ministry, Poppa, and then use the car," David said. "I need a Valium."

The driver took Saul Abaddon to the Ministry. David waved to his father as he walked away from the car, then he was driven to the Abaddon house, where he asked the driver to wait.

When he was alone in his room, David removed the small sphere from his suitcase. He placed the precious article in his backpack, picked it up, and walked out to the car. He was driven back to the funeral home.

The rabbi was compassionate when the young American asked to be alone with his mother. After the rabbi was gone, and David was certain he was alone in the room, he went to his mother's body and simply stared at her. He thought, "They've done a remarkable job. She looks so natural." David bent over and hugged her tenderly. Then he lifted her head, and removed the plastic bag of Israeli earth always placed there before the funeral of a Jewish person who would not be buried in Israel. He put the small bag in his backpack, and took the ball-shaped object from the backpack. He pressed it into the hollow bneneath her head. Gently, he lowered his mother's head and looked intently at her face for a moment, then turned quickly to leave. Outside, he told the rabbi he was ready to take his mother home to New York, for a Jewish burial.

David called Ruth, and told her how Fate had touched his life again. Ruth wanted to be with him, and Poppa Saul, too. David said to meet them at the funeral home.

Ruth came at once and provided the touch of feminine gentleness David needed. He was afraid of slipping into a black madness, but Ruth knew torment too, and stayed close for the sake of David and his father.

They stood and watched as the rabbi supervised the loading of the casket into the rear of the hearse. When that was done, they thanked Ruth. She stood, a resolute Sabra, while the two men got in the back seat of the long vehicle, and waved as they drove off to Tel Aviv Airport.

The driver had obviously been briefed, because he knew exactly where to go. He drove to a C-5 Galaxy aircraft. Colonel Logan, dressed in blue military uniform with five rows of ribbons under his command pilot wings, was waiting. He greeted Saul, and then David, and said he was conveying to both of them the deep concern of the United States government about what had happened.

Saul thanked the colonel, asked if they would please proceed. Logan nodded to the crew chief. The American airmen went to work. In a matter of minutes they had Sarah Abaddon's casket secured with thick white nylon straps to metal rings fastened at flight deck level at the rear of the aircraft, near the tailgate, and so was one passenger seat. The crew chief had thought of David's need for privacy. The master sergeant told David, "You can always walk up front to the cockpit to talk to us if you want to." David smiled, nodded to the blond, blue-eyed airman.

Saul motioned for David, and they walked alone to the side of the huge craft. They hugged each other for a long time. They kissed, and Saul said, "God go with you." They said nothing else. Their tears said the rest.

Empty, except for the fuel and the people, the C-5 easily flew non-stop from Tel Aviv to Torrejon Air Base, in Spain. There, the fuel tanks were filled, and they were off to Lajes Field, in the Azores. David asked, while the aircraft was being refueled and checked, how many hours the crew could keep flying. He was told that their crew had had crew rest in Israel, and that they could go for twenty-four hours, from the time they left Tel Aviv. When David asked how many pilots, navigators, and crew members were on their C-5, the airmen changed the subject. David quickly gave a Woody Allen line. Everyone laughed, and things loosened up again.

The last leg of the flight, from Lajes to New Jersey, seemed to David to take almost no time at all. "Just like that, we're home," David told the crew.

Customs officials at McGuire Air Force Base glanced at David's passport, then at Sarah's, and handed them back to David. They quickly looked through David's luggage, and one of them asked David for his backpack. The official found the Israeli bag of earth. David's heart began to pound after he'd explained the significance of that, and where it would be placed. Both officials walked to the casket, lifted the lid, then quickly closed it, nodded understandingly to David, and said he was cleared to leave.

The master sergeant crew chief watched for a signal from David. When he gave it, the airmen removed the nylon restraining straps and carefully moved the casket down the rear ramp to ground level. A blue Air Force half-ton truck was waiting, and the casket was gently placed in the back. David thanked all the members of the crew and told them how much he appreciated their anticipating every need. They told him it was their job. They were glad to help and very sorry about the circumstances.

David walked to the right side of the truck, opened the door and climbed inside. As he closed the door, he turned to the driver and asked, "What happens now?"

"I'm to accommodate you, sir. Those are my instructions," replied the black airman.

"Is there a phone where I can make a long distance call?"

The airman said there were pay phones in base operations, and David asked to be taken there.

It took three minutes. The driver stopped on the flight line side of McGuire AFB Base Operations, and saying he hoped it wouldn't be too long, David walked inside. He went to the information desk and got change. Smiling at the first U.S. coins he'd held in his hands in almost six months, David walked to the pay phones that lined one wall. He dialed a collect call to his grandfather. When he answered, David started to tell him everything, but Zada stopped him, told him that Poppa Saul had called. All he needed to know was, "Where are you?" David said he was at McGuire Air Force Base, eighteen miles southeast of Trenton.

Samuel Klein said he had a chartered jet standing by, and David heard his grandfather's voice breaking as he spoke.

David hung up the phone, went to the information desk and asked to speak to a senior officer. The airman buzzed and spoke into the phone. Then she suggested that David sit in one of the chairs to the left.

In a matter of minutes a black officer, wearing silver eagles on his light blue shirt, walked up to David.

"Hello, I'm Colonel Bob Overbrook. May I help you?"

Polished and professional, was David's instant impression. He stood and said, "I'm David Abaddon. My mother was killed at sundown on Monday, in Jerusalem, Colonel. Her body is in a casket, in the truck out there," pointing to the flight line. "A chartered jet will be coming to fly her body, and me, to JFK. Is there something more I should do, or someone else I should talk to?" David asked.

The Colonel reassured David, said their staff would alert the control tower and operations staffs.

David worried, "Sir, it'll be a civilian aircraft. This is an Air Force base. Will it still be all right, sir?"

Overbrook smiled, and David knew he'd take care of everything. David relaxed.

Colonel Overbrook nodded pleasantly, and disappeared into the office behind the information desk. David said almost out loud, "If everyone in the military was like that gent, it'd be super. Maybe it's that he's Air Force. What a pro!" David suddenly remembered he'd called the man "sir" several times, and thought, "When they're that good, they deserve it!"

In less than an hour, a Lear-jet pulled up in front of base operations. The airman at the information desk paged David on the loudspeaker, and she said all was ready for the flight to New York City. David thanked her, asked that she thank Colonel Overbrook. She smiled and said she'd have to do that tomorrow night, because the colonel had left. David nodded to her. As he walked toward the flight line door he was convinced of the relaxed efficiency of the Air Force staff. "No wonder," he thought, "with a man like Overbrook leading."

The airman driver, with help from both pilots and David, loaded the casket onto the jet. David shook the airman's hand and thanked him.

David got in the back of the Lear, and the pilots closed the side door and went into the cockpit. In less than ten minutes they were airborne; and in just over half an hour, they taxied up and shut down the engines in front of the fixed-base operations office at JFK.

A Cadillac hearse was waiting. Two ground attendants were standing next to the Lear's side door when the pilots came back and opened it. They removed the casket and loaded it into the hearse as David watched. He thanked Chief Pilot Ken Jensen and asked if there were any other details to see to. Ken smiled, told David that everything had been arranged by the chief executive officer of the Klein Department Stores. David nodded, and shook hands with both pilots.

During the ride in the hearse to the Jewish funeral home, he was remembering. They were back in New York, and Sarah Vida Klein Abaddon had come home. And she had not been just anybody.

David insisted on escorting the body of his mother at every moment. When the driver stopped the hearse at the receiving entrance of the funeral home, David told the night attendant that services for Mrs. Abaddon had to be that afternoon. "All arrangements have been made," David was informed. After the driver and night attendant had moved the casket inside, David asked for "a moment alone, to say good-bye to my mother." The two employees nodded understandingly and left.

Once he was certain he was alone, David took off his backpack and reached inside for the packet of Israeli earth. David gently lifted Sarah's head, removed the sphere of plutonium, and replaced it with the bag of earth and tenderly positioned his mother's head over it. Then he put the plutonium into his backpack. As he put his arms through the carrying straps and the backpack settled into place, David breathed a sigh of relief. Now they could bury her.

David started to turn and leave. Suddenly he stopped. He faced his mother again. Bending over, he looked carefully at her face, staring full into it. She seemed to David to be quite beautiful then. He looked at her, proabaly as never before. There was the gray creeping into her dark hair, the lines around her eyes and near her mouth, on her upper lip and neck. David thought, "Ah . . . but time's been good to her. She has aged so gracefully. My mother's quite a lovely woman even now." And as the tears flowed, he whispered to her, "Aging is the caress of time, Momma. It happens to all of us."

The night attendant called a taxi. When it came, they loaded David's two large suitcases into the trunk. The driver asked for directions and was told to go to Brooklyn Heights. David had decided to stay with his grandfather.

Samuel Klein was waiting for his only grandchild. He paid the cab driver and tried to help David with his luggage. Once inside, he embraced David, and told him how glad he was to see him. "You are my only blood now surviving," he said. And he said some words in Hebrew that David didn't hear.

"I haven't slept very much, Zada," David told him. "Can we talk later?" he asked politely.

His grandfather said he understood and nodded toward the upstairs.

Dragging the two heavy bags onto the elevator, David took it to the second floor. He pulled the luggage into his bedroom and closed the door.

He showered, letting the warm water run over him. It was soothing. It had been a long journey.

At noon, there was a gentle knock on the door. David awoke with a start, asked who it was. The maid answered and said that his grandfather wanted David wakened and reminded that the funeral would be starting in two hours. David sat upright, thanked her.

He went to the phone and dialed the international operator. She helped him with a person-to-person call. Saul Abaddon was in a meeting, in the War Room, but he said he'd take the call. He walked to his office and picked up the phone.

"Hello, this is Saul Abaddon," he said.

"Go ahead, please."

"Poppa, it's me. Everything worked out perfectly. Are you okay?"

Saul was exhausted, said there was a lot of work ahead, but that it would be done. He expressed love for David, said to give his regrets that he could not be at the funeral.

David assured his father that everyone would understand why he could not possibly be in New York, and promised to write about everything that happened. They said good-bye and hung up.

David hid the plutonium in the closet, and readied himself for the funeral.

The Brooklyn Heights Synagogue was filled with people, some that David and his grandfather hadn't seen in years. Rabbi Jacob Goldman arranged the services, and all was done in Orthodox Jewish tradition, with sincerest encomium for Sarah Vida Klein Abaddon.

Later, there was not a place to park at Knollwood Park Cemetery, or on the adjacent Cooper and Cypress Avenues. Mourners were everywhere.

Samuel Klein had sought special permission to bury his martyred daughter in New York City's oldest Jewish cemetery, next to the eighteen Jewish soldiers who had served and died in the Revolutionary War, but his request was denied. The First Cemetery of the Spanish and Portugese Synagogue Shearith Israel had been closed since 1833.

Knollwood's choicest location, on a small knoll in the Klein family plot, now held the body of Sarah.

Rabbi Goldman had made certain that the close friends of the family knew they were invited to the house in Brooklyn Heights to be together, to visit with father Sam Klein and to talk to son David.

Late in the afternoon, after everyone had left the house, David and his Zada visited in the sitting room. The old man told his grandson how happy he was about David still being a practicing Jew. David smiled weakly, then changed the subject, said he wanted to stay overnight again to accommodate to the time change. Grandpa had the maid bring hot tea, and they visited about Israel and Poppa Saul.

At dinner time, David asked to be excused, saying he wasn't really hungry. Politely he said good night to his grandfather and went upstairs to his bedroom. He closed and locked the door. Resting on the bed, after taking off all but his shorts, he told himself that he couldn't do another thing with anybody. He needed time alone, to slow down. He got up, took two Valiums with a glass of water, went back to the bed, and sleep came.

Nathan Moss sat in his office in Jerusalem and glared at his two assistants. He said, "The loss of even one piece of plutonium is the most serious problem Mossad has ever faced. Let's examine the knowns again."

He reviewed facts with his two best agents, Levi Rifkin and Isaac Switzsky. They were looking for at least two people. No one person could have done it. The weapon used on two of the Israelis was a 9mm Luger. Ballistics would be a plus, when they found the weapon, because one of the bullets had an almost perfect bore pattern they could later duplicate. No fingerprints of value had been taken from the wood or metal straps of the crate that had been opened; but—maybe—they had one thumb print from the wheel of the jeep, and strands of hair not belonging to any of the four dead Israelis had been taken from the cap found in the jeep.

They had sufficient clues, Moss said emphatically. Mossad agents would find them. Wherever they were—in Israel, or anywhere else.

Moss dismissed the two agents, with orders to "Find them!" Rifkin and Switzsky got up and left. But Moss kept thinking, "Why had they taken only one warhead? Why?"

David slept for over ten hours. He felt groggy, but after black coffee, he was more himself. He visited briefly with his grandfather, and then said he would have to go to his apartment to call his ICM bosses.

He took a taxi to get the two large suitcases and backpack to his Brooklyn apartment. David closed and locked the door and went at once to his computer room. All was untouched. All was as he had left it.

He dialed ICM. Jeff's secretary answered. They said hello, and then she buzzed for Jeff.

"Hi, Dave. How are you and where are you?"

David explained everything. He started with the suddenness of the attack by the Arabs, and ended with the details of the funeral of his mother.

Jeff was shocked, said David should take some time off.

David thanked him, said he'd keep in touch.

After hanging up, Jeff thought to himself, "That guy's life is a soap opera. It goes from one thing to the next. I don't think I could stand it. Not the way Dave Abaddon does!" And Jeff turned back to the papers he'd been reading to get his mind off David.

David unpacked everything, took his laundry and a few items to the cleaners, then he went shopping at the supermarket and got groceries, packed them so he could manage the three bags. Once he was back at the apartment, he put the food away and made certain the front door was locked.

Then he went back to his computers, and turned the system's master switch on. He sat at the console and typed the password on the keyboard. The CRT suddenly displayed the graphic he'd been thinking and thinking about. It was perfection, right down to the label at the bottom. *IMPLOSION DEVICE*. He studied all of it, again and again.

David shut off the computers and went out and sat in the easy chair in his sitting room. He glanced at the closet door, thought about the sphere that he'd hidden there—and he was sure he could build a bomb.

He did not, however, think about what he would do with it, once he got it built. *It was October tenth.*

P A R T
FOUR

14

DAVID WAS SITTING at his desk when Jeff came in. He grinned and said, "Welcome home, mister. We're glad to see you."

"Thanks, Jeff. I'm feeling pretty well, and it's good to be back."

Jeff invited David into his office. David shut the door and sat down, as Jeff went around behind his desk. Jeff sat in his chair and leaned back. David took the cue, talked about the tragedy of his mother's death. He was deliberate, let his boss know all was okay. Then David talked about total satisfaction, as far as he knew, on the part of the Israelis. Jeff explained that the final project report had been prepared by the three others. All Jim Bannion would need were David's quick assessments, and the final acceptance date by the Israelis, for purposes of the contract. David said he would call Bannion the minute he got back to his desk.

Jeff then talked about the new project for the Air Force. It was Top Secret, called the Defense Support Program—DSP—and it was a system for orbiting satellites equipped with sensitive infrared cameras, so that whenever anything of intelligence value was intercepted, such as a Russian missile launch, data was telemetered back to earth automatically, when the orbiting satellite was later in proper position to transmit to receiving stations on the earth's surface. ICM was being asked by the Air Force to improve the digestion of the data, by the computers, once it was received. David would be working on that, Jeff told him.

David was delighted. "Thanks! Just let me get some details from the trip to Israel completed, and then I'll be ready." They smiled at each other, and David left.

Back at his desk, David called Jim Bannion on intercom. Bannion told David he was about to put him on the recorder. "When I do, give me your final report comments, anything unusual that happened after Curtis, Barker and I left, and the final acceptance date," Bannion directed, and hung up.

David heard the recorder beep, and complied with Bannion's directions. He hesitated only when he got to the "anything unusual" portion. There, he smiled to himself but made no comment. He gave the final acceptance date as October eighth. At the end of the recording, he made a public relations annotation thanking ICM for giving him the opportunity to serve the company in Israel.

David read his office mail, then visited with ICM staff members he hadn't seen for six months. Each one expressed sympathy and support in the tragic loss of his mother. Before leaving, he stopped to ask Jeff one question he'd been thinking about all afternoon, "How many satellites are in orbit supporting DSP?"

Jeff frowned and said, "More than one and less than one hundred."

As David walked out of the Institute, to the subway to visit Father Donovan, he thought, "I've hit another sensitive area with my question. Wonder if I'll ever learn."

Father Donovan was sitting in his study when David walked in. They exchanged greetings, then David talked about his trip to Israel, installing the computers, and the death of his mother, and added the details of the jet trip home and the funeral. Then he asked, "Father, could we go into the confessional, please?"

Donovan smiled, nodded and rose. They went into the church, and David walked in and closed the confessional door. Father got in on his side, and they began. David explained how he'd just had no way to go to church, or take part in any of the sacraments during his stay in Israel, and he asked Father to take that into consideration. Donovan said that he would, under the circumstances. Then, David talked about the plutonium. He didn't bother to mention that he'd killed four Israelis to get it. That would only make Father very angry. But he did tell his priest how he had smuggled the plutonium into the U.S. David then explained that he would be building an atom bomb, and that he'd chosen Father as the person he would talk to about it all, because he knew it would be safe to do so.

Donovan gulped, assigned penance, forced himself to remain calm.

David left the confessional, after promising to begin attending mass again. He walked to the front of the church and began penance. Father got up slowly, went from the box to his study and closed the door. He did not know what to do. He kept hoping this was some kind of dream.

Saul Abaddon welcomed his long-time friend Nathan Moss to the ministry. Both had served Israel early in the Haganah. They'd risked their lives on missions together for the underground, and when Mossad became a reality, both became part of that, too.

"Please sit down," Saul said, closing his office door, and Saul sat in a chair next to his. Moss said, "We need to talk more about the loss of the warhead."

Other agents of Mossad had visited earlier with Saul, and he was hoping that the reason for Nathan's personal visit would be news that the warhead had been found. Obviously, from Moss's tone of voice, it had not.

"So?" Saul asked.

The two of them discussed for several hours how it might have been possible for anyone to have known the exact schedule for movement of the warheads. It had been highly classified, and labeled *Dispersal for the Survival of Israel.* Saul could not shed a ray of light on the critically serious situation. Moss had him explain twice where and how the action code words were protected, and both were satisfied that all was proper in Saul's office.

As he got up to leave, Moss said, "We're looking for other possible leaks. I'll be in touch."

Saul Abaddon had told Nathan Moss that the computers had to have stored in their memories the Most Secret data about the movement of the nuclear warheads. "The whole concept is based on instant last-second reaction. We dare not risk telephone conversations. So the best solution, with these given parameters, is scrambled electronic transmission directing dispersal. Thus, there would be no way for anyone to intercept," Saul had emphasized.

"I think someone got information from the computers," Moss guessed to himself. He walked downstairs and into the secure computer area. He asked for the supervisor. Daniel Abrashkov came in and introduced himself.

"What can I do for you?" Abrashkov asked.

"I'm Nathan Moss, a friend of Mr. Saul Abaddon," Moss said as he showed his I.D. Abrashkov instantly recognized the *Special Access* printed on the identification card. He knew Moss wasn't there simply to chat. Moss continued, "Please show me around. Let's discuss how these computers work. Oh, and tell me how the security of all the data is maintained."

Abrashkov swallowed hard, and began the tour. Moss watched

every move his guide made, listened, didn't miss a word that was said. When it was finished, Moss thanked Daniel and left, but he kept thinking, "The man was too nervous, much too anxious. Why?"

Early next morning, David met with Jeff. They talked all about the Defense Support Program. Jeff placed special emphasis on the security of the DSP. He told David, "I guess the guys in the Department of Defense even have a special yellow cover sheet that has to be on top of every single document pertaining to the project. Special individual clearances are required, too, for even limited access. DOD is really protecting this baby."

"I won't tell anyone about it, Jeff," David said, pretending Woody Allen. "I promise!" Their laughter echoed in Jeff's office, and in the hall as David walked to the 370 console.

David understood his role in improving the process of digesting the data once the computers received it. He knew it would be a challenge, and an interesting one.

He spent the rest of the day brainstorming the project.

Later, at the apartment, David could not concentrate on anything but the bomb—he was obsessed with it, so he labored, intricately, accurately. He was pleased that he had been able to locate and purchase everything necessary to construct the bomb from commercial outlets in New York City.

Worrying himself to sleep late that night, he thought, "I'll call the bomb HER. A perfect nickname!" *It was October twentieth.*

Nathan Moss tapped his pencil on the desk in his office. The intercom buzzed.

"Yes?" he answered impatiently.

"Sir, Agents Rifkin and Switzsky are here," his secretary said.

"Send them in," Moss directed. They came in and shut the door. They sat in chairs in front of his desk. Moss explained his theory of where the information leak had occurred. "Somehow, the computers are involved in the compromise. When the head programmer took me through the tour. I thought he was going to have a heart attack. He knows something!" The three agreed to pursue that possibility.

Saul Abaddon was working at a table in his office when his secretary announced that there were three visitors to see him. Saul walked out to the reception area and invited them into his office.

They sat at the table, and Saul shut the door. "What can I do for you?" he asked.

"How well do you know Daniel Abrashkov?" Moss inquired.

The three Mossad agents and Saul talked for over an hour. Then, Moss told Saul he wanted to talk to the head programmer. They summoned Abrashkov. He came at once to the intelligence chief's office.

Moss took the lead. "Tell me. If there is a special password used by each person who has access to data in the computers, wouldn't there be a record of who had made requests? When they'd done it? And exactly what data the computers surrendered?"

Abrashkov nodded. Little beads of sweat appeared on his upper lip. He shifted from one foot to the other.

"Why don't you tell us all about it?" Moss said as he stared into the man's eyes.

"About what?" Abrashkov asked.

Moss calmly told Abrashkov the penalty for treason. He added, "If there was a mistake, that's one thing. If you are part of some plan, or a group, tell us now. Save yourself some trouble, my friend. Talk!"

Daniel Abrashkov looked at each of them, then told the four men what had happened. "Brina was my mother's name," he said. "She's buried in the Ukraine. I was certain no one would ever guess the word here in Israel. But David Abaddon accidentally learned it when he and I were doing final checks on the terminals for the new computers. That's the only breach I know of."

The room became ominously quiet. Then Moss dismissed Abrashkov, said they'd be in contact with him soon.

After he'd gone, Moss told the two Mossad agents to wait in the outer office. As they closed the door, he said to Saul, "I want all the history of who did what with the computers!"

Saul assured Moss that he would have the complete history of all BRINA-demanded computer runs printed in the Ministry of Defense.

Moss said, "Get it done! Have data in this office by eight tomorrow morning." Saul nodded, glanced at his calendar. He noted that would be October twenty-first.

Early next morning, David was wide awake, driven. "I need to get finished," he thought. He got up and made coffee, took it into the computer room, turned the system's master switch on and entered his passwords. The atom bomb graphic flashed onto the CRT. He spread the various components on the floor where he could see each item, and then he began.

He worked slowly, methodically, on the final steps. Each move had to result in near perfection, he knew, or all his work would come to nothing. He anticipated each move, compared that with what the graphic showed as being reliable, then brought the needed materials close by. Cross-checking the Los Alamos notes, he arranged and secured the components in place.

By that night, David had made significant progress. He was obsessed, couldn't stop himself. He called Jeff and lied that he had the flu. "I'll try to come in later," he said, but he knew he'd be in his apartment, doing what he had to do.

He went to bed at eleven that night, but couldn't sleep. He tossed and turned, thought about HER. He dozed off, but by five in the morning he was back in the computer room, in only his Jockey shorts, constructing. "My biggest-by-far challenge of a lifetime," he knew.

Saul Abaddon and Daniel Abrashkov had the computer runs on the table and fully studied by the time Nathan Moss arrived. Saul gulped for a full breath of air, but his lungs just wouldn't fill properly. It was his anxiety. He stared at Moss, and said, "I've got some bad news, Nathan. BRINA was used to get data from the computers at six forty-four on Sunday morning, October seventh. We have not verified his story yet, but Abrashkov, here, says he was with his family then. He swears he didn't come to the ministry until later that day."

Moss told Abrashkov to leave, warned that he was to discuss the investigation with no one. Any violation of that order would result in most serious consequences.

After Abrashkov had closed the door, Moss said, "What data did the computers surrender to the requester?"

Saul shook his head. "We don't know. We only know the computer was activated by use of the password BRINA. To find out if the Action Code Words and Computer Authentication Procedures were used, we would have to enter them into the computers, too. That's so because the data for dispersal of the warheads are all on a totally secure, independent program."

"Get them," Moss ordered.

Saul got up, shoulders drooping, and walked to the security files. He dialed the combination and opened the drawer with the nuclear folders in it. As he lifted out the folder with the Action Code Words in it, Moss studied him, and Saul felt it. He opened the folder to the place where the Code Words were and handed it to Moss.

As he took the folder from Saul, Moss said, "Do you own a German Luger?" And he never took his eyes from Saul's face, even as he fingered the folder on the table.

Saul nodded and mumbled, "Uh huh."

Moss glanced at the paper in the folder, then quickly raised his eyes to look at Saul again. "Where is your son, Saul?"

Saul reminded Moss of Sarah's death, David's almost instant departure for the U.S. and the funeral in New York City. Moss listened intently, and then said, "Let's go get your Luger."

David was imaging the reaction that was set off in a nuclear explosion. He was sure the high explosive he'd learned about from the unknown man at Du Pont would crush the plutonium into a beryllium-polonium core. That would create an awesome atomic explosion, like Hiroshima and Nagasaki. Those thoughts were inspiring, and he was obsessed with finishing HER. David completed as much of the bomb as possible before he had to remove the protective cover from the plutonium. When the moment finally arrived, he put on the face mask, the lead apron and gloves. "At least I'll get some protection," he thought.

The time of day, or of night, became mixed in David's mind as he worked on and on. He did eat once in a while, and drank water in gulps when he became unbearably thirsty. But other than using the bathroom and napping some on the floor of the computer room, he built HER.

He wasn't sure exactly when he first realized it, but suddenly he knew: HER had become a reality. All was finished, and he could rest a little.

Saul Abaddon and Nathan Moss rode in the rear seat of the staff car. When the driver stopped at the Abaddon house, the two of them got out and went in together. Saul led the premier Mossad agent into the sitting room and to his desk. He removed the Luger from the drawer and handed it to Moss. He examined it for a moment, then stuffed it into his pocket and jerked his head toward the door. The two of them walked out to the waiting car.

During the ride to the central offices of the Mossad in Jerusalem not one word was spoken, but once they were in Moss's private office, with the door shut, the room was filled with sound.

Screeching like a banshee, Moss demanded, "How could you be a part of such a thing, Saul? Why? In God's name, tell me why you and your son did this nightmarish thing?" He glared at Saul, then slumped into a chair and pointed to another for Saul.

Saul sat down and said softly, "I have done nothing wrong, Nathan. You have my word from over all the years on that. As far as David is concerned, I cannot believe my boy would ever be involved in this! Tell me why you feel it might be David."

Moss stared thoughtfully, and then answered, "The strands of hair found in the cap that was in the back seat of the jeep are not from one of our people. We were able to get a footprint from the area where the thieves parked their vehicle. Unfortunately, the ground was dry and no really good tire tracks could be obtained. Anyway, the footprint we got didn't match any of the four dead Israelis. But it would match someone about David's size. We know he knew the password BRINA, and we are aware that he had ample opportunity to use the computers. He obviously had access to your Luger. The one thing we're not sure of is the Action Code Words. If he did have those, he must've gotten them from you." Moss focused his eyes then, with total intensity, on Saul's, who stared back at Moss, but gently; and Saul emphasized again that he knew nothing of the matter.

After several moments, Moss stood up and so did Saul. They went out to the car and got into the back seat. Saying nothing, they rode to the ministry, and walked upstairs to Saul's office. Moss picked up the folder with the code words in it, and the two of them went down to the secure computer area. Saul motioned everyone to stand clear of the main console. Nathan Moss sat down and typed. He entered the Mossad password, while Saul faced away, then the action code words and authentication. Instantly, the printers began to chatter, and the two of them had confirmation. Printout sheets verified that at 6:44 A.M., on 10/7/73, someone had requested, using the password BRINA and exact authentication, Most Secret data about the dispersal of the Israelis' nuclear warheads. Unfortunately, the computers had dutifully supplied the information.

Saul stared into Nathan's eyes and, in a whisper, swore with the Haganah Oath that he had not betrayed their country.

Moss, just then, believed Saul, and he said to him, "We're going to New York. Now! We'll use the United Nations special passports and entry visas. Go pack for a two weeks' stay."

After Saul had gone up the stairs to his office to tell the Minister of Defense and his staff about the trip, Moss walked out to the waiting staff car. He was driven back to his Mossad office. He handed the Luger to his assistant and told him to have a ballistics test completed. "This may be the murder weapon," he said. Moss already knew that it was.

Saul and Nathan met at the ministry two hours later and were driven to Lod Airport. They were on the next El Al jet to JFK. They cleared customs and took a taxi to Brooklyn Heights. *It was October twenty-fourth.*

David had slept soundly, he wasn't sure for how long, but suddenly he was wide awake and determined. After he got the coffee percolating, David shaved and showered. He noticed a more than normal amount of hair lying at the shower drain. Shrugging that off, he dressed in sports clothes, and gulped down two cups of black coffee. Then he called Father Donovan and said, "I must see you right away. It's imperative." Donovan told him to go to the study, at the church, said they'd meet there.

David's watch read eight-fifty. He carefully locked his apartment door. After all, it had in it his HER. He took the subway to St. Thomas More. When he got to the study, Father was waiting for him. Smiling weakly, Donovan asked, "What is it, David?"

"Father, can we please go into the confessional?" Donovan nodded, noting that David looked pallid, but he said nothing as they walked together into the church. When each had seated himself in the box, David began, "Bless me, Father, for I have sinned. This may be my last confession!"

Donovan's heart began to pound. "What do you mean?"

David told him the bomb was finished. "You ought to see HER," emphasizing the word.

Father was speechless.

David continued, "I've decided to fly HER over D.C. I want to demonstrate two things. *First,* I want to dramatize that if we allow the New Holocaust to happen, *everyone* will be Jewish, like my people were in World War II, and they'll experience the horror of Nam, too. *Second,* somehow I'm hoping that my actions will demonstrate how easy it is to build a bomb and start a nuclear war on a fluke or by accident. I live in morbid fear of that, because, as a nuclear physicist, I'm terrified about something. Let me explain. An atom bomb is a simple *fission weapon.* That is, the splitting of atoms occurs in those explosions. They're measured in kilotons. *But* the latest big-power nuclear warheads are *fusion weapons.* They explode in *megatons.* When that happens, hydrogen atoms are changed into helium atoms, just like what's happening on the surface of the sun millions of times over every moment, right now. Anyway, my awful fear is justified. If enough megaton weapons, launched by the super powers, explode at once or nearly simultaneously, maybe all of the free-floating hydrogen in the world will be converted into helium—at the same time! And during that fusion the whole earth could be blown up, and all of everything vaporized!"

The hair raised on the back of Donovan's neck. His flesh crawled. He could not speak. He was terrified! He had never before heard such madness. There was only one course of action left. "David, you must agree to come with me now. We will go together to talk with Doctor Silber. Let's get out of the confessional, and meet in my office."

David's voice reflected an infinite calm. He said, "No way, Father. I won't. And I know you can't say a word about this to anyone!"

Father pleaded, again and again, but David refused, and his serenity only served to further upset the priest. Donovan was filled with panic.

"Father?" David called softly. "Are you there?"

Donovan had walked out of the confessional. That was the first time that had ever happened, but he had to be alone. He went straight for his study and quietly closed the door behind him and sat down at his desk. With hands folded, and head bowed, he began to pray.

Hours later, when the custodian arrived for work, he quietly opened the study door and found Father Donovan there, praying.

Samuel Klein was pleased, surprised to see Saul, and happy to have as a house guest Nathan Moss from Israel. He showed them into the living room and told the maids to see to the luggage. Saul explained that he and Nathan were in the United States on business, at the U.N., for the Israeli government. Samuel asked if their business had anything to do with the cease-fire proposed by the U.N.'s Security Council. "I saw on the TV where both Israel and Egypt had accepted it on the twenty-second of October," Samuel said, grinning.

"Yes, it is about the war, Zada," Saul lied. "And we will be very busy because of that. I know you'll understand." They then talked, almost in whispers, about Sarah.

Later, Saul explained he would be taking a car and be gone for the day. Samuel smiled, nodded, shook their hands and watched them walk to the garage. As the two drove away, he thought to himself how nice it must be for Saul to still be young and a part of the latest Israeli victories, and to have such an exciting life, although he had noticed how tired Saul's face seemed. "That's probably because of Sarah," the old man thought.

David suddenly felt queasy in the confessional. He thought he might vomit. Then, just as suddenly, the nausea and a slight dizziness disappeared. He dismissed the episode, attributing it to anxiety because of his plans.

David left the confessional, deciding to move quickly now. Back at his apartment, he went to work packing HER. He used two large suitcases, but was able to get most of the bomb into one, and the remaining support devices in the other.

David called a taxi. He watched through the front window, and when it pulled up and stopped David waved to the driver. He lugged the two bags down the stairs and out to the curb. Only then did the driver get out to help put the bags in the trunk. "Typical," David mumbled to himself. He got in the back seat, said to go to the nearest Hertz Rent-a-Car place.

As the driver turned the taxi at the corner to head east, David saw what he thought looked like a familiar rust-colored Cadillac go past on the other side of the street and turn in the direction of his brownstone apartment building. For an instant, he imagined the driver was Poppa Saul. But that couldn't be, he knew, and he thought about what kind of rental car he'd want.

When they stopped in front of the Hertz Agency, David jumped out and handed the driver five dollars. He thanked David, but not with much enthusiasm. David had another "typical" thought. He took the bags inside and asked to rent a two-door Ford sedan with a large trunk. He told the redhead with the green eyes behind the counter that he'd bring it back Sunday night, unless he decided to leave it in the Hertz drop-off at National Airport in D.C. She completed the paperwork, had him sign his name four times, and handed him a copy. Then she gave him directions to the pick-up point in the garage. Attendants had the engine running and the driver's door open for David. They loaded the two suitcases into the trunk, closed the lid and wished him a good trip.

Driving to D.C., David was thinking, "That's much better public relations."

Saul couldn't get anyone to answer the phone at David's apartment. He worried. He and Nathan called everyone Saul could think of to try to find David. Finally, he and Nathan drove to the brownstone. Nathan had the security door downstairs, and then David's apartment door, open in no time. "Amazing," Saul told him. "You've never lost your touch."

Inside David's apartment, they examined everything. They went into the computer room last. The system was on, and there was a graphic on the CRT. It verified the developing horror story.

Saul had an idea. He walked quickly to the phone, and called the operator. She got him the Schreiber residence in Ithaca. As casually as he could, Saul asked for Mr. Schreiber. Jack said, "Speaking." Saul then explained who he was, and he asked if, somehow, they might know where David could be reached. Jack told Saul he had no idea where David might be. Saul explained where he'd be staying, thanked Jack, and hung up. "It was worth a try," he said to Moss. "But what do we do now?"

Nathan said, "We'll go back to your house. It's imperative that we find him!"

David drove to the parking lot next to the fixed-base operations office of Capitol Flying Service at Hyde Field, near Clinton, Maryland. He parked, went in and talked with an instructor. David mentioned the name of his flying instructor, Mac McCallum, who wasn't there anymore. The young receptionist behind the counter remembered hearing David's name from some of the other instructors when she'd first come to work for Capitol in 1968.

David leaned on the counter and charmed her. They chatted about flying. He asked if he could take a quick look at the Cherokee Archer he'd learned to fly in. She nodded, handing him the keys. "Of course. Go listen to the radios, or whatever."

He walked out and found N38394, his bird, parked on the ramp. David climbed into the cockpit and sat in the pilot's seat. He turned on the communications radios, listening to the calls of the air traffic in the D.C. area.

Later, when he went back to the office, the receptionist was busy. He didn't return the keys. But he did ask, "Is the airplane in commission to fly?" She told him it was. David left then to get something to eat. It was almost five o'clock, and that was closing time at Capitol.

It was dark at nine o'clock when David drove back to the Capitol Flying Service parking lot, and the place was deserted. He stopped the Ford beside Archer N38394. It was still parked on the edge of the ramp. David got out of the car, climbed up on the right wing, and unlocked the door. Then he pushed the latch at the top of the door, and pulled the one just below the side window to open. After leaning in and turning the cockpit reading light on, he jumped down and got the two big suitcases from the car. He dragged them along the ground to the trailing edge of the right wing. He pulled them, carefully, one at a time, into the back seat of the plane. There, he began assembling the contents of the two bags.

David had deliberately and cautiously designed the detonation system. There could be no mistake. He had included a timer, as well as an atmospheric pressure device. Both were wired to the electrical harness and, in turn, would eventually allow energy from the power source to flow to the detonators and the high explosives. David had built the system so the timer would be the primary control. He reassured himself, "I need it as a safety device. I'll set it, and as the time goes by, I can always change my mind. Later the atmospheric pressure device will become primary."

He carefully set the hands on the timer to allow him sixty minutes, and he thought of the "tick, tick, tick" of the stopwatch on the program that had recently become so popular on CBS-TV. Only when the timer was obviously working properly did David connect the atmospheric pressure device to the electrical harness. Then, he closed and latched the lids of both suitcases.

David knew he would not detonate the bomb. That had never been his intention. But he did want to demonstrate that it could be built, and flown. He was ready!

It was late evening. David's ears began to ring. He felt uneasy, nauseous. He had fleeting thoughts about radiation sickness, but ignored them, and forced himself into the pilot's seat. He adjusted the seat so his feet rested on the rudder pedals and fastened himself into the seat belt. Then he reached into the pouch at his left knee and took out the pilot's checklist. Following it, step by step, David started the engine. He carefully checked, then cross-checked, everything. After completing the before-taxi checklist, he tuned the VHF communications radio to the International Distress Frequency, 121.5. "Everyone will hear my voice when I transmit on that," he said aloud.

David cautiously, slowly, taxied the aircraft out to the end of the southwest runway. The moon and the landing light on the nose wheel illuminated the way. He pointed the plane straight down the white center line on the runway.

After the engine run-up showed all was ready, David glanced up at the star-filled sky. He gave each cockpit instrument one last look and advanced the throttle to full. He steered the nose wheel with the rudder pedals. The plane rolled down the runway on a heading of 230 degrees. When the airspeed indicator read sixty knots, David pulled back on the wheel. The Archer rose gently into the air, climbed steadily. *It was October twenty-fifth.*

15

FATHER ROBERT DONOVAN sat at the desk in his study, praying. He'd been there all day. The seal of the confessional was absolute. If he were to violate that most sacred trust, it meant automatic excommunication, so he tried to imagine some anonymous way to alert the police about David Abaddon's unbalanced behavior. Donovan knew law enforcement officials would doubt the story—he was sure that would be true even if he identified himself, presented his credentials, convinced them that he was authentic.

Donovan was in a state of great anguish.

After he had gone out to the altar to pray one last time, he knew he had to do it. He hurried back into the study, picked up the phone and dialed "O." The operator came on the line, and Donovan said, "Please get me the Washington, D.C. police right away. It's an emergency!" The operator called long distance to the D.C. police switchboard operator. Father said he urgently needed the chief. He was told to stand by.

"Hello, this is Police Inspector Craig Scott. May I help you?"

Donovan anxiously told the inspector the story of David Mikhael Abaddon's plan to fly an atom bomb over D.C. that night. Father Donovan convinced the inspector there was probably a real possibility the flight would take place. Scott asked for Donovan's home and office telephone numbers. Scott promised that he would notify the proper authorities of the danger, and said that the Father should remain calm.

After he hung up, Scott did some fast thinking. They were ready. They had to be. Law enforcement officials had to take such threats seriously, but the evacuation of people? Beginning at what level of government? It was evening, on a Friday. Most people were either sitting at home watching TV or out socially. What to do? What should we do?

He dialed the Pentagon switchboard, got the operator. Scott asked for the Command Post. He knew it was over there somewhere, underground.

A voice came on the line, "May I help you?"

Scott explained everything, said he thought the reliability of Father Donovan was probably good.

The voice from the Command Post asked, "May I please have phone numbers for Father Donovan?" Craig Scott gave them, heard a thank you, and the line went dead.

After the Army non-commissioned officer explained the call he'd just gotten, Colonel Drew Darke reacted quickly. He got Donovan on the phone. Drake listened intently to Donovan's every word and was convinced that the priest believed what he was saying. However, the question would later be raised about probabilities, so Drake began only initial actions, as outlined in the Department of Defense emergency checklist.

Air Force General James Shaw served as Chairman of the Joint Chiefs of Staff. He and Colonel Drew Drake had known each other when the four-star General Shaw was Commander of the Seventh Air Force in Viet Nam and Drake had worked in the Combat Operations Center on Tan Son Nhut Air Base in Saigon. Drake had just gotten the silver eagles of a colonel, and Shaw had heard almost daily briefings on the Viet Nam war situation from him. Now, working together again at the highest military levels in the U.S., Shaw had implicit faith in Drake's judgment. After telling Shaw the facts he had learned so far, Drake said he intended to alert, low-key, the Combat Commands. "Just in case the thing is for real, and because there is always the chance the Russians are in this someplace," he said. Shaw agreed, emphasizing that he was to be kept advised.

Drake used the hotline to call the North American Air Defense Command Combat Operations Center. The Senior Officer on duty deep under Cheyenne Mountain in Colorado Springs came on the line. He listened to Drake, acknowledged, then hung up.

NORAD, the Joint and Combined Command involving the country's Canadian allies, as well as U.S. Army and Navy and Air Force and Marines, handled the communication of the matter—"with the speed of light," they always joked, while setting up simultaneous conference calls with the Air Defense Regions that divided up the North American continent. The senior staff officer in each region was in instant contact with the various military commands needed to defend against whatever threat had been recognized.

When the NORAD senior officers on duty were finished with the calls, the Commander-in-Chief of the U.S. Navy's Atlantic Fleet knew; so did the Commanders of the Strategic Air Command, Tactical Air Command, Aerospace Defense Command, as did star-rank officers flying high above Washington, D.C., for the Pentagon itself, on board *Silver Dollar*, the National Emergency Airborne Command Post four-engine jet; and already flying Generals in *Looking Glass*, the airborne command post, somewhere high over the midwest for the Strategic Air Command.

The military's finest had been advised, and they were ready—if Father Robert Lee Donovan was correct.

David gently banked the single-engine plane toward the center of Washington. He climbed to 3,000 feet, then leveled off. "It's been a couple of years—my God, it's been five years," he thought, "since I've been at the controls. Ah, it's like swimming or making love—once you know how, you've got it." As he flew over the Capitol, he looked down and had a strange thought. He could almost hear a choir singing, "Lead Me, Lord. Make Thy Way Plain Before My Face." David whispered, "R.S.V.P.?" And smiled.

He looked at the Potomac, watched the lights of the cars moving along Pennsylvania Avenue. There was the White House, the Washington Monument, and the Lincoln Memorial. "It really is beautiful," he thought.

He pressed the communications microphone to his mouth. "This is Archer 38394. Does anybody read me?"

"Archer 38394, this is the Air Traffic Controller at Washington National Airport. You are broadcasting on the International Distress Frequency, 121.5. Are you having difficulty?"

David hesitated, then said, "Washington National, this is 394. I have an atom bomb on board this airplane, and I have a few things I'd like to say."

The Air Traffic Controller was struck dumb, but there were other ears that heard, and they were ready.

Colonel Drew Drake called General Shaw on the hotline. He notified the President, at once—OPERATIONAL EMERGENCY—stating there was imminent danger to the huge population centers of the greater Washington, D.C. area, to say nothing of the buildings, grounds, archives, everything that Americans hold dear.

President Nixon asked General Shaw detailed questions about

the defense posture the armed forces were in. Nixon had recently visited NORAD's Combat Operations Center, and was intimately familiar with what Shaw was describing.

Nixon paused, then ordered a world-wide alert. "We're going to a full-scale *DEFENSE CONDITION 3*, General Shaw. Issue the orders. *Now!*" And he told Shaw to be prepared for a higher state of alert later. If that became necessary.

Respectfully, Shaw asked what reason to give, saying, "The media will be all over that, Sir."

"Tell them it's because of the unstable situation in the Middle East," Nixon directed. Then, he told Shaw he was going to the Pentagon Command Post and to meet him there.

By the time the President and General Shaw got to the underground Pentagon facility, DEFCON 3 had been transmitted all over the U.S. Military World, and that included the full complement of armed forces overseas. It had always been done that way. Combat aircrews, ships and crews, marines, and grunts in the army were called to a state of war readiness. Fighting men always said to each other as each arrived at their posts of assignment, "Is it an exercise, or the real thing?"

David knew that, and he wondered if they did believe he had an atom bomb what was being said to the combat troops.

President Nixon ordered Drake to call the other members of the Joint Chiefs of Staff and tell them to come to the Command Post at once, and Drake did, with a calm, efficient resolve. "Professional," Nixon noted.

"Washington, this is Archer 394. Did I lose you? Over."

"394, this is Washington. We are standing by. Over," said the concerned radar traffic controller. He had no idea if the guy talking on the radio was even up in the air, let alone if he had a bomb.

"Washington, I'd like to talk to the President. I want to explain a few things to him. Over."

"394, please stand by. We will call for Mr. Nixon, right away. Meantime, 394, do you have a radar transponder aboard? Over."

"Yes, I do, Washington. Do you want me to transmit so you can track me on radar?"

"394, please squawk 7500."

"Understand I'm to squawk 7500," David acknowledged. He tuned the frequency into the radar transmitting device.

"394, this is Washington. We have positive radar contact. You are three miles north of the Washington National Airport. Please say your altitude and intentions, 394."

"This is 394, I'm at 3,000 feet, leveled off. And my intentions are to talk to the President about some things that've been on my mind for some time. Over."

"Roger, 394, we're still attempting to get Mr. Nixon on the phone. Say your fuel and number of souls on board, 394."

"I have full fuel tanks, and I'm alone, Washington."

"Roger, 394. Stand by," the controller said.

"394," David dutifully replied.

By then, the President and the Joint Chiefs had decided on their course of action. Colonel Drake called Father Donovan, and the priest asked if there was some way he could talk to David. Drake explained how they could simply patch him through from the phone to the transceiver of the Washington Radar Controller, and Donovan and the pilot of the Archer could talk back and forth over the radio and telephone electronic connection. Drake told Donovan to go ahead.

"David? Can you hear me?"

"This is 394. Who's calling? Over."

"David, this is Father Donovan. Go back and land the airplane. Don't do anything with that awful bomb. David?" Father pleaded.

"Father, just relax. I've planned this thing for a long time, and what must be done, will be done. Just keep calm. I'm gonna talk to the President, to get some things straightened out."

Donovan was quiet. He couldn't think of anything else to say.

Drake told Donovan to stand by. He turned to General Shaw and said, "Sir, why don't we set up a conference call. Let's get the names and phone numbers of as many of David's family and closest friends as we can. Then we'll have the staff get each of them on the phone to explain what's occurred. I'm sure they will all try to talk him out of anything . . . ah . . . God! You know, Sir."

Shaw nodded to Drake. He put Donovan back on the Command Post loudspeakers so the staff could hear their conversation. He asked Donovan for the names of David's family, close friends, and where each lived. Father thought first of Jack and Lisl Schreiber in Ithaca. He told Drake. He nodded to his top NCO, who completed the long distance call, got Jack on the line and told him what was happening. Jack Schreiber told the NCO that David's father was at the Klein-Abaddon home, in Brooklyn Heights. Poppa Saul and Zada Klein were called and held on the line, with Nathan Moss listening on an extension.

The process went on for twenty minutes, while the radar controller talked to David on the radio from time to time, asking him to remain calm, trying to stall him to the point of using up his fuel, so that, sooner or later, he would have to find a place to set down. Then, maybe, they could reason with the young man, face to face.

After another three minutes, Drake's staff had Grandpa Samuel and Poppa Saul holding on long distance telephone. Jack, Jeff, and Father Donovan, also. Each of them had expressed disbelief as they were informed of the situation, but all had said they wanted to try to help.

David keyed his mike again, and transmitted, "Washington, this is Archer 394. What's the hold-up down there? I told you, I want to speak to Richard Nixon. Over!"

"394, Washington. Roger. We're trying to get him to the phone now. Stand by one."

Admiral Phillip Nolan was called at his Norfolk, Virginia living quarters. He was told the Chief of Naval Operations wanted him to call the Pentagon Command Post. OPERATIONAL EMERGENCY was the priority. Nolan told the Atlantic Fleet Command Post controller to connect him to the Pentagon Command Post. An Air Force NCO answered, and asked Admiral Nolan to wait. The NCO looked for the glance of the Navy's top four-star, Admiral John Coventry. He got it, and courteously motioned for the admiral to take the call at a side telephone. When Coventry pointed to the blinking button on the telephone console, the NCO nodded.

Picking up the phone, Coventry said, "Phil, we've got a cliff-hanger up here." And he explained the entire situation. Then he directed, "Let's have three F-4s up over him in fifteen minutes. I want some eyes on that guy through the rest of whatever happens tonight."

Nolan said, "Yes, sir. The Phantom crews will use our UHF Navy discreet radio frequency for communications, and they'll monitor the Archer pilot's VHF transmissions at the same time."

"Thanks, Phil." Coventry hung up. No time for chatter.

When the Navy senior controller at Norfolk came back on the line, Nolan told him, "Scramble three F-4s to circle D.C. at flight level two-zero-zero. I'll be down there in the Command Post in ten minutes. We can call the pilots on the radio then. I'll explain later."

The controller acknowledged, but the line had gone dead. Nolan had hung up and was running for his staff car, to rush to CINCLANT headquarters, minutes away.

By the time Admiral Nolan got to the Navy's Command Post in Norfolk, the aircrews had been scrambled. The three F-4s were off the ground, climbing to altitude, in formation, headed to D.C. Nolan had the senior controller contact the three aircrews, on the Navy discreet radio frequency, and explain the mission. When the jets began circling over D.C., at about 20,000 feet, they had a radar picture of David's plane.

Archer 394, a Cherokee-series aircraft manufactured by the Piper Aircraft Corporation, was now flying at 3,000 feet over the nation's capital with, in all probability, an atomic bomb aboard.

David Mikhael Abaddon didn't know it, but special HIJACK radar code 7500 that he was transmitting from his radar transponder was lighting up his image like a neon sign on every aviation radar screen in greater Washington, D.C.

Drew Drake called the supervisor on duty in the Washington offices of the Air Traffic Control. He coordinated with the FAA executive to now allow the Pentagon Command Post staff to assume control of the situation, and, critically important, control of the VHF emergency radio frequency the pilot of 394 was using. Barry Crist, FAA's supervisor at Washington National, told Drake to go ahead.

Electronic switches, activated in the underground Pentagon Command Post and in the FAA's offices at Washington National Airport, completed the connections. Drake now had operational command of the International Distress Radio Frequency. He could hook up a conference call on 121.5, whenever he chose to.

The Pentagon's Staff was working overtime, still trying to locate two more people. The VA had been contacted, and they were searching for Doctor Louis Silber. Poppa Saul had suggested that and, urged by Donovan, the Army Office of Personnel Operations was frantically looking for the one person David might listen to: Kelley!

It was too quiet in the underground Command Post. General Shaw stared at Drake. He pushed the control switch and said, "Archer 394, this is Colonel Drake in the Pentagon Command Post. How do you read me? Over."

"394 here, Colonel Drake. I read you five by five. How me? Over." And David thought, "Now we're getting somewhere!"

"David, I'm Drew Drake," the Korean and Viet Nam veteran jet fighter pilot calmly transmitted. "There are some people we've contacted on long distance who wish to speak to you. I'll put them on the air now. Over."

"This is 394, go ahead, Colonel."

Drake nodded to the senior NCO at the main console. He tripped switches on the Command Post console like an astronaut about to be launched into orbit. Suddenly, the voices of all of those who had been holding on long distance lines went live.

"David, this is Poppa. Zada is on the extension here, too. Land the plane, son. Come, talk to us. Blood is thicker than water. Come down! I beg you!"

"Poppa, I need to talk to the President. There is an awful situation that has developed in the world. It's the New Holocaust— total annihilation, just like it almost was for our people in World War II. Don't you see, Poppa? Over."

Grandfather Samuel tried next. Then, Jack Schreiber and Jeff Piedmont talked to David, and Donovan came on once more, this time appealing to "the love of Christ you professed to me earlier this year."

David reasoned with each one, in turn. He explained, "You're doing nothing to save the world. We are in a perilous spiral, heading to nuclear war." And he dismissed their arguments, one by one.

David was becoming frustrated. This was wasting time, and most importantly, fuel. He pressed the microphone to his mouth to transmit. "Colonel Drake, this is 394. I want to speak to the Commander-in-Chief. Now! Over."

The President took the phone out of Drake's hand. "David, this is Mr. Nixon. Go ahead, son."

David Mikhael Abaddon poured his heart out to the President. He spoke of the three holocausts, the original holocaust of World War II, and the symbolism of it. He told of his personal holocaust in Viet Nam. He explained, "That's another example of what man does to man when the *Beast of Awful* in each of us is turned loose, Mr. President. I call it all *The Great Hate.*"

David emphasized that he had built and was now flying the bomb to bring attention to the nightmare that was fast developing in the world.

"David, this is Mr. Nixon. Land the plane, son. And you and I will go to the Oval Office to talk this important subject through, for all of our fellow Americans. Okay?"

David vomited on himself. He hadn't eaten, so it was just water, bile, stomach acid that burned his mouth and nose. The stench made him ill again, but there was nothing more. He got the dry heaves.

His hands began to tremble. He felt dizzy, the instrument panel momentarily blurred. Then he was able to focus again.

David could deny 'it no longer—the plutonium had poisoned him.

Senior officers on duty in the Pentagon's Army Personnel Office found Father Joe Kelley. He was confined to a hospital bed at Fitzsimmons Army Hospital in Denver. Now on what the Medical Staff felt was his death bed, David's long-time friend was suffering from brain cancer.

In 1970, after he had been promoted to Lieutenant-Colonel, doctors had discovered a small melanoma just above Kelley's left ear. It had been removed that same afternoon; and for more than three years the priest with the cherub face enjoyed good health, but sixty days ago Kelley had been found sitting at his desk in the Fort Carson Chaplain's office. He was staring at a picture of his Irish mother and could not speak. An ambulance had rushed him to the Air Force Academy Hospital, the closest Department of Defense medical facility. They'd taken X-rays and immediately had him transferred to Fitzsimmons. He had already undergone Radiation Therapy, and currently the Army's finest doctors were giving him chemotherapy.

Kelley had five lesions on the left side of his brain. They were of sufficient size to be inoperable. One of the most loved and admired men to ever serve his country, everyone agreed, was critically ill.

The moment Kelley was informed, he asked, "Can you get me patched through to David?"

When David would not respond on the radio to President Nixon, Colonel Drake took the phone.

"David, this is Drew Drake again. There's someone on the line who wants to speak to you."

"Hi, bro. What's happening, kid?" Kelley said in his inimitable style.

"Hello, Father Joe," David managed to say.

"Tell me about it, bro."

David struggled through the story.

Kelley paused, and then he said, *"You've got to take Lang Vei back now.* I can't remember it for you anymore, fella, and you're gonna have to be strong enough for both of us from now on—to build the better world we both believe in, and to make sure there are no more Nams. I'm not much longer for this old world, Dave. Got the Big Casino. Got black cancer inside this ole noggin." And Kelley told David, quickly, the story of what was going on, explaining that he suspected Agent Orange was surely a part of what had happened.

David hesitated, unsure now. He hadn't expected to involve all these people, and certainly not Kelley. Slowly he said, "What should I do, Father?"

"Land the plane, brother. Come out here to God's country and let me see you one more time. Come and sit by my side, Dave, please. I'm asking you to do this one thing for me."

There were tears in David's eyes, and he was scared, he was sick. The atmospheric pressure device was to set the bomb off at 1,500 feet.

"Father, I can't. I'm not sure I can land this bird. The bomb may explode. I'd come out to see you, if it was possible. But, what about this bomb? I can't descend," David said, now feeling great panic.

Kelley's thinking processes had never diminished. Crystal-clear thinking had always been one of his major strengths. "Take it out over the ocean, bro, as far as you have to, and then just dump it over the side. Pull some connecting wires loose first, so it doesn't pop off on you. If you can't do that, disarm it in some other way. Sound okay, Dave?"

Drew Drake broke in. "Dave, this is Colonel Drake again. I've got over 5,000 pilot hours. Let me help you now."

"Go ahead, Colonel."

"Were the fuel tanks full when you took off?"

"Almost, sir," David confirmed, sounding weaker now.

With that military response, and David's tone of voice, Drake felt that he might be gaining control of the awesome situation. "Dave, that means you had roughly four hours of flying time when you left the ground. You've been airborne since when, Dave?"

"I've been flying for an hour, Colonel. Over."

"Fly out over the ocean, Dave. We can have Navy jets fly cover for you. They will have to stay well above you to conserve their fuel, but they'll be there."

Taking a chance that David would respond now, he said, "Turn to a heading of 090 degrees and remain at 3,000 feet, Archer 394."

"Understand I'm to turn to 090 and stay at 3,000," David acknowledged, turning the plane toward the east coast.

Drake asked all the people on the conference call to stand by, and thanked each of them by name, using his incredible memory for names that had always served him so well.

Radar controllers in the entire D.C. area began to breathe a little easier. The brilliantly flashing radar image each had been monitoring for what seemed a lifetime, was moving across their screens in an easterly direction. Flying at over one hundred miles an hour, "that thing" would soon be far enough away to eliminate the horrible threat.

As soon as Drake was certain the Archer was moving out over the water, he alerted the Strategic Air Command to have a KC-135 refueling tanker rendezvous with the F-4s. At high altitude, each would be individually refueled. "Then they'd have more than enough jet fuel to last for the duration," Drake thought. "Whatever that means."

Within half an hour, each F-4 had full fuel tanks.

Archer 394 was over ocean water, and a host of concerned people had lowered anxiety levels. Maybe, just maybe, it would work out.

"Colonel Drake, this is 394. Over."

"Go ahead, David. This is Colonel Drake," maintaining military distance.

"Sir, please tell Father Kelley I'm gonna get rid of this thing. Then I'll fly back, land at Hyde Field, and return this plane to its owners. I can be on an airliner out of Washington National and at his bedside early tomorrow. Over."

"394, Father Kelley heard your transmission. He's just told me to tell you that you're in his prayers now. And he'll see you when you get safely back and out to Colorado."

"Colonel Drake, 394. Thank you, sir."

David wondered how he would fly the plane, disarm the bomb, and open the only door to throw the bomb out. Without an autopilot, he knew he'd have to exercise the utmost care, now that he had decided to dump the bomb.

His thinking had been rational, he felt, through the whole thing. After all, he had gotten the attention of the highest level of government authorities. The President himself had talked on the radio, and said he would meet with David in the Oval Office, but David knew that meeting couldn't happen until after Colorado. Father Kelley came first.

When the lights of the east coast had disappeared behind him, David transmitted.

"Colonel Drake, this is 394. Over."

"394, you are barely readable, but the crews of the three F-4s above you can hear what you say, and they'll relay any messages, so just key your mike and say what you want us to know. Over."

"Roger, Colonel."

After almost an hour, David was well off the east coast, over international waters. Cross-checking, David knew he was out seventy-five to eighty miles. He was ready to open the door, and push HER overboard.

With the imminent danger past, the lead pilot of the three-ship jet formation decided they should climb for higher altitude to conserve fuel. He so informed Air Traffic Control, got permission to climb. Each pilot pushed his two throttles forward, and the noses of the jets rose gently above the dark horizon. Their ability to monitor the location of Archer 38394 was absolute—it was the only pattern on their radar screens.

When the three jets leveled off, they were flying at flight level four-zero-zero.

Colonel Drake kept the entire group ready for another conference call. Even if he couldn't speak directly to David, the F-4 aircrews were monitoring.

Drake came on the phone live, now and then, and told the group David's position, altitude, that all was proceeding according to plan. Each time, Drake reassured them that he felt the situation would soon be resolved. His intentions were to be comforting. It had long been obvious to him that each person listening on long distance held David Mikhael Abaddon in high esteem.

Nixon told Shaw he was leaving, decided the Joint Chiefs of Staff could return to their quarters on Fort Myer, in Virginia. Shaw walked with the President to the guarded exit. As the Commander-in-Chief nodded to him, Shaw said, "I'll be on Fort Myer in my quarters at 14-B in ten minutes, sir, if you wish to call me." Nixon turned and walked out. And Shaw wished he hadn't tried what might even slightly resemble humor.

David decided it was time. He was over an hour of flying time from the east coast.

The large suitcase had to be dragged up to the right front seat. He knew there was no other way. He couldn't turn completely around and try to open it to disarm HER. The plane might go out of control.

He reached over to the underside of the copilot's seat and pulled up on the lever. The seat slid all the way to the front. Then, flying with his left hand on the pilot's wheel, he reached around with his right hand and pulled on the handle of the huge bag with HER inside. It would slide forward only to the back of the right front seat. David didn't have the strength to drag it up over the hump that seat had become.

He knew then that he would need both hands and shoulder strength to get the suitcase up where he could disarm HER and push the thing out. He trimmed the Archer's control surfaces for hands-off flying, as his flight instructor had called it. The plane was maintaining 3,000 feet, according to the altimeter. The heading indicator showed it was on a course of 090 degrees. The vertical speed needle was pointing to zero.

He unhooked the seat-belt and shoulder harness, and turned his upper body to the right. Stretching, he couldn't quite get the leverage needed to force the big bag up front. He twisted, as hard as he could to the right, bracing his feet against what he thought was the side of the cockpit, but he was, in fact, pushing, with both feet, on the right rudder pedal. It went to the full forward position. In seconds, the aircraft began a sharp skid to the right, went over on its right side and almost fell into a spin.

When the aircraft was finally back under control, David was soaked in perspiration. He fought against waves of panic.

The engine spluttered, coughed, then began to run smoothly again.

David knew he had to switch to the other fuel tank. He'd forgotten that. He reached down with his left hand to the fuel tank selector handle, tried to twist it. His hand was trembling, lacked strength. The handle wouldn't move. He tried again. The handle moved only part way toward the new position, which would provide two more hours of fuel.

With no warning, the engine quit.

David used both hands on the fuel handle, struggling to get it properly positioned.

The Archer began a slow descent.

Commander Brad Hoyle led the three-ship jet formation through a left turn at 40,000 feet. They rolled out on a westerly heading. Hoyle glanced at his radar scope image of the Archer over seven miles below them. He started to say something, but he never got it out, for suddenly, the sky became like the brightest summer day— *white light*, too brilliant, was everywhere, filled everything. All six jet-aircrewmen instinctively shielded their eyes. It was too painful to do anything else.

Hoyle screamed into his mike, "Get the hell out of here!" He directed the pilot on his left wing to *"Break formation left! Climb at take-off power! Use afterburners!"* Hoyle ordered the right wingman, *"Break right, go max power!"*

Hoyle flew his Phantom straight west, pushed both throttles wide open. Within moments all three jets were flying at almost twice the speed of sound toward Norfolk.

Drew Drake simply said good-night to everyone on the conference call, then called General Shaw.

It was October twenty-sixth.

EPILOGUE

FATHER ROBERT LEE DONOVAN sat at the desk, in his study. The same question went through his mind, over and over: *"Did I do the right thing?"*

And, he thought, "I believe David was trying to set an example. The whole world is threatened. My little friend wanted everyone to dump their plutonium—somewhere. People *must* learn to live together in peace."

He was certain. Something must've gone wrong when David tried to disarm HER. David did *not* set that bomb off. David had wanted to sit by Joe Kelley's side, just one more time.

The phone rang once. It was Archbishop Peter Casini's secretary calling. Father was to be in the office of the Archbishop the following morning, at eight o'clock sharp.

Father Donovan hung up the phone, and asked himself again, *"Did I do the right thing?"*

EPILOGUE